COLD
BLOODED

COLD
BLOODED

Toni Anderson

This one is dedicated to fiercely talented Romantic Suspense author, Rachel Grant.

She excels at exuberant friendship and superb Chocolate Martinis. Or maybe exuberant Chocolate Martinis and superb friendship?

It all gets a little warm and fuzzy...

PROLOGUE

H E ENTERED THE lab, wearing full protective gear. The screeches and rattling of cage bars reassured him the animals were alive. He held his breath as he went around each cage, noting the individual demeanors and facial expressions of the rhesus macaques. He fed them fruit and made sure their water supply was sufficient, noting the bright eyes and interested gazes of these fascinating creatures. Sometimes they appeared so human he had to look away in shame, but not today.

There were no dead monkeys.

A frisson of excitement shot through his nerves. Even more exhilarating, there were no sick monkeys. In all his past experiments, the monkeys who'd been exposed to SA-HCAM45-65 had died within twenty-four hours despite being given the vaccine. But this new vaccine worked.

It worked!

Finally.

Finally, he'd figured it out, but he held back the feeling of triumph.

It was the weekend and he'd offered to care for all the animals in the lab which he did periodically when he didn't want any prying eyes. Officially no experiments were going on, so someone simply needed to feed and check the animals at regular intervals.

He took blood samples then exited the monkey room, showering in his suit before heading into another restricted area. An emergency isolation unit that few knew existed and even fewer could access.

Macaques shared ninety-three percent of their DNA with humans but there was enough difference in the remaining seven percent that more extensive tests needed to be done with the vaccine before it would be declared safe for people to use. Unfortunately, the law prohibited testing efficacy on human beings.

The light above his head buzzed and flickered, making him pause.

He peered through the glass into the shadowy isolation chamber, the small secure room shrouded in darkness. The primate lay on a bed inside a plastic tent, restrained, inert, face averted from the window. It looked dead.

His heart thumped disturbingly hard.

Disappointment? Frustration? Anger?

No one ever said science was easy.

He heaved a great sigh that fogged up the inside of his mask.

It looked dead.

Just like all the other test subjects.

Pushing the despondency aside, he entered the room through a locked, sealed door. The subtle brush of air being drawn into the room felt like an indrawn breath and prevented the escape of any microbes.

The rustle of sheets had him freezing in place. A movement from the bed as the creature attempted to sit up almost made him piss his pants.

"Where am I? What happened?" Her voice was small and scared.

Oh, my God. Oh, my God. Oh, my fucking God! It worked. He'd gotten it to work. He wanted to pump his fists but held on to his decorum.

His pulse pounded. This was it. This was *it*!

"Who are you?" she asked. "Where am I?"

Thankfully she wouldn't remember anything, this runaway he'd picked up off the street and offered a warm meal. She'd offered to suck his cock in payment but he'd wanted something else. Something far more valuable. He'd brought her here, tranquilized her, infected her and never expected her to live past midnight.

She started to struggle against the restraints as her panic bloomed.

"You're okay. You're okay now," he told her calmly. "You were sick. Very sick but I made you better. You're going to be just fine."

He withdrew his hand inside his suit and used a small digital camera to take a short video as proof of life, then stepped forward and picked up another dose of anesthetic, injecting it into the cannula he'd inserted into her vein on Friday night. She stared at the needle but was hopeless to do anything except watch the clear liquid enter her vasculature.

"You're going to be okay," he assured her. "Actually, you're going to be absolutely fantastic."

She smiled slightly before her eyes drifted shut.

This changed everything.

He closed his eyes for a moment. Everything would be okay. He wouldn't be a failure anymore.

He took blood samples with clinical efficiency, storing

them in small vials that he'd analyze along with the monkey blood. He checked the subject's pulse. Waited for her heart to slow. Slower and slower until it was barely a murmur. He gave her another dose, just to be certain she wouldn't wake up again.

He unzipped the plastic tent and removed the cannula, undoing the restraints which clicked open.

He lifted her limp body. She was light, easy to carry. He held her tightly as they entered the chemical shower, getting dowsed and sanitized, turning them so every micrometer of their surface was sterilized. After two minutes the spray stopped. He opened the door into the suiting up room, then placed the girl on a metal gurney while he stripped off and hung up his suit before wheeling her into the next shower station. Once they were thoroughly clean, he dried them both and covered her in two big towels. The biggest danger was bumping into someone unexpectedly so he peeked out into the changing area before he brought the gurney.

No one was here.

And that was why he worked in the middle of the night.

He quickly got dressed and grabbed his belongings. Then he checked the corridor before pushing his precious cargo down to the incinerator. He touched the delicate blue vein of her wrist. Traced his finger over the tip of her nose and across her soft lips. Memorizing her features so he never forgot this moment of triumph.

He placed her inside, trying to be respectful. She was so tiny there was plenty of room.

He closed the door and turned the machine on. It took time to reach 1500 degrees and he made himself wait patiently just as he had with the others, although the others had been

4

hidden inside doubled up amorphous black body bags to contain their deadly cargo of germs. This one posed no danger though he wished he had more time to study her.

Once the incinerator hit the necessary temperature to burn bone, he turned and walked away.

Everything was about to change.

CHAPTER ONE

T HE SOUND OF magazines being snapped into place echoed around the bullpen in a metallic symphony of governmental firepower. Anticipation tightened his gut as he checked his SIG Sauer and backup Glock. FBI Special Agent Hunt Kincaid of the Atlanta Field Office was locked and loaded and ready to party.

Hunt reached down for the arrest and search warrants and handed them over to Agent Mandy Fuller.

"Thank you kindly, Agent Kincaid." She batted her eyes dramatically as she took the documents. Fuller was blonde and pretty and deceptively sweet looking. She'd been undercover for the past four months and deserved to be the one to put their main suspect in cuffs after the number of times the elected official had fondled her ass.

"My pleasure, Agent Fuller."

Today was the culmination of a fourteen-month-long investigation into corruption at City Hall. It had been a long and laborious process that involved thousands of hours of stakeouts, surveillance, poring over bank details, electronic communications, and chasing down smaller prey to get them to flip on larger targets—all without the man at the top of their suspect list becoming suspicious. Fuller's work had produced a cooperating witness, and surveillance had finally garnered enough rock-solid evidence for a judge to sign off on warrants.

Councilor Jim Crowley and four of his lackeys were going down.

Hunt checked his spare ammo and put another three magazines into his vest pocket. He wasn't expecting trouble but he sure as hell was prepared for it.

His buddy, Agent Will Griffin, came over and gave him a nod. Will was on the Enhanced FBI SWAT team and surreptitiously checked over Fuller's vest and equipment. Fuller gave her boyfriend a pointed look and the other agent heroically managed to suck back whatever piece of advice he'd stupidly been about to offer.

Hunt and Fuller might currently be assigned to the white-collar crime squad but they were both field agents with extensive experience. SWAT would act only as backup during these arrests.

Fuller headed over to their immediate boss, the Supervisory Special Agent of Atlanta FBI's White-Collar Crime Unit and showed him the paperwork.

Hunt smirked at Will who stood watching the female agent leave. "Did you want to check my vest, too?"

"I was actually thinking of confirming its bullet resistance capacity." Will's teeth flashed in a forced smile that quickly faded. "I used to be okay with Mandy going out there every day, but…"

"That's what love does to you, pal. Makes you weak."

Will rolled his eyes at the suggestion, his brown cheeks darkening with heat. He was still in denial about the depth of his feelings but Hunt had seen it before. The guy was toast.

"What does she think of you applying to HRT?"

Will grimaced.

"You didn't tell her yet?"

"I haven't found the right moment."

Hunt snorted. "She's gonna know as soon as the call goes out. Especially with all this training we're doing."

Will stared at him miserably.

Hunt backed off. He didn't intend to get caught in the middle of the personal lives of two agents he liked and respected, but he for one, had no intention of being caught in the relationship trap.

Eyes on the prize, and that prize was making it into the FBI's elite Hostage Rescue Team.

The head of his squad shouted across the bullpen. "Time to go."

Adrenaline spiked through Hunt's veins as he checked the chamber one last time. Didn't matter how often he'd arrested people during his five-year tenure with the Bureau. This never got old. He grabbed his raid jacket off the back of his chair. Strode down the corridor toward the stairs of the new field office. Twenty other agents joining them in addition to the SWAT guys. This was gonna be fun.

"Kincaid!"

The strident bellow startled him out of the zone and stopped him in his tracks. He turned.

Shit.

Caleb Bourne, Special Agent in Charge of the FBI Atlanta Field Office, stood yelling down the hallway at him.

Hunt hadn't realized the SAC even knew his name. Neither did anyone else, judging from the surprised glances people were throwing his way. He didn't have time for this. Surely the SAC knew what was happening? Suppressing a curse, Hunt broke away from the gang and headed back toward the bullpen.

"Boss?"

SAC Bourne raised his voice at the rest of the team. "You guys are going to have to go on without Kincaid."

What?

Hunt drew in a deep breath and held on to the words that would get him another letter of censure in his file if he didn't rein it in. "With all due respect, sir, I've worked on this case for over a year. I deserve to be on that arrest team."

"Yes, you do." Bourne's cool gaze settled on his face, but the man's expression didn't alter. "Unfortunately, it's not gonna happen. I need you with me."

The SAC turned on his heel and strode away.

Hunt threw a pissed-off glance at Will who was staring at him open-mouthed with a *what-the-fuck* expression.

Left with little choice, Hunt followed Bourne, catching up just as the elevator doors opened. He calmed his anger long enough to wonder what the hell was going on. Since when did the SAC run his own errands? Since when did the SAC take an agent away from a potentially dangerous, high-profile takedown where a show of overwhelming force was the best way of making sure the suspects came quietly?

Had Hunt fucked up?

He tried to think of any rules he'd bent lately but came up with nothing.

Dammit, he wanted to see the look on Crowley's face when Fuller slapped on the cuffs. Wanted to see the fat bastard sweat when he realized the FBI had him on the corruption charges, threatening behavior, abuse of power, RICO counts—

This couldn't wait a fucking hour?

Hunt kept his mouth shut.

As a former member of the FBI's Crisis Negotiation Unit, the SAC of the Atlanta office was notorious for using silence to his advantage. Bourne simply stared at people and they started confessing sins he'd had no idea they'd committed. Hunt wasn't going to blow everything by opening his big mouth. He checked his wristwatch. With luck he might be able to rejoin the team in time to make the arrests.

Hunt strode after the SAC and past curious faces of the assistants and secretaries who helped run this massive field office to the big corner office with a fantastic view of Mercer University campus and surrounding woodlands. A view Hunt had never before had the privilege of seeing.

Bourne sat down behind his desk. "Shut the door. Sit down. Shut up."

Okay then.

It didn't sound like he was up for any awards.

Bourne pressed some buttons on his laptop and a screen on the wall sprang to life. On it, a guy in a dark suit, hands in his pockets, lounged in front of an array of monitors showing various maps behind him. He straightened when the feed went live, eyes careful and shrewd.

"Agent Hunt Kincaid meet ASAC Steve McKenzie from SIOC."

Pronounced *"sigh-och,"* SIOC was the Strategic Information and Operations Center based at headquarters in DC.

What the hell was going on here?

A small smile quirked ASAC McKenzie's face. "Sorry to drag you away from your other duties. It looks like you were about to have some fun."

Agents didn't usually sport Kevlar and thigh holsters in the office. Hunt nodded, not bothering to hide his frustration.

The video link split in two and Hunt recognized the legend that was Lincoln Frazer appear on the right-hand side of the monitor.

Frazer was a big deal in the FBI. He'd taught their classes on serial killers during New Agent Training five years ago. Hunt got a tickly feeling between his shoulder blades that usually meant something major was about to take place. Whatever this was, it was serious.

A gorgeous, dark-haired Asian woman in jeans and t-shirt climbed up from beneath Frazer's desk.

"That should work now," she told Frazer. "Don't fiddle with anything."

Fraser cleared his throat a little self-consciously as he became aware of his audience. "Thank you, Agent Chen. Tell everyone the team meeting is delayed until noon."

The woman raised an eyebrow in what Hunt interpreted as a "*do I look like your secretary*" face, but diplomacy won the day, "Yes, boss."

Hunt was obviously working in the wrong office.

Bourne formally introduced them, then said, "Gentleman, Agent Kincaid is Atlanta's WMD coordinator, as requested."

Hunt cocked his head and narrowed his gaze. Every office had a WMD coordinator. Weapons of Mass Destruction— because people needed bigger and better ways of killing other people. Hunt had taken over the WMD coordinator role a month ago when one of his colleagues had gone on maternity leave. Rose Geddy had told him not to get comfortable and he'd replied he had no desire to sit in endless Public Health planning meetings, especially after this stint in white-collar crime. He'd rather bathe his eyes in acid.

McKenzie, McKenzie…

The name clicked into place and Hunt sat up straighter. McKenzie and Frazer had both been involved in foiling the attempt to bomb FBI HQ back in February. That tickly feeling turned to a full-on itch that he couldn't scratch through the impeding layers of nylon, cotton and Kevlar.

"What do you know about anthrax?" McKenzie asked abruptly.

Hunt snapped to attention. "It's a Category A biological agent, sir."

Category A signified the most potent bioweapons—terrible, insidious, death machines. Other Category A agents included such dainties as smallpox and Marburg virus. Nasty shit.

"The anthrax sent through the US Postal System in 2001 caused eleven people to develop the inhalation form of the disease." McKenzie's tone suggested this information was going to be relevant to the rest of Hunt's day and a chill stole over him. "Five of those people died."

Hunt nodded. The AMERITHRAX case had been studied in detail at the academy. The investigation had lasted more than eight years and the FBI were convinced the bioterrorism was the work of an Army scientist out of Fort Detrick.

Not everyone concurred. The scientist had killed himself before he'd gone to trial.

Hunt wasn't about to mention the merit of that case as career suicide wasn't on today's to-do list. Then again, neither was a lecture on anthrax.

"What you're about to hear is strictly confidential and on a need-to-know basis. You're getting read into this case as is every other WMD coordinator in the country," McKenzie told him.

So, it wasn't just him, though Hunt had a feeling he was amongst the first to be briefed. His location probably had a lot to do with that. At least two maximum biosafety level containment laboratories (BSL-4) were within a short drive of where he sat, one of which was at the CDC, the Centers for Disease Control and Prevention, the other, Georgia State.

"A few grams of normal *Bacillus anthracis* dispersed in a certain way have the potential to kill up to a hundred thousand people." McKenzie looked grim.

Normal Bacillus anthracis?

Frazer took over. "Less than a week ago, an illegal arms broker named Ahmed Masook tried to sell what he claimed was weaponized anthrax on the black market."

"Weaponized?" asked Hunt.

"Heated up in the lab." Frazer pressed his lips together as if containing his anger. "They claimed it was faster acting and more virulent than natural strains. Disperses more easily on the wind. And is resistant to current vaccines."

Unease scratched deeper down Hunt's spine.

"Last week we got lucky. We intercepted the transaction and prevented the sale of the bioweapon. Unfortunately, the arms dealers didn't survive the experience so we couldn't question him about the supplier." Frazer's smile grew razor sharp.

But if that was the end of the story Hunt wouldn't be here while the rest of his squad conducted the most important arrests of the year.

"One of the conversations we overheard suggested this new strain came from a US source. We found some online correspondence but the supplier made a big effort to cover their tracks." Frazer was being frustratingly frugal with specific details.

Hunt sat forward. "If you prevented the arms deal I assume you have whatever it was they were trying to sell?"

Frazer nodded cautiously.

"And you've had it since last week. So, I presume you had it tested?" Hunt wasn't sure of his position in this room. Didn't even know if he should be opening his mouth or just nodding and doffing his cap. But the FBI hadn't hired him for his looks.

"Not yet." Frazer's cool blue gaze frosted over. "The bioweapon and the vaccine that accompanied it were...appropriated...by an agent from a foreign nation. We exerted considerable pressure and they finally sent us samples to analyze."

"Can you trust them to send the real thing?"

Frazer nodded. "I believe so. Our interests align and we have considerable leverage. We're waiting on special transportation permits from CDC and USDA. As soon as they are approved, samples should be hand-couriered and in-country by tomorrow morning."

Frazer continued. "One sample is going to USAMRIID." The United States Army Medical Research Institute of Infectious Diseases. "Another to the CDC. CDC will organize a subsample for DNA sequencing, see if we can track the genetic fingerprint of the anthrax in question."

It made sense to take precautions and also not to send the samples to just one lab. Last time the FBI had run this sort of investigation some initial help had come from the man who'd ultimately become their prime suspect. FBI expertise and preparedness regarding bioterrorism had increased dramatically since that time, but no one wanted to leave anything to chance.

Technology had been radically refined and accelerated because of the AMERITHRAX case.

"Do you believe this supplier has sold previous batches of weaponized anthrax to terrorists?" Which might explain the sudden urgency. Not that the idea of someone heating up anthrax to sell to terrorists wasn't horrifying enough.

"We don't believe so." McKenzie twisted his lips to one side. "The sort of money being discussed during this exchange suggested a high value was being put on the product and part of that value would come from exclusivity—presumably of both the bacterial strain and the vaccine. We'd have heard about a cluster of victims if the material had been released. The intelligence community is pursuing the possibility though. We are digging deeper into communications and bank records of all the people we know are involved, searching for a link."

Okay. "So how did the anthrax supplier contact the arms broker?" It wasn't like these people hung a shingle over the door.

"Dark web. We have leads we're tracking there," McKenzie told him. "We're obviously coordinating with the WMD Directorate, but POTUS ordered a Joint Terrorist Task Force to be set up for this investigation and I'm in charge. Initial signs are pointing to the Southern US."

Hunt's eyes widened. POTUS? The President of the United States, Joshua Hague, was involved? This was a real and ongoing threat.

"What do you need from us?" Bourne interrupted. Technically he was senior to the two men on the screen, but it was obvious he wasn't calling the shots.

"We want FBI WMD coordinators from around the country to reach out to everyone whose work involves or has involved *Bacillus anthracis*. The CDC maintains a current list."

"Won't that send the bad guy to ground?" Hunt tapped his index finger on his boss's desk. "They might get rid of evidence."

"We'd rather them destroy any stocks of anthrax than produce more of it." Frazer's tone was grim.

"Unless the suspects are computer hackers, it's only a matter of time before we figure out who is involved," said McKenzie.

Lincoln Frazer eyed Hunt critically. "We want you to check onsite records to see who is spending a lot of time in labs working on anthrax and to make sure they know you noticed. Look for any potential red flags in their behavior."

"We've got numerous high-level government facilities, universities and private biotech companies within a stone's throw of this office," Bourne pointed out.

McKenzie nodded. "And you don't even need a level four lab to work with anthrax. Level two labs can work with inactive strains."

"Inactive strains aren't worth millions on the black market," Frazer argued.

Bourne ran his hand over his short hair. "Do you have any idea how many highly trained microbiologists reside in our jurisdiction with the knowledge and capability to produce large batches of this microbe?"

"Hundreds," said Frazer.

"If not thousands," Hunt said helpfully.

"We need more people," Bourne suggested.

McKenzie shook his head. "Not yet. We don't want to start a mass panic so we need all the WMD coordinators to reach out to researchers as part of their normal duties. We're prioritizing coordinators who live in areas with BSL-4 labs and working our way down the list. That means you're first. Agent Kincaid is new. He can go introduce himself and suggest the FBI is thinking of overhauling the rules of who will be allowed to work on these substances in the future. That normally gets people extolling the virtues of their research. As soon as you leave they'll be on the phone or email to their cronies asking what the hell is going on and how to stop it. Word will spread. The bad guys might panic, in fact we're counting on it. We've got a room full of analysts at SIOC poring over data and monitoring activities. We'll track your contacts with the scientists and examine the ripple effect."

"Track?" Hunt said, startled. "You're monitoring my work cell?"

"Not hot-mic-ing," Frazer assured him. "But logging GPS, call times and emails so we can map your movements and communications in relation to the activity of the scientists. It's more efficient. We will monitor the activities of all our WMDs with a little help from a supercomputer and our friends at the NSA. Any objections?" Frazer raised an imperious eyebrow.

"No, sir." Even though it was gonna be a little weird to be tracked.

McKenzie checked the time. "You have a meeting with a unit chief at the CDC in thirty minutes to triage which individuals to talk to first and then begin your enquiries. A Dr. Jez Place. I've sent the details to your cell. Contact me directly if anyone raises your suspicions. The WMD coordinator in San Antonio is up next on our list. Stay vigilant."

Hunt relaxed a little. Georgia wasn't the only state to be saturated with mad scientists, although they had more than their fair share.

Anthrax was an invisible, indiscriminate killer. How could someone create something that could potentially kill thousands of innocents, for cash? The thought was an anathema to decent human beings and made him uneasy in a way he couldn't pin down.

He waited to be dismissed, then changed out of tactical gear and back into one of his many business suits, adjusting his tie in the eerie quiet of the building.

It looked like he was back behind a desk or in the field, talking to scientists. Hell, he might not survive the excitement. The sooner HRT selection began the better.

That tingling feeling was back between his shoulder blades, though, and he scratched the hell out of it. It didn't disappear and he finally figured out what it was.

Dread.

CHAPTER TWO

I T WAS ONLY April, but in rural Georgia at nine o'clock in the morning it was already hot enough to fry eggs on the hood of Pip West's aging Honda. Sweat trickled down her back and she pushed her hair from her damp brow. The car bottomed out on a rut. She winced.

Her anxious gaze swung to the angry red light of the engine and the steadily rising temperature gauge. Dammit. Less than quarter of a mile to go. If she stopped now her car might never start again. She gritted her teeth and put her foot on the accelerator.

It didn't help the sedan was jam-packed with all Pip's belongings. At twenty-eight years old her entire life's possessions could be condensed into an eighteen-year-old Civic. She didn't know whether to be impressed or horrified.

Last night, Cindy had texted that she'd finished her thesis. The joy of Cindy's momentous achievement had been overshadowed by their recent argument and Pip was ashamed that she hadn't been the first one to reach out.

Saying sorry had never been easy for Pip, but she and Cindy had always been honest with one another. Twelve days ago, they'd been a little too honest.

But Cindy had been right.

Pip had quit her job and packed up her life in Tallahassee.

Now homeless and jobless, the only reason she wasn't destitute was because she had a best friend who was compassionate, understanding and forgiving.

Pip needed to figure out how to say the words, "I'm sorry" and stop holding onto old hurts. It wasn't a pattern she needed to live by any more.

"Come on. We've got this." Pip patted the steering wheel in desperate encouragement. If she could make it to the turn-off, she could coast down the dirt road to the cottage and collapse in a heap.

Pip took a corner and shrieked in surprise, jerking the wheel hard right as a black SUV screamed around the bend, half on her side of the road. Grit showered her windscreen like dirty rain. Her pulse hammered and her heart gave a nasty squeeze as she struggled to keep her vehicle on the gravel.

"Asshole!" Pip didn't let up on the gas. She eyed the temperature gauge as steam started to curl from the grill. The driveway appeared up ahead on the left, dust rising along its length, suggesting another car had recently traveled the quiet track.

Pip frowned. She'd tried to call Cindy before making that final decision to move to Atlanta, the way Cindy had been urging her to do for years, but her friend hadn't answered. Pip assumed she'd turned off her phone and gone to bed. Hopefully she hadn't already left for the city.

Pip's fingers clenched the wheel and she barely slowed as she took the turn. She rumbled crazily along the overgrown driveway toward the cottage, teeth-clattering, bones rattling. Killing the engine to save it, she coasted down the rutted path. The building came into view, set back from the lake on a short, steep rise. The car traveled hard over the uneven ground, going way too fast. She stomped repeatedly on the brakes and finally came to a shuddering halt beside the cherry-red SUV Pip had helped Cindy pick out at Christmas.

Intense relief washed through her and she sat, breathing hard, though she'd done nothing more strenuous than drive all night. She gently honked her horn to let her friend know someone was here.

Pip wanted to fall apart. She wanted to walk into Cindy's embrace and sob and curse and rage and celebrate and apologize and promise never to say anything judgmental ever again. To never make another mistake.

The engine hissed. Steam wafted from beneath the hood in great Apocalyptic white clouds. The death of her car seemed like a fitting metaphor for the current state of her life.

Popping the door, she climbed out, waving away the steam and stretching out the kinks of an all-nighter behind the wheel. She needed to check the radiator and call a mechanic, but the engine had to cool down regardless and the car could wait. She wasn't planning on going anywhere anytime soon.

Grabbing her purse and cell phone from the passenger seat, she climbed the steps at the side of the cottage and knocked on the main door. She listened attentively. Nothing. She walked around the wraparound porch to the front of the cottage where huge picture windows opened up onto the quiet peaceful lake.

"Cindy?" She tapped on the glass of the sliding door that led from the deck into the living room.

No answer.

She tried the handle and was surprised when it moved. Cindy was a stickler for home security. Pip opened it an inch and called inside. "Cind? Are you home? It's Pip."

Still no answer. Pip pushed the door farther open. Cindy would forgive her, but hopefully she didn't scare her friend half to death first. And hopefully Cindy wouldn't shoot Pip with the gun she'd bought for self-defense last summer.

"Cindy?" she called.

Swallowing the lump in her throat, Pip took out her cell and dialed the number to the landline of the cottage—she *really* didn't want to get shot—and heard the incessant ringing of the phone in the kitchen. It was one of those old-fashioned numbers with a stretchy cord that must be fifteen feet long. She could see it from where she stood.

No groggy, grumpy Cindy came stumbling out of the bedroom and down the stairs. No one stirred from the office. Pip tried Cindy's cell again. Tilted her head to one side and listened for the gentle chiming. Nothing.

Maybe it was on silent, or the headphones were plugged in. Pip glanced at the SUV. Cindy must be here somewhere. Maybe she was in the shower.

Pip stepped inside, then quietly closed the screen door behind her because her friend hated mosquitoes with the force of a thousand suns. "Cindy?"

Nothing, except a grackle calling from the trees.

Pip looked around. The place was clean and tidy, but for a bottle and an empty glass on the coffee table. It wasn't like Cindy to leave a mess. Cindy was precise and meticulous about hygiene and clutter, her work life mirroring her personal life.

Pip's mouth dropped open in shock when she spotted white powder residue on the glass table top. Next to the powder lay a straw.

What the hell?

No way. No frickin way.

Cindy was way too smart to snort chemicals.

Did she have a new boyfriend who was into that shit? They'd both dated their fair share of losers over the years, but this wasn't like her friend. Pip wasn't about to judge, but she was gonna help kick this loser to the curb.

Maybe Cindy was under more stress than she'd let on and their fight had tipped her over the edge? Guilt rose up. Pip should have let go of her anger and contacted her friend. What sort of horrible human being held onto annoyance simply because she couldn't take what she was dishing out?

Her sort, apparently.

She walked through the living room and past the small kitchen nook with its ancient breakfast bar. "You here, Cind?"

As she headed to the office at the back of the house, floorboards creaked under her feet. She paused, the small hairs on the nape of her neck lifting—as if a ghost were trailing a cold hand across her skin.

"Cindy?" Her voice trembled.

The room was empty. The air in her lungs rushed out and she held onto the doorjamb feeling lightheaded. "Ninny."

Cindy was going to laugh her ass off when she heard how freaked out Pip was. Pip didn't frighten easy, but the last few weeks had reminded her monsters existed.

Pip squared her shoulders. This was crazy. Maybe Cindy had gone back into the city in a different vehicle and had forgotten to lock up. Or she'd needed something from the store and had biked into town. Or maybe she was out shagging the hot guy from the neighboring cottage they'd met last year.

Pip winced at the memory of their fight. And if Cindy had hooked up, that was her business.

She'd mentioned not feeling well last night. Perhaps her BFF was in bed, helpless, with a fever.

Pip ran up the stairs, calling out her friend's name as she went. There were two small bedrooms at the back of the house and the main bedroom that had been Cindy's parents up until the summer before last.

The thought of Mr. and Mrs. Resnick and Cindy's little brother Richie brought a lump to Pip's throat but she forced it away.

The bed in the main bedroom was made as was the norm for her neat freak friend. No sign of Cindy though. Pip was reassured by the sight of her friend's makeup arranged tidily on the vanity. Pip walked to the small balcony overlooking the lake and stared down at the smooth surface of the water. The view was dear and familiar and usually soothed her heart. But not this time. This time she was too worried about Cindy.

Where was she?

The tin boat was tied to the dock. The yellow kayak Cindy liked to paddle around the shoreline was pulled up next to the big oak.

Something broke the surface beside the dock and caused concentric ripples to spread through the water.

A fish, probably.

It surfaced again.

Something pale.

Almost white.

Half under the dock.

Wrong shape for a fish or a turtle. It looked like a bark-stripped tree branch. Pip squinted against the light reflecting on the water.

Realization streaked through her body like a flash of

white-hot lightning. Panic erupted. Every nerve. Every blood vessel exploded into action. Her pulse punched her throat.

She bolted down the stairs, careening across the smooth wooden floor, slamming through the sliding door. Running as fast as she could though she felt like she was in slo-mo, rocks skittering as she hurled herself down the steep path. She tossed her purse and cell on the bank and threw herself into the water, half swimming, half floundering, desperate to catch hold of the person floating face down in the cold lake.

Pip knew it was Cindy before she turned her over. She knew her size, her form, the short blonde hair plastered to her skull. Her lips were blue. Sobbing, Pip caught her under the arms, muscles burning, back straining, using every ounce of strength to get her out of the water, up onto the bank.

The only thing Cindy wore was her tattoo. They'd both gotten one at Christmas. Cindy's said "Mind" with a line beneath it, and the word "Matter" below that.

Mind over Matter.

Pip used that philosophy to haul Cindy's larger frame onto the bank.

Where were Cindy's clothes?

Had she been assaulted?

Blood pounded in Pip's ears.

Horror crawled through her stomach and up her throat and spilled out in a yell. "Don't you dare die on me, Cindy Resnick!"

Cindy wasn't breathing.

Pip ignored the hopelessness that wanted to turn her into a useless mess and instead called on the lifesaving skills she'd learned to help fund her way through college. She angled Cindy's head, sealed her lips to Cindy's mouth, forcing warm air into still lungs. She pressed two fingers to ice-smooth skin, searching for a pulse.

Nothing.

She tried again, tears bubbling to the surface, getting in the way of her efforts. She wiped her wet hand on the grass and reached for her cell, quickly entering the code when her thumbprint didn't work.

"Nine-one-one, what is your emergency?"

"Ambulance. My f-friend. I just pulled her out of the lake. She's not breathing. Please send help ASAP. I can't talk. I need to do CPR." She reeled off the address and started chest compressions, her cell on speaker beside her. She avoided Cindy's sightless eyes and concentrated instead on not falling apart.

Please, God, help me save her and I will never ask for anything ever again.

Miracles happened.

The lake was cold.

Thirty chest compressions. Two breaths. Watching the artificial rise and fall of Cindy's chest filled Pip with hope. She would breathe for her. As long as it took. Again and again until her limbs shook with fatigue and her lips cracked and split.

Each second lasted for a million years and yet time ran away like sand in a storm and her friend still didn't take over. Didn't cough or draw in her own hoarse breath. Didn't push her own blood around her inert body.

Fear set in. Pips hands shook. Her arms ached. Her knees hurt.

Her lungs burned with a need for more oxygen but she didn't give up. Cindy was the one person in the world who mattered to her.

"I'm here, Cindy. I've got you." *Don't die.*

Pip loved her so damn much.

Don't let her die. I'll do anything.

It took almost an hour for the medics to arrive. Pip never stopped trying to revive her friend. She'd keep going forever if there was the slightest hope Cindy could be saved.

Just *breathe!*

When the paramedic gently urged her away she rolled onto her side in the dirt, too exhausted to move, sweat coating every inch of her body as she stared up at the limitless blue sky.

Her efforts were for nothing. Cindy was dead.

HUNT BOUNCED ALONG the rutted rural road near Lake Allatoona searching for the right address. Will Griffin and Mandy Fuller had both texted him saying that Crowley and his cronies were in custody, bleating like sheep about this being a massive mistake. Until they'd realized that the first one to roll had the best chance of saving himself. Needless to say, they'd all rolled.

Will had wanted to know what was up with the SAC, but Hunt had been sworn to secrecy and couldn't tell him.

After a quick trip to CDC he'd gone to Blake University on the southeast edge of the city, to speak to staff and students who worked on *Bacillus anthracis.* Professor Karen Spalding, head of the Microbiology Department, had been showing him around their brand-new biosafety laboratories when she'd received an urgent call from the departmental secretary.

Visibly upset, Spalding had explained that a grad student from the department had been found dead at her lake house an hour north of the city. Cindy Resnick had been working on a new vaccine against anthrax—a double whammy on his investigation checklist. The timing was too much of a coincidence to ignore.

He'd left his card and contact information with Spalding and called McKenzie at SIOC to fill him in. He'd been passed to an analyst named Libby Hernandez who was compiling background info on the dead girl to see if there were any links to the case, which had been codenamed BLACKCLOUD.

Hunt checked directions on his phone. Definitely in the boonies now. Sparse trees lined the road with scrubby underbrush creating an impenetrable screen. A group of whitetail deer scattered up ahead and he slowed his tan Buick—the ugliest car in the FBI Atlanta Field Office's fleet— to a crawl. His idea of adventure didn't involve a deer through his windscreen.

Local detectives were supposed to meet him at the scene.

The area was vaguely familiar. He and Will had taken canoe trips and white-water rafting adventures in some of the nearby rivers. Quiet green woodland surrounded him. Tall broadleaf trees stretched all the way to the shore.

He rounded the corner and finally reached the turnoff for the cottage. After a short drive the lake came into view and the dazzling reflection of light off the water made his eyes sting.

Short dock. Boat. Kayak. Rustic, but well-maintained cottage. Red SUV parked next to an older model sedan that was sun-baked and worn. His gaze sharpened on the Florida plates.

He pulled to a stop beside a cute-looking outhouse, wood

stacked neatly in the lean-to. Six pairs of eyes watched his progress as he got out of his Bureau issued vehicle—his "Bucar" in agency slang. An ME and his assistant stood over the body down by the water. A dark-haired woman sat on a stump, hugging her knees in the shade of the trees. The fact she had a pretty face was probably the main reason a deputy was hovering over her like an overprotective shadow.

Another deputy held a logbook near the steps of the property.

"Agent Kincaid." Hunt spoke quietly and flashed his badge at the man and signed the log.

A cop in plainclothes came over and introduced himself. Detective Lance Howell. They shook hands. Hunt had spoken to him on the phone.

"What do you have?" asked Hunt.

"Twenty-eight-year-old female, name of Cindy Resnick, found dead in the water. Suspected drug overdose. Friend," Howell nodded to the dark-haired woman down by the water, "Pippa West, claims she arrived from out of town and found the vic lying face down in the water at 9:05 AM when she immediately called 911. Paramedics found West doing CPR when they arrived an hour later. Vic was already dead."

It was now noon and these people had been waiting all morning for him to arrive, which would make him the least popular man at the party.

"Vic was naked?" Hunt eyed the pale body against the dark earth.

The detective nodded. "Some minor bruising on the arms but not enough to clearly indicate trauma." The detective's eyes held no sympathy, only annoyance this was taking up so much of his time.

"Next of kin been informed?"

"According to Ms. West the vic didn't have any living family. We're looking into it." Howell rested his hands on his belt. He wore a denim shirt and faded jeans and made Hunt feel stuffy and overdressed.

"Photographer's in the cottage, she already took shots of the body. Frankly, we don't usually put much effort into cases like this but when the FBI said they wanted to get involved…"

The man wanted to know what was going on. Hunt wished he could tell him.

The heat was stifling in the midday sun so Hunt took off his jacket. He opened the car door and hung it over the back of the seat. Felt eyeballs on him and turned to find the woman who'd discovered the body, watching him intently, clearly trying to overhear what he and the detective said.

She didn't look away when he caught her staring. Oval face with brown-black eyes and hair the deep, blue-black of a clear night sky. Her eyes were intelligent—weighing and measuring everything from his badge to the detective's sour expression.

Another scientist?

The ME rolled the vic onto her side and the woman's gaze darted back to her friend, looking anguished.

"What makes you so sure she ODed?" asked Hunt.

The detective grunted. "Found traces of white powder on the glass table inside."

White powder… Ah, shit.

The detective would have run a color test that indicated the possible presence of cocaine. That didn't mean it *was* cocaine. And even if it was cocaine, it didn't mean it was *just* cocaine.

"Looks like someone had a few drinks and did a few lines.

She might not have ODed," the detective conceded with his exaggerated Georgia twang. "She might have gotten high and decided it was a good idea to go skinny-dipping and drowned. But it's still drug related, and it still frustrates the hell outta me." His shoulders pulled back, high and tight.

But it might be more than just a drug thing. Cindy Resnick's death might be connected to the attempted sale of a bioweapon to international terrorists.

A light breeze rustled the leaves on the nearby trees. Thoughts of anthrax spores floating invisible on the air had Hunt glancing uneasily in the direction of the cottage. The ache in his arm from the vaccination he'd been given at the CDC earlier suddenly didn't hurt so bad.

Each person who'd attended the scene was gonna need to be vaccinated as a precaution, including the civilian—although if McKenzie and Frazer were to be believed, the current vaccine might not work on this particular strain of the deadly bacteria.

Hunt eyed the friend. Something told him she was going to be trouble. She reached up and touched the deputy's hand and the guy practically preened under her attention. Yep. Serious trouble.

"Why are the Feds involved?" Howell asked straight out when he'd been silent too long.

Hunt wished he could flat-out tell him, but it was restricted, need-to-know. "I need to get clearance to bring you in on this. Let me talk to my boss."

Despite being unhappy Howell nodded and backed away. Hunt dialed McKenzie and updated him on the situation.

McKenzie swore. "Work it as a suspicious death. I'll contact CDC and they can send in a team to do an immediate

TONI ANDERSON

sweep for anthrax spores. I have a HMRU team heading to Atlanta and another staging in LA." HMRU—the Hazardous Materials Response Unit—were usually based at Quantico. "They can collect evidence at your scene just in case it is anthrax."

Some kinds of evidence were more ephemeral than others—fingerprints, for example, deteriorated over time. If Cindy Resnick was a terrorist instead of a recreational coke-head, they needed to figure out who else was involved with her. He looked at the friend.

"Spin it as routine." McKenzie meant lie.

Great.

Hunt got off the phone and faced the detective, keeping his voice low, aware that the friend—Pippa West—watched them keenly.

He gave his back to the woman. "Remember the anthrax letters sent through the mail just after 9/11?"

Detective Howell pulled a face. "Who doesn't?"

Hunt nodded. "Since the AMERITHRAX investigation the USDA instigated a bunch of new regs."

"They do love their regulations. What does that have to do with this?" Howell's eyes narrowed.

"That includes what happens after the suspicious death of anyone researching certain pathogens, which is why I'm here."

The detective's gaze sharpened. "Vic was a researcher?"

"Ph.D. student."

"Studying…?"

"Anthrax."

Howell put his thumbs in the loops of his jeans and made a face. "Which is a white powder. *Shit.*"

Hopefully the detective hadn't tasted the powder the way

32

some narcs did.

"With your permission the Feds will take over processing the scene as a precaution and we'll also give everyone who visited the scene a vaccination just in case." And hoped it worked against this new weaponized version of the disease. "We are not expecting to find any spores here," he didn't want to start a panic, "but we don't want to ignore the possibility." Hunt stared at the cottage. "We should probably get the photographer out of there until it's declared safe. I'd like copies of the images she's taken if possible."

Howell nodded, looking pissed.

Hunt tried to reassure the man. "I'm sure it's exactly what you think it is. A drug-related fatality with no risk to yourself or others. The CDC will come out to test the powder to make sure it's just coke. I'd appreciate help interviewing any potential witnesses around the lake or in the local community. Track down the vic's movements for the last week or so. Figure out where she got the drugs. I'm just one agent…" He raised his hands with the implied message. *This isn't important enough for the Bureau to put much effort into and I need help.*

The detective's expression turned from freaked to irritated. "It's not contagious, right?"

"Nope. Not contagious." Of course, the bioweapon that some asshole had tried to sell to the highest bidder was an unknown entity. Hunt eyed the woman who'd supposedly tried to save her friend. He wondered how contagious a pathogen was if someone gave an infected person mouth-to-mouth.

"Thing is…" Hunt lowered his voice. "If anyone spots the CDC here, next thing you know we'll have an Ebola outbreak in rural Georgia."

The dark-haired woman was staring at him so hard he was starting to think she could read lips.

"Can I ask you to talk to your deputies, and the other people who attended the scene? Assure them this is routine? CDC doc can head down to the police station or local hospital to give everyone who attended their shot and some antibiotics. They can sign a waiver and refuse if they want to." *No pressure. No big deal.*

The detective glanced over at the pretty friend. "What do you want me to do with her?"

Hunt frowned. People who found bodies were always suspects in murder cases, but this didn't appear, at first glance, to be a homicide. But it was possible it was something far more sinister.

He called Hernandez at SIOC, gave her the license plate and name and asked her to run a quick background check and to get back to him.

"I'll need to question her after I've assessed the body and the scene, which will take some time because of the new regs, which in this case requires the scene to be tested for the presence of pathogens. We need to crosscheck the time of death with Ms. West's story."

"I can take her back to the station." Howell nodded to the Honda. "That's her vehicle. The shit heap. She said she had engine trouble on the way in. Might need to tow it into town. That might be a good way to slow her down for a few hours while convincing her we're the good guys."

Hunt eyed the stacks of boxes in the backseat and wondered what else was inside. "She moving?"

The detective smoothed down his mustache. "Just left her job in Tallahassee. Claims she was planning to stay with the vic until she decided what to do next."

Now the friend was dead.

Was it possible she'd supplied the vic with whatever had killed her? Had they fought? Had Cindy not wanted the other woman around?

Or was the vic selling weaponized anthrax to international terrorists? Maybe this was a suicide because she'd figured it was only a matter of time before the FBI tracked her down. And if that was the case it was also possible she'd left them a bioweapon bomb as some twisted form of revenge.

"We should try to check whatever Ms. West has packed in her car before we let her leave." He was thinking potential biohazard but could frame it as a drug search. Hunt motioned with his chin at the crammed Honda. "In case she's not telling us everything."

Howell nodded slowly. "She's a suspect?"

"Everyone is a suspect," Hunt said tiredly. "Until they're not. We'll know more after the autopsy."

The detective went off to handle the photographer and let the others know what was going on. Hopefully they'd clear out of here before the CDC turned up. Because nothing screamed, "No need to panic!" like men in space suits.

CHAPTER THREE

A TALL, BROAD-SHOULDERED, slender-hipped guy in a lightweight gray suit had turned up and was clearly calling the shots.

"Who's that?" Pip asked the uniform officer who'd first questioned her when he'd arrived on the scene then had hovered like a shadow ever since. She didn't know if he thought she was going to run away or start a rampage.

Part of her wanted to crawl over and wrap her arms around her best friend, shielding her nakedness from these strangers' eyes. She stuffed her fist against her mouth to hold back a sob. She hoped Cindy forgave her for letting them do their jobs.

The deputy shrugged noncommittally, apparently unimpressed by the newcomer.

"You don't know?" she prodded his ego.

"Fed." His lips twisted. He was young and cleanly shaven. He stood with his hands on his equipment belt, one hip cocked.

Oh, God. He was trying to impress her, she realized. Not understanding that even on a good day her heart was as impenetrable as steel.

She looked away, her eyes drawn back to the new arrival. He carried with him a natural air of authority even though he wasn't that old. Her age, maybe a few years older. He shrugged out of his jacket and put it in his car, careful not to wrinkle the material.

Anger seeped through the cold numbness that encased her.

Her friend was lying dead in full view of everyone and he was worried about wrinkling his suit?

The Fed spoke to the detective, both of them eyeing her like they were measuring her for handcuffs.

Screw them.

Pip eyed the new guy's short, sandy-brown hair, crisp white shirt, shoulder holster and shiny gold badge clipped to his belt. Combined with the confidence of his stance and the reaction of her minder, Fed made sense.

DEA? In her experience they rarely looked so neat and shiny.

She'd told the cops fifty times that no way had Cindy taken drugs and she was too good a swimmer to drown. Pip had thought they didn't believe her. Perhaps they did and had called for a second opinion.

But a Fed?

The ME and his assistant turned Cindy over. Pip watched the strangers manhandle her friend wishing she could somehow protect Cindy from all this. The moisture in her mouth turned to hot tears that wouldn't quit.

Pip had only had the strength to drag Cindy halfway up the bank. Her friend's feet were still in the water. Pip desperately wanted someone to pull Cindy's toes out of the cold lake, but she also knew that the moment they did, Cindy would be hauled off to the morgue and Pip would have to face the bleak reality that her friend was gone forever.

She reached up and touched the deputy's hand to get his attention. Asked in a rough whisper. "Can't they cover her up? Please?"

The deputy's gaze flickered over her friend's naked body but he made no move to do as she asked. She drew her hand back into her lap.

The Fed gave her a hard stare then turned to make a phone call. She couldn't hear what he was saying though she tried. He turned back to look at her with a new expression on his face, this one piercing her to the bone. Whatever someone was telling him wasn't good. She shivered and looked away. Which of her sins had he discovered, and why did any of them matter?

After a few minutes, the newcomer walked down to where Cindy lay on the wet grass. He studied her intently, eyeing her friend's tattoo, before crouching and looking even closer at the private places of her friend's pale and vulnerable body.

Bile rose in Pip's throat.

Cindy would hate this. *She* hated this. The ignominy of death. The casual callousness of the observers. Death should be something that made them all look away in shame. Instead they stared.

"What happens now?" she asked the cop.

She was usually good with people, especially cops and blue-collar types, single moms and students working two jobs to get through college. They were her people. That's where most of her information came from. Normal, decent, hard-working folk. At least that's where it had come from.

After her last big story, she doubted anyone would trust her with their secrets again.

At least my job doesn't get people killed...

"Depends," the cop told her, snapping her attention away from the past. He had white blond brows. A patch of red was forming on his neck where his skin was getting fried by the sun. "Most drug overdoses don't warrant an autopsy."

A sob caught in her throat.

She'd witnessed a postmortem and knew how objectively death was evaluated. She was torn between not wanting her friend's body desecrated and a burgeoning anger that law enforcement might not consider Cindy's death worth investigating.

The county probably couldn't afford to autopsy every suspected OD, but this was different.

"Cindy didn't do drugs," Pip repeated. No one took any notice and she was starting to feel invisible. Maybe if she started screaming she might get their attention. Then they'd call her hysterical and ignore her for that reason instead.

"Ms. West?"

Pip looked up to meet a direct blue stare. Thin gold bands circled the irises like rings on a small planet. She pressed her palms against her chilled thighs to stand so she wasn't at such a massive height disadvantage. Her movements slow and stiff.

The uniform faded away to where the detective—Howell—stood watching them from the deck.

"I'm Agent Kincaid." The Fed held out his hand. "I'm sorry for your loss."

"Pip West." She accepted his handshake, her fingers so numb she barely registered the squeeze of his. She caught the scent of him, some sort of fresh pine combined with the subtle odor of laundry detergent. It beat the smell of swampy lake water that permeated her clothes.

She shivered.

"You're cold," he observed.

Her bones felt like icicles ready to snap. She gritted her teeth and glanced at Cindy. Cold didn't begin to describe the state of her being.

"Can you walk me through what happened earlier today?" He had a nice voice. Deep, but not gruff. Smooth—as if the rough patches had been sanded out by a good education. She couldn't place his accent and she was usually good at that.

She told him how she'd found Cindy earlier that morning. "Which agency did you say you were with?"

The smile around his mouth didn't reach his eyes. "Federal Bureau of Investigation."

"Since when do FBI agents investigate single person deaths?"

He ignored her answer. "Ms. Resnick wasn't expecting you?"

She shook her head. Gooseflesh rose on her arms and she rubbed her roughened skin.

"You were planning to move in with her anyway?" The words had a slight bite and she started.

She nodded, unable to speak. Her teeth started to chatter. Her damp top clung to her chest and she was suddenly aware her nipples were clearly visible against the cotton. She crossed her arms over her chest. Mortification seeping between slivers of grief.

"I need a sweater from my car." The numbness of finding Cindy was beginning to wear off. Tiredness from a sleepless night and an hour of CPR started to make her feel dizzy.

He matched his stride to hers as they walked up the hill to her battered Honda. She went to the passenger door and grabbed a red fleece that was draped over a box of photo albums and knickknacks sitting on the front seat.

Two potted plants Cindy had given her for Christmas were on the floor. Cindy had said she needed more friends.

God.

Tears filled her eyes.

Agent Kincaid didn't even notice. His gaze was all over the contents of her car, but it was nothing to get excited about. A box of kitchen pots and plates was crammed next to her printer and TV. The haphazard mess was covered by a crimson duvet. She had two suitcases of clothes and all her documents and books in the trunk. She'd left her furniture for the next tenant back in Florida.

Kincaid didn't say anything and she had no idea what he was thinking. Did he know who she was? They'd have run the plates but would they have made the connection between her and the journalist who'd run a story on a dirty cop and gotten her source killed?

Her stomach cramped.

Agent Kincaid took a notebook out of his pocket. "When was the last time you spoke to Ms. Resnick?"

"We texted last night. I don't remember exactly when we actually spoke."

"Try." The edge in his voice suggested he knew she was lying.

Twelve days ago.

She looked down at her bare feet covered in dirt and bits of dead leaves. Her wet socks and sneakers were drying in the sun beside the old tree stump she and Cindy had often used as a table between two deck chairs during the sweltering heat of a Georgia summer.

Her eyes shifted to Agent Kincaid's feet. He wore good

quality black leather shoes that had a lot of miles on them.

People who worked for the government generally weren't in it for the money. Hopefully that meant he'd do the right thing by her friend.

Her eyes hurt from the effort of holding in her grief. "I tried to call her last night after we'd texted," she said gruffly, avoiding his question. "She didn't answer."

Had she already been dead?

Her hand covered her mouth. She couldn't do this. Not now.

"You quit your job?" His eyes were back on her belongings.

"Yeah." A harsh laugh escaped. "Quit my job. Quit my apartment."

Two weeks ago, she'd been the golden girl at the small paper about to break a massive story about police corruption. Now she was nothing.

"Cindy would never do drugs," she told him.

"What about you?"

Her chin snapped up. "I don't do drugs, either."

Those eyes of his were hard. "So how do you explain that arrest for possession when you were seventeen?"

She took a step back as if he'd physically assaulted her. "I was charged with a misdemeanor."

His gaze drilled into her like this mattered.

This was bullshit.

She gritted her teeth and felt the muscles in her jaw flex. "They weren't my drugs, but no one ever believed me."

"You pled guilty."

"My shitty court-appointed attorney told me I was lucky it was my first *offense*. I was actually still sixteen at the time and my *boyfriend* shoved his stash into my coat pocket when the cops pulled him over for running a red light. He said they wouldn't search me, and that even if they did I was a juvenile so they'd let me go." She looked away. "They did search me, and they didn't believe me when I told them the truth so I stopped trying."

"Prisons are full of the cries of the innocent." He didn't quite sneer and she didn't quite glare.

It was an experience that had pushed her toward journalism. Trying to tell the truths of other people who'd stopped trying.

"When did you speak to Cindy last?" he asked, forcefully.

She looked at her dirty toes again. "Twelve days ago. We had an argument."

"About?"

She brought her nose down to the softness of her fleece and closed her eyes.

You work too hard. You don't eat properly. You hook up with guys you barely know.

You don't know everything, and at least I'm not too terrified to date. At least my job doesn't get people killed!

"Nothing. Stupid stuff."

When she opened her eyes, his penetrating gaze made her look away. Cindy's words had cut deep and Pip had hung up on her. The next day, Pip had quit her job and tried to figure out what to do next. If only she'd figured it out a day earlier Cindy might still be alive.

"Last night she texted to say she'd finished her thesis and then she said she wasn't feeling well. I'd already given notice for my job and apartment, so I thought I'd surprise her this morning. I have the texts on my phone. I'll show them to you."

That grip tightened around her throat again. "I tried to call but she didn't answer. I figured she'd probably gone to bed and I wanted to be here by the time she got up in the morning so I just started driving."

Had she been so caught up in the drama of her own life that she'd completely missed something was going on in Cindy's? She knew Cindy had been hiding things from her lately. It was one of the reasons she'd pushed her friend during their last phone conversation.

What's going on with you?

Nothing.

Liar.

Drop it, Pip.

"She completed her thesis?" Agent Kincaid asked.

"Yeah." All that work for nothing.

"Do you know the nature of what she was working on?"

Pip closed her eyes as Cindy's laughter rang clearly through her mind.

"Anthrax." She caught a tear with a knuckle. Pretended it wasn't there. "She was developing a new vaccine." She drew in a shaky breath. "It always freaked me out that she studied something so dangerous. I know she was good at what she did but we rarely discussed the details."

"Why not?"

"Because the science is so far over my head it's like a comet passing through the outer atmosphere." Pip propped her hands on her hips. "She just needed a break from it sometimes."

Pip hadn't told Cindy every detail about her work, either. She wasn't the only one whose work could be dangerous. Pip swallowed the rest of her tears. Stuffed them down. They did no good and revealed a weakness she didn't want exposed. "She was the smartest person I ever met."

Agent Kincaid frowned, obviously not convinced. "What about her family?"

Grief was like a rusty nail driven into her gut. She wanted to curl into a ball and howl at the unfairness of it all, but she had to get through this, for Cindy's sake. She needed to know what had happened to her friend. "Her parents and younger brother died in a car wreck seventeen months ago."

Those blue-gold eyes narrowed with a mix of sympathy and suspicion. She couldn't hold his gaze and her eyes dropped to his chest. His navy tie had teeny tiny handcuffs on them. The gun he wore looked frightening and lethal.

"You were close to the family?"

She nodded.

"What about other relatives?"

Pip pressed her lips together. "Cindy's dad had a half-brother up in Alaska and her mom had a few cousins dotted around the south. They never made it to the funeral." Which had pissed Cindy off, big time.

"Did Cindy have a boyfriend?"

"I don't think so, but I'm not sure. It's the first thing that crossed my mind when I saw the things on the coffee table," she admitted. "Cindy is a neat freak and always cleaned up immediately—even if that meant doing it at four in the morning. But she didn't mention a new man in her texts and she'd come here to work, not play."

"People don't always plan to hook up." A gleam of something that spoke of late nights and tangled limbs flashed through his eyes.

Heat spread over her cheeks. "But she said she wasn't

feeling well. I can't imagine that she went from there to partying."

"Maybe she was lying so she didn't have to chat. You always told each other when you hooked up with someone, even for one night?"

Pip didn't want to talk about her sex life with a stranger. And talking about it with a guy she'd have been attracted to if she'd met him in a bar? Uh, uh.

"We told each other everything, but not always straight away," she admitted reluctantly. "She'd have told me if she was dating someone new though." Wouldn't she?

You don't know everything.

"You don't look too convinced," he said.

Her stomach clenched.

"Can you tell me the name of her last boyfriend?"

Most murder victims were killed by someone they knew. Most were killed by someone they were in a relationship with. Did he think Cindy had been murdered? The thought was horrific but made more sense than Cindy suddenly experimenting with narcotics.

"Dane Garnett. I never met him but I spoke to him a few times on speaker. He seemed okay." Pip's lips were dry and cracked. She rubbed the rough skin. "Cindy said he was handsome and ripped, but not that smart."

Pip felt embarrassed to be sharing Cindy's intimate confessions but she wanted this officer of the law to have enough information to find out exactly what had happened.

He gave her a faint smile. She'd have had to be blind not to notice he was ripped, and from the assessing light in his eyes he was also smart.

"Where'd they meet?"

"They hooked up at a bar. But he was also in her running club. They only dated for about a month. Broke up at the beginning of March."

"She was a runner?" Agent Kincaid made a note in his spiral notebook.

Pip nodded. "Five miles every day. She got me into it in college. Used to drag me with her so she didn't have to go out alone at night."

All those years of being careful.

"Is that where you two met?" he asked.

All those years of being safe.

"Freshmen in college. Yes." Pip couldn't think about their shared past without breaking down. She changed the subject. "She dated another guy for a couple years in grad school but found out he cheated and dumped him. They were pretty serious." *The asshole.* "Pete Dexter. She thought they were gonna get married and have babies."

Pip watched the Medical Examiner and his assistant tuck Cindy's body into a black body bag. Paper bags covered Cindy's hands—to preserve evidence, Pip knew. The two men, with the help of a deputy, hoisted Cindy onto a stretcher. Pip took an involuntary step forward to help.

Strong fingers curled around her upper arm, knuckles accidentally brushing the side of her breast. She jolted and her eyes swung to his. His mouth twisted with apology but he didn't let go.

"They'll take care of her," he said quietly.

Her stomach lurched as she watched them load her best friend into the back of an ambulance.

"Was she raped?" She forced the question through gritted teeth. It had burned through her mind every time she looked at her friend's naked body.

"I don't know."

She released a pent-up breath. At least he hadn't lied. He let go of her arm and she turned to face him. "What happens now?"

"I need you to go with the local cops and make a written statement. And because Cindy worked on anthrax and we found white powder at the scene we're treating this as a suspicious death and giving everyone involved an anthrax vaccination. Just in case."

Pip was appalled by the idea that the white powder could be anything more deadly than cocaine.

"Cindy would never be so reckless with anthrax spores. She was extremely safety conscious."

"It's standard procedure." Agent Kincaid looked at the sky. "Since the anthrax letters post 9/11."

She lifted her chin and narrowed her eyes. "Is that why you're here?"

He nodded.

It actually made sense, which made it highly unusual for a federal agency.

The ME slammed the doors of the ambulance and tapped the back of the vehicle and she jumped again. The engine started up and the rig began its slow grind up the dirt road.

Pip started to shake. The ice in her bones starting to splinter and crack. She didn't know how she was still standing up. "What happens to her now?"

"We'll do an autopsy before releasing her body for burial." He sounded so matter of fact while her world crashed around her feet.

"I want to make the funeral arrangements."

"You the executor of Ms. Resnick's will?" The blue eyes with their flash of gold were cool and assessing.

She probably shouldn't fantasize about smacking the guy around the head. "I don't know."

They'd never talked about it. They'd talked about hot romance, dream men, and perfect vacations.

Things that didn't matter anymore.

But the idea of someone else arranging Cindy's funeral?

Screw that.

Pip would get a job or a loan, or both, and make it the best goddamned funeral Atlanta had ever seen.

"Can I go now?" The need to get out of here was suddenly overwhelming though she didn't know where she'd go. She looked at her car. Would it even start? Could she get water for the radiator? Cindy had an outside hose. Hopefully no one would object if she used that.

Kincaid's voice trapped the part of her that wanted to escape. "The detective mentioned you had car trouble on the way in."

She nodded. "I rolled in here thinking it was my last stop for a while and then..." Tears jammed her throat and she couldn't speak. She blinked them away. She'd already shown too much weakness in front of these people.

"I'll arrange for the car to be towed to the station then you can call a garage in town and have them take a look at it. One of the deputies can give you a ride back so you can make your formal statement. I'd like to talk to you again later today if possible..."

She saw something move across the back of his eyes. Some

glint of mercilessness. "And if I don't?"

"Then I'll have you arrested on suspicion of manslaughter." His smile didn't reach those pretty eyes. He shrugged dismissively. "Your choice."

CHAPTER FOUR

B Y THE TIME the CDC specialists in their protective gear finished taking samples the sun was starting to glow behind the trees on the western ridge.

Hunt flashed back to the look of contempt Pippa West had thrown at him when he'd suggested the manslaughter charge. No flicker of fear. Just pure unadulterated scorn for him and his badge.

Interesting.

Did she hate law enforcement in general, or was it just him who pissed her off? And what had she fought with her friend about? Something personal or something criminal...?

His cell rang. It was Libby Hernandez from SIOC.

"Got some more information on the woman who found the body. Lives in Tallahassee and was a reporter for the Tallahassee Free Press."

A wave of dislike moved over him. A journalist. Shit. He'd known she was trouble just from looking at her.

"Was?"

"She resigned just over a week ago. There was a big scandal when a dirty cop she exposed murdered his family and then killed himself. A lot of bad feelings stirred up. She got death threats and something tells me that the local cops wouldn't have protected her."

So, it was all law enforcement rather than just him she detested. He had a reciprocal distaste for journalists so they were even.

Dr. Jez Place—Hunt's contact in the CDC—came toward him, having been doused in disinfectant in some sort of portable decontamination plastic tent that looked like it should be in a field in freaking Africa.

"I have to go, Hernandez," Hunt told the analyst. "Thanks for the information. I appreciate it."

The microbiologist had stripped off his plastic suit and wore sweat-stained scrubs. The smell of bleach on the afternoon breeze made Hunt's eyes water.

"Our field sensors didn't indicate anthrax and I did a preliminary exam of the white substance. Looks like some sort of non-biological reagent."

"Not anthrax?" Relief hit Hunt like a fist to the gut. He hadn't even known how much he'd dreaded the idea until now.

"It's only preliminary, but no, not anthrax. We'll run it through the mass spec and see if we can grow any bacterial colonies to confirm."

"How long will that take?"

"Tonight, or tomorrow morning on the mass spec, a few days at most on the latter, but I'm fairly confident. We swabbed the desk, kitchen, bathroom. Any flat surfaces that might have been utilized as a home laboratory, but the sensors didn't indicate anything suspicious. This looks to me like recreational drug use."

And a giant waste of time and resources.

HMRU were due on scene within the hour. They'd lift fingerprints and take DNA samples. They'd also bag phones,

52

computers and anything else they could examine for trace or digital information to be sent to the lab. None of this would be necessary if some asshole hadn't tried to sell weaponized anthrax to terrorists.

Hunt bit back his annoyance. Cindy Resnick was probably just another loser who'd gotten the balance wrong between high and dead. So much for being smart. But the fact she worked on anthrax vaccines was too pertinent to ignore. The FBI had to keep an open mind in this death investigation while selling the idea to local cops and interested parties that it was just routine.

The victim's friend's anguished face flashed into his mind. Damn.

Why did people do it? Chase a high that so often spiraled into a bad decision and wasted dreams?

"Ironic that the only reason we're here is the fact there was white powder on the table." Jez Place commented dryly. "Endospores of *Bacillus anthracis* are about one micron in diameter. You can fit a hundred across the width of a human hair."

Hunt grunted. "It's not the only reason we're here."

Jez knew about the bioweapon and the fact all researchers involved with anthrax were being put under the FBI's own microscopic examination. Especially those who also worked on vaccine development.

Jez scuffed an orange Croc over the grass. "We're doing the right thing treating this site with caution. I know it's probably overkill, but easier to defend that than explain why we didn't take the threat seriously." Jez pulled a face. "It's important to follow procedures, even though it's time consuming and expensive."

"Did you know her?" Hunt asked.

Jez shook his head. "I saw her at conferences a few times—she was hard to miss. Tall. Blonde. Insanely attractive."

Hunt hadn't noticed. Corpses weren't his thing. He had noticed her friend was hot though. She was also a petite little thing so it was surprising she'd managed to drag the dead girl that far out of the water—assuming things had gone down the way Ms. Pippa West claimed. Assuming she hadn't had an accomplice.

The FBI didn't operate on unsupported assumptions.

"Resnick never presented any scientific data and I'm a happily married man, so I didn't pay her much attention. Her supervisor, Trevor Everson, was a top guy in vaccine development about fifteen years ago."

"What's he like?"

The CDC specialist considered for a moment. "Nice enough. A little disillusioned by the federal funding of research in this country, and the way universities are saving a buck by hiring sessionals rather than tenure-track professors."

Hunt's ears sharpened.

"Don't look so intrigued. It's not an unusual point of view. In fact, the opposite would be true. Even I find it difficult to hire grad students knowing they might find it hard to make a living wage if they go into academia. I guess we all hope it's going to change, but so far no sign." Jez shook his head in frustration. "Then there's the fact funding bodies want an accounting for every cent scientists spend. Can't blame them, but…"

"But?" asked Hunt.

"It's put a stranglehold on research for the sake of research." The man's eyes flicked to his face. He looked a little embarrassed. "The natural inquisitiveness of scientists, which has led to so many vital discoveries, is stymied by dollars and cents." He shrugged. "Maybe it keeps us focused."

"What about private labs? Or industry."

"Oh, there are jobs out there, but a lot of really good scientists want to tackle important questions and that generally depends on getting a good academic position and solid funding." A deep crease formed in Jez's cheek. "Pharmaceutical companies don't care about curing disease, they care about shareholders and stock dividends."

"But they still do research, right?"

Place looked unimpressed. "They're looking for drugs that will make profits for decades to come. There is no profit in eliminating the problem. Some research is funded by charitable donations, but I don't understand why research that could save the country billions in health care costs has to rely on charity—" The man cut himself off. "I'll shut up before I start talking about the financial burden of healthcare versus that of developing cures for common ailments."

Hunt raised his brows. "I think you just did."

Jez grimaced. "Back to Everson. He doesn't present much at conferences and hasn't in a few years. He publishes less. Looks like he's counting the days until retirement. Cindy Resnick was the last student left working in his lab that I'm aware of."

"Did you see a copy of her thesis in there?"

Place shook his head. "It's probably on her laptop and hopefully backed up on several different servers. Although I've heard of students who lose everything and have to start over from scratch. Geniuses gonna genius."

One of the CDC team shouted to the microbiologist.

"Looks like they're ready to head back."

Hunt looked at them loading up gear. "Who'll do the autopsy?"

"Probably the senior pathologist."

"I'd like to observe but I'm not sure when I'll be done here." Jez Place knew how to contact him. "We need the results ASAP, so don't wait for me."

Jez nodded and walked away with a raise of his hand. The CDC team left the decontamination tent and some gear for the HMRU people.

Quietness settled around Hunt when the van finally trundled out of view.

He put his hands on his hips and looked out at the millpond flat surface of the lake. Only a few cottages were visible half a mile away on the opposite banks. No speedboats destroyed the peace of the afternoon. The lake had a pensive atmosphere that matched his mood. Only the memory of the dead girl disturbed the quiet.

He thought about Pippa West. The determined look in her eyes and the jut of her chin. He needed to go talk to her again at the police station. Needed as much information as he could gather to finish this investigation and get back to interviewing other scientists who worked on anthrax. This case looked more and more like an accidental overdose, which was a crying shame. Regardless, for the time being the FBI would continue to examine the evidence under the hastily written guidelines someone at CDC was currently throwing together regarding deaths of researchers of Category A substances.

News of the FBI's interest in Cindy's death *might* prompt the bioweapon producer into action. As long as it was getting rid of evidence rather than producing more anthrax, Hunt was okay with that. McKenzie seemed confident the people at SIOC would track them down eventually.

Professor Trevor Everson was at a conference in Nashville. He'd been informed of Cindy's death and was returning early tomorrow morning.

Hunt stared up at the cottage and blew out a breath of frustration. He wanted in there but wasn't authorized until HMRU finished. Same deal with the house in Atlanta, which seemed stupid when CDC had virtually given it the all-clear.

Something thumped and bumped along the track toward him, getting louder and louder until a big-ass suburban came into view and pulled up sharply outside the cottage. Six people piled out of the vehicle and came over to greet him with a barrage of questions.

HMRU had arrived.

———————————

PIP RUBBED THE injection site on her arm. Her skin was warm to the touch and the flesh beneath throbbed slightly. Even after five hours of incessant waiting, she still fumed.

Manslaughter?

Man-*fricking*-slaughter?

They were seriously considering her a suspect? She shouldn't be surprised. She'd investigated enough cases where the minimum amount of police work had been done to close a case, cops seemed to forget the real aim of law enforcement was to catch the *actual* offender, and not just get the case off the books. The anger was grounding compared to the grief that left her anchor-less and adrift in an unfriendly world.

She slumped down in the hard-plastic chair, exhaustion

pulling at her eyelids as she waited for Agent Kincaid to deign to show up. She'd made a statement about the morning's events. She'd shown the locals her phone message history with Cindy, allowed them to print out their exchanges and emails. They'd asked permission to search her car, which she'd denied. Now they were looking at her like she was guilty of something besides losing the person she loved most in the world.

She had files in her car and on her computer that she didn't want anyone to see. Contacts. Sources. The last thing she needed after everything that had happened in Tallahassee was to expose her informants, although some would say that ship had already sailed.

The knot in her stomach tightened.

Nausea roiled inside.

She hadn't eaten anything except a donut in the middle of last night when she'd felt herself flagging and needed a sugar boost. But the idea of food made bile churn and she pressed her hand to her chest to try to calm herself.

Pip took a sip of the bottled water the cops had given her three hours ago and fought to banish the memory of Cindy lying dead in the dirt. She forced herself to think of Cindy alive and vibrant. Grinning at a bar when a good-looking guy asked for her number. Scowling over an experiment that didn't work the way it should.

What was taking the cops so long?

Theoretically she could walk out the door. She hadn't been charged or arrested for anything although people who found the body were always suspects.

Manslaughter.

Honestly, right now she felt capable.

But they wouldn't talk to her if she pissed them off and she wanted to be kept up to date on the status of the investigation. She wanted to be kept informed. She wanted them to turn over every stone and shine a light in every corner.

Her anger deflated.

They should be questioning her motive and her alibi. If they'd allowed her to drive off into the sunset they'd be truly lousy cops.

Maybe they were lousy. She'd soon find out.

Cindy wouldn't have done drugs, but she might have drunk too much and gone skinny-dipping. So maybe there was a new man on the scene and the coke belonged to him. They'd partied and then climbed in the lake for a quick swim.

Had Cindy known what was happening? Or had she just gone to sleep and sunk beneath the surface? Had the guy panicked and run?

Pip pressed her fingernails into the skin of her palm.

After a lifetime of avoiding recreational drugs, Cindy would be pissed that people were labeling her a junkie. Pip owed it to her to figure out the truth even if the law dropped the ball. After another swig of water, she got up and tried the door. Maybe they'd forgotten about her.

She poked her head out and bumped right into the hard chest of Agent Kincaid. Ouch. She drew back and rubbed her brow.

His brows rose with a grin that seemed to catch them both by surprise. "Looking for the escape hatch?"

His face settled back into guarded lines as he held out a cardboard cup of coffee that he'd balanced on top of another one.

She took it reluctantly. Caffeine might get her through the rest of the day. She doubted it would stop her from crashing tonight.

He followed her back inside, sat at the bolted down table and started leafing through a bunch of papers.

He had big, capable-looking hands.

Her heart gave an unsteady knock against her ribcage as she imagined Cindy's throaty laugh at her observation. Pip crossed her arms over her chest, knowing she was giving him negative body language but so what. He already thought she was capable of killing her best friend.

"You provided a statement to the locals." Kincaid held up the sheaf of papers.

Was that a question?

"You refused to let them examine your vehicle?"

She gritted her teeth. "If they want to check the engine they can knock themselves out."

The outside edge of his lips lifted. She hated the fact she liked his face.

She reached for the coffee cup. Wished her hands didn't shake when she raised it to her lips.

"What time did you get to the Resnick property?" He looked at those notes again but he was bullshitting. No way had he forgotten. He was making sure she had her story straight.

She was suddenly so tired she regretted not curling in a ball on the floor and catching a nap earlier. They would probably have offered her a cell if she'd asked for one. She smiled humorlessly. "Do I need a lawyer?"

"I don't know, do you?" His long legs stretched out under the table. She made sure she didn't accidentally brush against him.

She had spent enough time around court cases to know

she probably did need a lawyer but couldn't afford a good one and didn't want some inexperienced court-appointed sap.

Her brain wanted to scratch and spit about her rights as a citizen, but her body was spent. "I didn't have anything to do with Cindy's death, but I am glad you're investigating it properly. Don't fuck it up."

"I'm just supposed to take your word for it? You admit to having fought with the victim, you have a drug conviction"—her eyes narrowed into murderous slits—"and you're the one they found hunched over the body."

"I was trying to revive her. I'm the one who called the paramedics!" Emotion surged but she pushed it aside.

Those interesting blue eyes with their thin gold bands watched her steadily. Straight brows and dark brown lashes framed them prettily. A lean jaw and a stubborn looking chin underscored a nose that was possibly a fraction too narrow. He was handsome and appealing, or he would have been if her best friend hadn't just died and he hadn't accused her of having something to do with it.

He raised a brow. "I find it a little surprising that you seem to be impeding the investigation."

An exhausted laugh escaped her. "Impeding? I'm impeding jack. I'm trying to help. No way did Cindy OD. I'm the one who's been telling you this from the start. Not without help, anyway—and not *my* help." She held his flat cop stare.

He looked unconvinced. She really wanted to kill him now.

"So why not let us look in your car?"

Her chin lifted. "You know what I do for a living, right? The FBI are surely smart enough to have figured that out by now?"

Of course, he did. That's why she was in here sweating and why they wanted to toss her car. Make her life as miserable as possible whether she was guilty or not.

Too late. Life was already as low as it could go.

"You're a journalist." An edge of derision escaped into his carefully controlled voice.

"Was. I quit." She didn't know if she'd ever work as a journalist again.

"How come?"

"I messed up." She blinked and swayed a little in her seat. She was starting to feel lightheaded, probably from lack of food.

"Tell me what happened," he repeated. He crossed his arms loosely in front of him. Patient as Job.

It shouldn't make her so crazy. "Leaving the paper doesn't have anything to do with Cindy's death."

"It gives me insight into your state of mind," he said.

"Which is irrelevant."

"Nothing is irrelevant in a suspicious death investigation." She clenched her teeth. "This is."

"Tell me, anyway." That tone of his was so condescending.

"Go to hell." She tangled her hands together and squeezed so hard her fingers turned red at the tips.

He leaned forward. "What is it you don't want us to see in your car, Pippa?"

"Pip," she corrected automatically, like it mattered. She bit her thumbnail. The idea the cops thought she might be involved in Cindy's death was crazy, but she couldn't have her cake and eat it. If she wanted them to investigate she had to accept them investigating everything.

"Fine. You can look at my car," she conceded. "And

through all my belongings. But you can't read any of the paper files or get into any of my electronics."

"Okay—"

"*And* I get to observe."

He hiked his brows. "That's not standard procedure."

"I don't care. You want to do this quick and dirty and without a warrant then I get to observe. If you refuse I want a good lawyer and you keep your hands off my stuff until a judge okays it."

He considered her slowly and thoroughly. It made her uncomfortably aware that she probably looked like a drowned rat who'd been dragged through hell.

She ran her tongue over her teeth and raised a brow to match his. "I have better things to do than sit around here forever. I'm assuming you're in the same position."

"Fine." He took a sip of coffee. "You can observe."

"And *you* conduct the search. Only you."

"You're kidding?" Now he sounded pissed which was fine with her. "As you pointed out I have better things to do."

Nothing was more important than figuring out what had happened to Cindy.

"I don't trust the locals," she admitted.

"Why?"

"Because two weeks ago a veteran cop killed himself rather than face the allegations of corruption I'd uncovered."

Agent Kincaid's nodded slowly, confirming he knew why she'd left Tallahassee.

Here was something he might not know. "But not before he somehow figured out my informant was his wife. He shot her and each of their three kids before turning the gun on himself. I won't put my other contacts in the same sort of danger."

His only response was an almost imperceptible widening of pupils.

No one, not even her editor, had known who her source had been until after the disaster that had unfolded. Somehow Detective Frank Booker had figured it out.

The disgraced detective had been spotted driving past Pip's apartment at dawn the morning he'd killed himself and his family. If she'd been at home rather than asleep at her desk, she'd have likely been another victim.

At least my job doesn't get people killed...

How could a story be worth so much bloodshed? Did truth really matter that much? Her brain said yes, but her heart wasn't so sure anymore. Dizziness swirled and she braced her arm on the table to stop herself face-planting.

"Ms. West? Pip? Are you okay?" The Fed was behind her now, with his palm pressed gently against her back. She was aware of the warmth of his fingers. Of the scent of his body.

She drew in a long deep breath and shook away the disorientation. Today had lasted a lifetime and she wanted it over. "Let's get this done."

CHAPTER FIVE

HUNT LED THE way through the police station fielding unfriendly glances and pissed-off cop vibes directed at the woman behind him.

Cops really didn't like reporters, especially reporters who specialized in police corruption. He'd left HMRU collecting evidence and they'd promised to pack up the decontamination tent and drop it back at the CDC when they were done. The cottage would remain a sealed crime scene until they figured out for sure whether or not Cindy Resnick had been illegally dealing anthrax.

He checked his shoulder to make sure he hadn't lost Pip West. Her skin was so pasty she looked like she was gonna pass out and only grim determination held her upright. He had to fight the desire to offer support.

But maybe she was manipulating him the way she'd played the deputy who'd watched over her earlier. She was attractive and she must know it. That little touch he'd witnessed, of her hand on the deputy's. Drawing attention back to her when the guy hadn't answered her question to her satisfaction.

Maybe he was jaded.

No *maybe* about it, but he didn't intend to fall for the fragile creature act.

Although someone *should* have stayed with her, especially

since she'd received a vaccination. But it was a small department and Detective Howell and many of the other officers were canvassing people who lived on the lake, at Hunt's request. The locals simply didn't have the manpower to babysit a journalist and they certainly hadn't wanted one in the bullpen.

A journalist.

ASAC McKenzie had blown a gasket when Hunt had found out and told him. Hunt had assured the ASAC he could handle her. He'd better.

As soon as the news had come through as to her connection to the investigation into police corruption in Tallahassee, the attitude of the police department here had shifted toward her. Hardened.

Hunt got it.

In LA, he'd spoken to a journalist he'd thought of as a friend, strictly off the record. She'd asked about the rumor UC Irvine might have a serial rapist operating on its campus. The journalist had run the story and quoted an unidentified FBI source and their chief suspect had got on a plane that same day and headed home to his mega-rich parents in Switzerland.

Hunt had confessed his unwilling involvement to his SAC and received a letter of censure for his trouble. The journalist had called him up again a few months later. She'd thought it was trivial and funny and got annoyed that he wouldn't talk to her anymore. But he wasn't just pissed, he was atomic-bomb fucking furious. Because of her a rapist had gotten away. All those victims had been left with no closure. No justice.

So, yeah, he didn't like reporters—not even when they filled out tight blue jeans and a fitted t-shirt like a wet dream. Not when the stakes were this high.

The cops had towed Pip West's car to the fenced compound at the back of the station. Someone had set up klieg lights. Hunt went back inside and grabbed a chair and placed it where Ms. West could observe without getting in the way. Sooner they got this over with, the sooner everyone could go home.

She lowered herself gingerly into the seat, wobbling slightly.

He frowned. "When was the last time you ate?"

She stared at him, mutely, big eyes filled with a mixture of grief and defiance.

He went back inside and grabbed a can of soda and a cheese salad roll he'd picked up on his way through town earlier, but hadn't had time to eat yet. His stomach growled in protest but the last thing he needed was her collapsing on him.

"Here." He handed it to her. "Eat."

She muttered a thanks and began pulling the roll apart, eating it slowly, bit by bit.

He nodded with grudging satisfaction. If she was telling the truth she'd had a truly awful day and he didn't want her to faint on him. If she was lying they'd figure it out. No need to be an asshole.

A K9 team were due to arrive any minute and another officer was videoing the whole thing as per Hunt's instructions. The crime scene photographer was also on hand to document the search if anything turned up. Hunt wasn't going to get accused of impropriety or making a mistake if he found a flask full of weaponized anthrax hidden somewhere inside this vehicle.

Except he couldn't see how a reporter from Tallahassee might be involved with selling a bioweapon to international terrorists, especially when she was so keen on exposing police corruption. But what did he know?

A van pulled up and the K9 handler jumped out. Hunt pulled on a Tyvek suit, face mask and latex gloves while the drug dog went over the vehicle and indicated nothing. There were ways of obscuring scent from hounds.

It would tie up the case with a nice pretty bow and let him get back to his real job if Pip West had given her BFF some coke to party with and accidentally gotten her killed.

He glanced at the woman.

Her ravaged eyes told him she thought she knew exactly what he was looking for and resented the hell out of him for it. But she'd insisted Cindy's death be properly investigated and he was obliging by doing his job.

So much for not being an asshole.

He saw the deputy from earlier today come outside and lean down to whisper something in Pip's ear before placing his hand on her shoulder and giving her a little squeeze.

Hunt turned away.

Do the job. Arrest her or send her on her way.

The photographer stretched out a large blue tarp on the ground to keep Pip's belongings out of the dirt.

Hunt started with the plants. He knew what cannabis looked like but apart from that he was clueless. His stepdad would know. His stepdad funneled grief into his garden to the extent Hunt's mom now called it "the other woman."

Hunt shoved thoughts of his parents aside. Losing focus could result in missing something.

"Any needles in here? Sharp objects?" he asked loudly.

Pip West's expression was derisive, but she answered clearly for the video. "Small scissors and a nail file in my toiletries bag. Kitchen knives and big scissors are in a Tupperware container in a kitchen box."

He started in the front seat. Cardboard coffee cups and a brown paper food sack, presumably from the road trip, were in the foot well of the passenger side. His stomach grumbled again and he glanced at her. She'd finished the cheese roll and some of the awful pallor from earlier had receded. Grief still marked her features and she looked like a gentle breeze would knock her off the chair.

The set of her jaw suggested she'd climb right back on again.

He pulled out a box of books and flicked through them quickly and efficiently. Lots and lots of books. Tiny TV, computer, pots and pans. Bed cover. It was deep crimson and the image of her lying on it, wearing nothing but a seductive smile flashed through his mind.

Obviously lack of food was making him delusional.

She was a suspect, for both her friend's death and the bioterrorism thing. But an unlikely one. She hadn't had to call 911 that morning—frantic and afraid. She could have driven away. A terrorist probably would have.

She'd provided receipts from two convenience stores on the way from Florida and Hunt had asked local agents to go to the gas stations to find timestamped surveillance footage to help verify where she was when her friend died.

It all depended on what Time of Death the ME established. In the meantime, Hunt couldn't afford to give her the benefit of the doubt. Someone somewhere was weaponizing anthrax to sell to people who liked to indiscriminately kill as many innocents as possible.

He pulled out a coffeemaker and a random assortment of

mugs. One had a smiling photo of Pip West and Cindy Resnick at one of the big theme parks. He put another stack of books to one side. He'd taken a look at their message exchanges and needed no further proof that Pip West and Cindy Resnick had been good friends.

But they had argued.

Or the overdose might have been accidental. Celebrating finishing her thesis and partying too hard.

Shoes, lots of shoes, were scattered on the floor of the back of the car. He pulled them out, one by one. Spiky heels and sparkly sandals. He indicated the K9 handler come over and take the dog over the interior again while he moved on to the trunk. He hefted out a suitcase and opened it up on the tarp.

He shook out every piece of clothing and placed it in a black plastic bag so it didn't get dirty.

He could feel his own face heat, and an expression of outraged horror crawled over Pip West's features. He wasn't a shrinking violet, but women were normally lovers or dead by the time he was handling their lingerie.

He grabbed the second enormous case. More clothes. Down the side were several make-up bags. He had no clue why women put so much crap on their faces, especially when they were already knockouts. He was grateful he could shower, shave and brush his teeth and consider himself ready for the day.

Although he did have to wear a tie.

Another good reason to dedicate everything he had into his quest to join HRT.

He searched the cases quickly, efficiently. No obvious sign of drugs or drug paraphernalia. No freaking anthrax.

Last, but not least, he pulled out a pink teddy bear that he examined carefully before tossing it to Pip.

She caught it easily.

"Cindy gave this to me," she said softly, stroking the pink fur. "She bought it at a teddy bear museum in England when she visited a few years back with her mom and dad." She hugged it and looked close to tears again.

He said nothing and then felt like an asshole, but what *could* he say? Sorry? What good did sorry do?

He went back to checking the spare tire and the jack. The K9 team did another once over of the car but found nothing to wag their tails about.

Hunt stepped away from the Honda and started stripping off his protective gear, tired and inexplicably relieved. "You're clear to go, Ms. West."

She nodded expressionlessly and stared at the mess he'd made before slowly pushing to her feet.

Hell.

He began stuffing her clothes back into the cases but she squatted beside him and nudged him aside with the sharp end of her elbow.

"I'll do it," she insisted.

Instead, he loaded the boxes back inside the car while she repacked her clothes. When he'd finished stowing her possessions he raised the hood. He went over to his Bucar and grabbed some coolant from the trunk, filled her radiator, checked the oil, and climbed behind the wheel to start up the motor. He damn near castrated himself with the steering wheel, but he didn't adjust the seat. It took two tries before the engine caught and rolled over. He watched the temperature gauge for a minute or two, but the warning light didn't come on.

"I wouldn't go too far until a mechanic checks the engine."

"Thank you." The words were polite but bitter. She closed the suitcases with a firm snap.

He grabbed them before she could insist on doing it herself and slid them into the trunk. "Next time, check your fluid levels before you set off on a road trip. You're lucky your engine didn't seize."

"Yes, Dad." She snorted a laugh but her eyes remained sad. Dark circles underscored her exhaustion.

He cleared his throat. "Where will I be able to get hold of you if I have more questions?"

"Call my cell. I'm sure you have the number." She climbed in to the seat, then combed her hair back from her face with wide-spread fingers. Hunt couldn't help noticing they trembled slightly.

Should he call her a cab rather than let her drive tonight? "It might be a good idea if you stayed local…"

"Don't leave town?" Her lips parted in surprise, then she slumped. "I'm too tired to drive anywhere tonight or fight with you about it. I'll find a motel." The onyx in her eyes seemed haunted and the pale pink of her lips was vivid in comparison to the paleness of her skin.

He pulled out a business card, forcing himself not to think about the fact that if she was innocent in all this she'd had one of those days that became seared into memory as one of the worst moments of your life.

"I'll probably have follow up questions tomorrow. Call me if you think of anything that might be relevant." Hunt cleared his throat. "Hopefully the ME can shed some light on your friend's time of death. We'll have information from the gas receipts you provided. As long as you were telling the truth everything should be fine."

Tears shimmered like diamonds spiking the tips of her lashes. "My best friend is dead, Agent Kincaid. Nothing will ever be fine again."

They held each other's gaze even though the pain in hers made him uncomfortable. He closed her door and she drove away.

After a few seconds he got in his car and followed, half worried she'd fall asleep at the wheel, half worried the rust-bucket she was driving would break down and leave her vulnerable on the side of the road.

She pulled up at the first motel she came to. He parked at a store across the street and watched her drag one case and then her computer and TV into the crappy motel room.

He told himself he was watching in case some dubious looking dudes appeared out of nowhere or Pip West decided to split. He used the time to update his SAC and the agents in DC. No one came to her door. After an hour Pip West's light went off and he started his engine and headed back to the police station.

As far as DC was concerned this was an FBI case until he figured out whether or not Cindy Resnick's death had anything to do with the sale of illegal anthrax. Which unfortunately meant Pip West was very much his problem.

———————

PIP SLEPT DREAMLESSLY, until she woke up and discovered she was still stuck in a nightmare. She'd dropped off her car at the local garage for a service. Now she was in the local diner, forcing herself to eat.

Going through the motions.

The restaurant was busy, loud. Wood paneling. Blue and white gingham drapes. Sunshine so bright it hurt her eyes.

At eight AM, Agent Kincaid slid into her booth just as she pushed what remained of her breakfast away. He wore the same suit, with a fresh white shirt, blue striped tie. His short sandy hair was ruffled in a way some men spent hours trying to achieve. His looked stress induced.

"Ms. West." He inclined his head across the table, then raised a hand to the waitress who came over with a coffee pot and a smile much bigger than the one she'd worn when she'd served Pip her bacon, sausage and eggs. He pointed at Pip's plate. "I'll have whatever she had."

The waitress left with a swing of her hips and a roll of Pip's eyes.

"Do you have news? Has the Medical Examiner finished the…?" She couldn't force the word autopsy out of her mouth. It was too bloody, too cold, too final.

She found herself lifting her chin to meet the challenge of his eyes.

"I just got the preliminary report. Your friend drowned, but there was enough alcohol and cocaine in her system to stun an elephant. If she hadn't drowned, the fentanyl mixed in with the coke would probably have killed her."

Pip flinched.

The cops were right…

No.

No way.

Pip didn't care what the report said. Cindy would never have taken drugs. She was a microbiologist with a joint major in biochemistry. She understood the risks too well to snort something she bought on the street from a stranger.

Agent Kincaid reached over and stole a piece of toast from her side plate. She didn't care. She wasn't hungry. "Did you find more cocaine in the cottage?" she asked.

He bit into the toast. Chewed slowly. "You know I can't reveal any details of an investigation."

She gritted her teeth. "But you are quite happy to pump me for information."

"I'm an FBI agent. It's what I do." His direct gaze unnerved her. "You want me to figure out what happened to your friend? This is how it works."

She looked away. Of course, she wanted to know what happened to Cindy. She just didn't have a lot of faith in law enforcement.

"Any idea where she might have gotten the drugs?" He watched her closely, no doubt looking for hints of deception.

"This is what I've been trying to tell you." She was so exasperated. Why wouldn't he believe her? "She detested drugs. I never saw her do drugs, not even in college when everyone else was doing them."

"Including you?"

She stared back, trying hard to hold back her resentment. He didn't know her. He just saw she'd pleaded guilty to possession when she'd been too young and too vulnerable to speak the truth. His skepticism bolstered her determination to be taken seriously. Cindy didn't have a voice any longer. Pip would be her voice.

"I grew up in foster care, Agent Kincaid. When I was sixteen I dated a guy a few years older and thought I was cool. I even tried a couple things because I was young and miserable and stupid. But I didn't like dope or cigarettes or alcohol for that matter. Until that day when the cops stopped him I didn't know the jerk I was with was on probation. He shoved those baggies into my jean jacket pocket and begged me to not say anything." He'd used her. And let her take the fall. It wasn't a mistake she'd made twice. "By the time I started college I was an A student on a scholarship who had no fallback position if I screwed up. So, I never did drugs. And I went to every lecture and completed every assignment. I worked hard. So did Cindy."

That fist in her throat was back and it was expanding. Air became trapped in her chest and she couldn't swallow. All Cindy's dedication had been for nothing. All those hours poring over textbooks and sweating exam results and lab experiments and written reports. Worthless. Her airway got tighter, her breath started to wheeze in and out of her chest. *Oh, God...*

"It's okay. You're okay. Breathe." Kincaid's much larger hand closed over her fist as it rested on the table. Her eyes shot desperately to his and he squeezed, just firmly enough to ground her in the here and now. "Breathe deep but slow. Slower."

He was probably worried she was going to pass out or have a panic attack. That hadn't happened in years but her mind was overloaded and her emotions felt like they were shorting out.

She made an effort to shake off the grief that wanted to overwhelm her. Concentrated instead on forcing the muscles of her ribcage in and out, fighting that destructive need to hyperventilate. She took in a drag of air and held it.

His skin looked lighter than the tanned bronze of hers. She concentrated on the feeling of strength in those long, blunt fingers. Took another gulp of air and held it, trying to slow down the reflex.

Cindy had helped her get through college. She'd taught her to run, taught her to study, taught her that the only thing that really mattered was integrity and no one could take that from you.

Except someone was trying to steal Cindy's integrity.

Pip took another deliberate breath and her heartbeat started to settle. Her chest lost that tight constriction that spelled panic.

Agent Kincaid's firm grip was warm and reassuring. She looked up and caught his gaze. For the first time since they'd met, he wasn't looking at her like she was a suspect. Either he knew something he wasn't telling her, or she was more pitiful than she'd realized.

After another minute, he removed his hand and she looked away.

"Sorry." She let out a slow, steady breath that told her she was back in control of her body. "It's just hard to believe she's actually gone." She swallowed. "When will the Medical Examiner release the body?" Last night she'd done some research and was pretty sure she knew who Cindy's lawyer was—assuming it was the same guy Cindy's parents had used. She'd ask him the name of Cindy's executor because she needed to help organize the funeral.

"It's going to be a few days." His vague answer pissed her off. "Losing her family must have hit Cindy hard."

Duh.

"Could it have sent her off the rails?"

Pip bristled. "Losing her family did hit her hard, but it was nearly eighteen months ago. We'd done all the anniversaries that sneak up without you realizing and then hit you in the solar plexus like a punch from a dodgy ex—"

"Dodgy ex?" His eyes burned.

"Like I say, I grew up in foster care and didn't always make great choices." She pressed her lips together. "Cindy was coping with her loss even though it hurt. She wasn't suicidal." Her tone was sharp.

"I'm trying to get a feel for her and her state of mind." Gone was the patient man who'd held her hand. The Fed was back.

"So you can justify saying she did something completely out of character?"

"Drugs or suicide?" he asked.

"Both," she bit out.

He lowered his chin, clearly looking for a different angle of attack. "You said you had a fight. What was it about?"

She huffed out a resigned breath. "Lifestyle choices."

"What do you mean?"

You work too hard. You don't eat properly. You hook up with guys you barely know.

"Nothing important." She fiddled with her napkin.

"Could you have missed the fact that something was bothering her?" His voice had an edge now, as if he thought she was lying.

You don't know everything...

What was it Pip hadn't known? What had she missed by being so consumed by her own search for truth?

"It's possible." She exhaled, and guilt rose up all over again. They'd both been busy. She'd been caught up in a case that should have launched her career. Instead innocents were dead. She hadn't even told Cindy she'd quit.

Kincaid leaned back when the waitress brought out his food and coffee. He smiled and Pip found herself caught off guard. He was a really good-looking guy.

The waitress left with a flirty wink that Kincaid didn't seem to notice. Pip bet he had women throwing themselves at him all day long.

"She finished her thesis?" he asked, stirring his coffee.

"Day before yesterday. Around six she texted me to say it was done. She planned to submit Monday morning which was another reason I wanted to get to the cottage early before she left for the city."

Pip drained the last of her tea. All that effort wasted.

It put Pip's life in perspective. Sure, in a democracy truth mattered but at what cost?

The FBI agent was wolfing down his food as if he hadn't eaten in days. Pip remembered the cheese roll he'd given her yesterday.

She couldn't let one small act of kindness derail her from her goal. "You're thinking she got high because she finished her thesis."

"How long had she been working on it?"

"Four years. She'd completed her masters in two."

"Seems like a reason to party to me."

"Except it would have been completely out of character to snort coke."

"Says you." Blue eyes pinned her.

"Says me," she agreed. He was right. He had no idea how accurate her version of Cindy's life was. "But say you're right and Cindy decided to celebrate. Where'd she get the drugs for this impromptu celebration? Because *I* know it wasn't from me."

"She had the champagne," he pointed out.

"She always had champagne."

"Perhaps a new boyfriend you didn't know about supplied the drugs?"

Did he know something he wasn't telling her? Pip took a sip of water to ease the soreness of her throat. "It's possible. Men tripped over themselves trying to get her attention and often used me to get to her."

He gave her a frown.

Then she remembered something. "Hey, before I got to the cottage yesterday I was almost run off the road by a big black SUV going too fast on one of those blind bends. And when I got to the driveway I noticed dust rising up, you know how it does on a dry gravel road after a car has just gone over it?"

Kincaid frowned harder and Pip tried to ignore the way it made little lines fan out from the side of his eyes. The small signs of age looked good on him.

"The car could be a coincidence. A vehicle traveling along Cindy's driveway might have turned in the other direction. You wouldn't have seen them."

"But someone was there," she insisted. She couldn't believe she hadn't remembered this yesterday.

He shrugged one shoulder, apparently unconvinced, and kept on eating.

He didn't believe her. Anger started to grow.

"What time did she die?" Her stomach turned. How could she be talking about this so casually as if her world hadn't disintegrated into ruined ashes? She didn't want to be sorting through the sterile facts of Cindy's death, but there was no one else to champion her friend.

Kincaid's fingers curled around his coffee mug. Long tapered fingers and clean, blunt nails. He swallowed, then opened his mouth to blow her off.

Her lip twisted derisively. "Don't bother with the 'I can't reveal information' bullshit. I'm the biggest asset you have when getting to know the victim."

"Which might matter if this had been deemed a homicide but there are no obvious suspicious circumstances."

How could he say that? "What about the vehicle I spotted? The fact Cindy never used drugs?"

"To your knowledge." He pointed his coffee mug at her, which made her clench her teeth together and inhale deeply through her nose. "If it was a homicide, you'd be the chief suspect."

"Because I found her?"

He drank and put down the mug. "Partly that, and partly the fact you had the most to gain from her death."

"Gain?" Grief catapulted into her gut and made her want to curl into a ball and sob. Instead, she searched her wallet for a twenty and tossed it on the table. "I lost my best friend. The only person in the world who cared whether I lived or died."

He wiped his mouth with a napkin as she grabbed her purse and started to edge out of the booth.

"I spoke to Cindy's lawyer, Adrian Lightfoot." His words stopped her. He slid a piece of paper with a phone number written in pencil. "You need to call him. Apparently, you're the executor of Cindy's last will and testament. You inherited everything. The house in the city, the cottage on the lake, the SUV, the trust fund." Those blue eyes with their thin gold rings pinned her in place. "So if this was a homicide investigation, sweetheart, all the smart money would be on you."

CHAPTER SIX

TWO HOURS LATER, Hunt was glad to be back in Atlanta. He parked in the visitor lot of the Blake University building where Cindy Resnick had worked and where her supervisor was now waiting for him. No signs of anthrax at the cottage, nor in her house in Atlanta, nor in her body.

According to the ME, if Cindy had died from the disease, lymph nodes in her chest, and other locations, would have been swollen and blackened like over-ripe plums. Cindy's lymphatic system appeared normal. Nor were there signs of long-term drug abuse. It appeared the woman had gotten drunk, gotten high and drowned.

But they couldn't afford to ignore the timing.

ASAC McKenzie had decided to let the local cops in Allatoona run the investigation into Cindy's death with Hunt assisting in his official WMD coordinator capacity while he continued to prioritize interviewing living scientists. The labs would analyze all the evidence and direct pertinent results back to the BLACKCLOUD taskforce before sending it to the cops. Publicly, the FBI would play down Cindy's death as accidental. Privately, they were considering all options.

Was Pip West involved? Was she after a story? Or did she have something to feel guilty about? She'd refused to tell him why she and her friend had argued. *Lifestyle choices* wasn't exactly specific.

His phone rang as he was crossing the service road. Libby Hernandez from SIOC.

"Parents and younger brother died in a crash September before last. Drunk driver piled into them doing ninety on the I-85. Concertinaed their car and a fuel leak caught fire before the Resnicks could get out."

Burning to death in a car wreck had to be near the top of the list of horrendous ways to die. Right next to contracting a deadly disease like anthrax. Tragic as those events were, it meant Pip West had just become a very wealthy woman. But the look in her eyes when he'd told her the news about her inheritance had been one of intensified grief, not greed or satisfaction.

Maybe Pip was good at lying. Maybe she'd purposely bought toxic cocaine and encouraged her BFF to suck it back and then go swim in the lake so she could inherit the cash. People did worse things—ever single day.

The Medical Examiner put a time of death of between midnight and two AM. They were still trying to pin down Pip's exact location at that time and agents were examining surveillance tapes from the gas stations and crosschecking cell tower information.

Hunt wanted Pip eliminated from this case, and not just because he liked the look of her dark eyes and soft mouth. He had more important things to investigate, like looking for a bio-terrorist willing to sell out his or her country and the lives of its fellow citizens, in exchange for cold, hard cash.

"What happened to the other driver?" he asked Hernandez, climbing the steps.

"Died on impact. Guy named James Roma. Seventeen

years old," said Hernandez.

The insanity of youth.

How had that loss affected the sole survivor of the family? Could it have turned her into a terrorist? But there were no red flags. No weird internet searches. No virtual private network or alternative online personas. No suspect connections. No obvious need for cash.

"Anything on the laptop or cell phone?"

"HMRU sent everything to Quantico last night. They also took swabs and sent them to USAMRIID and they are waiting on final results from CDC before they proceed."

Which meant the lab hadn't even started processing the electronics yet. Hunt stowed his frustration. He didn't want to put anyone at risk. It was difficult to process evidence quickly when dealing with a potentially deadly infectious material even though the general consensus was the cottage was clean.

"What about those BLACKCLOUD samples?" The so-called bioweapon. "Did they make it to the CDC and USAMRIID?" Until it was confirmed the substance was anthrax rather than his grandmother's talcum powder this might all be for nothing. A con they'd all fallen for.

Wouldn't that be fucking awesome?

"Cleared for import and arrived late last night. Scientists got straight to work. Initial reports suggest weapons-grade anthrax."

So much for the hoax theory.

"They're doing more studies to see if they can identify the strain. DNA is being sequenced as we speak."

And in the meantime, the bad guy might be mass producing this microbe and doing who knew what with it. Or burrowing down so deep they'd never find him.

"Any other leads?"

"Not yet. Whoever it is covered their tracks. But we're watching. We have some seriously talented cyber security people helping us out."

He grunted. They were basically playing hide-go-seek with a brainiac.

The scientific component of the case frustrated him because it was out of his control. He didn't know as much as he wanted.

"Thanks anyway. Oh, one more thing…" He felt guilty for a split-second before reminding himself he was looking for a heartless terrorist. "Can you run a deep background check on Pippa West?"

"The girl who found the body?"

If he called Pip a "girl" most women he knew would flay him alive. "Yeah. The woman who found the body."

"No problem. I'll start on that today."

Hunt rang off, headed to the departmental secretary to get a visitor badge and directions to the professor's office.

He found the man surrounded by shelves full of text books, and a desk piled high with folders and forms. The door was ajar.

Professor Everson was bald with deep set features and prominent cheekbones that made him appear emaciated. The eyes were sharp, though. Observant and wary.

"Agent Kincaid?"

Hunt nodded and stepped into the room. "Professor Everson."

They shook hands.

"You're here about Cindy." The professor sagged in his chair. "I can't believe this has happened. Such a terrible loss.

Please, take a seat." He pressed his lips together and looked down at his desk.

Composing himself? Or hiding something?

Hunt took a seat and let the professor take the lead. Hunt sometimes flaunted his authority and sometimes he reined it in. Whatever got results.

"Can you tell me how she died?" the professor asked.

"I'm afraid I can't release any details at this time."

The professor frowned, bushy brows meeting to form a solid line. "She was a wonderful young woman. Brilliant, hard-working, dedicated. I can't believe she's gone. I just spoke to her on the phone day before yesterday and she said she was ready to submit." His fingers curled and uncurled into fists.

"You were in Nashville?"

The professor nodded. "NAMS meeting. I was president for a few years, so I always try to go and support it. It's a small meeting, but a friendly one."

"There are unfriendly ones?" Hunt asked conversationally.

"You better believe it." The professor's knee bobbed up and down in a nervous rhythm. "Can I ask why the FBI is involved in Cindy's death?"

"What was Cindy working on?" Hunt asked instead.

The professor got up and closed the door. "The information is a little sensitive."

"I'm not about to spill your scientific secrets, Professor Everson."

Everson sat back down and Hunt waited him out, pencil poised over his notebook.

The professor cleared his throat. "We've been keeping it very quiet. Cindy was developing a new type of vaccine for anthrax. One that might revolutionize the field."

Hunt was surprised. From his talk with Jez Place from CDC Cindy had never so much as presented her work. "Why so much secrecy?"

The professor shifted and huffed. "The work has wide-ranging implications."

Hunt played dumb. "Like what?"

The professor shrugged. "Medical. Research. Military. Terrorism."

For some reason Hunt flashed back to Pip describing that big black vehicle she said had almost run her off the road.

The professor's mouth twisted into a cynical knot. "We've been told not to talk about it."

"Who told you not to talk about it?"

"The university. They're set to share the monies generated from the patent and intellectual property rights with myself and Ms. Resnick. They forbade us to discuss our results or methodology with our colleagues until Cindy was ready to submit, by which time the patents should have been granted." His voice dropped lower as if someone might be listening in. "They didn't want anyone stealing our methodology."

Hunt dipped his chin. "Does that happen a lot?"

Everson shook his head. "Not at all. Scientific research and breakthroughs depend on shared knowledge. But her idea was so incredible, so simple—"

"Cindy's idea?"

"Yes. Yes. I never pretended otherwise." Everson nodded. "I was getting ready for retirement and this young grad student comes up to me with an idea she wanted to discuss. I thought I was doing her a favor even listening to her, intending to put her out of her misery and correct the course of her experiments." His eyes were wide. Arms animated. "Her idea blew my mind. She ran a few trials and once we realized what we had on our hands, I went to the IP office because I wanted to bring other institutions onboard for greater funding and clinical experiments. Instead they put a virtual gag order on us." Bitterness laced his words.

"What about freedom of speech, and publish or die, and all that?"

The professor shook his head. "You either learn to work with the administration or you get the hell out."

The same ideals held true within the Bureau.

"So how much is Cindy's idea worth, do you think?"

Everson's eyes held a gleam. "Millions."

Hunt must have looked skeptical.

"Who is the biggest buyer of anthrax vaccine?" the professor asked.

"The military."

"And during a conflict? The need for vaccine goes up exponentially. Also, her idea might work for vaccines for other diseases, too, although that's pure conjecture. So that patent is potentially worth millions to the university. Hundreds of millions."

Enough to kill Cindy for?

"We agreed to not publish any of our findings until all the preliminary work for Cindy's Ph.D. was completed and she'd submitted." The professor looked angry. "I understood why the university did it. They do have a business to run. But they denied her some of the experiences she should have had as a grad student. And now she'll never get the kudos she deserved."

"So no one else knew about her discovery?"

The professor shook his head.

"Not colleagues or friends or co-workers?"

"No one." The professor was emphatic. "Just Cindy and I and the IP people and the patent office. They made us sign an NDA that would have bankrupted us both had we violated it, but neither of us wanted to be scooped in our discovery."

"You ever meet a friend of hers, Pip West?" asked Hunt.

Everson nodded. "At Cindy's family's funeral. Dark-haired, pretty little thing. I know Cindy was close to her." Those eyes grew sharper. "Why? Did she have something to do with Cindy's death?"

Hunt ignored the question. "What happens to the research and patent if a student doesn't submit?"

The professor scratched the back of his neck. "I honestly don't know. I will submit her papers to peer-review journals. Income from patents will pass on to whoever her beneficiary is." He swallowed tightly. "There will probably be endless meetings as admin figures out how to bend this to their advantage."

Hunt leaned forward. "Is Cindy's death advantageous to the administration?"

The professor laughed. "I can't see the suits from IP putting a hit on the girl. She was probably worth more to them alive than dead, especially if she stayed on at Blake."

At Hunt's expression the professor sat up straighter. "Don't tell me someone murdered her."

His expression morphed from amused to horrified, but Hunt couldn't get a solid read on the guy. Was he hiding something, or just socially awkward?

"Can you tell me anything specific about Cindy's work?"

The professor considered for a moment. "When Ken Alibek left Moscow in the early nineties, he gave us an insight into just how vigorously the Russians had lied about, and were pursuing, a biological-weapons program. It was terrifying. Strains were being heated up in the lab, spliced, and made resistant to traditional vaccines. It was probably only the fact that there were no vaccines available, no cure, that stopped them being used as weapons. Cindy's work might change that."

Hunt felt a growing sense of dread at the range of threats out there and the importance of the researchers countering it. "This vaccine of Cindy's works on even resistant strains of anthrax?"

The professor took a breath, as if considering how much to dumb down his explanation.

Hunt set his teeth.

"We think so. She developed a DNA vaccine where she incorporated the gene that encodes the lethal factor of the plasmid pX01—also known as the pathogenic island of the anthrax molecule—into a plasmid we then used to inoculate mice. We tested the vaccine against every strain we could get our hands on." He looked away, avoiding eye contact. "Obviously it's possible it wouldn't work on people or against certain strains—we haven't been able to conduct clinical trials yet." The man sounded annoyed with this fact. "But because she used one of the key proteins that contributes to the bacteria's virulence, we hypothesize it will work against even the most deadly variants."

That sounded promising.

Worth killing for? Hunt would say so.

"It wasn't just Cindy's *idea* of developing that specific DNA vaccine, but her technique cut down production time by half. I can't go into more detail than that without talking to the

IP department."

If Hunt came back with a warrant the IP department could go fuck themselves.

The professor stood and rested his hands against the window glass as he stared out across the campus. "Cindy was an incredibly bright young woman." He swallowed loudly and turned around. "Her technique could also dramatically speed up research into many other diseases, including cancer." The man's eyes went diamond bright. "Do you have any idea how big this is?"

Hunt nodded. "Curing cancer. Got it." *Nobel prize* big. And the lead architect was dead after snorting cocaine laced with fentanyl and then going for a midnight swim.

But maybe that worked for the professor. Now he didn't have to share the glory.

"Can you show me your laboratory?" asked Hunt.

The professor let out a surprised chuff. "There's nothing to see from the outside and there's a strict policy about who can enter. We've just moved into a new facility—"

"I realize that. Professor Spalding showed me some of the new labs yesterday." Hunt didn't bother saying he was the WMD Coordinator, instead he let Everson mull over the information that he'd already spoken to the man's boss. Hunt wouldn't recognize anthrax from yeast cells so there wasn't much point in him insisting on a site visit—yet. "You keep logs of the people working on anthrax in the labs?"

The prof nodded.

"I'd like to see those logs. For the old labs as well as the new."

"How is that related to Cindy's death?"

Hunt just stared at the man without saying a word.

Everson cleared his throat. "The departmental secretary will be able to give you a copy of that information."

"I'll also need a copy of Cindy's thesis. I'm assuming you have one?"

The professor shook his head. "That's not possible, I'm afraid. Didn't you hear what I told you about the restrictions?"

"I'm looking into a young woman's death. I can get a subpoena if that makes it easier for you?"

This time the professor didn't budge. "You'll have to. I'm not having that work end up in some FBI file for anyone in the government to read, not without going through official channels." Everson's jaw muscles flexed and his eyes narrowed. "What about Cindy's computer? That must have a copy on it. Where is that?"

"If you think of anything else feel free to contact me." Hunt stood and handed over his business card with all his contact details. "My colleagues will be in touch."

The professor frowned down at the card, clearly annoyed. "What about Cindy?"

Hunt didn't understand the question. "What about her?"

"Well, how did she die?" the professor asked impatiently.

"I'm afraid I'm not at liberty to discuss an active investigation, Professor." Hunt stood.

"Active investigation?"

Hunt pressed his lips together and nodded again. The analysts on the taskforce would be following every move these people made in the wake of the Resnick woman's death and hopefully the bioweapon manufacturer would reveal themselves. Hunt just hoped Pip West didn't figure out the real reason the FBI were still interested in Cindy's death.

CHAPTER SEVEN

P IP PACED THE floor of the tiny motel room in Allatoona waiting for the mechanic to drop her car back. They'd done a full service and oil change and although the Honda wouldn't win any beauty pageants it should get her where she needed to go.

Her cell rang and she snatched it up. She kept hoping someone was going to tell her this was all a big mistake, some dark, grim, horrid practical joke.

"Ms. West? This is Adrian Lightfoot. Cindy Resnick's lawyer?"

How'd he find her number? Pip had avoided calling him. Ignored what Kincaid had told her as it hurt too damn much.

"Perhaps you remember me? We met after Cindy's parents and brother died?" There was a forced cheerfulness to his tone, but underneath he sounded fraught.

He wasn't that old. Early forties. Movie star handsome. The son of Cindy's father's original attorney, Cindy had often joked Adrian Lightfoot was too hot to be a lawyer.

Pain twisted in Pip's stomach and she sank down onto the lumpy mattress. She missed Cindy's mom and dad and kid brother more than she missed her own blood. Now she got to miss Cindy, too. Life really wasn't fair.

Pip's mouth felt arid and her voice came out croaky. "I

remember."

There was a long pause, as if he wasn't certain how to proceed. "I know this is a difficult time. I understand you found Cindy's body?"

"That's right."

He cleared his throat. "I'm so sorry. It must have been awful. The authorities aren't telling me how she died except to say it wasn't suicide and doesn't appear to be foul play..."

Silence filled the air but she didn't know what to say. Nothing made sense to her either.

"Well," he continued after an awkward moment, "the thing is, after Cindy's parents died, I urged her to make a will. She said she didn't have time and she'd leave everything to you anyway. I told her to put that in writing otherwise you'd never see a dime."

Her nails bit into her palm. Kincaid had been telling the truth. She was probably a wealthy woman and she had this man and Cindy's untimely death to thank.

She didn't want it. She didn't want any of it. She wanted her friend back.

"There will be a period of probate but if you can come into the office today to sign some papers I can get the process started for transferring Cindy's bank account details, etc. Before you go home to Florida."

Pip bent over at the waist and wondered if grief could kill you. It hurt so much.

"Or I can come to you if that makes it easier." Emotion laced his voice. "Where are you staying?"

Pip stared numbly at the stained carpet. "Right now, I'm in some crappy motel, hoping this is all a horrible dream. I left Florida. I had planned to stay with Cindy until I figured out my next move." Her tongue felt thick and dry. Her eyes like something was scratching the backs of them with sharp claws.

"How about I arrange a hotel room for you downtown and bring the papers by this afternoon?"

"I don't have money for a hotel." Her former employer owed her a month's wages but she wouldn't see it until the end of the week. She could use her credit card but hated spending money she didn't have.

"The estate will take care of the bill until you're able to move into Cindy's house. I know you're good for it."

She shrank away from the idea of spending Cindy's money, or of moving into Cindy's house without her. The thought of selling up was worse. She felt stuck. Numb. Shock and grief rendering her unable to make decisions she usually made with ease.

Pip pushed her hair out of her face as one thing came into focus. "I need to organize Cindy's funeral."

"We can go over that this afternoon. How about I meet you at six? I'll text you with the hotel details…"

"Okay," she said uncertainly. What else could she do?

"Drive safe." Lightfoot rang off.

Pip's legs trembled. A fresh wave of tears made her want to crawl back under the covers and sleep for a week.

A knock on the door had her jumping to her feet. She glanced at the digital display on the clock. 11:03 AM. She was supposed to checkout by eleven.

At the door she found a man standing there with a form to sign and credit card machine. He held out her car keys.

After he'd left, Pip grabbed her purse and the box containing her computer stuff and took it out to her car. In the few seconds she was gone, the maid nipped inside and started dragging the linen off the bed.

Pip paused for a moment, watching the woman work.

It was stupid to feel unwanted and as if her life was out of control simply because a maid was getting on with her day, but…

Snap out of it.

Meeting with Adrian Lightfoot would be the first stage of organizing a fitting memorial for her friend. She had a lot to do. People to contact. Details to arrange. Cindy wouldn't care about the money or even the house. She would care that the cops thought she was stupid enough to die of a drug overdose.

Pip's specialty was finding out the truth.

She went back into the room and politely claimed the last of her belongings and left the maid a tip. She got into her car and her fingers curled tight around the wheel as her journalistic instincts began to emerge from the numbness of grief. Kincaid had told her he didn't believe Cindy's death was a homicide, yet the FBI was still investigating. Kincaid said it was routine because Cindy worked on anthrax.

Kincaid's reasoning didn't quite ring true, and when things didn't ring true they were generally bullshit.

Pip needed to figure out what had really happened to her friend and why it so interested the Feds. And one thing was for damn sure, FBI Agent Kincaid was no more likely to keep her in the loop than he was to declare his undying love.

She'd do it on her own terms. Screw the FBI.

IT WAS EARLY afternoon when Hunt drove to the small private research facility on the outskirts of North Druid Hills, fifteen minutes from the new FBI Atlanta Field Office, and five minutes from the CDC.

The headquarters of Universal Biotech Ltd was made of mirrored glass with solar panels on the roof. The overall effect was slick with a lot of dazzle.

He gave his name at the gate and drove his senior-style Buick inside the secured area and slid it into a bay between an Audi A8 and a Mercedes-Benz CLS.

He got out of the car, raised his sunglasses and eyed a sun-baked blue beast across the lot.

Pip West's beat up Honda.

What the hell was she doing here?

He shook his head, locked his car and headed toward the building.

Heat shimmered from the newly laid black asphalt and pressed against the soles of his shoes. If this was April, July was going to be a slow roast in hell.

His reflection in the mirrored door showed a distinct lack of sleep and too much caffeine over the last thirty-six hours. He dropped the glasses back into place and rubbed a hand over his chin. At least he'd been able to shave on the way over. Hoover might not be around anymore but there were definite standards of appearance street agents were expected to maintain.

Yet another reason to apply to HRT. Shaving every day sucked.

Inside the glass and chrome building he hit a welcome wall of cold air. And the unwelcome sight of Pip West in the arms of another man.

A bolt of something disturbing and unpleasant shot through him.

The guy looked about her age, late twenties, six feet, one ninety, overlong black hair and thin wire-framed glasses. Wannabe hipster, which was right up there with emo as Hunt's least favorite vibe. The man wore a dark blue suit with a burgundy t-shirt and black converse trainers with no socks and he was hugging Pip West like a Burmese python hugged a goat.

And Pip West...

Holy hell.

The side view was eye-popping.

She'd applied makeup, masking the dark circles and adding a subtle glow to her skin. Her eyes looked bigger, darker, and crimson stained her lips in a way that made his thoughts turn strictly unprofessional. Her long hair was up in a silky-looking bun, leaving her neck bare except for soft tendrils of dark hair. She'd changed from old jeans and t-shirt into a tight-fitting skirt that framed a knockout ass, and a flowery blouse that clung to her slim waist and full breasts in a way his hands wanted to touch. His mouth went dry. The skyscraper heels had last been seen on the floor of the backseat of her car. They'd be a deadly weapon in the wrong hands. He wasn't convinced she wasn't the wrong hands.

Get a grip, Kincaid.

Hunt stood saying nothing until they finished their touching exchange. Then Pip pulled away from the guy's clasp and half-turned, acting as if she'd just spotted Hunt standing there, but he was pretty sure she'd been aware of him since the moment he'd walked in the door.

Or maybe that was his ego talking.

He angled his head and raised his brow, expecting her to acknowledge him. Instead, she ignored the questions in his eyes and brushed past him as if she'd never seen him before. A ripple of sensation flashed over his skin in response to the fleeting touch of her arm against his. Then she pushed open the Windex-bright front door and exited the building.

What was she up to? He'd find out later.

Hunt stepped forward and sidestepped the assistant who arrived five seconds too late to guard the gate. Hunt wasn't leaving without what he'd come for.

"Mr. Dexter?" He recognized the guy from the company website. Cindy Resnick's former longtime boyfriend.

The guy's eyes were red, as if he'd been crying. Kincaid took an instant dislike to the man and told himself it had nothing to do with grabby hands.

"It's Doctor Dexter, actually." Dexter's self-deprecating chuckle grated across Hunt's nerves.

"Exactly who I want to talk to." Hunt ignored the correction. "I'm Special Agent Kincaid from the Federal Bureau of Investigation. I need a moment of your time."

"Sorry." Dexter wiped his eyes. "This isn't a good…" Dexter looked wildly at the assistant who opened her mouth to try and take control.

"I made an appointment to talk to your PA, Ms. Grantham?" He nodded to the redhead. "As she said you weren't in the office this afternoon." Hunt smiled at the young woman who was trying to get a word in. "Obviously your plans changed."

Dexter rubbed his forehead as if being questioned by the FBI was a minor inconvenience. "I'm—"

"I'm afraid Dr. Dexter has just heard news of a terrible loss," Ms. Grantham finally cut in, "and won't be able to meet with you today, Agent Kincaid. We can reschedule for tomorrow—"

"This won't take long." Hunt should feel a little ashamed he was using a woman's death to get inside a private company, but it gave him a perfect opportunity that he wasn't about to pass up. McKenzie had been all over the idea once he'd found out where Cindy Resnick's long-term ex had worked.

Perfect opportunity.

Dexter blew out a shuddering breath, then swallowed loudly. "It's fine, Bea. I don't want to waste the FBI's time. Come this way, Mr. Kincaid. I can spare you five minutes."

Hunt ignored the lack of title from a man who obviously valued them. His gun and handcuffs and power of arrest worked just fine, regardless of what someone called him.

He glanced around at the spotless checkered floors and fancy framed monochrome photographs that lined the hallway. The lighting was LED but sunlight sparkled in reflected light from a window at the end of the corridor. They hit the elevator but Dexter didn't make conversation. His shoulders slumped. Expression turned bleak. As if he really had just lost someone he cared about.

They strode down another long corridor. Hunt didn't see any sign for labs or biohazard warning signs.

Dexter unlocked the door to his office—interesting that he locked it in his own building—and waved him inside.

Dexter lowered himself into a chair behind a desk empty of papers. The computer wasn't on. There were a couple of generic pictures on the wall.

Not the CEO's office, Hunt realized. Maybe it belonged to an associate who'd left or was ready for a new recruit. Or where they conducted interviews? But it raised Hunt's suspicions. Why didn't Dexter want Hunt to see his office?

What was he hiding?

"Please take a seat, Mr. Kincaid."

"*Agent* Kincaid," Hunt corrected him this time. "I assume you've heard about Cindy Resnick's death?"

A spark of anger lit Pete Dexter's brown eyes. "Her best friend, Pippa West, came and told me about it. That's who I was talking to down in the lobby. It's all a bit of a shock to be honest."

The fact Dexter called Pip West "Pippa" made Hunt irrationally smug. "Can you tell me the status of your relationship with Ms. Resnick?"

"We dated for a couple of years but broke up before Christmas."

"You weren't involved in her life at all anymore?"

Dexter winced. "If you're here to make me feel like shit, you just scored a direct hit." The man looked genuinely upset.

"When was the last time you saw Cindy?" Hunt pulled out his notebook which Dexter eyed warily.

The guy rolled his shoulder. A shark's tooth necklace hung around his neck. "The day she dumped me. I'm not sure of the date exactly." He brought up an electronic calendar on his phone. "There we go. December twelfth. Shit." He rubbed his eyes. "More than four months ago." He swallowed hard. "We'd gone up to her cottage."

"Why did you break up?"

"Is that really FBI business?"

"I'm just trying to figure out what happened to Ms. Resnick."

"Why?"

"Why?" Hunt asked curiously.

"The FBI doesn't usually investigate drug overdoses, does

it?" Dexter flexed his fists.

Hunt raised his brow in question.

"Pippa told me," Dexter admitted. "She wanted to know if I'd ever seen Cindy using drugs when we were together."

So, she was pursuing this. Interfering with his investigation and digging her nose in where it didn't belong. Damn. "You good friends with Ms. West?"

Dexter shrugged. "I wouldn't say good friends."

Dexter had looked pretty damn friendly downstairs.

"She was Cindy's confidante, not mine. They spoke all the time. I was jealous at first. I think Cindy loved Pippa more than she ever loved me. I guess that's obvious now. I'm surprised she came to see me, but I'm grateful. I guess she recognizes I was an important part of Cindy's life for a long time."

"Why'd you two break up?" Hunt pushed.

Dexter looked out the window and a pink stain hit his ghostly pale cheeks. "She found out I slept with another woman."

"You cheated on her?"

Dexter's mouth tightened at his blunt terminology. "Yes."

"Who with?"

Dexter held his gaze. "I'd rather not say. It was a hookup. We got drunk and slept together. I loved Cindy." His fists clenched again.

Hunt let his skepticism show. A man in love didn't cheat. "How'd Cindy find out?"

"I told her. Stupidly." Dexter huffed out a strained laugh. "The guilt was eating me up inside. I wanted to propose, but felt I needed to come clean first. I should have kept my big mouth shut. She might be alive today." He gave a bitter smile.

"She wasn't very understanding about my mistake."

"Smart women don't like to be messed around."

"And she was smart." Dexter looked at him with earnest brown eyes. "She was the smartest person I ever met."

Hunt kept hearing that but he found it hard to believe. Maybe she was book smart. "Where'd you two meet?"

"Grad school. We had the same supervisor."

That was news.

"I was in my final year when she started so we didn't overlap by much. I fell in love after just one conversation. Prions. She was perfect for me."

"Until you nailed another woman in a drunken haze."

Dexter picked up a pen and gripped it tightly. The muscle in his jaw flexed with suppressed anger. "I made a mistake that I'll regret for the rest of my life. Why do you care so much, anyway?"

Possibly because Dexter had had his lousy hands all over Pip West when Hunt had walked in the door. Not that it really mattered. Not that it *should* matter.

"You knew what she was working on?"

"Yes and no. We spoke in general terms but she'd never go into great detail with me."

"That must have burned. Finding a soulmate who was your intellectual equal but who wouldn't share her work?"

Dexter just looked at him. "She wasn't allowed to talk about anything because of the university administration." He held his hands up and indicated the building around him. "I run a private biotech firm. I can understand why she wouldn't cross that line."

"You'd use her findings?"

"To cure deadly diseases?" Dexter pressed his lips together. "Damn straight."

It might be more noble if the guy didn't drive that fancy Audi sitting in the parking lot.

"What do you actually make here?" Hunt had read the website. He knew.

"Vaccines."

Hunt cocked his head. "Same as Cindy?"

"It shouldn't be a big surprise that we were both interested in creating vaccines considering where we met." Condescension tinged his voice. "The grad students at Blake are a social group. We spent a lot of time together."

"Did you also study anthrax?"

Dexter held Hunt's gaze at that question. "Yes. It's Professor Everson's main focus."

"You work on that here, too?" asked Hunt.

"Yeah, we've been developing new vaccines. Also, for HIV, influenza and prions." Dexter sounded defensive. "Do you know what a prion is?"

"As a matter of fact," Hunt's feral smile probably wasn't in the FBI handbook, "I do. I should have mentioned. I'm also the new WMD Coordinator at the Atlanta Field Office. Took over from Rose Geddy while she's on mat leave. I'd appreciate a tour of the facilities if you can arrange it."

"Of course." Dexter straightened his shoulders, suddenly more deferential. "I'll ask Simon to give you a call and arrange a tour."

"Simon?"

"Simon Corker. One of my partners who handles the PR and admin side of things. I spend most of my time in the lab. He's not in today."

"How many partners do you have?"

"Simon and another scientist, Angela Naysmith. She was also at Blake."

"You guys cover a lot of different specialties."

"We have other virologists working for us." Dexter looked defensive. "We're good at what we do."

Hunt thought about the fancy office building. Hell of an investment to make in someone who'd only recently finished their doctorate. Hunt would get Libby Hernandez to check into the company financials in-between the five billion other things she had on her plate.

"Did Cindy ever do drugs when you were together?"

Dexter reared back like Hunt had slapped him. "No."

"Never? You're sure?"

"I'm sure."

"What about you?"

Dexter laughed. "I'm a partner in a multi-million-dollar startup. Do you think I'd admit taking drugs to an FBI agent?"

"You'd lie?" Hunt pushed.

Dexter glared. "No."

"I'm not interested in harming your reputation. I'm interested in how Cindy died." And in shaking up this guy a little so the people at SIOC could monitor his response.

"I still don't understand why the FBI is looking into her death if it were an accidental drug overdose."

"Are you refusing to answer the question?"

Dexter looked flustered. "I never said that. I don't do drugs."

Hunt noted the careful use of present tense but let it go. "And you're sure about Cindy?"

The long pause was telling. "I know there were other students in the lab who did drugs and they were friends of

Cindy's. I never saw Cindy touch anything, but I have no idea what she did after we broke up. Now I really am busy and have a lot to take care of even though I'd rather just take the day off." Dexter raised his eyes to the doorway where the assistant appeared like magic.

Hunt nodded and shook the man's hand which was firm but damp—Hoover would not have approved. Hunt followed the assistant along the corridor and into the elevator. She sported a tight bun that had a pencil sticking out of it.

"You enjoy working here, Ms. Grantham?"

Her fingers curled tighter around her oversized cell. "I do."

"Well paid?"

Blue eyes shot to his. "Not bad."

"Good bosses?"

Her expression seemed amused. "I like my job, Special Agent Kincaid. I like my bosses."

He wondered if she was the other woman. "Did you know Cindy Resnick?"

"Only in passing," she replied. "I haven't been here that long."

"Not going to rock the boat?"

A flirty smile touched one side of her mouth. "Not even a ripple."

They got to the front door and he nodded his thanks. He didn't think the next woman he spoke to was going to be quite so frank about her intentions, but the last thing he needed was a journalist catching scent of a bioterrorism threat.

He needed to make sure Pip West stayed well out of his way.

He climbed into his Bucar and started the engine. Maybe

he could feed Pip just enough information to keep her occupied while he got on with doing his job of keeping the American public safe from harm and bringing the bad guys to justice. Feed her a few crumbs to keep her satisfied.

He cursed himself because the idea of keeping Pip West satisfied appealed on many different levels, and most of them had nothing to do with his work at the FBI.

CHAPTER EIGHT

I T WAS LATE afternoon and Pip had claimed a loveseat just outside the main bar area in the hotel lobby where she'd arranged to meet Adrian Lightfoot. The lawyer had texted to say he might be delayed. She didn't want to go to her room. She knew enough about herself to know if she did, she might never come out.

She busied herself tracking down contact details for as many of Cindy's friends and workmates as she could find using her friend's social media profiles. Pip messaged the people she'd met over the years, and one grad student had said she was coming to the hotel to see her.

Pip hoped the lawyer and student didn't both turn up at the same time.

She'd emailed Cindy's Ph.D. advisor but he hadn't gotten back to her yet. She'd met Professor Everson at Cindy's parents' and brother's funeral. He'd been awkward but seemed well meaning. Cindy hadn't always agreed with his opinions, but she'd admired him and he'd seemed to respect her. Hopefully he'd do a reading at the service. Something that would enable others to appreciate just how brilliant her friend had been.

Pip had fended off several unwanted advances by being completely absorbed in what she was doing and politely but firmly saying "no" when someone sent her a cocktail.

When someone sat down in the seat beside her even though there were other chairs available she gritted her teeth. She sank slightly toward the middle of soft green leather sofa and looked up to see a familiar face.

Huh.

"How'd you find me?" she asked.

"FBI, remember?" Agent Kincaid's eyes glinted with humor.

A huff of laughter took her by surprise. It was the first in weeks. She sobered. She'd expected him to contact her. She hadn't expected him to track her down in person. "You needed to speak to me?"

"What were you doing at Universal Biotech earlier?"

"Yippee. It's my turn to get grilled again." She settled back against the arm of the loveseat. "Why are you so interested in my movements, Agent Kincaid?" She tilted her head to one side and batted her eyelashes at him, but she couldn't maintain the facade for long. Her grief seemed to have stolen the happy pieces of her personality, anything that wasn't nailed down with misery or sadness.

"Assuming you weren't breaking any laws," he countered.

"I kept it under the speed limit every step of the way."

"Traffic offenses are the least of my concerns," he murmured. "It's your mouth I'm worried about."

He hadn't meant anything dirty but the temperature shot up twenty degrees and she wanted to fan her suddenly burning cheeks. She cleared her throat. "I'm not allowed to talk now?"

He grunted. "You can talk as much as you want. But you're not allowed to interfere with my investigation."

There you had it. Classic law enforcement bullying. Trying

to shut down and shut up anyone questioning their authority.

"What exactly *is* your investigation?"

Those intriguing eyes of his watched her, revealing nothing.

"Why'd you go see Dexter?" he asked, feigning casual about as successfully as she feigned meek.

"I was trying to get a feel for what he knew about Cindy's death."

"Which had been my intention until someone beat me to it. Something I'm trained for."

"Well, I didn't know you were going to talk to him." Her voice rose defensively.

"Now you do."

"Look, Kincaid. I'm a journalist—"

"I am well aware."

She ignored the snark. "And I'm trained for it, too. I'm not a mind reader. Unless you give me a list of all the people you don't want me to talk to, I'm flying blind."

Kincaid sat there silently regarding her.

She forced herself to calm down. She needed to find the truth behind Cindy's death and this man could help her. "I talked to Dexter about preparations for the funeral. Asked if he had any ideas about input for the service." Not that she'd take them. Cindy would hate the idea of her cheating ex orchestrating anything to do with her memorial, but she wanted the guy onside.

Kincaid raised a cool brow at her. "Is that why you were making out with him in the foyer?"

"*Making out?*" She gaped. "You've either been married too long or forgotten what 'making out' looks like."

The blue in his eyes darkened. "Not married and I haven't

forgotten a damn thing about anything except to avoid doing it in public."

She rolled her eyes even though her pulse skipped a little. So, he wasn't married. So what? Federal agent, *remember*? A man who'd yesterday threatened to arrest her for manslaughter if she didn't do as he said. A man who'd searched her car for drugs that might have been responsible for the death of her best friend.

Not exactly relationship material.

"Pete grabbed me in a bear hug and wouldn't let go," she admitted grumpily. She hadn't enjoyed the experience, but she hadn't wanted to reveal her true feelings about the guy by pulling away and dousing herself in Lysol. Pete Dexter knew things about Cindy's world she needed access to, and if her willingness to use him made her a bad person, so be it.

Kincaid leaned forward and picked up a coffee off the table. He eyed her across the top of the curling steam. "So, what did you make of Dexter's reaction?"

"He cried." She shifted uncomfortably. Dexter's tears had seemed genuine enough. "A normal reaction." The lump in her throat appeared out of nowhere and threatened to choke her again. *God.* "Honestly—I never really liked the guy. He's conceited and a bit of an ass. He always treated me like the dumb kid sister who needed small words and a pat on the head. What did you make of his reaction?"

Kincaid's expression remained neutral. He wasn't falling for her invitation to share.

"Cindy knew I wasn't that fond of him but I didn't diss him to her. She loved him."

"You sound like you were in love with her yourself." Kincaid sipped his coffee.

"I was." The shock and flicker of disappointment in his eyes had something hot and forbidden rolling low in her abdomen. "If we'd been lesbians we'd have found our soulmates and the search for true love would have been over. Unfortunately, we weren't lesbians."

His expression didn't change but the tension in his fingers eased. He might not want to admit it, but he was a little bit attracted to her. He also didn't like her very much.

"I loved her," she told him. "Platonically."

"So, the search for true love continues?" Cynical amusement edged his tone. His eyes dropped to her lips for just a moment and a buzz of warmth lit her skin.

Pip hadn't given up on the concept of dating, just the practice. Some people were more lovable than others. And not everyone found their soulmate.

"Neither of us based our life decisions on love or men or relationships," she told him briskly, although strictly speaking that was a lie. After college, Pip had moved to Miami to be with a guy. He'd cheated on her and gotten another girl pregnant. Now they were married with two kids and Pip was still single.

"Cindy planned to work in developing countries to eradicate some of the deadliest diseases on earth. It took guts to do what she did and she had no intention of stopping even when she found the right guy." She sucked in a lungful of air, trying to quiet the constant hurt that raged inside. "She didn't work on deadly diseases because she needed the money. She did it because she was passionate about helping people."

"What are you passionate about?" His thumb stroked the side of the cup in a way that made her skin tingle.

"Me?" She laughed self-consciously. "I don't even know

anymore." She looked away from the FBI agent's piercing gaze. She wasn't about to admit she felt adrift in this world and that she no longer knew what she was going to do with her life. Short term was easy. She was going to figure out the truth about Cindy's death if it killed her. But long term?

"Cindy sounds like she was a good person," Kincaid said eventually, filling the silence that stretched between them.

"She was." She sniffed. "You'd have liked her."

He gave her a questioning look.

"You both want to save the world."

He grimaced. "I do not want to save the world."

"Why else become an FBI agent?"

He shifted in his seat. "For the cool badge and gun?"

She snorted, crossed her legs and saw his gaze catch on her spiky black heels.

He looked up. Their eyes met.

A shiver ran down her spine. She pressed her thighs together and the silk of her stockings caused a rush of unwanted sensation to slide over her flesh.

"What are you working on?" He nodded to her laptop, derailing that uncomfortable rush of desire with a big slap of guilt.

"A list of people to contact about the funeral. And Cindy's obituary."

Words that had to stand testament to the life Cindy had lived.

Pip looked at the screen. They weren't enough. They'd never be enough.

Kincaid stared up into the hotel's enormous atrium with its futuristic-looking glass elevators zipping up and down. Then he met her gaze again. "I'm sorry about your friend. I guess I never said that."

Fickle tears wanted to rise up but she fought them back. She'd shed her tears in private from now on. "Does this mean I'm no longer a suspect?"

"Surveillance cameras place you miles away when Cindy overdosed."

The relief Pip felt was overshadowed by irritation. "I keep telling you there's no way Cindy took drugs."

"Yet the ME found coke in her system."

Anger warmed her blood. "Maybe someone helped it get there. Without Cindy's permission."

His look turned pitying. "And sometimes people keep secrets."

Pip drew in a deep breath trying to dampen her underlying annoyance. Hell, she'd been angry for days now. But he didn't know Cindy. He didn't know *her*.

"I keep asking, but you're not saying. Why are you examining Cindy's death?" She was sure he was hiding something. "Don't give me that bullshit about it being SOP for people who work on controlled substances."

"It is SOP for people who work on controlled substances."

He was playing with her.

"I don't believe you."

He leaned closer. "I don't care what you believe. You need to back off."

"Cindy was my friend," she bit out. "And I don't think she took drugs."

"And maybe you're trying to make something out of this because you argued with your friend and there's no other way you can figure out how to make amends."

She flinched.

"What did you argue about anyway?" he asked.

"Work. Men," she said bitterly.

"Boyfriend troubles?"

Pip looked away. "She was telling me I needed to get out more."

"How come?"

She fiddled with the hem of her shirt. "I haven't dated in a couple of years."

"Why not?"

"Bad experience."

"What kind of bad experience?" His voice lowered to a tone that made her shiver.

"Just a crappy relationship. I tend to have terrible taste in men." She looked up. His gaze locked onto hers and for a moment the air between them sizzled.

Federal agent, remember?

"What did you find out at Universal Biotech?" she asked instead.

"Not a lot." His gaze landed fleetingly on her mouth. He leaned closer and she held her breath. "Leave it alone, *Pip.* Else I'll have you charged with obstruction."

Rather than backing away, this time she inched toward him until their lips almost brushed. Playing a game of chicken with their mouths.

"Freedom of the press. Remember?"

He narrowed his gaze before backing away. She'd won that round.

He scratched his head and she thought she heard him mutter "pain in my ass" but wasn't sure.

"I actually came here because I spoke to the Medical Examiner," he said and immediately her attention shifted to his words and not his mouth. He stretched his legs out under the table in front of him and leaned his head back, staring up at the forty floors worth of balconies. "The body should be released by the end of the week. You can arrange the funeral now."

"What if I want a second autopsy?"

He turned to look at her and frowned. "That's up to you. I can ask the ME to recommend someone if you'd like…"

She raised both brows and didn't bother to hide her skepticism.

He laughed. "You don't really think we'd invent the water in her lungs and drugs in her system, do you?"

His words were like a punch to her stomach. This was Cindy they were talking about, her best friend, not some Jane Doe.

He sat up and raked his hand through his short hair, looking contrite and troubled. "Sorry. I keep forgetting this is personal to you."

She wiped her eyes, glad she'd worn waterproof mascara. Dammit, when was she going to stop crying?

"I know what the evidence is saying, but it isn't the whole story. It can't be. I know Cindy. There's no way she snorted coke. Not unless someone forced her do it."

He sighed and climbed to his feet, wrote a number on a piece of paper and handed it to her. "That's the number for the ME. The people there can help with arrangements to transport the body wherever you want it to go."

She nodded. She wasn't trying to be difficult. She just wanted the truth. If that truth turned out to be that Cindy made an error in judgment, she'd accept it. Eventually.

His lips formed an unhappy line. "You're wasting your

time, Pip."

"It's my time to waste." And, let's face it, she didn't have anything better to do.

He stared at her long enough to make her uncomfortable. Finally, he spoke. "If you come up with anything more solid than blind belief in your best friend, give me a call. I'll look into it."

"You'll take me seriously?" she asked in surprise.

He laughed. "Lady, I already take you seriously. I'm just not sure about your motive."

"Does truth need a motive?"

"Is truth always worth the cost?" he countered.

Her mouth dropped open, knowing he was talking about what happened in Tallahassee. "Are you saying I should have let that go? Information on a corrupt cop?"

"Why didn't you take the tip-off to the Feds?" His tone was soft, curious, rather than accusing.

"Lisa didn't want me to. Said she'd only talk to me as long as I printed the truth on the front page. Said that once Frank was exposed he'd never be able to crawl back into the shadows."

"Lisa?" he asked.

"Frank Booker's wife. She was my informant."

Surprise and then understanding entered his gaze. "And Frank Booker somehow figured it out."

"I warned the chief of police he needed to pick up the detective before the story ran, but he didn't believe the allegations." It was her fault they were dead. Her, the police chief, and that miserable sonofabitch Frank Booker. "Why do you hate journalists?" she asked suddenly, knowing there was a story there.

He pulled a face. "I don't hate journalists."

"Liar," she said softly.

"I just don't like being manipulated."

"Liar," she repeated. And the shadow that moved over his eyes proved she was right.

Breaking their connection, a young woman came and stood behind the chair opposite and waved at Pip, trying to get her attention. It took a moment for Pip to recognize her. Sally-Anne Wilton, a friend of Cindy's from the lab but her hair had been purple last time Pip had seen her at Christmas. Pip opened her arms to embrace the other girl. Immediately she was clamped in a needy hug.

Eventually Sally-Anne let go and took a moment to compose herself. Pip introduced Agent Kincaid and watched Sally-Anne's eyes grow round at the mention of the FBI.

The agent handed Sally-Anne a business card. "In case you need to talk to anyone about Cindy's death."

Her brows pitched high. Were the FBI some sort of therapy support group nowadays? She didn't think so. But Kincaid was advertising his involvement in Cindy's death investigation loud and clear.

Her cell phone rang and she reached for it, but it was actually Kincaid's. They had the same ringtone.

The agent checked the screen but didn't answer. "I need to head back to the office."

"No rest for the wicked," Pip commented dryly.

"Me or the criminals?" The amused gleam in his eyes made her wonder what it might have been like to meet him under different circumstances, but she thrust the thought away. He'd still hate a reporter.

"Ms. Wilton." He nodded to Sally-Anne before turning

back to Pip. "Remember what I told you."

Which bit? The *don't interfere with an FBI investigation*, or the *if you come up with anything more solid than blind belief, call me*? Before she could ask, he was walking away.

She realized they were both standing there admiring the rear view when Sally-Anne fanned herself dramatically. "Do all FBI agents look like that?"

"I doubt it," Pip said honestly.

Sally-Anne smiled and sniffed. "Cindy would have thought he was hot, too."

"Just because he's good looking doesn't make him hot," Pip argued.

"With those eyes and that ass? Give me a break." Sally-Anne gave her a sideways glance and grinned. "Plus, I saw the way you were looking at him. Same way he was looking at you. If you weren't all cut up about Cindy's death I'd have told you to get a room."

Pip ignored the comment.

"Cindy would have liked the idea of something good coming out of her death. She worried about you. Thought you worked too hard and played too little."

Pip hugged herself around the waist. "She worked harder than anyone I knew. You probably do, too."

Sally-Anne shrugged and sat down, waving over a waiter. "We all work too hard. And that's why sometimes we need to let our hair down. I want a bottle of champagne, please. Two glasses." She told the man when he came over.

Pip slumped heavily into her seat. "Champagne?"

"Yep." Sally-Anne handed Pip her laptop off the table. "Put that thing away. We're going to raise a couple of glasses to our girl and not bawl our eyes out. She wouldn't have wanted that. Cindy would never have wanted that."

A few minutes later, Pip forced her hand to remain steady as she raised a toast. "To Cindy. The best friend in the universe."

"To Cindy. And to hot FBI agents who can handcuff me to the bed anytime." Sally-Anne clinked her glass hard.

Pip felt her cheeks heat. "To Cindy," she repeated. No matter how "hot" she thought Kincaid was she wasn't going to toast him or think about handcuffs in any way.

"Why are the FBI involved, anyway?" Sally-Anne asked, already refilling her glass.

That was the million-dollar question. "He said it's SOP for suspicious deaths of anyone working on certain bio-agents."

Sally-Anne's eyes went wide. "I wonder if Hanta virus is on the list."

That was what Sally-Anne worked on, Pip recalled now.

"I have no idea but let me know if you find out." Pip put her glass down.

"How did Cindy die?" The whites of Sally-Anne's eyes were streaked with red, and her lip wobbled.

"They're saying drowned, but she had coke in her system."

Sally-Anne stuffed a napkin against her pale lips and then blew her nose. "I never saw her take anything but you never really know if someone is using."

And just like that Sally-Anne believed Cindy was a cokehead.

Pip had learned to compartmentalize her emotions in order to be able to separate herself from painful stories in the past. If she hoped to figure out this mystery she was going to have to do it again with Cindy's death. She needed information from the other grad students. The people who'd seen her on a daily basis. She couldn't afford to scream at the world at the unfairness of it all.

"Cindy told me your parties got pretty wild?"

Sally-Anne laughed and scratched her throat before finishing her second glass of champagne. "This is true."

"Do you think that's where she might have gotten the drugs?"

Sally-Anne frowned. "I don't remember. I get pretty wasted at most parties and my memory gets really fuzzy. Sometimes a few of us bring something besides booze. It isn't a big deal. I mean everyone tries it once, right?"

Pip didn't judge the woman. As a teen she'd tried weed and Ecstasy before getting framed with her boyfriend's cocaine. She'd never touched anything after that and had avoided people who did. She'd seen what happened to some of those less fortunate than she'd been. One girl she'd met in foster care had progressed from weed to heroin to meth within two months and was dead by three. The kid had been searching for something that might make her feel better and had lost herself in the process.

"I can't believe she's gone." Sally-Anne refilled their glasses though Pip had barely drunk out of hers. "I keep expecting her to walk in here laughing at this massive joke she's played on us all."

If Pip hadn't seen her friend with her own eyes she probably wouldn't have believed it, either. But the feelings of desolation and loneliness were very real—feelings she remembered well from her early teenage years. "She wasn't depressed, was she?"

It was an option she hadn't wanted to consider, but if she truly wanted to discover the truth she needed to be objective, to face every possibility, not just the ones that suited her.

The idea she'd missed the signs of depression and that Cindy might have purposely ended her life…

You don't know everything.

What was it Pip hadn't known?

"No. Not that I could see, anyway." Sally-Anne drank the whole glass and poured herself another. She wiped her nose on a napkin. "She was excited and happy to be almost done. We were planning a surprise party for her when she submitted. Obviously, she didn't know about it." She laughed, tears suddenly streaming down her face.

Pip was emotionally wrung out. There were no tears left inside her anymore. "Do you know who might have supplied the drugs to her?"

Sally-Anne shook her head. "I'm not getting my friends in trouble with the FBI."

"I'm not going to tell the FBI." Pip pulled a face and played it cool. "I doubt the FBI cares if a bunch of grad students get high. But the coke Cindy took was laced with fentanyl. I don't want anyone else taking that stuff."

Sally-Anne's bottom lip wobbled. "She didn't get that from anyone we buy from. Hanzo prides himself on the purity of his product and one grad student even ran a sample through the HPLC. High grade stuff."

Hanzo.

Sally-Anne downed another glass of bubbly and checked her watch and gathered her purse. "Sorry. I need to head. I have to TA at nine tomorrow morning and I left my notes back at the lab." She stood and leaned over for another hug. Her fingers dug into Pip's back. "It wasn't your fault, you know. She was probably exhausted and not thinking straight."

Emotion wedged in Pip's throat. What if Kincaid was right and Pip was in denial because they'd argued and she could never make amends?

"I'll call you when I've finalized the funeral arrangements." Pip squeezed Sally-Anne's icy hands. "Thanks for talking with me. Just, be careful, okay?"

Sally-Anne shouldered her bag. "I will."

The woman was a frickin' virologist. She didn't need Pip to spell it out for her.

"Ciao, Pip." Sally-Anne leaned down and kissed Pip's cheek. "Keep your chin up. Remember Cindy loved you—that's all that really matters."

She wiggled her fingers in goodbye and disappeared out the door, and Pip was left alone in a crowd of strangers.

CHAPTER NINE

H UNT SAT AT his desk going through the full autopsy report on Cindy Resnick, wishing he could get Pip West's grief-stricken face out of his mind.

The results from all the samples they'd tested at CDC were also in. No anthrax had been found in Cindy Resnick's body or in her house in the city or at the cottage where she'd died. The second autopsy Pip West had requested could now go ahead in a standard mortuary. Hunt didn't think Pip would like the results.

On top of the coke and alcohol, the first autopsy revealed Cindy had traces of spermicide inside her, suggesting she'd had sex with someone wearing a condom the night she died. Evidence teams had also found male DNA on the sheets of her bed. Pip hadn't thought her friend was involved with anyone, but obviously she was wrong.

Maybe Cindy had other secrets… Maybe she'd killed herself rather than face the consequences of some of them.

"Hey, what happened to you?"

Hunt jolted out of his thoughts.

Will Griffin appeared beside him, dressed in running gear.

"I got sent on a lead for headquarters." Technically it wasn't a lie. "How'd it go yesterday? Anyone give you trouble?"

"Nah." Will grinned. "You should have seen Crowley's face when we walked in and Mandy read him his rights. I think he pissed his tighty-whities."

"Wish I'd been there." Crowley had been in his crosshairs for over a year and he'd missed the big takedown. But he'd barely thought about the case since this anthrax thing had come up. Nothing like the lives of thousands of people to put white-collar crime into perspective.

"Kincaid." Will clicked his fingers in front of Hunt's face.

Hunt rubbed the back of his neck and yawned. "Sorry. Didn't get a lot of sleep last night." Or the night before that come to think of it.

Will looked at him critically. "And not because you got lucky."

Hunt grunted. "I wish." Pip West's face flashed through his mind. No doubt about it, she was a beautiful woman. And totally unsuitable despite the spark of attraction that flared between them.

Will tossed an apple in the air, then caught it and started eating. "Most of the City Hall arrestees are out on bail. Except Crowley. I heard another woman came forward with a complaint he sexually assaulted her. Now his wife refuses to pay bail."

Crowley's wife controlled the purse strings and, as far as they'd been able to ascertain, wasn't involved in the corruption scandal. "The guy is slime."

"No kidding. Every day Mandy worked with him made me crazy."

"She can look after herself. Plus, she had backup." Hunt, to be precise.

"Yeah, but it wasn't me." Will crunched his apple. "And I

can't say anything about it without her getting pissed. Damn prickly woman."

"That's why you love her," Hunt needled him.

"That's *not* why I love her, but she keeps me on my toes." Will caught sight of the autopsy report on Hunt's desk and leaned closer. "You're looking at a drowning vic? That's your lead? How does it relate to white-collar crime?"

Hunt closed the file. "I'm off the white-collar squad for now." He accepted a high five from his buddy. "I'm liaising on this investigation with HQ as part of my WMD coordinator role." It was as much as he could say without overstepping security clearances. "The drowning vic is probably a coincidence."

"What's the investigation?" Will asked, interest lighting his eyes.

"Can't say."

"Why not?"

Hunt laughed. "Can't say."

Will was eyeing him funny. Hunt thought of Cindy Resnick being told the same thing by her university. How much strain had that put on the grad student and her relationships?

Will gave up grilling him. "Got your application ready?"

They were waiting for HRT to announce they were open for submissions to the next selection program. It should be soon.

Hunt's application had been ready for months. "Yup. You?"

Will nodded. "We should up our physical training. Wanna go for a run?"

"Now?" Hunt would rather stick needles in his eyes.

Will nodded again.

Hunt looked at the folders of paperwork associated with various different scientists sitting on his desk. He still had a lot to do. "Pretty busy with this. Maybe tomorrow?" Until they figured out whether or not this bioterrorism threat was coming from the Atlanta region Hunt didn't think he'd be getting much time for ten mile runs.

A smile curled the side of Will's mouth. "No point applying if you're not one hundred percent committed. I'll send you a postcard from Quantico."

Smug fuck.

"I'm committed." But it was after seven and Hunt was wasting his time on a woman who'd probably snorted too much toxic coke and then gone for a swim—alone—at night. It probably had nothing to do with the illegal sale of weaponized anthrax. The scientists were all tucked up at home. The analysts at SIOC were doing their thing. Hunt had another group of researchers he'd lined up to speak to tomorrow morning at Georgia State. "Fine. Give me five minutes to get changed."

"Hurry up. Some of us have plans for later, bro. Let's do this before our bodies atrophy and we both start looking like Reinhold."

Bob Reinhold was bald and fat, but Hunt was pretty sure he'd been born that way.

"Whoever wins buys beer." Hunt shut down his computer and locked his files away.

"I have time for you to buy me a quick beer." Will smirked.

Hunt shook his head as he went to the locker room. Will was athletic but built for sprinting. Fourteen months ago, Hunt had consistently beaten the guy over longer distances, but then he'd broken his leg in a motorbike accident—that's when he'd been transferred from the enhanced SWAT team to white-collar crime. Now Will mostly had the edge on him. A weakness he couldn't afford if he hoped to make it through selection. Hunt threw off his clothes, stored his creds, wallet and gun in a locker and pulled on running shorts and an old gray tee.

Guilt that he wasn't working on the case started eating at him, but HRT had been his dream since he'd been seven years old. He needed to do his job, but it didn't mean he had to sacrifice his long-term aspirations. Time to figure out how to do both.

He flashed to the image of Cindy Resnick's dead body on the banks of the lake. You never knew when your time was gonna be up.

PIP STARED AT the empty bottle of bubbly now floating in a sea of melted ice. The celebration had felt good in the moment and Pip knew Cindy would have approved, but now that Sally-Anne was gone Pip was once again left with that gaping hole in her life. A shotgun wound where her heart used to be.

A man came and stood opposite her and held out a small tray of coffees. "Sorry I'm late. Wasn't sure how you took it so I opted for black." He eyed the champagne bottle. "But maybe you'd rather something stronger?"

Adrian Lightfoot wore a moss-green sports coat over a white shirt and tan pants.

"No, this is perfect." She took a coffee and placed it on the table in front of her. "Thank you, Mr. Lightfoot."

"Call me Adrian." He sat opposite and Pip got a blast of blond-haired, green-eyed good looks, although there were dark shadows under his eyes, as if he hadn't slept.

She nodded to the bubbly. "One of Cindy's friends from the lab came over to commiserate. Insisted on raising a toast to Cindy." It probably looked awful to him, she realized. Like she was celebrating the cold hard cash of her inheritance.

He gave her a soft smile. "Cindy did love champagne."

"Yes. Yes, she did." A bittersweet ache shot through her chest. She was so grateful he knew that about Cindy. It made dealing with him easier.

He put a briefcase on the table and flicked open the latch. "I'm sorry for everything that's happened." His fingers were shaking. "The fact you found her. Well, it must have been awful…"

Pip looked away. Yup. It sucked. And it was not how she wanted to remember her friend. She wanted to remember the pajama days, the hard runs, the good nights out. The bottles of Moët shared in happiness rather than sorrow.

"Have the FBI indicated how she died?" he asked.

Pip went to take a sip of coffee.

"Careful," Adrian warned. "It's hot."

She blew on it and took the tiniest sip. He was right. It was scalding so she put it back down.

"I spoke to an FBI agent who said the ME indicated she drowned. They also found fentanyl-laced coke in her bloodstream," she said.

His eyes widened. "She'd taken drugs?"

Pip gritted her teeth. Why was everyone so quick to believe the worst? "I want a second autopsy."

"What?" He looked non-plussed. Tension infused his body

129

as he slowly sat up straighter and his voice rose. "Were there signs she was assaulted?"

"No," Pip said, frowning.

Adrian sank back into his seat. "I can probably request a second postmortem on your behalf. They aren't implicating you in this, are they?"

Was he suspicious of her? Did he think she'd murdered Cindy for financial gain?

"My alibi has been verified. I'm thankfully on surveillance cameras hundreds of miles away when she died." Sadness welled up but she fought it. It was hard to swallow back the tears and she was sick of crying.

She tried to be kinder to herself. Cindy died *yesterday*. Pip was allowed to grieve, she just wasn't allowed to wallow.

"They searched my car—"

"They what?" Adrian sounded alarmed.

"For drugs. Yesterday at Allatoona."

"You agreed to that?"

Pip nodded. "I found the body. They naturally suspected I might have supplied the cocaine." She smiled slightly at his outraged expression. "Anyway, there was nothing to find so it worked in my favor. Although if I had supplied the drugs that killed Cindy and was too chickenshit to admit it, I'd have poured them into the lake or buried them in the woods. I wouldn't have stashed them in my car."

"You better not let the FBI hear you say that."

"They aren't stupid. They know. Anyway, like I say, I was nowhere near the cottage when Cindy died." Her breath caught and her voice cracked. "I wish I had been."

He reached across the table and squeezed her hand, just like Kincaid had at breakfast that morning. It seemed like a thousand years ago now.

"I was very f-f-fond of Cindy." He cleared his throat. "I'm so sorry she's gone. I'm so very sorry you had to find her that way." His touch was warm and comforting. "But I'd like to understand. Why exactly do you want a second autopsy?"

"I knew Cindy for over a decade, and I never once saw her do anything as stupid as take drugs. They either made a mistake or they missed something."

"Cindy also had a wild side." Adrian seemed to be cautioning her.

"I am well aware."

"And no one could ever force her to do anything she didn't want to do."

Cindy had been just as stubborn as Pip.

"Would drugs be so completely out of the realms of possibility?" Adrian asked softly.

Pip thought about the crazy stuff they'd done together over the years. Reluctantly she shook her head, though she didn't really believe it. Being wild was one thing. Being reckless was something else entirely. But maybe Cindy had blurred the edges after months and years of hard work. Maybe the death of her family and rift with her best friend had tipped her over the edge of one bad decision. She still didn't believe it though.

Slowly he released her hand and gave her a pat. "I do remember Cindy having a low opinion of people who did stupid things." A wrinkle marred his perfect brow. "Which is why she dumped that boyfriend of hers."

"Dane?" Pip didn't know Dane at all. He ran with a different crowd from Cindy's other friends.

"I meant the other one. Dickster?" There was a hard glint

in Lightfoot's blue eyes.

"Ah, a different stupid thing." She laughed. "But yes. She didn't tolerate fools or betrayal."

Adrian Lightfoot scratched his head. "He kept asking Cindy to invest in his firm but I advised her against it. Not that it was my place, but with her father gone, I figured it wouldn't hurt to give her a little fatherly advice about men who were only after her money."

Adrian wasn't that old and was seriously handsome. Pip doubted Cindy had considered him a father figure.

Had Cindy ever tried to seduce him? Pip wouldn't put it past her. Cindy liked men and since her breakup with Pete had had a string of one-night stands. It was one of the things Pip had tried to caution her against.

And now she was dead and Pip wished she'd never mentioned it.

"I'd be happy to advise you professionally once probate is settled, but I'll understand if you already have an attorney or want someone different. I knew the Resnicks my whole life. I might be a painful reminder…"

Pip hunched her shoulders and the cold rush from of the hotel's A/C gave her goosebumps. She wanted that connection. She wanted that reminder. The last thing she desired was to forget them. "I don't have a personal lawyer. I've never needed one before." And wouldn't have been able to afford one even if she had. She frowned. "I'm happy for you to advise me, but the only thing I want to do right now is give Cindy a decent burial."

He nodded. "We can do that. You were a good friend. I know she appreciated and valued you. She spoke about you often."

That stupid argument weighed on Pip's soul. The fact she'd criticized Cindy's choices. She'd only done it because she worried, but she'd been way out of line.

"I need to do what's right by her. I need to figure out what happened. I owe her that." She hesitated, then admitted, "I'm not sure I can afford to do everything I need to. How much does an autopsy cost? How much is a decent burial?"

Adrian looked startled. "Inheritance tax is going to take a big chunk out of Cindy's money, but—"

"I'll use every penny if necessary." She clenched her fists. "And I can get more. I was offered a good job in Denver…"

Adrian held up his hand, shaking his head. "I don't think you quite understand the extent of Cindy's assets. Her father's patents alone generate hundreds of thousands of dollars annually." Cindy's dad had worked in the pharmaceutical industry and done very well for himself at a young age with a series of patents for drugs used to treat hypertension. "And Cindy filed her own patent that might also be worth a lot of money in the not too distant future."

Pip had forgotten about that.

"You might have to mortgage one of the properties or liquidate some stocks to pay the inheritance tax in the short-term, but there is still a considerable amount of money left over. You don't have to take the job in Denver unless you want to." He leaned closer to her so his voice wouldn't carry. "I don't know what your aspirations are, but you never need to work again."

"What?" Pain creased her stomach. Pip hadn't realized grief could physically hurt so much. Cindy had made her a wealthy woman, but all she really wanted was her best friend back.

She heard the leather creak as Adrian came and sat next to her, then he hugged her gently, rocking her as tears began to flow.

"Come on. Let's go somewhere more private," he urged.

She grabbed her bag. He picked up his briefcase and together they shuffled to the elevator, abandoning the coffee and the empty champagne bottle to the wait staff. In the elevator he pressed her cheek to his chest as she started sobbing so hard she couldn't see. On her floor, he led her to her door and stood aside as she fumbled for the keycard.

She went inside the large suite he'd booked and curled up on one of the comfy chairs, wiping her eyes. Grief was a sledgehammer that kept hitting her over and over out of nowhere. One minute she was dealing with it, the next she dissolved into ashes.

Adrian stood uncertainly near the door. "Can I come in for a moment?"

"Sure." Dammit. She hated weakness. So much for no more tears. May as well tell the waves not to lap the shore. "I'm not sure I'm up to dealing with anything important though."

He pulled a sheaf of papers from his case. "Just read and sign this top page and I can start the process and you can start organizing the funeral and I'll request a second autopsy with the best private medical examiner in the city. The sooner the legalities are finalized the better. Cindy was a big believer in getting things done."

Pip huffed out a soft laugh. It was true. Cindy hadn't liked to waste time. Pip scanned the letter quickly and signed. The feeling she was betraying Cindy wouldn't go away.

"We had a fight," she admitted, needing a confessor. "I said some things I regretted and I never got the chance to properly say I was sorry." She swallowed noisily. "She might not have wanted me to have her money after that."

Adrian's lips formed a sad smile that didn't go near his eyes. "Cindy loved you like family. And family's fight. There's no one else in the world she'd rather have inherit her things or take care of her funeral arrangements than you. I hope you'll let me help."

He took the signed paper from her hand and pulled her against his chest for one more hug.

"Get some sleep, Pippa. I'll get started on the paperwork. You concentrate on the funeral arrangements and think about where you want to live. The FBI released the house in town—"

"The FBI searched Cindy's home?"

Adrian nodded and put the papers back in his briefcase. "Making sure there were no signs of anthrax."

She frowned. "Isn't that a little odd?"

"Claimed it was standard procedure for researchers working on nasty diseases."

"Did you believe them?" she asked.

He ran his hand over the back of a chair. "I did. It made sense. Also, it felt reassuring once they raised the possibility of something like anthrax being on the premises. The fact they didn't find any will make resale easier."

His attempt at humor fell flat for both of them.

"I'd like to visit the house. Go through some photographs, sort some clothes..." She couldn't finish the sentence. Sort some clothes for Cindy to be buried in. The idea was too final. Too...wrong. She stared at the carpet.

"Of course. You have keys?"

She nodded.

Adrian asked softly, "Will you be all right?"

She looked up and gave him a sad smile. Of course, she wouldn't be all right. But what choice did she have except to go on?

The moment he left she closed her eyes and wanted to sink into the bed and hide from the world. Instead she pulled out her cellphone and started looking for a drug dealer named Hanzo.

CHAPTER TEN

H E SAW THE girl standing in the rain desperately searching for a gap in the traffic so she could sprint across the road and catch her bus. He tapped the car horn insistently and snagged her attention. She took a step back from the curb and eyed the vehicle warily as he pulled up alongside and rolled down the tinted window.

"Oh, hey. I didn't recognize the vehicle." She laughed nervously, color high in her cheeks.

Even from this distance he could smell the alcohol on her breath. Perfect. "I saw you standing in the rain and thought it would be cruel not to offer you a ride. Get in."

Rain drenched her hair and dripped off the end of her nose. She raised her laptop bag and laughed. "That would be great, saves me from getting my computer wet. Thanks."

Sally-Anne Wilton climbed inside and pulled on her seatbelt.

"You hear the terrible news about Cindy?" he asked, knowing it was easier if he brought it up.

"Yeah. It's awful. The cops think she ODed." Sally-Anne huddled into her damp fleece.

"I still can't believe it." It wasn't the police he was worried about. Why were the FBI asking questions?

She nodded. "I spoke to her friend earlier. You know, the

journalist."

He pulled out into traffic in the direction of Sally-Anne's apartment. "I remember her."

Hard to forget the small, dark-haired woman with her hourglass figure and inquisitive eyes.

"She's organizing the funeral." Sadness was written in Sally-Anne's anguished eyes and pale lips. "Wanted to know if anyone at the department took drugs."

"What did you tell her?" he asked.

She gave a defensive little shrug. "That a few of us had tried it at parties, but we weren't stupid or addicted."

Cindy's death was supposed to have been treated like a regular drug overdose but instead the Feds were all over it. So was the nosy journalist. His fingers tightened on the steering wheel as he maneuvered through the rain-drenched streets.

Since the arms broker had disappeared off the face of the earth a week ago, he'd been in clean up mode. Nothing could lead back to Atlanta. He hadn't spent this many years working his balls off to lose everything now.

All communication had occurred via the dark web with cloaked identities. Untraceable.

It had been a calculated risk, selling that anthrax and the vaccine on the black market. One designed to induce panic and stir up interest. Unfortunately, it had backfired and now he had to get rid of loose ends and throw the authorities off the scent.

It didn't take long to get to Sally-Anne's apartment. She lived in a cramped one-bedroom dump. The main advantage was she lived alone.

"Thanks for the ride." She undid her seatbelt and prepared to climb out of the SUV he'd borrowed from a friend.

"Can I come in for a drink?" he asked. "I don't want to be alone just yet."

She looked reluctant but her expression softened. "I can feed you some frozen pizza if that'll help? But I have an early start tomorrow."

"That would be great. Thanks."

She led the way and he followed her through the main entrance that had a security door, but no cameras. He kept his head bowed anyway, just in case. He was careful not to touch anything.

They walked up the stairs to the third floor. The carpet was dirt brown but stains were still visible.

Sally-Anne unlocked her front door, dumped her coat and bags on the nearest chair and turned on a lamp rather than the main light. Piles of text books and photocopies of papers were stacked on the coffee table.

"Sorry about the mess. I wasn't planning on having anyone over." She started to clean up.

"Don't bother on my account."

She looked unsure, then shrugged. "Find a spot on the couch. Beer or wine? Full disclosure...I opened the wine yesterday but hopefully it's still good."

"A beer sounds good."

She retrieved two bottles and set them on the coffee table. She started to clear away the text books.

"I'll move them. You get the pizza."

She gave him a sad smile. "Thanks. I'll put the oven on. It still hasn't sunk in, you know?"

She meant Cindy's death.

But she was wrong. Cindy's death had sunk in. The ramifications of the investigation into her death was why he was here.

He watched Sally-Anne go back into the kitchen and turn on the oven, throwing in a frozen pizza. He took a plastic vial from his pocket, flipped the cap and poured the white powder into her beer bottle when she wasn't looking. He wiped the lip of the bottle with his thumb, mentally noting to wipe it clean later.

When she came back she curled her feet underneath her on the couch and raised her bottle high. "Here's to Cindy."

"Cheers." They tapped bottles and both took a healthy swallow.

"I've already drunk too much." She cradled her skull. "I'm going to be the TA from hell tomorrow."

"Cindy could drink like a fish and never get drunk."

Sally-Anne gave a soft groan. "I can't believe she died right before she submitted. I mean, she worked so hard. It just seems wrong."

"It's the definition of irony."

"A good reason to get my thesis finished, STAT." She laughed louder this time.

He leaned back in the sagging couch. "Maybe it's a sign never to put off those things in life we want to try."

"Like?"

Was this wrong? To bait her? "I don't know. Bungee jumping? Seeing the Grand Canyon? Diving the Great Barrier Reef while it still exists? Sex against a hotel window. Bucket list items. What's on your bucket list?" He watched her take another long swallow. Her cheeks were flushed now though the apartment was cold.

"Walking the Great Wall of China. Seeing the Amazon." Sally-Anne pressed her lips together and grinned. "Going down on someone in a darkened movie theater?" She blushed. "You asked."

"Do it. Cindy's dead, Sally-Anne. You might be run over by a fucking bus tomorrow."

Her eyes were unfocused. Mouth a little slack. She wasn't used to hearing him curse but he was under a lot of stress.

"Want another beer?" he asked, climbing to his feet.

"Why not? I'm already drunk. One more won't make me more drunk."

He used his sleeve to cover his hand when opening the fridge and wielding the bottle opener. He slipped a second vial of powder into her drink.

He brought the bottle back and handed it to her.

Her eyes held his and there was a gleam in them that told him she was aroused. Whereas before she'd looked tired, now she looked wired.

When he sat back down, she unzipped his pants with a sly grin. She always got horny when she got high. She just didn't realize she was high. And she rarely remembered what she'd done when she woke up the next day. It was one of his favorite things about her. He grabbed her hair and ran his teeth down her neck.

He'd make it good for her. Really good. Until her heart cracked wide and her veins exploded from sheer bliss.

And the scariest thing about this was how much he enjoyed it. What had at first been a necessity was now giving him a kick, a bigger kick than anything he'd ever got from cocaine.

Who knew?

Murder was addictive.

CHAPTER ELEVEN

T HE ALARM SYSTEM wasn't armed, and Pip felt like a burglar as she walked through the front door of the Resnicks' Sherwood Forest home. Ghosts danced over her skin with footsteps as soft as cats' paws. Even without the bright silver of the moon she knew every inch of this house and there was a catch in her chest at the empty silence that greeted her.

She eased off her running shoes—a house rule—and closed the door before moving into the foyer. She flicked on the tiffany lamp that had been Cindy's mom's pride and joy. Muted jewels of light dappled the ceiling.

Cindy had kept the essence of the home the same since her parents died. Same furniture and wall coverings. Same pictures on the wall, same drapes and blinds. The idea of replacing her mom's choices had sat heavily on Pip's friend. Now it was Pip's problem.

A family portrait hung on one wall.

It was a big canvas of all four Resnicks in happier times. Cindy had always groused that it made her look dumpy, but she'd made no move to remove it after her parents and brother died. They wore denim and autumnal colors and were surrounded by fallen leaves, sitting out the front of this house. Cindy's mom had her arm wrapped possessively around both of her children and Cindy's dad stood behind them looking proud and happy. Their love for one another shone through that two-dimensional image and echoed through Pip's heart. That's what she'd been talking about when she'd spoken about the search for true love. That's what Cindy had been looking for.

Pip knew without a doubt she'd keep that portrait until the day she died. They were her family. Not the alcoholic mother, or the absent father. These people.

She'd first met them when Cindy discovered Pip didn't have anywhere to go for the holidays that first year at Florida State. Cindy had dragged her home and they'd virtually adopted her.

Now they were all gone.

Loss washed through her but she didn't let it bring her to her knees. Not this time.

She looked around. There were no signs that the FBI had been searching for anthrax. They hadn't made a mess, which was different to how most police departments operated.

Surely if Cindy had cocaine lying around the FBI or CDC, or whoever the hell was involved, would have found it? What did Pip really expect to find here?

She'd tried to track down the drug dealer but none of her contacts knew who he was and there were no arrests in that name. She'd cruised down to "The Bluffs" with some inane idea about asking around but had just kept driving. The area was a notoriously deprived and dangerous place. A woman like her asking questions about specific drug dealers in that part of town—she'd wind up lying next to Cindy on a slab.

She'd come here instead, drawn by memories and that aching sense of loneliness.

Though Adrian had told her the place had been released

by the police they hadn't removed the crime scene tape from the front door yet.

Pip wandered into the kitchen area and checked the freezer. Given Cindy's nature and her profession, that was the most likely place her friend would store chemicals. No obvious baggies. Not even an open box of baking powder. A conservatory sat on the back of the house where Cindy's mom had nurtured and raised many of the flowers that grew in the garden. It was Pip's favorite spot in the place with its comfy rattan furniture and large lazy fans. The moon shone brightly and she didn't bother with any more lights.

The idea that this house was hers was unsettling. Pip shook her head. She couldn't think about that right now. Once she'd taken care of Cindy's funeral she'd think about what to do about everything. The houses. The vehicles. The money.

Bigger questions loomed. What was Pip going to do with her life? Where did she want to work? What did she want to do?

The obvious choice was getting another gig with a paper, but even the thought made her stomach knot.

Don't think about it. Concentrate on figuring out what happened to Cindy and honoring her. One step at a time.

She was looking for a way to track down this drug dealer. She'd tell Kincaid the name Sally-Anne had dropped, but not until she'd squeezed as much information out of the grad students as possible. If Cindy did do drugs it was possible she had contacted the dealer somehow. Pip didn't have access to Cindy's cell phone but Cindy kept paper copies of her bills, a holdover from her father who was always worried what might happen if a company's system glitched or the U.S. was hit by a massive EMP. She'd trace the phone numbers on the bills and see if any of them came back to unknown sources and she'd check those out. Without walking around the bluffs and getting her throat cut.

She headed into Cindy's dad's old study with its dark polished wood and open fireplace. There was a TV and a green leather loveseat where Pip had once accidentally caught Cindy's parents making out.

She'd been mortified but they had barely been phased. She'd loved how in love they'd been even after thirty years together. It was a rare kind of love. A true kind of love.

She wouldn't settle for anything less. But doubted she'd find it.

Maybe there was something wrong with her. Something fundamental. Something that made her essentially unlovable.

Didn't matter. Not important.

She forced the thoughts out of her head and went to the filing cabinet in the far right corner and opened the drawer where Cindy kept the household bills. Cindy was such an organized neat freak there were folders for everything, clearly labeled, doubled up for both this house and the cottage. The phone bills were in order of date and Pip pulled the ones for the year so far, for the house, cottage and Cindy's cell phone, and folded them and placed them in her purse.

She glanced at an oil painting on the wall. Would Cindy have kept a stash of coke in her father's safe? Had the investigators known it was there?

Pip took the painting off the wall and keyed in the code. Cindy's mom and dad's wedding anniversary. Cindy hadn't changed it.

Inside were old passports and various official documents. Some rolls of cash and foreign currencies, and jewelry boxes full of Cindy's mom's diamonds. Pip shied away from the idea of owning these things. It was too big of an emotional burden. She moved aside some papers, and something big, black and lethal stared back at her.

Cindy's dad's gun.

Pip had totally forgotten he'd owned one. Cindy had bought a Glock for self-defense. She spent so much time alone at the cottage and walking to and from campus late at night she'd wanted something to make her feel safer.

Pip hated guns.

Being a crime reporter, she'd seen the damage they could and did inflict. Slowly she reached out and touched the cold metal of the barrel. Tentatively she reached inside and pulled the pistol out of the safe. It felt heavy and awkward and she needed two hands to hold it steady.

Since the Booker shooting she'd had several threats to her life. She was positive some of them came from Booker's fellow cops. Lack of confidence in the local police department's willingness to help her should she be attacked had been one of the key factors in play when she'd decided to leave Tallahassee.

She turned the weapon over and ran a finger over "Remington" stamped on the metal.

She had no training. She didn't even know how to load the thing. But she was gonna learn she decided, straightening her spine. She was gonna learn how to defend herself. She slipped it into her purse, along with a box of bullets. They were heavy suckers. She'd find a gun range and pay someone to teach her how to shoot.

Agent Kincaid's cynical smile flashed through her mind. He'd probably advise her to avoid danger by keeping her nose out of other people's business. But she couldn't do it. She couldn't rest until she figured out why a woman who'd just finished a four-year project that she'd been dedicated to had immediately snorted coke and died.

Pip closed the safe and replaced the painting. Were the cops even looking for the drug dealer? From what Kincaid had said, she assumed so, but the Feds seemed more worried about the potential threat of the disease Cindy had worked on, rather than what had killed her.

Did they think Cindy had brought anthrax home? Or maybe they were worried she'd inadvertently carried it here on her clothes?

Pip knew the precautions Cindy took in the lab. It didn't make any sense.

Or, more likely, the powers-that-be had established sweeping new regulations that covered all Category A agents. Blanket procedures for everything from anthrax to Ebola.

Pip wandered through the kitchen, to the hallway. A formal lounge sat off to the right. Used at Christmas and Thanksgiving and if the family was entertaining. Pip was pretty sure the only person who'd been in there since the wake was the Resnicks' longtime cleaner.

God, she now had a cleaner. No way could she fire the woman.

She went to the front door and fingered the mail. Bills and flyers. Her bills now, she realized. Perspiration broke out on her forehead. She wasn't used to such responsibility. Hated getting into debt or buying things on credit—hence the poor state of her car.

She squeezed her hands into fists. The Resnicks would want things handled properly. Affairs sorted. Bills paid. She would do that for them.

She headed up the wide staircase to Cindy's room. Unlike at the cottage, Cindy hadn't moved into the master bedroom here, preferring her own large girlhood room down the hall. She'd redecorated it a deep green with flowery watercolors on the walls.

Pip hung on the doorframe and flicked on the light.

The image of Cindy sitting on that double bed hit hard and fast as a prison shiv. Pip forced herself to step inside. Cindy used to keep a journal and although Pip didn't want to pry she really wanted to know if she'd missed anything important.

You don't know everything.

The words ran round and round inside her mind on a loop. What was it she didn't know?

She opened Cindy's bedside table. There was her journal for last year but not this one. It was probably at the cottage. She put her hand on the hardcover and then picked it up even though she didn't want to. The answer might be in this book, but the idea of snooping into Cindy's innermost secrets…?

Pip wasn't judgmental about sex, but she wasn't sure she wanted to read Cindy's most intimate innermost thoughts or any graphic details. Pip would never judge her. Considering where *she* came from? The idea was a joke. But what if she read things about herself she didn't like? Her fingers clasped the journal tight. She needed to face the truth, whatever that truth was.

The house creaked in the wind. Pip had never felt vulnerable here before but she'd never really been alone. She slipped the journal into her bag next to the reassuring weight of the pistol.

Pip went over to the chest of drawers and checked out the

cork board resting against the wall.

She searched through the photographs, most of which were dear and familiar. Many were of the two of them goofing around, or Cindy's family. A postcard with a bare-chested cowboy was stuck to the center. Pip had sent it last month after a work trip to El Paso. Her throat hurt with the effort of holding back emotion.

She would not cry.

She pulled the postcard off the board to read what she'd written. Some stupid inane comment that she'd hoped would make her friend laugh.

Behind the postcard was a picture of Cindy and a really good-looking dude. Dane.

Could Cindy have gotten back with him? Pip tugged the photo free and tucked it into her bag along with the journal. She scanned the room for anything else.

A book sat on the other bedside table. *Gone With the Wind*, by Margaret Mitchell.

Not Cindy's usual reading material.

Pip walked over and picked it up. Some of the page corners were folded, a habit Pip abhorred, but Cindy preferred. She'd definitely been reading it.

Pip flicked through it and saw a handwritten inscription in the front.

"Dearest Cindy, I 'do' give a damn." Signed with a love heart.

The bookmark was from the Margaret Mitchell Museum downtown. Pip frowned and wondered who had given it to her friend. Cindy was a romantic at heart. She'd wanted happily-ever-afters, not the rather bleak ending of this particular novel. Bitterness and anger threatened to well up inside Pip and expanded through her chest and wanted to spill out of her mouth because her friend would never get her happy ending now and it wasn't fair.

Pip flicked through the pages for more clues as to who'd given it to her. Nothing.

Pip couldn't see Dane giving it to Cindy but what did she know about the guy? Not a lot. Pete might. He was pretentious enough and arrogant enough to try and worm his way back into Cindy's good graces even though Cindy would never forgive infidelity.

Someone else? Someone new and exciting?

Agent Kincaid's handsome face flashed through her brain again.

Federal agent! Not new or exciting, just annoyingly handsome.

Pip laid the book down on the table and turned around to leave. She needed to track down this Hanzo character, but not alone at night. She'd speak to Dane Garnett tomorrow—see if he or the drug dealer drove a black SUV. She had a clear plan and it made her feel better, gave her renewed purpose. Maybe now she could sleep.

The creak of a door hinge downstairs had her heart catapulting into her throat. She edged to the doorway and flicked out the light. Was that a footstep downstairs? Dread shot through her. Had she forgotten to lock the door when she came in?

She couldn't remember.

She listened harder, heart thumping so violently against her ribs she felt physically winded. There were no other sounds. She stayed still and counted to a hundred. No footsteps, no doors opening or closing. Nothing moved. Maybe it was a draft catching one of the interior doors?

Okay. She released a big breath of relief.

It was her overactive imagination and a big dose of paranoia giving her the heebie jeebies.

Still she pulled her cell from her pocket and dialed the first two digits of the emergency services. She crept carefully out of the bedroom and inched silently along the hallway. Shadows danced over the walls as the wind rustled the bushes and trees outside.

She was being a chicken, but she couldn't shake the sensation she wasn't alone. The shadows seemed sentient and the sensation of being watched crawled over her skin. She reached for the handgun in her purse, fingers curling around the grip as she pulled it out.

Armed with the gun and her cell she checked the front door, locked it, deciding to go out through the kitchen, the closest exit to where she'd parked her car near the double garage at the back of the house. She slipped on her sneakers.

Determined to be brave she turned off the lamp and headed along the corridor toward the kitchen. She could see easily enough and knew her way. She'd arm the alarm on the way out just in case any burglars got the bright idea of robbing the place while it was empty.

The only warning she got that she truly wasn't alone was a quick brush of air before she was caught around the waist, the attacker's arm trapping her left hand to her side. He grabbed her right hand jerking it upward, the gun coming out of her grip before he twisted her arm behind her back and shoved her into the nearest wall.

And it was very definitely a "he" attacking her.

She screamed as terror rushed over her. She didn't want to die.

CHAPTER TWELVE

HUNT STOOD IN semi-darkness holding onto a wriggling mass of terrified female who seemed determined to pierce his eardrums with her vocal cords. At least she hadn't blown his brains out.

"Ms. West. Pip. Pip! It's okay." He relaxed his grip on her arm, trying to reassure her. His other arm was still around her waist and his fingers hit bare skin which scalded his hand like a naked flame. "It's Agent Kincaid." He carefully released her, but kept hold of her gun. Just in case.

She stumbled away and turned to face him. "Kincaid? Oh, my God. Oh, my God!" Her hand went to her chest. "You scared me to death. I could have shot you."

She was sucking in air like an asthmatic and he belatedly remembered the panic attack she'd had that morning. It had been a hell of a long day.

"What are you doing creeping around?" she asked.

"I wanted to take another quick look at the house before the scene was released." He lived in Ansley Park just south of this Sherwood Forest neighborhood and knew it would likely be his last chance.

"In the dark?"

He grimaced. "It's bright enough to see you scowling at me."

"You could be completely blind and know I'm scowling at you," she snapped.

He suppressed a smile. It was getting harder and harder to maintain his dislike of her even though he wasn't sure of her motives. "There was a light on in the hallway when I arrived. I had the light on in the study but I didn't know anyone else was in the house. Where're you parked?"

She shifted the bag she had draped across her body and nodded toward the back of the house. "By the garage where I always park."

After his run with Will—and the quick beer Will had paid for—Hunt had received a message from his contact at CDC. Dr. Jez Place had wanted to give him Cindy Resnick's autopsy photographs. All biological evidence had been sent to the FBI's lab at Quantico for storage. Jez had also given him the house keys for this place along with Hunt's promise to return them to their rightful owner—Pip.

"What were you looking for in the study?" Her voice was all breathy. He knew he'd given her a scare. She'd nearly given him heart failure when he'd seen a figure walking past him carrying a gun.

He flicked on a light switch behind him hoping to dispel the sense of intimacy that was developing between them. She blinked at the brightness, all tousled and disheveled as if she'd just climbed out of bed.

Should have left the lights off.

"I was looking for a copy of Cindy's thesis." He figured he'd at least try and read the introduction and discussion sections to get a grip on the science behind it. He wasn't a total moron. He had a degree in engineering.

"Did you find one?" she asked.

He shook his head.

"I could have shot you," she said quietly.

He checked the older model handgun he held in his hands. "Not unless you turned off the safety and added a few bullets."

Her expression fell. "I don't know how. I don't know anything about guns," she admitted. Her shoulders slumped. "I could have killed you by accident as much by design."

"You'd probably have got away with self-defense too, except for the fact this scene is still sealed off."

She set her jaw in what Hunt was coming to recognize as imminent stubbornness. "Cindy's lawyer told me the scene had been released."

He checked his watch. "In another thirty minutes or so, he'd be right."

"Well maybe you should give me the gun back and I'll just wait for half an hour." She sounded pissed again.

He hid his smile. "Did you just threaten a federal agent?"

He was pretty sure she growled. "Gonna arrest me?" She thankfully realized he was kidding as there was a trace of humor in her voice.

"Where'd you get the 1911?" he asked, turning the piece over in his hands. Looked old.

"The what?"

"The weapon."

"It's Cindy's dad's." The corners of Pip's mouth turned down. She looked tired.

He wondered if Cindy's dad had been in the Army.

"I found it in the safe."

He glanced at her sharply. "Safe?"

"You want to take a look in the safe?" she guessed.

"You offering?"

She huffed out a laugh. "Seems to me you still have twenty-nine minutes of federal authority left. I'd make you order me to but I resent being bossed around."

"I noticed." He sent her a wry smile.

"You prefer submissive women?" Her cheeks burned red as her words took on other meanings. "I didn't mean—"

He barked out a laugh. "Forget it. I like many different kinds of women."

Her eyes narrowed.

He squeezed the bridge of his nose. Now he'd made himself sound like a manwhore, and from her expression she wasn't impressed. She started walking through the house, turning on all the lights along the way.

He purposely kept his eyes off her very ripe ass.

He did like different kinds of women, and never ventured beyond superficial relationship territory. Sex and fun times. No sticky emotions.

So maybe he was a manwhore.

He certainly wasn't ready to settle down. He wasn't sure he was built for serious relationships. He'd seen what his mother had gone through when his dad had been murdered. He knew what he'd suffered as a child without a father and as a young man losing his step-sister.

It was easier to be alone.

And so what if Pip West wasn't impressed by him. Was his ego really that fragile?

The study was old-fashioned and classically cool. A hardwood floor and dark wainscoting. A hunter-green leather couch and wingback chair gathered around an open fireplace with a large screen TV off to one side.

What would Pip do with the place? Sell it for fast cash?

Settle down and raise a family?

He ignored the irritation the thought brought with it, unsure from where it stemmed. The fact she'd felt good in his arms even if he'd been holding her for all the wrong reasons? The fact he found her attractive but had no intention of acting on it? Or the sense she wasn't the sort of woman who'd go for a brief no strings fling?

He shook his head at himself. He must be more tired than he'd realized to be thinking of flings. She was a journalist and he wouldn't trust a journalist if they were bound and gagged.

Pip walked over to an old-fashioned looking oil painting and took it down off the wall. He followed and watched as she typed in a six-digit code and opened the door.

She pulled out a box of ammunition from her purse and stuffed it inside the safe.

"I didn't see a paper copy of her thesis, but she might have put a backup drive in there at some point. You may as well replace the gun, too. I'm obviously a liability until I learn how to use it."

He put the gun to one side and methodically emptied the contents of the safe onto a sideboard. Old passports, birth and death certificates. Cash. Jewelry boxes that he'd bet held the real deal. Pip had inherited the motherlode. He glanced at where she stood, biting her lip and watching him. She didn't look too happy about it. He knew all too well, money didn't replace the people you loved.

His fingers wrapped around something cool and plastic. A small black data stick. "Can I take this?"

She hesitated, then nodded, arms crossing tight over her chest. "If you promise to tell me if you find any evidence of where she got the drugs from?"

He stared at her suspiciously. "Why?"

"Because I don't believe she took them willingly," she conceded. "I'd like to talk to the person who sold them to her to confirm."

Like anyone would admit to that.

She looked away. "And maybe you're right and the reason I can't accept it is I'm feeling guilty about the argument we had." Her throat worked as she swallowed. "But I need to know."

"I can't make that promise," he said regretfully. He held out the thumb drive toward her. "I won't jeopardize any ongoing or future investigations."

Her shoulders slumped in defeat as she exhaled. She shook her head. "Fine. Just take it."

The fact he was taking advantage of her exhaustion should have bothered him. It didn't. He'd do whatever it took. He loaded everything else back into the safe. Held up the weapon. "You sure you don't want this? I can show you how to load it and how to turn off the safety."

The muscle in her jaw flexed and she seemed to lose color. "I hate guns."

"Why did you take it then?"

She didn't answer him.

He frowned. "You have reason to believe you're in danger?"

She shrugged.

He wasn't getting anything more out of her. He double-checked the pistol was unloaded and placed it gently in the safe. He closed the safe door and pressed "lock" on the menu and the thing beeped. He replaced the painting.

Out of the corner of his eye he saw Pip walk over to the

printer that sat on top of a low file cabinet behind the desk. She gathered up a thick stack of paper from the printer tray. His pulse started to beat a little faster. She turned the stack toward him and showed him the title page.

"Is this what you're looking for?"

Cindy's thesis. *Jackpot*. He went to take it but she held up a finger. "I want a copy, too."

"The university might object."

She raised an eyebrow. "They'd like you having it even less."

This was true and from the angle of her jaw he'd run out of free passes. It took ten minutes to duplicate the thing on the printer-copier that was fancier than the one they had in the field office.

When they were done they left the house via the kitchen door, each carrying a copy of Cindy's apparently groundbreaking research. Pip armed the security panel and he walked her to her car, handing her the house keys the cops had borrowed from the neighbors on Monday.

He and Pip had spent the last hour communicating without arguing which marked progress. So maybe she wasn't digging for a story. Maybe she was genuinely trying to find a way to deal with her loss. He remembered the devastated little boy he'd been when his father was killed. The only thing that had dragged him out of it was meeting an FBI agent and being told the bad man who'd murdered his father during the bank robbery had, in turn, been killed by an HRT sniper.

Perhaps she was simply pursuing the same sense of closure, but he wasn't ready to trust her yet.

She climbed behind the wheel, but before she could close the door he stopped her. "Stay safe, Pip."

She opened her mouth to say something but changed her mind. She closed the door and drove away.

He wished he could tell her something to put her mind at rest about her friend, but he doubted she'd listen to him when she wouldn't listen to a well-respected medical examiner. And, of course, there was no way he would let a journalist sniff out a link to bioterrorism that might jeopardize innocents. He ran his finger around the inside of his collar and climbed into his truck parked near the curb. Best if he kept far, far away from the sexy and intriguing Pip West.

Eyes on the prize.

CHAPTER THIRTEEN

T HE PHONE CALL at three-thirty in the morning sent a jolt
through Hunt's bloodstream.

He grabbed his work cell from where it was charging and
unplugged it. The name of an Atlanta PD detective he knew,
Cyril White, flashed up on the screen.

"Kincaid here."

"I have a dead body down here with one of your business
cards in their wallet."

An image of Pip West burst through his brain. Sweat
broke out on his cold skin and he knocked a glass of water
over on the nightstand. *Fuck*. The glass rolled onto the floor
and shattered.

"A young woman named Sally-Anne Wilton. Anything
you can tell me?"

Hunt covered his mouth with his hand and breathed deep
for a moment. The strength of his reaction surprised him. Pip
West had snuck under his skin. He couldn't afford that
weakness or attraction. He rolled over to the other side of the
bed where he started pulling on pants.

"Give me the address. I'll be right over."

Thirty minutes later, Hunt stood outside the doorway of
the cheap one-bedroom apartment and signed the crime scene
entry log sheet held by a uniformed Atlanta PD officer with a

clipboard. The flash of a photographer's camera came from inside the apartment. Other residents loitered in their doorways to see what was going on.

Nothing good.

He slipped white paper booties over his shoes even though first responders had tromped all over the place when they'd first arrived. Atlanta PD was calling it another drug overdose in an epidemic that was out of control. The problem wasn't just heroin or cocaine, it was what dealers put in those drugs. Fentanyl was supposed to create a more "euphoric" high and was a hundred times more potent than morphine. The opioid crisis was making the cocaine influx of the eighties look like training camp.

He stepped into the room. The scent of burnt food mixed with the familiar odor of death.

It was an ugly scene.

At least Pip had been spared this, he thought grimly. The lake had washed off the physiological trauma of poison and rendered Cindy Resnick's death clean and sterile. She'd looked almost peaceful lying on the banks of that lake.

Pip hadn't had to see her friend like this.

This girl was bone thin and very naked. Her clothes were scattered around the floor as if she'd ripped them off and thrown them away. A vibrator lay next to the couch and a bottle of olive oil beside that. She was lying on her back, a fine dusting of what he hoped was coke, rather than weaponized anthrax, coating her skin.

Blood dripped from her nose. The whites of her eyes were shot through with crimson and the sharp scent of vomit permeated the atmosphere.

The stink of death hit him unexpectedly and he moved

into the kitchen to try and distance himself from the stench. Sally-Anne Wilton who he'd met at the hotel when talking to Pip. She'd worked in the same department as Cindy Resnick. Coincidence? Unlikely.

Dumb fucking smart kids.

Hunt popped some latex gloves from the box on the counter and pulled them on. Checked the fridge.

It was full of diet cola. An open bottle of white wine. Cheese—strong cheddar. Brown bread. Margarine. Free range eggs. Some homemade smoothies. He looked in the freezer. Frozen pizzas and chili. No dope.

A pizza box and wrapping sat in the recycle bin. He touched the top of the old electric ring stove. Slightly warm. He opened the oven door and there was a burnt-out piece of cardboard.

The woman's coat was on a chair near the entrance. Her phone was on the counter. A beer bottle lay overturned on the carpet.

So...she'd gotten home, horny and hungry after her meeting with Pip at the hotel, stuck a pizza in the oven and decided to get high and masturbate during the twenty minutes it took to cook?

"Did someone turn this oven off?" he asked the room in general.

The cop near the door piped up, "Smoke alarm was screaming and the neighbors complained to the custodian. He let himself in, turned off the oven, and called the EMTs."

The sight of the dead girl turned his stomach and he knew it was wrong to be so repulsed, but...the fact that this had been her own choice drove him crazy.

Nothing would ever induce him into the drug scene. Hell,

he'd even avoided painkillers as much as he was able during his rehabilitation after his motorcycle accident. It was too easy to get hooked, especially with doctors over-prescribing and exacerbating the problem.

Detective Cyril White walked up to him in the kitchen. They'd worked together before on the City Hall investigation and on some bank robberies when Hunt had first transferred to Atlanta. Cyril knew more about police work than Hunt could ever hope to learn.

The detective had endured Katrina and its aftermath. Had grown up in the ninth ward and watched his parents' house get destroyed by the floodwaters before moving to Georgia.

"Why did she have your card in her pocket?" the detective asked.

"I met her today at a hotel downtown. She was the friend and co-worker of a young woman who was found dead after taking cocaine out at Lake Allatoona day before yesterday. I didn't interview Sally-Anne. Spent about sixty seconds with her before I had to leave so I gave her my card in case she had anything she could tell me."

"Any similarities with your DB out at Allatoona?"

Hunt eyed the white powder. "Yeah, lots. But dissimilarities, too. They were both working on their doctorates at Blake. Same department. Different supervisors and specialty areas. Lake victim was also naked but the body was found outside and manner of death was drowning. My vic had money— cottage at the lake and a house in the city. ME found traces of fentanyl in the coke at Allatoona. It would have probably killed her if the water hadn't."

And both victims had known Pip West, he realized. Could she be involved?

"Foul play?" the detective asked.

"Still unclear." Hunt shook his head.

"Why're the Feds looking at it?" Cyril asked bluntly.

"I'm the FBI's WMD coordinator and the vic worked on a Category A listed substance. We decided caution was warranted."

"Anything I should be worried about in this case?" White stared warily at the white powder on the vic.

Hunt pressed his lips together. Sally-Anne worked on Hanta virus, not anthrax. He'd run her background when he'd left the hotel earlier.

"I'll talk to my boss but it looks more and more like these women scored some dirty coke, possibly from the same source. We'd better figure out who the dealer is before more people wind up dead."

White shook his head. "This shit is getting worse rather than better."

The sight of Sally-Anne's lifeless body depressed Hunt. Why would she risk getting high right after her friend died?

What a goddamned waste.

"You informed next of kin?" Hunt asked the detective.

White shook his head. "They're in Maine. Someone's going there now."

Hunt said nothing. He remembered a faceless cop coming to his door when he was seven years old to tell them his dad had been shot dead, and more vividly at his mom and stepfather's door telling them Hunt's step-sister had died in action. Different uniform. Same fucking pain.

"How do you want to handle this?" Cyril asked him.

Hunt thought about the likelihood of this being drug related versus bioterrorism. Pretty damn high. "I think this is a case for APD to try to figure out where this shit is coming from. FBI can assist and I'll pass on any relevant information from the Lake Allatoona vic pertinent to the drug angle."

Cyril raised his salt and pepper brows. He'd heard everything Hunt wasn't telling him.

"Can I get a dump of her phone?" Hunt eyed Sally-Anne's phone and laptop.

Cyril nodded. "I'll send it over as soon as I get it."

Hunt thanked the man and headed out the door, dialing McKenzie despite the hour. Although unlikely, if McKenzie wanted to treat this death as a biological hazard, things were about to get a hell of a lot more public and panic was guaranteed. No one wanted that, but no one wanted to be infected with anthrax either.

The proverbial choice between a rock and a hard place.

CHAPTER FOURTEEN

INSISTENT KNOCKING ON Pip's door had her blinking awake and groggily sitting upright. The room was pitch-black so she fumbled to switch on the reading light above her bed. She nearly dislocated her jaw with a yawn as she peered at the display on the digital alarm clock.

Five AM. Who the hell was knocking on her door at this time in the morning?

She flung back the covers and staggered to the door. She stood on tiptoe but couldn't see through the peephole that was apparently designed for people over nine feet tall.

The knock came again.

Pip put her hand on the handle, hesitated. "Who is it?"

"Kincaid." He didn't sound happy but her heart gave an unexpected leap of excitement, and not just because he was FBI.

Stupid heart.

She flicked off the security latch and opened the door.

His eyes traveled down her soft, pink, sleep-rumpled pajamas and quickly back up to her face.

"Can I come in?" he spoke quietly.

She didn't feel like she had much choice so she let him slip inside before closing the door behind him. She followed him into her room and refrained from apologizing for the mess. A bunch of her belongings were stacked between the bed and the bathroom wall. She'd left boxes of books and non-essential items in the trunk of her car. Her open suitcases were on the bed she wasn't using and she'd set up her computer on the desk.

He glanced around the room with a frown. "How long are you here for?"

She'd transferred from the suite to a double room last night. No point in wasting money, especially money she didn't yet have. "Until after the funeral. I guess I'll stay at Cindy's house after that."

"You gonna keep it? The house?" His eyes were still scanning the room. Maybe it was a law enforcement thing. Maybe he was just nosy.

"I don't know yet. It's difficult to imagine being there without Cindy." Pip wasn't a morning person. She needed coffee before she could handle the FBI. Especially this particular FBI agent. She grabbed a coffee filter and then filled up the in-room coffeemaker with water and turned it on.

He stood beside her desk and she saw him scan her notes. Damn it. She went over and closed the file folder.

"You're interviewing people who knew Cindy?" He stood way too close.

She was hyperaware of everything about him and that made her nervous and jumpy. "Not interviewing, just writing down impressions and thoughts." She moved away from him. She felt self-conscious in her pajamas while he was once again wearing full federal armor. "I told you I'm trying to figure out where Cindy got the drugs."

Pip scrubbed her fingers over her face, struggling to wake up. She'd been up until two after her run-in with Kincaid at the Resnicks' house in Sherwood Forest. Making lists and notes, unable or unwilling to close her eyes, knowing today would be just as empty as yesterday and trying to prolong the horrible inevitability of it all.

Kincaid stared at her for a long time, searching her face but she had no idea what he was looking for. Guilt? Innocence? Absolution? Finally, he asked, "Mind if I sit?"

She shook her head. The man looked exhausted.

"Did you sleep yet?" She winced. The question sounded too intimate. It wasn't her business. What if he was tired because he'd been tearing up the sheets with a lover? He'd told her he was single, not that he was celibate. He'd told her he liked *many* different kinds of women. An equal opportunity kind of guy.

She'd fallen for his type before. In fact, he was exactly her type, good looking, confident, verging on arrogant.

"I got a few hours. Enough." He ran a hand over his hair, making it stand up. "Got called out in the middle of the night."

"That happen a lot?"

He shook his head. "Less than you'd imagine. Up until a few days ago I was working white-collar crime."

"What changed a few days ago?"

He gave her a tight smile that didn't reach his eyes. He obviously wasn't going to tell her.

Her journalistic instincts were twitching. The smell of coffee was making her brain slowly inch awake, but not fast enough to figure this out.

"Why are you here, Agent Kincaid?"

He was watching her carefully. It was hard to read the expression in his eyes in the dim light. "Did Sally-Anne tell you anything useful yesterday?" He kept his voice low.

Noise traveled through these walls and she liked the fact he was considerate to other guests, but she wasn't sure why he was here asking her about Sally-Anne.

"Not a lot. She said that some of the students did occasionally do recreational drugs at parties. She'd never seen Cindy take drugs but was quick to believe she had." If Pip sounded bitter she couldn't help it. Did she tell him the dealer's name or not? What was more important, finding out the truth about Cindy or getting fentanyl off the streets? "She let slip the fact one of the other students had tested a sample and it came back pure so they trusted the dealer." Pip took a breath.

"She say which student?"

Pip shook her head. "She was spooked because the FBI are involved. I'll ask her again next time I see her, but I don't think she's gonna tell me. I'll probably have better luck with one of Cindy's other friends—"

"Don't," Kincaid said sharply. "Let the experts handle it."

She jerked at his tone and resented the fact he thought she was an idiot. "Sally-Anne also let slip a name for the dealer. Hanzo. I never heard Cindy mention him."

His eyes widened slightly at that. "She told you all this downstairs in the lobby, yesterday?"

She nodded. Why she wanted to impress him she didn't know.

"What time did she leave?"

"Six forty-five. She said she was picking up something from the lab before heading home. I stayed in the lobby until Cindy's lawyer arrived."

"Your lawyer now."

She shrugged. What difference did that make?

"What did you do for the rest of the evening?"

It sounded almost like he was checking an alibi. What did he think she'd done this time? "After Adrian left I ordered room service, switched rooms, and then took a shower. That's when I decided to drive out to Cindy's house about ten thirty."

"You didn't go anywhere on the way?"

She thought about her drive through the bluffs but wasn't stupid enough to admit to it. She shook her head.

"And you came straight back here last night?"

"Yeah. You're literally the last person I spoke to between then and now. Mind telling me why you're interrogating me?"

He was watching her again, his unwavering gaze making her nervous. "Sally-Anne Wilton was found dead in her apartment last night. Apparent drug overdose."

Pip sank onto the bed beside him. "Th-that's impossible."

"Trust me. It's not."

Silence loomed between them, filled only with the gurgle of the coffee pot. Whatever he'd seen had left a mark.

"You have a link to both victims," he said slowly.

Gooseflesh raised on her arms. Did he really believe she was capable of murder?

She swallowed her hurt and stared numbly at the hotel wall. "So does everyone who works at Blake."

Otherwise she might be in serious trouble. The idea made her nauseous.

The coffee finished brewing and he walked over to the machine. "You take it black or with milk?"

"Milk. No sugar," she said quietly.

He brought it to her and wrapped her fingers carefully around the white, ceramic mug. Then he went and loaded the coffee machine again. He winced when he caught sight of his reflection in the mirror. She didn't tell him he didn't need to worry. He still looked hot. Sally-Anne had thought so, too.

Pip couldn't believe the girl was dead. Not after just having commiserated with her over Cindy.

Cold stole over Pip. She had told Sally-Anne about the fentanyl, right? She had. She knew she had. But the woman hadn't believed she was at risk, or believed the risk was worth it.

Kincaid squatted at her feet, brushed her hair out of her eyes. "For what it's worth, I never really thought you murdered your friend. But law enforcement always looks hard at the person who reports the body. They're often involved with the crime. You know that from your work as a reporter."

Her brain felt numb. "Good thing I didn't stumble on Sally-Anne then."

"Yes," he agreed firmly.

"You know," her voice came out scratchy, "if I had given Cindy the drugs I could have dumped any leftovers into the lake. Or down the toilet."

The mattress sank when he sat next to her on the bed. "Did you?"

She sipped her coffee, hands trembling. "I'm just saying." Damn. The idea Sally-Anne was dead was unreal. Two bright, beautiful women dead. "How could this happen?"

Kincaid shook his head. He looked angry, too. "Whoever sold them the drugs—and I will pass on the name to the detective in charge of the case—has a lot of questions to answer. Ultimately the women chose to take cocaine. They knew the risks associated. Or maybe they were already addicted and at the mercy of the disease."

Could Pip have missed that?

You don't know everything.

Was that what she hadn't known about Cindy? Had it been a cry for help?

The coffeemaker buzzed again and the fresh smell of coffee filled the air. Kincaid stood and poured milk into his mug and took a slug even though it had to be scalding.

Pip held his gaze across the room. "I know you think I'm crazy but I still don't believe Cindy took those drugs."

He glanced away. She caught the pity in his eyes. At her unwillingness to accept facts. Maybe she *was* delusional.

"I shouldn't be telling you this, but as you've requested your own autopsy you'll find out soon enough anyway. The ME found traces of spermicide inside Cindy's vagina and also some unknown male DNA on the coffee table. It's likely she had sex the day she died."

Pip sat there frozen. "But—"

"They also found a second male DNA profile on the bed sheets."

"What?" Her shoulders sagged. Cindy had been involved with two guys she hadn't told Pip about? "Could she have been raped?"

"No sign of sexual assault. She might have been having a series of one-nighters."

"Cindy wasn't like that—"

"Maybe she was, Pip. And maybe she hid that side of herself so you didn't judge her for it."

Pip recoiled. *You work too hard. You don't eat properly. You hook up with guys you barely know.*

"We all have things we don't want people we care about to find out."

Hot tears burned the back of her eyeballs but she would

not let them fall. "Like what?"

"You tell me."

Her lip curled. "I suspect you know everything there is to know about me. How about you reveal something personal about yourself for a change?"

He sucked back another gulp of coffee and put down the mug.

Her jaw dropped when his hand went to his belt and he lowered his suit pants.

"Not that personal," she croaked.

His shirt covered his boxers. He pointed to a massive scar and a red slice that went from the top of one muscular thigh, curled down the side of his knee and then around the back of his calf.

Holy crap.

"Motorcycle accident fourteen months ago. Semi jack-knifed on I-85 and I had to put the bike down doing about sixty and slide right under the rig to avoid plowing into the side of it. It probably would have looked good in a movie but in reality, it hurt like a bitch. Thankfully I was wearing full leathers. It was a miracle I survived, but I fucked up my leg. At first, they thought they'd have to take it off, then they said I might never walk again." His voice deepened. "I was back at work six weeks later." He pulled his pants back up.

She stared at him, horrified at what he'd gone through. Not just the pain of the accident or recovery, but the fear that he'd lose his leg, his ability to walk, his career. Things that clearly defined him, made him the man he was today.

"I'm sorry you went through that."

He shrugged as if he hadn't revealed something important, but she knew he had. That wound was more than skin deep.

"I'm just saying maybe Cindy had her own scars she didn't want anyone to see."

Maybe she had. The thought put another crack in Pip's already fractured heart. She finished her coffee and walked over to the blinds and looked out onto the downtown streets. It was still dark outside. The city lazily waking from slumber.

"Are you investigating Sally-Anne's death?" she asked.

He moved up behind her, a quiet shadow that she was achingly and increasingly aware of. "No, Atlanta PD is. I shouldn't even be here…"

And yet he was. She turned her head. Knowledge flashed between them that their relationship had somehow shifted and they both looked away again.

He cleared his throat. "Expect a Detective White to contact you with questions at some point."

"I thought it was SOP for the FBI to investigate unexplained deaths of people who worked on dangerous substances?"

"Only Category A substances." He moved away. Picked up his mug again. "Hanta virus isn't on the list."

She watched him in the reflection of the window. But he wasn't giving anything away.

"Will you contact me when you hear back from the ME regarding the second autopsy?" he asked. "I'd like to see the report. Make sure we didn't miss anything."

She nodded and clenched her fingers into a fist. "I'll get him to send you a copy."

Would Cindy have told Pip if she was sleeping with more than one guy, or had started doing drugs? Suddenly Pip wasn't so sure. It was out of character, but she hadn't seen Cindy in person since Christmas. Pip would have tried to get Cindy to straighten up her act. And Cindy would have done the same if the situation had been reversed. Was that being judgmental, or being a good friend?

"I'd like to attend the funeral. If you're okay with that?" Kincaid said softly.

Law enforcement attended funerals of victims all the time, but he seemed insistent about the idea Cindy had died from an overdose. So why would he want to be there?

She didn't get it, but she liked the idea of him being there, of seeing him again. *Fool.* "I'll let you know when I've finished organizing it."

He drained his coffee and went into the bathroom and she heard him run the mug under the tap. He brought the clean mug back out and put it on the console.

House trained.

He was obviously ready to leave. She walked him to the door. He turned just before he got there and suddenly they were standing much too close. She looked up at him, her breath catching, pulse fluttering unsteadily through her veins.

His gaze rested on her bottom lip and his nostrils flared, but he made no move to close the gap. The air between them was charged with vibrant uncertainty.

She held herself very still. Emotionally she wasn't in a good place to start anything, especially with a federal law enforcement officer and she was a little worried she might throw herself at him if he stared at her like that for much longer.

"If the person who supplied Cindy and Sally-Anne with coke finds out you've been asking questions they might not be happy."

She blinked. That's not what she'd expected him to say.

"But the cops have already linked the two deaths. Why would anyone come after me?"

"No one ever said drug dealers were smart. Be careful, okay?" He reached up and cupped her cheek, brushed his thumb across her bottom lip. Electricity sizzled through all her layers—pajamas, skin, flesh, bone—pinging off atoms along the way.

She held her breath and thought for a moment he was going to kiss her. But he didn't. He dropped his hand and stepped away.

She locked the door behind FBI Special Agent Kincaid and tried to untangle all the emotions that churned inside her. She didn't have time for the complications he posed. She didn't have the desire for a broken heart.

Two women were dead, and Pip still didn't have any of the answers she needed.

CHAPTER FIFTEEN

O FFICIALLY, ASAC MCKENZIE ordered Hunt to leave the death investigations of the two grad students to local police and concentrate on speaking to scientists working on anthrax. Use the two deaths as an excuse to search for abnormalities in the Microbiology Department at Blake while analysts at SIOC continued to monitor the situation and search for suspicious activity. Unofficially, the FBI were also conducting their own deeper examination of these drug deaths just in case there were connections to BLACKCLOUD.

No red flags yet. Whoever had done this was obviously a pro at anonymous communication and surfing the dark web.

The lack of progress was making Hunt tense. The idea some bastard was out there refining an already deadly disease into an unstoppable killing machine pissed him off. But he'd stopped being surprised back in elementary school by the depth of some people's evil.

"We've sent out an email to all the grad students and undergraduates to keep them informed and to warn them about the dangers of taking drugs," the departmental secretary, Lenore Daniels, told him. She reminded Hunt of his mom. Tough but maternal. Someone who'd kick your ass for screwing up and then give you a hug because you were upset. "And we arranged counselors to be available for anyone who needs to talk."

Good call.

"Did you ask them to contact the cops with any information they might have about anyone who sold drugs to students...?"

Lenore pulled a face. "I put it in the draft of the email...the administration took it out."

He held back a curse. "Can I ask why?"

"I don't know. They said it wasn't the university's place and they didn't want to put anyone in a dangerous position or create an atmosphere where students felt they couldn't trust one another."

"That's—"

"Horseshit. I know." She glowered at him in mutual irritation. Her phone rang and she held up her hand. "Let me just get this."

Hunt had spoken to the people at the Intellectual Property office before coming here and they'd presented a professional unified front, but had been more concerned with protecting the university's assets than worrying about how their students had died. The more he'd pushed about Cindy's work the more they'd pushed back with threats to bring in the lawyers. They said they'd given him all the documentation they had on file but it hadn't amounted to much. A thesis proposal and a well-written introduction. Hunt didn't believe they'd lodged a patent based on that alone.

He hadn't mentioned he already had a copy of what was probably the final version of Cindy Resnick's dissertation. What they didn't know wouldn't hurt them. The university wanted Cindy's laptop but it was stuck in the FBI's evidence laboratory. After that it would be turned over to Pip. The university lawyers could fight it out with Cindy's estate. In the meantime, he'd keep his lips firmly sealed.

He'd spoken to McKenzie about the piranhas in the IP office at Blake. McKenzie decided the best bet was to play it cool. Chances were the terrorists selling weaponized anthrax to international arms dealers were not two stick-up-their-ass suits in IP. Even so, their attitude pissed Hunt off. They didn't seem to care about the young woman who'd died. Just what she was worth to them. A lot, apparently.

Could Pip have been conning him about not knowing she was Cindy's beneficiary or about the fact she wasn't thrilled at the idea of all that money? His inherent cynicism seemed to have been won over—although perhaps he was kidding himself. Perhaps he'd been disarmed by her curvy figure and lush mouth in that incredibly dumb moment before he'd left her hotel room at dawn when he'd wanted to kiss her.

Thankfully self-preservation had kicked in.

But guilty people did not, in his experience, order second autopsies when the first one had cleared them of wrong-doing.

Hunt had a conference call in a couple of hours in his boss's office with SIOC to see what they'd discovered so far. It suggested to Hunt they still thought Georgia was prime territory for the bio-terrorist location.

The two dead girls had taken up most of his time. Hell of a coincidence to die now…and he hated coincidences.

He'd told Pip about the DNA evidence that suggested Cindy had been involved with at least two men to try and distract her and prove she didn't know her friend as well as she thought. He didn't want her in danger and couldn't afford for her to start digging around in his investigation. Hopefully she'd accept the autopsy findings and back off.

The secretary finished her phone call and turned back to him.

"Were you able to get those logs of lab use for me, Lenore?"

She passed him a brown nondescript folder. "If you tell anyone I'll deny it under oath."

He grinned and thanked her and set off down the corridor. He went up to Professor Everson's office but the door was locked and no one was in. What he really wanted to do was get into all the labs and search for a flask full of deadly spores, but there were simply too many places someone with the right knowledge and a basic setup could do the work. Plus, he didn't have a fucking clue what he was looking for and would probably get himself and others killed.

Jez Place from the CDC had assured him that once they figured out the DNA sequence of the specific parent strains it would narrow the suspects and shouldn't take long to figure out who might have had access to it.

Hunt had learned patience while recovering from his broken leg. It didn't mean he was good at it. *Christ*, he couldn't believe he'd dropped his pants and told Pip about his accident. It was a wonder she hadn't run screaming from the room, but Hunt had never been bashful about his body. He'd only considered the possible accusations of sexual harassment later.

Hopefully she wouldn't figure out he didn't discuss the accident on a casual basis. He usually kept his weaknesses on the down low.

He had a feeling that Pip West could make him do a lot of things he wouldn't normally contemplate, but next time he dropped his pants in front of a woman she better either be his physician or already naked.

He was walking back to his Bucar when his cell rang. "Kincaid."

"Hunt. This is Cyril White. APD."

"How's it going?"

"For once, it's going pretty damn good. Found the drug dealer, Hanzo, who was reportedly selling coke to the students at Blake, real name of Marcus Colton."

Hunt stopped walking and stared up at the blue sky. He'd texted the information Pip had given him that morning to the guy. "DA discuss charges?"

The detective gave a gusty sigh. "Hard to charge a dead man."

Hunt frowned. "Did he sample the goods?" He couldn't think of a more just end to the guy.

"Nah." The New Orleans drawl was out in full force now. "Nine-millimeter to the back of the skull."

What the fuck? "Got a shooter?"

"Nope. No witnesses, either. Guy was found in his car in a quiet wooded area, southwest of the city. No cell phone found at the scene. I figure the killer took it. I doubt we'll find records because the chances of it being registered in his own name are slim to none. We found coke in his car that we'll test against the samples found at the vic's apartment."

"Got a TOD?" Hunt couldn't help holding his breath for the answer. He'd checked the hotel security tapes before he'd spoken to Pip earlier that morning. Underhand? Perhaps. But she hadn't lied about when she'd left and returned to the hotel. She might have had time to rush over to kill the dealer before she headed to Cindy's house to put the gun in the safe—which was when he'd bumped into her. But the metal of the Remington pistol had been stone cold, and it hadn't smelled like it had been recently fired.

"Eleven thirty-seven. Local resident reported a gunshot but cops didn't find the body until sun up."

And at 23:37 he'd been helping Pip West photocopy Cindy Resnick's thesis.

The relief he felt was overwhelming which meant he should stay far away from the pretty dark-haired woman from now on. No more showing off his scars while they were alone and she was in her pajamas.

Idiot.

"Any CIs in his circle of friends?" Confidential informants might be the only way of figuring out who'd had a beef against the man.

"Nah. Last guy who fed us information from that area ended up floating face-down in the Flint River."

Hunt swore again.

"I just wanted to update you. Nice to have him off the streets even though there are another ten to take his place."

"I appreciate the call." Hunt uttered his thanks and rang off.

Cindy and Sally-Anne's cases were pretty much closed even though the evidence was all circumstantial.

The chances of APD solving the murder of the drug dealer depended on exactly how dumb the perpetrator was and how much effort the cops put into solving it. The vic had been dealing drugs, a high-risk profession on the mean streets of Atlanta. But Cyril was a good cop. He'd at least try.

That niggle between his shoulder blades was back—maybe because the person who'd developed weaponized anthrax and tried to sell it to terrorists was still out there, walking around anonymously, possibly planning to do it again in the near future.

Hunt's phone rang with another incoming call, this one from McKenzie. The ASAC wanted to move the conference call up by an hour. It was time to get back to the field office and see if anyone had figured out this mystery.

"WHAT'S THE SITUATION with the dead students?" McKenzie demanded via monitor as Hunt walked into his SAC's office.

Hunt took a seat next to the guy from CDC and recapped the overdoses and dead drug dealer as quickly as possible.

McKenzie frowned. "Any other deaths in the city attributable to this dealer's product?"

"Not that we know of, sir." That bothered him.

"It is a hell of a coincidence," Frazer acknowledged from the other side of the screen. "For them to die of drug overdoses the week after an attempted sale of an anthrax bioweapon."

"The second fatality didn't study anthrax," McKenzie stated.

"Still…" Frazer sounded intrigued.

"And according to her supervisor Cindy worked on cutting edge vaccine research. The college is secretive about the details of her thesis because of pending patent registration. They don't want us to read it."

Dr. Jez Place sat up straighter. "Seriously?"

"We presumably have a copy of her research on her laptop?" asked McKenzie.

Hunt nodded. "I assume so. We're waiting on analysis back from the lab." He shifted forward. "But," he cleared his throat, not sure how this would go down, "I managed to obtain a paper copy from Cindy Resnick's Atlanta residence last night."

"Legally?" his SAC asked.

"Yes, sir." Hunt tried not to be insulted. "With permission from the new owner."

"The journalist?" said Bourne.

"Pip West."

Bourne seemed to hate the idea of journalists even more than Hunt did. Or maybe he was thinking about that letter of censure in Hunt's file from the Office of Professional Responsibility. Hunt gritted his teeth.

Onscreen McKenzie pulled a face. "Is she going to be a problem?"

Hell, yes, she was gonna be a problem. For *Hunt*.

"She insists her friend would never willingly do drugs and has ordered a second autopsy, but that was before Sally-Anne Wilton was found dead."

"Interesting," said Frazer. "And her alibi is solid?"

"Rock. I don't believe she's involved in BLACKCLOUD."

Not that Hunt would finger Pip as a suspect anyway. It wasn't her grief—even murderers sometimes experienced genuine grief. It was her determination to discover the truth. That was a trait he could admire even when it wasn't associated with an attractive woman. Pity that her version of public service involved exposing potentially damaging information in the name of transparency.

Bourne looked at him from beneath thick brows. "Keep an eye on her."

Exactly what Hunt was hoping to avoid. "I have over two hundred scientists left to contact. I don't have time to babysit a journalist on top of that."

He did not want to be that close to temptation.

"He's right. We need to concentrate on finding the anthrax supplier," said Frazer.

"We cannot afford for this story to break in the press," warned McKenzie.

None of them looked like they'd gotten any more sleep than Hunt had.

"I'll get someone pulling data from Resnick's laptop and cell today," McKenzie said. "Make sure there's nothing of interest there that the journalist can uncover. Can we get a sample of whatever vaccine Cindy Resnick developed to test against what we found in BLACKCLOUD?"

"Not without raising a lot of noise and suspicion from Blake officials," Hunt said honestly.

McKenzie narrowed his eyes. "Perhaps Dr. Place would be willing to take a look at the thesis for us?"

Jez shrugged. "I don't mind looking, but the college administration might balk. They'll see me as the competition."

"As long as we keep the information to ourselves and don't violate any patents we'll go ahead with our assessment of the material and beg forgiveness later."

Jez leaned forward. "I've never heard of this much secrecy over a doctoral thesis before. Maybe I can get a look at the patent filing, too?"

McKenzie wrote a note to himself on a tablet. "I'll arrange it. If the university admin doesn't know you're looking at her thesis they can't give you any flack. If they do, refer them to me." Something in McKenzie's expression suggested he wouldn't take any prisoners or put up with BS.

They were dealing with the lives of thousands of people and a possible act of war if this biological agent turned up in the wrong hands.

"Where are we at with the DNA sequence?" McKenzie stared at Jez Place.

Jez started talking fast. He was clearly nervous which, considering what he did for a day job, was a bad sign. "We had a machine malfunction last night and it slowed us down. The sequence is almost complete but we aren't there yet."

"Understood." McKenzie looked pissed. "ETA?"

Jez scratched behind his ear. "Realistically? Tomorrow morning. We're running multiple samples for comparison. I want them to hurry, but I don't want them to rush. They're good scientists, so I'm trying not to hang over their shoulders. There are some things you can't speed up no matter how urgent the circumstances."

McKenzie took a big breath. "We don't want any mistakes. Tomorrow is good enough."

"It shouldn't take long to find the parent strain—assuming we have a reference sample." Place shifted uncomfortably. "The anthrax could have come from a source we've never examined before. Like the Soviet biological warfare program or a defrosting wooly mammoth up in the arctic."

Everyone's eyebrows raised.

"Growth rate is substantially faster than standard anthrax which means this weaponized strain is potentially a lot deadlier than the ones we're used to dealing with."

"Otherwise what would be the point?" Frazer said dryly. "What about the analysis of the BLACKCLOUD vaccine?"

"It's a much slower process." Jez shifted uncomfortably in his chair. "We want to make more of the material before we do any destructive testing because if this strain of anthrax is released into the wild we need to be prepared. We were only sent a few milligrams to work with. It'll take longer than the sequencing."

"A day? Two?" McKenzie demanded.

Dr. Place shook his head. "We can start replicating it straight away, but a full analysis will take at least a week."

"Get every available help you can with this," McKenzie ordered.

The idea of having a population completely vulnerable to this disease for that amount of time sent a shudder of unease through Hunt.

"Whoever made this bioweapon had to also create and test a vaccine. It seems like a more complex skillset," Hunt commented, thinking of Cindy and her ex, Pete Dexter.

"Assuming the vaccine works." Frazer's smile was grim. "Personally, I wouldn't want to be that guinea pig. Once the money was transferred to the anonymous seller via cryptocurrency and Swiss bank accounts, the anthrax producer could disappear. Most of the players would be dead before they figured out the vaccine didn't work."

"The seller might not even know if it works or not. Human clinical trials of this nature are banned," said Jez Place.

"Something tells me legalities are the least of their concerns…" said Frazer.

"You think they might have used human guinea pigs?" Bourne's expression grew even more concerned.

"Nothing to stop them picking up runaways or homeless people and testing it on them." The more Hunt thought about it the more abhorrent the whole thing was, and the more likely. "We need to start looking into any suspicious disappearances—"

McKenzie raised his face to the ceiling. "We're going need

more agents."

"Maybe bring in APD or GBI," Hunt suggested. "Detectives on the ground have a better idea about any missing person cases—assuming you have good reason to believe that ground zero for the anthrax production is in fact Georgia."

"I agree." McKenzie wrote another note to himself. "And, yes," he looked at Hunt. "Some of the internet activity has been linked to the Atlanta region, though we can't completely rule out a ruse."

Shit. They sat in silent contemplation for a few moments.

"How did the seller transport the bioweapon?" Jez asked.

"What do you mean?" asked Bourne.

"Did they courier it? Standard mail? Hand delivery?"

McKenzie dipped his chin. "Good question. I don't know. French police are processing the scene. I'll ask about any boxes found onboard or any suggestion the arms dealer picked up packages locally."

Onboard? So, this had gone down on a boat or a plane? There'd been some hoopla involving some sort of terrorist activity on the Riviera last week. Hunt figured this had to do with that.

"You could try backtracking your arms dealer's movements and cross reference any travel made by US scientists," suggested Hunt.

"On it." McKenzie nodded. "I have another group of analysts and a supercomputer working that route. This is the Bureau's number one priority."

"It's taking too long." Bourne sounded impatient.

"Compared to the AMERITHRAX case this is going at lightning speed." McKenzie pushed back.

Bourne looked pissed. "It's still not fast enough. What's to stop them from running?"

"Nothing," McKenzie admitted. "They might have already split. But we're watching airports and monitoring activity of everyone who is registered or has been known to work on anthrax. And we're getting closer. A cyber-geek found the page on the dark web where the supplier reached out to the arms dealer and we're tracking all participants of that forum."

Anyone hanging out with arms dealers and terrorists on the dark web was probably someone worth the FBI's time.

The silence grew tense.

"I got hold of all the lab activity logs from Blake today," Hunt told them.

"Without a warrant?" McKenzie asked in surprise.

"I used my charm," Hunt admitted.

McKenzie grinned and Frazer pulled a face.

"Whoever purified and created this anthrax would have had to spend long hours in the lab," Jez Place added.

"Go over the records. See if anything pops."

"But I haven't even started at Georgia State, yet." They'd set him an impossible task and he didn't appreciate the fact his SAC was glowering at him. It spelled trouble he didn't need.

"This is about elimination of suspects so the pool of potentials is more manageable. Once we narrow it right down we can take cracks at interviewing them more aggressively." McKenzie was getting another call but he shut it off. "They're already emailing one another wondering what changes the Feds are thinking of implementing. It's working."

"We're assuming this is motivated by money rather than ideology?" asked Hunt.

Frazer pressed his lips into a thin line. "Seems you'd have to be pretty desperate for cash for that to be your only motivation but look at the narcos and the lengths they go to get their millions."

"Motive is fuzzy," McKenzie bit out. "It doesn't matter—"

"It matters if they decide they've got nothing left to lose," Hunt cut in.

Frazer's cool gaze landed on him with the tiniest inkling of respect.

Hunt finally got it. "Which is why we aren't coming down hot and heavy." They were narrowing the suspect pool while giving the bad guy an escape route that the authorities could track without the villain feeling desperate and cornered and might-as-well-take-out-the-nearest-city with a crop duster.

"I'll get Hernandez to contact you if anything interesting comes up on the Resnick laptop or comms," McKenzie told him and then the screens went blank, leaving the room in sudden silence.

"I'll get back to the lab." Jez Place stood and nodded.

Hunt got up to follow but Bourne stopped him before he reached the door.

"I know you're planning to apply to HRT, Agent Kincaid. It would be a shame if the journalist caused any problems with your application." His boss had the subtlety of dynamite.

A wash of resentment flowed through Hunt, but he nodded and left Bourne's office. He couldn't help the feeling Pip didn't deserve the suspicion everyone was throwing at her. Then he remembered the trouble he'd gotten into after the last journalist he trusted. He couldn't afford more if he hoped to stay in the Bureau.

CHAPTER SIXTEEN

P IP RETURNED TO the hotel after a long run, during which she forgot everything except for the beat of her own heart. After a quick shower she dumped her belongings on the bed and dragged on tight jeans and a pair of red converse sneakers and her favorite Wonder Woman tee. She forced herself to apply makeup and put her hair up in a high ponytail. The whole effect made her look younger. Young enough to be in college. Then she slipped the photograph of Dane with Cindy, her cell phone and some cash into one pocket, and her hotel keycard and credit card into the other before heading out the door.

Pip had done a little research that morning and discovered Dane Garnett worked at a popular Mexican restaurant that catered mainly for the tourist trade. It was a five-minute walk from her hotel.

At the door of the restaurant she scanned the dimly lit interior. Dane Garnett was tending bar.

"How many for?" A perky blonde with bright pink lips asked with a smile.

"Just me." The words cut through Pip with sadness.

Her server brought her a glass of water and Pip ran a finger through the condensation. Had Dane known Sally-Anne?

She put in an order for nachos and watched Dane Garnett while he served customers and cleaned the bar. Cindy had said he was a model and trying to get into acting. Pip couldn't believe he had any trouble getting work. The photo of him with Cindy hadn't done him justice. In the flesh Dane had the sort of male good looks that intimidated and made it hard to breathe. Cindy had definitely been his equal in beauty, and they'd have made a striking couple. He had long ebony hair, dark chocolate eyes. Straight nose. Dark brows but not too thick or unibrowed. Broad shoulders looked like they were sculpted in the gym. Physically, he was probably the best-looking guy she'd ever seen if one went for tall, dark and handsome.

Pip wasn't sure what her type was, but didn't appreciate the fact a sandy-haired federal agent popped into her brain when she tried to figure it out.

She stared at Dane. She wanted to know who had given her best friend drugs but wasn't sure the best way to go about it. This sense of uncertainty and lack of confidence was unnerving. It was the fallout from Cindy's death and the mess in Florida and the awful realization that her work had gotten Lisa Booker and her children killed. She was a good investigative reporter. She trusted her instincts and looked below the surface, behind the words that came out of people's mouths, and she wasn't afraid to dig. Growing up in foster care, and before that in the house of an alcoholic mother whose taste in men ran toward the abusive, her instincts had been honed until they were sharp as razor blades.

Being an investigative reporter was the only thing she really knew how to do, and she wasn't even sure how to do that anymore.

She looked around. A couple sat in a back booth, holding hands and looking at one another all doe-eyed. A man in a suit worked at another booth on his laptop. She could see the server taking a break through the glass porthole in the door that led into the kitchen area, waiting while Pip's nachos were put together.

Dane wasn't likely to harm her in this public space if she confronted him.

And Agent Kincaid had promised that if Pip found evidence that Cindy's death wasn't accidental he'd take it seriously. She just needed to find a way to prove someone had forced her friend to take drugs. She got up from her seat and headed toward the bar.

Dane eyed her expectantly, clearly waiting for her drink order. Then his brow crinkled. "Hey, I know you."

Pip opened her mouth, startled.

His face lit up in a friendly smile. "You're that friend of Cindy's. I saw photographs of you in her house."

Her cover was blown before she'd gotten started. He obviously had a good eye for faces—probably a good thing for a barkeep.

"Dane, right?" she asked. "I was hoping we could talk about Cindy, actually. Do you have a few minutes?"

He checked the large clock on the wall behind the bar. "Sure. I'm just covering for someone who called in sick until the owner turns up. She won't be long as I have a photo-shoot this afternoon. I'll see you at your table."

Ten minutes later, he came over carrying a large gym bag and a glass of water, an attractive blonde woman now serving behind the bar. He slid into the booth.

She held out her hand. "I'm Pip. Pip West."

"Cindy talked about you all the time. I feel like I know you already." His handshake was warm and firm but not a spark of attraction sizzled over her skin. Unlike when Kincaid had touched her lip with his thumb. That had zapped her like a cattle prod.

"You want something to eat?" she asked. "I can order something," courtesy of her credit card and Cindy's money, "or you can just dig into these." She pointed at the enormous pile of nachos that sat in front of her. Turned out she wasn't hungry after all.

Dane shook his head. "No thanks." He seemed nervous. "I'm trying to think of all the reasons you might want to talk to me."

"What did you come up with?" She hadn't mentioned the fact that Cindy had died and it dawned on her in sudden horror that, unless he'd had something to do with Cindy's death, he might not know.

Dark brown eyes way prettier than her own met hers. He swallowed. "At first, I thought maybe she wanted to get back with me, but she wouldn't have sent someone else in that case. Then I thought that maybe she got pregnant but didn't know how to tell me." His eyes lit up at that, then dimmed. "Or she got an STD and didn't know how to let me know to get tested—"

"Dane," Pip cut in, acid churning in her stomach. "I'm really sorry." Oh, God. "Cindy is dead."

"What?" The shock looked genuine, but he was training to be an actor.

Pip wished she wasn't so cynical but no one wanted to go to jail and whoever had supplied those drugs could face manslaughter charges or worse. "I went out to the lake to see her on Monday morning and I found her in the water." Her voice caught and tripped. It still didn't seem real.

"Cindy?" His eyes filled with tears and Pip's welled up in sympathy. Dammit. "No. No way."

Tears streamed down Dane's cheeks and he didn't try to wipe them away. His big fist clenched on top of the table. "What happened?"

"The cops say she was high and decided to go for a swim."

"High? Like drugs high?" He sounded incredulous. "No way."

"That's one of the things I was gonna ask you." She jumped on his response. "If you ever saw her do coke. Because I didn't. Not ever. And I knew her for a decade."

"I only knew her for a few months." His lips trembled. "But I wanted to know her for much longer."

She waited out his shock and grief. He needed a moment to process everything that had happened.

"Have you ever done drugs?" she asked.

He sniffed loudly and blew his nose. "A lot of people in the modeling and acting worlds use drugs but it's not my thing." His cheeks darkened. "I have a criminal record because a photographer roofied my drink and planned to assault me. I overheard him whispering to one of his creepy friends when I went to the restroom. I broke the bastard's nose. Now I always bring my own drinks wherever I go." He picked up and shook his water bottle.

Pip's heart went out to the guy. But she'd dig into that information regardless and make sure he wasn't feeding her a line.

"Do you know anyone with a grudge against her?"

"You knew her better than I did." He smiled sadly "I did

hear her going at it on the phone once. Super pissed. She told me it was something to do with college, but I don't know what it was about." He shrugged and then closed his eyes. "She was way out of my league but I kept hoping…"

Pip found herself wanting to comfort him. Even though he looked like a badass alpha male he was a big softy. She found herself liking the guy and wishing Cindy hadn't dumped him. He would have been good for her.

"Don't feel bad, Dane. She was out of my league, too."

He wiped his eyes. "Nah. As far as Cindy was concerned you were the most amazing person on this planet. Actually." His smile was worthy of a Hollywood premiere. "You're the reason she gave me a chance."

Pip frowned. Either he was falsely modest or half blind or truly didn't know what was in the mirror.

"I was raised in the foster system, too."

Ah. It was weird that this man knew private things about her. It wasn't something she advertised.

"I'm sorry." It was all she needed to say. *Sorry there was no one to love you. Sorry there was no one to look after you. Sorry there was no one to care…*

"We met at a club and started dancing. We hooked up." A blush stained his cheeks. "It's not something I make a habit out of but Cindy was stunning and I didn't want to miss my chance. When she got up to leave my place she noticed a picture of me and my foster family. They were good people. She told me about you and changed her mind about giving me her number. I guess it was pity, but at that moment I'd have done anything to see her again."

His earnestness made her hurt for him. But could that have turned to anger when Cindy dumped him?

"I know I wasn't her usual kind of date but I think she wanted something different from the type of guy she'd been with before. I tried to be that for her but it wasn't enough."

"She liked you." She decided to give him something back. "But this was a pretty intense time for her with her Ph.D."

"Yeah, I know her work was full on." Those brown eyes met hers, but they were cooler now. "But that's not why she dumped me. I wasn't the only guy she was seeing…"

"What?" Pip asked, genuinely startled. She'd never known Cindy to two-time anyone.

"I saw her with another guy and I followed them." His lips firmed and he looked away.

"You followed them?" Alarm raised the hairs on her skin.

He shrugged. "I'd gone to her work to surprise her with some flowers around the time I knew she usually left. I was just getting ready to text her and offer her a ride home when I saw her come out. She climbed into a black SUV and drove away."

Black SUV?

"I thought it was funny at first and figured she was just getting a ride home from a friend. I drove to her place and arrived just in time to see them go inside. He was kissing her and had his arm around her waist. Possessive."

Pip sat stunned.

"I stayed outside, feeling like a damned fool. And to prove I'm an idiot I texted her." He swallowed tightly. "She replied saying she was still at work and she'd see me tomorrow. I sat fuming in the car for a little while and then left."

"What did he look like? This other guy?"

"It was dark. I didn't really see his face. Wore a suit." Dane gave a shrug. He'd clearly been hurt by Cindy's actions.

198

Had he been hurt enough to want revenge?

"Why didn't you confront her about it?" Pip asked. Her mind was buzzing at the mention of the black SUV. Was it the same car that had nearly run her off the road the other day? Had the owner of that SUV given Cindy the drugs that had killed her and run away the next day when they'd realized she was dead?

He smiled bitterly. "I didn't want to lose her. Pathetic, huh? Especially when she dumped my ass a few days later."

But Pip understood. How many people turned a blind eye to what was going on because they didn't want to rock the boat? Lots.

"When was the last time you were at the cottage?"

He looked affronted. "You think I had something to do with her death?"

She shook her head. "I'm just trying to get a handle on her routine. I hadn't seen her since Christmas. She went out to the cottage in mid-March to write. I was curious the last time you guys were together."

He looked away, jaw clenched. "I never went to her cottage."

But his eyes wouldn't meet hers and she got the impression he wasn't being completely honest with her.

She ate a nacho to kill time and think, not because she was hungry. "Did you ever buy Cindy a book?"

Three small lines pinched the skin between his eyes. "What kind of book?"

"A novel. *Gone With the Wind.*"

Dane shook his head and looked confused by all her questions.

"I'm organizing her funeral." She changed the subject. "I'll text you the details."

He shrugged one perfect shoulder. "I don't think I should go."

"Why not?"

His smiled, all gorgeous and brooding. "Because all her friends are brainiacs and I make a living tending bar and modeling underwear."

Pip laughed softly. "I am not a brainiac. And, trust me, it doesn't make them better people." But she was familiar with the insecurities that dogged people who'd grown up in difficult circumstances, and foster care was mostly difficult circumstances. You never felt welcome. You never felt like you truly belonged. But she had with the Resnicks. That's why they were so important to her.

"I'd like you to come. I think Cindy would have wanted that, too. You can say your proper goodbyes." Plus, he might recognize the guy he'd seen at Cindy's that night.

He nodded slowly. "Fine. Okay. I'll be there."

They exchanged numbers and she walked out into a warm Atlanta afternoon and looked up at the vivid blue sky dotted with white fluffy clouds.

Her cell rang. Her mouth went dry when she saw it was the Medical Examiner she'd hired to perform the second autopsy. And it hit her all over again like a sledgehammer to the face. Cindy was dead and she wasn't ever coming back.

THIS TIME WHEN Hunt called for a tour of Pete Dexter's Universal Biotech company they were ready for him.

Simon Corker met him at the swanky glass doors. He had

light brown hair and clean-cut features. According to Hernandez, Corker had done an MBA and his father was a big deal military contractor who was the silent fourth partner who'd bankrolled much of the startup. Something Pete Dexter had failed to mention when they'd first spoken.

Corker was smooth and suave and accommodating. He took Hunt through several laboratories, storage facilities, walk-in freezers and showed him the liquid nitrogen stores. Assured him all safety protocols were stringently adhered to.

They didn't enter the containment labs, but from a window Hunt could see into a room within a room where several people were working in blue space suits.

"You couldn't pay me enough to do that job," Hunt admitted with a shudder.

"They're probably safer than we are. The rooms are under negative pressure and air is drawn into the labs to prevent microorganisms getting out. The protective suits have their own air supply that blows air outwards."

"And they're handling some of the deadliest diseases on the planet."

"Well." Corker shrugged. "If no one works on them we'll never find cures."

"I thought there was no money in cures?" said Hunt. All the time he'd spent with government scientists recently was rubbing off.

"It isn't all about the money. We are looking for cures to some diseases." Corker laughed and Hunt had the feeling the guy was playing him. Saying all the right things. That's what PR people did.

However, the FBI didn't take answers at face value.

"Imagine the publicity if we cured HIV? The value of our

company would go through the roof and sales for our other products with it."

They walked down a corridor, past a door with a red light over it that was set in close proximity to two sets of heavy fire doors on either side of them in the corridor. No door handle on this side and an emergency shower station overhead.

"Crash door," Corker explained with a patient smile that didn't quite reach his eyes. "If there's an emergency the scientists inside press a button and the fire doors either side of us close to automatically create a mini decontamination area. They can then enter this vestibule and the shower automatically starts. After two minutes the shower shuts off and they can exit through either fire door and out through the emergency exit at the end of the hallway."

"Is that door alarmed?" Hunt nodded at the crash doors.

Simon nodded. "As soon as anyone leaves via that door, or presses the button inside, a siren goes off, the fire department and CDC are notified and the shower comes on." He put his hand against a vent in the wall. "This section of the corridor has its own high-level filtration system so that air sucked out goes through HEPA filters and is decontaminated. It's a top of the line system."

Hunt nodded, impressed despite himself. He bet it was pricey as hell. "Where do you keep the anthrax you work on?"

"It's stored in the freezer most of the time." Corker raised one blond brow.

"Anyone working on it right now?"

"I don't believe so."

Hunt had been shown as much of the lab as he could without gearing up. But he didn't know what most of the equipment was, let alone what the microbes looked like. This visit was purely about pushing buttons and psyching people out. Next time he'd bring Jez Place.

Hunt decided to try out the latest cover story they'd decided to go with. "We're planning a large-scale training op in preparation for a terrorist release of an airborne pathogen in Atlanta. We'd like your company to have some input."

Corker's eyes gleamed. "Definitely. I can arrange that."

He seemed like a man who could arrange anything. Did that include arms deals on the dark web?

"I'd like to run it past Dr. Dexter before I leave today," Hunt said, getting into the elevator.

"I don't know if Pete is in."

Hunt pressed the button for the second floor where the partners' offices were, not giving Corker the chance to warn the other man. "Pretty sure his Audi was in the parking lot when I arrived."

Corker's lips tightened. "I think he had a meeting—"

"Let's go by his office and see, shall we? I had a couple of other questions I wanted to ask him."

"About what?"

Hunt gave him a blank look. "I'm afraid I can't discuss an ongoing FBI investigation."

The elevator doors opened.

"I thought Cindy Resnick's death had been deemed accidental?"

"Local cops are still investigating. Did you know her?" Hunt started walking toward the closed door that had "Dr. Peter Dexter, CEO" stenciled on a gold name plaque.

He gave a sharp rap on the door and waited. Corker's features remained tight.

A grinning strawberry blonde threw open the door, "Did

you—" Her question cut off when she saw Hunt.

"Angela, this is Special Agent Kincaid. Angela Naysmith is another partner in Universal Biotech."

"Along with your father, Rebus Corker, right?" Hunt watched Simon's expression. He didn't look happy.

"Correct." Corker's voice had lost any trace of friendly overtones. "You seem to know a lot about us."

"It's my job," Hunt said. He held his hand out to shake the woman's. She was greyhound thin and well-dressed. His gaze shot over to Dexter who lounged on a bright red sofa.

"Sorry to interrupt your meeting," Hunt said without inflection. "I have a couple of questions for you."

Pete sat up.

"The FBI want to invite us to get involved with a training op for a simulated biological attack on Atlanta," Corker explained quickly.

Looking relieved, Pete nodded. "Would love to. The private sector needs to be more involved in public sector stuff."

"That's great. I'll contact you with more details when I have them."

A small smile started to form on Dexter's lips.

"I also wanted to ask you a couple more questions." Everyone tensed. Hunt looked expectantly at Naysmith and Corker. "In private."

"They can stay. I have nothing to hide." Dexter stood and walked to his office chair, putting the desk between him and Hunt. Corker sank onto the red couch. Angela Naysmith sat demurely on the visitor chair facing the desk. No one offered Hunt a seat.

"We've been reviewing entry and exit logs for the BSL-3 and BSL-4 labs at Blake and it looks like you used your card to access Professor Everson's lab on three separate occasions over the Christmas period."

Dexter frowned and leaned forward. "What? No. Cindy had my keycard. I assumed she'd given it back to the department ages ago."

"I spoke to the departmental secretary," Hunt watched the guy's body language, which was tense, but that wasn't necessarily unusual. He was more worried by people who acted natural and easygoing in the face of questions from the FBI. "She never received the card."

"That's hardly Pete's fault." Angela was quick to defend the guy.

Was there something going on there? Was she the drunken hookup?

"So," Hunt said slowly, "you're saying you didn't access the labs at that time?"

Dexter's laugh sounded forced. "Why would I go there when I have my own, much better labs here?" He raised his hands. He was justifiably proud of this set up.

"Maybe to keep an eye on what Cindy was doing?" Hunt said casually.

"Cindy was pretty mad with Pete," Angela cut in. "I can see her using the access card on purpose just to try and get him into trouble."

Blaming the dead girl. Hard for her to defend herself.

"I'll have the laboratory techs check for it," said Hunt.

"Lab techs?" Angela came to her feet.

"Crime scene techs," he elucidated.

"I thought she overdosed?"

"We have new guidelines when investigating the sudden death of anyone working on a Cat-A biological agent."

"I hadn't heard about this." Angela's gaze darted off her partners in the room. "Why haven't I heard of this?"

"USDA is just rolling it out. Cindy Resnick is pretty much our test model. Well, thanks for your time. I take it you heard about Sally-Anne Wilton?"

Dexter nodded and looked upset. Angela nodded. Corker was watching her, as if waiting for direction. Hunt was starting to think Angela was the brains of this operation.

"We heard she also suffered an overdose." Angela squeezed her fingers together. "It's a terrible tragedy."

"I knew Sally-Anne took drugs occasionally," Pete said. "I just never knew Cindy did."

"Who knows what she did after you two broke up." Angela consoled him and condemned Cindy in one short sentence.

Pip wouldn't like Angela. Hunt would bet money on it.

"I'll be in touch about the training op," Hunt said. The whereabouts of that keycard was a mystery. He'd have to see if he could talk Pip into letting him search for it at Cindy's properties without an explanation or a warrant.

Sure.

"Thanks for showing me around, Mr. Corker. Doctors." Hunt nodded and headed out, spotting the redheaded PA with her neat bun and handy pencil. "Ms. Grantham." He nodded as she gave him an exasperated little sigh.

"Follow me, Agent Kincaid. You have a tendency to get lost."

"Am I causing trouble, Ms. Grantham?" he asked. She was cute. He wished he was even vaguely interested. Instead, the image of Pip West in her soft pink pjs filtered through his mind.

"I don't know, Agent Kincaid. Are you?" she asked archly.

He laughed as he headed outside the building into a scorching hot spring day.

He was definitely causing trouble.

CHAPTER SEVENTEEN

S OMEONE RAPPED ON the side window of Pip's Honda and she almost had a heart attack. She quickly unlocked the door.

"What are you doing here?" Her voice squeaked embarrassingly high.

Kincaid slid into the passenger seat, and raised a brow, the hot gold in his eyes glinting. "I could ask the same about my favorite unemployed journalist, except it's obvious she's staking out a local biotech firm."

She rolled her eyes even though her heart gave another embarrassing little hitch at being his "favorite" anything. She'd seen his ugly car enter the facility an hour ago, but was chagrined to admit she hadn't seen him leave, nor had she noticed the tan Buick pull up behind her.

"You mind if I...?" He pointed to the extra bottle of water she'd stashed in the console.

"Help yourself."

He took a long drink and wiped his mouth with the back of his hand. His gaze took in her clothes and ball cap and sunglasses she'd worn to prevent Pete Dexter from easily recognizing her should he happen to drive by. But she was parked down a side road, well away from their security cameras.

He tipped the bottle at her outfit. "Is this your incognito look?"

She eyed him narrowly.

"No hot blooded heterosexual male is not gonna notice you sitting here."

She rolled her eyes. He must want something. "Sure they are. Happens all the time." She was trying to pretend that intense sizzle hadn't zapped her earlier when he'd been leaving her room and she'd thought he was going to kiss her. More mortifying was the fact she'd wanted him to.

"Maybe you just don't notice them looking," he suggested.

She made a rude sound. "Are you flirting with me, Agent Kincaid?"

His widening smile pissed her off. "You'd know if I was flirting with you, Ms. West."

Her pulse did one of those disconcerting little skips. With those distinctive eyes, stubbled chin, and sandy-haired good looks the guy pushed every one of her buttons. She drew in a deep breath to calm the blood rush, pretty sure he was deliberately trying to put her off her game.

"Why are you here?" he asked.

"I wanted to see if anyone at the firm drove a black SUV," she told him calmly.

His eyes widened in surprise, but he still said nothing and she found herself filling the silence.

"I spoke to Cindy's other ex—"

"Mr. good-looking-but-dim?"

She sipped her water as guilt washed over her. "He's nice."

"*Nice?*" Kincaid turned in his seat to stare at her. "Wasn't he as gorgeous as your friend told you?"

"*Au contraire.*" She shook her head rapidly. "He's probably the most handsome man I've ever seen. Why do you care?"

"I don't." He flipped the sun-visor to catch a look at his reflection in the small mirror and winced theatrically.

Hot.

The voice in her head was Cindy's. She was pretty sure her friend was haunting her. "Dane said—"

"Dane?" Kincaid's cynicism leaked through.

"That's his name."

"Of course, it is." His lips curled even though he tried to contain his amusement.

"Dane said that he saw Cindy with another guy when he followed her home once, just before they broke up."

Kincaid grew serious. "And that didn't scream crazy stalker to you?"

She was close enough to smell the scent of Kincaid's skin and made a conscious effort not to lean closer and sniff. Talking of *stalkers*. "Yes, it did, so did the fact he has an assault charge on his record. But I checked his story and I don't think he lied to me. They were together at the time, but he didn't confront her on it."

She saw his mouth twist with disbelief. Ignored it.

"He said the other guy drove a black SUV with tinted windows." Kincaid's bland expression made her add. "Like the one that almost ran me off the road before I found Cindy." In case he'd forgotten.

"You know how many black SUVs are registered in the great state of Georgia? Over sixty thousand."

Her shoulders sagged. "You checked."

"I checked because I'm thorough, not because I believe the person in the car had anything to do with her death. She died between midnight and two AM. Remember?"

Unexpected emotion pricked tears behind her eyes but she blinked them away. This was just a job to him. To her it was the death of her best friend.

"Why are you *here* specifically?" he asked.

She shrugged, knowing she'd sound naïve. "I thought Pete Dexter might have a second car that just happened to be a black SUV."

"He doesn't have one registered to him."

"You checked that, too?" Pip didn't know why she was so surprised.

He nodded. "I checked that, too."

He hadn't dismissed her. He had followed up.

They sat in silence, that knowledge seeping into her brain as the quiet rush of traffic provided a gentle whoosh-whoosh of background noise.

He stared through the windshield. "Atlanta PD found the dealer who goes by the street name of 'Hanzo'."

Oh. My. God. "Did he admit to supplying Cindy or Sally-Anne?"

Kincaid shook his head. "APD found coke with him and put a rush on the analysis. We'll check it against that found at Cindy's and Sally-Anne Wilton's apartment."

"I'm impressed you found him so fast." Pip stared him. That was good work.

"Yeah, well, he was easy to spot with a bullet hole in the back of his skull." Kincaid ran a hand over his short hair as if feeling for an exit wound.

Her mouth went dry. "Dead?"

"Found in his car in a remote area of the city."

Pip shivered despite the heat. "Who killed him? Or did he kill himself?"

Kincaid shook his head. "It's not my case. Same guy who is running Sally-Anne Wilton's case is in charge. He's a damn good detective. I expect he'll be calling you at some point."

"I'll contact him."

Kincaid's lips canted sideways like he disapproved but he didn't say anything.

Good. She didn't need Kincaid's permission to do anything. She had questions. Lots of questions. "I got a call about the second autopsy earlier."

Kincaid lifted his chin, seeming to lock onto the emotion she was trying to hide.

"ME believes Cindy hadn't taken the coke that long before she died. She didn't find any benzoylecgonine in her urine."

"Meaning what?" Kincaid asked.

"Meaning I don't know," Pip cried out in frustration. Why did scientists have to spout geek rather than plain English? "The ME didn't find much cocaine in her bloodstream suggesting she drowned not long after inhaling it."

He shrugged. "The alcohol and the fentanyl—"

"Don't," she said sharply.

"Don't what?"

"Don't tell me all the things Cindy did wrong. Please, just don't."

He was silent for a few seconds. "ME confirm she drowned?"

Pip nodded.

"I'm sorry."

She took her sunglasses off and tossed them on the dash. "She's going to run more tox screens."

He turned toward her. "For anything in particular?"

"I asked her to look for any sedative-type drugs."

He frowned and looked irritated. "You think she was roofied?"

She shrugged, staring fixedly out the window. "She had sex with someone Sunday night before she died, but she told me she wasn't feeling well. Maybe someone heard she'd finished and went over to help her celebrate. Maybe he wanted sex but she wasn't in the mood. So, he gave her something to loosen her up and then broke out the coke."

"So why isn't he dead?"

"I don't know." She was exasperated. "Maybe he's taken it before and built up a tolerance. Perhaps Cindy took too much. None of this makes sense but neither does the idea that Cindy willingly took drugs. It could have been an accident. He passed out and she woke up and wandered off. Ended up in the lake. He sees her the next morning and boots it just before I arrive. Or it could have been deliberate, and he murdered her."

"You should write novels."

Pip gritted her teeth and pressed her nails into the hard plastic of the steering wheel. "These are all viable scenarios."

"So is your friend getting high and drowning—alone. How do you explain Sally-Anne?"

"How do you? Pretty convenient the dealer also turned up dead."

"Except if word got out his coke was killing people maybe another dealer decided to take him out of the game—or someone who knew both women? Overdoses are bad for business."

"My scenario is just as plausible as yours," she argued.

One of his brows lifted, but she couldn't read his eyes. "You're suggesting a triple homicide to cover up a rape."

When he put it like that it did seem a little farfetched.

She shrugged. She didn't care. "It's Cindy's money. I want to do everything I can to make sure I know exactly what happened on the night she died. I don't always want to wonder if I missed something."

He looked away then and his nostrils flared as he blew out a breath. "I get that."

"Liar. You think I'm nuts."

He put a finger on her chin to make her look at him and then let go. "No. I do get it. The need for answers." He drew in a deep breath and sadness touched his features. "My step-sister died in Afghanistan. I spent a lot of time tracking down Marines in her unit so I could learn what happened. It gave me the chance to say thank you to the people who comforted her when she was dying." He looked away, but she caught his hand.

"That probably meant a lot to them."

He shrugged a shoulder, staring out the window.

"I'm sorry about your sister."

His chin raised and mouth tightened. "Yeah. I am, too. But it doesn't change anything. Eventually you have to deal with the grief. You can only run away from it for so long."

She shied away from his words. "I'll deal with it once I've given my friend a proper burial. And once I have explored every avenue as to who might have been involved in her death. If it's this drug dealer then fine. I'll accept it. But I want to know who the sexual partners were. I want to know who was with her that night and who left her to die."

And she wanted to know if Cindy had forgiven her, she realized. Something she might never find out.

He stared at her, weighing her up in a way she wasn't sure she liked. "If you want me to take a look around her Atlanta home. See if I can find anything that gives me some insight into who her lovers might be, I can do that."

She blinked at the unexpected offer. "Thank you. Yes." He had resources she couldn't come close to. She'd take anything she could get. "I'd appreciate that."

A black SUV appeared suddenly at the security gate of Universal Biotech. It must have been parked around the other side of the building, out of sight of the main highway. Or inside the loading bay.

Pip turned the key and started the engine. "You better get out."

"You can't just follow people around, Pip," Kincaid warned.

"Sure I can."

"Ever heard of stalking?"

She snorted. "I think stalking involves more than trying to figure out who the owner of a vehicle is. In or out?" she insisted. "I'm leaving in three, two, one."

Kincaid stayed put and she floored it, getting to the main highway a couple of seconds after the other car.

Pip tucked herself two cars back and tried to see who the driver was, but the glass was tinted.

"I'll run the tags but do not get too close." Kincaid called the license plate in. The car came back registered to Angela Naysmith.

"Cindy didn't like her much," Pip told him.

"Your friend ever tell you who Dexter cheated with?"

"Cindy didn't know. She just found panties in his jacket pocket and threw him out."

"Panties?"

"Not her panties." Pip's lip curled but she couldn't help it.

"Dexter told me he confessed about his indiscretions because he wanted to propose."

"He confessed after Cindy found size four, black silk underwear in his jacket pocket. You think it might be Naysmith?" she said sharply.

"No idea." Kincaid shrugged, but looked thoughtful.

Pip tried to keep a discreet distance behind the SUV to avoid being noticed.

"You have a name now. You don't need to follow her home," Kincaid told her.

"Where's your sense of adventure?" she asked.

"Battling with memories of illegal and unauthorized surveillance laws."

"Nonsense. I kidnapped you."

He laughed and her heartstrings gave a little twang.

No. Nope. Not happening. She was not falling for this FBI agent who just a few days ago had threatened to charge her with manslaughter.

She concentrated on not losing the SUV as it turned into one of the more expensive neighborhoods, a new, gated community east of the city.

The car reached a guarded barrier and Pip swore and slowed right down. The barrier went up and the car sailed through. The barrier closed again.

"Head to the gate."

Pip glanced at him and he shrugged.

"We've come this far."

She took the turn and the guard stepped out of his air-conditioned box.

Kincaid flashed creds as the guard leaned in. "Can you tell me who was inside that black SUV that just went through?"

The guard made a face. "Dr. Naysmith. She lives here."

"Was she alone in the vehicle?" Kincaid asked.

The guy shrugged. "As far as I could tell, but I didn't look inside. You want me to call her—"

A weird sound made Pip look around.

"Gun!" Kincaid threw himself over her back, his heavy weight pressing her face down into the center console, crushing her. Glass shattered and rained down into her hair.

Bullets. The sound had been *bullets*.

The gunfire went on forever. Pip braced herself in anticipation of being hit. She couldn't move. Kincaid drew his weapon and returned fire. The noise was deafening. Pip couldn't think. She shook in terror. Someone cried out.

Tires squealed and the shots stopped. The smell of gunpowder filled the air, choking her. Finally, it was over.

It had felt like forever but had probably only lasted a few seconds. Kincaid lifted himself off her.

"Are you hurt?" he demanded.

"No. Are you?" she asked.

He shook his head but was already moving, getting out of the car. The guard was down on the ground, bleeding.

"Call 911. Tell them there's been a shooting involving an FBI agent. Of all the times not to have my fucking Bucar." He bent down and started CPR on the guard. Pip got out the passenger side and stumbled around to the injured man, calling emergency services as she went. She found the street address just as people started running out of their homes to help.

"Is he breathing?"

Kincaid ripped off his tie. "I need to tourniquet this leg wound. Anyone have a shirt I can use to pad the bleeding?"

Kincaid raised his voice and a man quickly pulled his t-shirt over his head before she could offer.

Kincaid torqued the knot tight around the top of the man's thigh and the guard cried out in pain, breath coming in small, shallow pants. Perspiration beaded the man's dark skin. At least he was alive. For now.

"Press down on this," Kincaid instructed Pip. "Hard as you can."

She scooted over to kneel beside him. Kincaid shifted slightly so they leaned against one another, hip to hip, thigh to thigh, as he ripped open the guy's uniform and found another wound seeping blood from his chest.

Oh, God.

Instead of looking at the gunshot wound she gripped the guard's leg and prayed. Was this some random drive-by shooting or had she or the FBI agent been the target?

A squad car screeched to a halt behind them. Seconds later an unmarked vehicle with men in t-shirts and jeans arrived, hands on their weapons, eyes cataloging the crowd. They looked relieved to see Kincaid alive and kicking.

FBI.

Kincaid called out information to the law enforcement people about the shooter. The vehicle make and model. The direction the shooter had taken off in. To her it had been a complete blur of noise and panic. To him it had been a normal day at the office.

She shuddered.

A paramedic eased her aside and she tried to stand, but her knees buckled. Kincaid grabbed her by the waist and dragged her onto the grass, away from the crowd of onlookers that the uniforms moved back. He pulled her t-shirt out of her pants and raised it so he could check her torso, then walked around her, looking at her body.

"What are you doing?" She struggled to pull away but he wouldn't let her.

"People don't always know they've been shot," came a stranger's voice.

Pip looked over her shoulder.

Kincaid looked up. "I can't believe she isn't bleeding out. Someone shot up that car up like an old tin can."

"What about you?" Pip cried out. "You shielded me from the bullets. Who's checking you for wounds?"

"I'm fine." He waved off her concern.

Tears welled in her eyes. "How could you have been so stupid?"

"Years of practice, right, Kincaid?" The man she didn't know thumped his fist into Kincaid's shoulder.

How could they joke about this?

She started to shake.

"This is Agent Will Griffin." Kincaid introduced them. "Pip West."

Agent Griffin was ridiculously handsome. He had close-cropped hair, rich brown skin and almost black eyes that were critical but compassionate. They nodded at one another as her teeth pounded each other like pneumatic drills.

"Are you gonna use this to get out of our run later?" Will asked Kincaid.

Pip just stared at him, aghast. He was worried about a run?

"Hell, no. I enjoy beating your ass into the ground too much for that." Kincaid quipped back.

She went to wipe her face, but her hands were covered in the guard's blood.

"Here." Kincaid's buddy, Will, held up a bottle of water and indicated they both hold out their hands.

He poured water over them and grabbed some paper towels and hand sanitizer off the paramedics who were already loading the victim onto their rig.

"Do you think he's going to make it?" Pip watched the paramedics slam the rear doors closed and the ambulance take off, sirens screaming.

Kincaid pressed his lips together. "We did everything we could for him."

Except maybe get him shot.

"This a random drive-by?" Will asked.

Pip looked at Kincaid.

"Not sure." Kincaid stared back at her.

"What were you doing here?" Will asked.

Kincaid pressed his lips together. "It's complicated."

Pip looked away. Had she gotten him into trouble? She hoped not.

She glanced at her car. Glass was scattered across the trunk and holes pierced the front and back windscreens which were held together by a fine network of fractured glass that looked like a million cobwebs that would shatter at the slightest touch. Holes the size of dimes dotted the trunk.

Had someone just tried to kill her? Or had they been targeting Kincaid. Or the guard?

Why would anyone shoot at her?

But she found it hard to believe it was coincidence, unless the Universe was really trying to send her a very loud message that the world was dangerous and not to get attached to anything because it could be wiped away in the blink of an eye.

"What do you have in there that stopped those bullets?"

Kincaid used the edge of his shirt to ease open the trunk. Inside sat several large boxes of books and photo albums that had formed a barrier between their bodies and the bullets.

Apparently, her Romance novel obsession had saved their lives.

Will nodded, impressed. "Next time someone asks me if I prefer digital or print I'll have a good answer for them."

"How can you joke about this?" Pip snapped.

A large pool of blood smeared the concrete next to the driver's side door. Pip felt like she was going to throw up. Kincaid came over to her, put his hands on both her arms. "It's okay."

"I thought you were going to die and it would be all my fault." She gulped back tears. She didn't want to lose anyone else, not even the annoying FBI agent who thought she was a pain in the ass.

"Let's get you out of here." He led her toward Will Griffin's vehicle. "I need a ride back to my car." Kincaid gave him the address.

"No problem," said Will easily, despite her yelling at him.

"Someone in the field office will be investigating the shooting but it won't be me," Kincaid told her, guiding her with a hand on the small of her back. "They're going to have to question you. Just tell them exactly what happened."

She got into the car and covered her face with her hands. "I didn't see anything. It was just a blur of bullets and glass and," she swallowed, "blood."

Kincaid got into the back seat next to her. Will got in the front and immediately pulled away from the scene.

"I don't understand. What just happened?" she asked.

Kincaid put his arm around her and drew her tight against

him. She saw the other agent watching them in the rearview.

"Someone just tried to kill us, Pip. I just don't know whether they were aiming at you, me, or the guard."

CHAPTER EIGHTEEN

"WHY THE HELL were you conducting unauthorized surveillance? And why were you with the goddamn journalist I told you to keep away from in the first place?" SAC Bourne's questions were like one-two punches into his gut and Hunt felt his career at the Bureau sliding away from him.

He lifted his chin. He hadn't done anything wrong. "I paid another visit to Universal Biotech after consulting with ASAC McKenzie and then arranging a tour of their facilities. I used the opportunity to ambush Pete Dexter with questions as to why his keycard had been used to enter the biosafety labs at Blake over the Christmas period when he'd left that university several years ago."

Bourne paused in what must have been a mentally re-hearsed rant. "Why wasn't the keycard deactivated?"

"That, I don't know."

Bourne looked like someone was gonna get chewed up over lax security.

"I planned to talk to the secretary at Blake and ask her but wanted to question Dexter first. He said Cindy Resnick had his keycard. He said he'd assumed she'd handed it back to the department months ago. One of Dexter's partners suggested Resnick had used his card to get him into trouble out of spite."

Bourne stared him down with a flinty gaze. "Any security

cameras to tell us who used the card?"

Hunt shook his head. "They have one that monitors the main entrance but they only keep the tapes for a few days." Which was frustrating as hell.

"You believe Dexter?"

"I don't know." Hunt wasn't sure where his dislike of the man stemmed from—machismo nonsense or finely-honed intuition? "He's into his status symbols—drives an expensive car and is a full partner in this firm at only thirty. I'd like to check into the firm's financing."

Bourne shook his head. "Keep to the plan, Kincaid. Ask SIOC to check the financials if you really think they might be the ones selling the anthrax but otherwise move on. Why were you with the journalist?"

"Pip West—"

"The journalist."

Hunt blew out a big breath, praying for patience. "Yes, sir, the journalist. I saw her car when I was leaving Universal Biotech. I wanted to tell her we'd found the drug dealer who'd supplied her friend the coke, ask if the second autopsy she'd requested on Cindy Resnick had produced any results. I also wanted to ask if she'd come across Pete Dexter's keycard amongst Cindy's belongings." He hadn't gotten that far.

"She just happened to be there?" The SAC did not sound convinced.

Hunt knew he was dangerously close to getting a verbal ass kicking for subordination but neither he nor Pip had been responsible for some asshole pumping multiple rounds of 9mm lead at them. Without Pip's love of print books, they'd both be dead.

Bourne stared at him. Waiting.

Shit. He was in for a roasting. May as well get it over with.

"She was watching the Universal Biotech facility for a black SUV. She says she saw one near Cindy Resnick's cottage on Monday, minutes before she found her friend's body."

"Why didn't you just run all the employees for black SUVs?"

"I ran Dexter to see what vehicle he drove, but no SUV. I didn't know what Pip was doing outside Universal Biotech until I got in the car with her. I had no reason to run everyone else at the company." Which would have taken hours of grunt work he didn't have time for.

The SAC still looked pissed.

A letter of censure could kill Hunt's hopes of being accepted into HRT selection, but begging would kill his pride.

Bourne straightened a piece of paper on his desk. "The journalist thinks Dexter is involved in her friend's death?"

"West—the journalist," Hunt said before the SAC could, "believes whoever had sex with Cindy the night she died probably provided the drugs. She was looking at Cindy's ex for that reason alone." Not because Hunt had told her anything about bioweapons or BLACKCLOUD.

Bourne shook his head. "Local cops are ready to declare Cindy Resnick's death an accidental drowning stemming from drug use. The dealer who probably sold her the drugs has been found dead. Check the dealer's DNA against the samples the lab took from the cottage. Maybe she knew the guy and asked him to come see her and bring a party bag. Maybe he expected a different kind of payment than what she had in mind."

Hunt wanted to argue that Pip said Cindy wasn't into drugs, but what if she was wrong? Did he want to screw up his career by sticking his neck out with his SAC? Plus, there was nothing wrong with checking the dealer's DNA. It was a solid idea. He'd also see if he could figure out a way to check Dexter's.

Bourne leaned back, deceptively relaxed. "So what happened?"

He meant the shooting.

Hunt relayed what had happened.

He was mad he hadn't got a license tag of the truck or a clear view of the driver. He'd returned fire and definitely put a few holes in the thing. He'd been hampered trying to protect Pip. Plus, the busy highway behind them had increased the chances of a civilian getting caught in the crossfire.

Bourne watched him with that legendary eagle stare. Hunt bore the silent appraisal. Chin up. Shoulders back. He was still wearing clothes smeared with blood and they itched against his skin. He didn't know if that worked in his favor or not. The guard was in surgery. No one knew if he was gonna make it.

"Who do you think they were shooting at?" Bourne asked finally.

Hunt cleared his throat. "We're running the guard for any gang affiliation or criminal history but he's the outside bet. Ms. West and I have both been asking a lot of questions, but shooting at me only makes the FBI dig deeper." He met his boss's gaze. "They followed *her* car. I suspect they didn't even know I was with her."

They'd been after Pip.

Bourne gave a sharp nod of acknowledgement. "You'll be questioned about the shooting, but I don't believe there's any issue with your actions. If you hadn't been there that journalist would probably be dead."

Hunt swallowed, fighting the bile that wanted to rise up

his throat.

"Are you involved with her?" Bourne asked bluntly.

"No, sir." He hoped the SAC wasn't the legendary mind reader some people believed.

"Good. Make sure it stays that way. She's dangerous." Bourne's lips formed an uncompromising line. "If she finds out about the bioweapon and writes about it, the ensuing panic could kill more people than an actual outbreak."

Hunt adjusted his stance and snapped his shoulders back further. "Even if we were *involved*, sir," he fought to keep his tone even despite the seething anger. "I wouldn't compromise an investigation by revealing classified information to anyone, let alone a reporter."

His SAC didn't throw the incident in LA at him. Instead he went for fresh blood. "Yeah, but you wouldn't be the first agent to blurt something compromising during an intimate moment."

Hunt felt his face heat. He was not discussing "intimate moments" with his boss, but he wasn't gonna let this ride. "I have no intention—"

The SAC laughed. "Intentions mean jack-shit. She's a beautiful woman. You're both single. She has an alibi for her friend's death, she isn't a witness to any of your cases, but it doesn't mean she's in the clear. She might be involved in the drug dealer's death."

Hunt didn't reiterate he was her alibi for that shooting, too.

"And she might have conspired with her dead friend to sell enhanced anthrax and some sort of super vaccine to terrorists."

The task force had checked her out in detail and there

were no solid links, but again, Hunt kept his mouth shut. She was involved. He couldn't afford to personally get entangled.

"Then there's that thing in Tallahassee…"

"Where she exposed a dirty cop." Which was what they'd have done, too.

"And a lot of innocent people died." The SAC watched him carefully and Hunt felt like he'd fallen into a trap.

"I don't think she's looking for a story right now," Hunt said. "I believe she's trying to deal with the death of her best friend in the only way she knows how."

"Reporters are always after stories. I'd have thought you'd have learned that after LA."

Bourne slashed a hand, cutting off Hunt's angry response. "Go get cleaned up. Make your report and then get back to work on BLACKCLOUD."

Hunt left the SAC's office angry and frustrated. He headed to his desk, found Will using his phone. Will looked up, finished his conversation and put the phone down.

"Mandy's taking the lead on your shooting. She's interviewing your girlfriend right now."

"She's not my girlfriend," Hunt said through gritted teeth. Part of him wanted to go watch the interview, tell Fuller to go easy on Pip, but that would be crossing a line both personally and professionally. As protective of Pip as he suddenly felt, he couldn't interfere in the investigation. He knew the BLACK-CLOUD taskforce would be burrowing even deeper into Pip's background, but why would she have called 911 at the lake on Monday? Why would she have insisted her friend didn't do drugs despite all the evidence to the contrary? If she and Cindy had been working together to sell weaponized anthrax, why keep pushing for answers? Why draw attention to herself?

He checked his phone messages. Information on the guard had come back negative for gang affiliation or priors. His gut told him Pip had been the target, but the question was why?

Dammit, he didn't have time to guard her, but the idea of anything happening to her... He squeezed his hands into fists and blew out a big breath.

"I need to clean up," he told Will.

He headed to the locker room and stripped, tossing what had been his best suit into a plastic bag in case evidence wanted it. He'd almost died today. Pip had almost died and another man had been shot and gravely injured. The hot water drummed over his face, against his eyelids as he stood there with one arm braced against the wall and let the spray heat his body. He needed to figure out how to protect Pip while still doing his job, and right now he had no idea how to balance the two.

PIP WATCHED THE female agent assigned to the shooting investigation drop down to a chair opposite her in the interview room. The space was sterile and nondescript and reminded her of the other room she'd sat in earlier this week. Had it only been a couple of days ago? It felt like a lifetime in terms of grief and anger.

"Ms. West. I'm Special Agent Fuller. I'd like to ask you a few questions about the shooting earlier today."

Pip nodded. The agent had sleek, long, blonde hair tied back in a ponytail so tight it pulled at the corner of her unfriendly blue eyes. She wasn't much taller than Pip herself and wore her gun and badge like a declaration of hostile intent.

"Do you have any reason to believe Dr. Angela Naysmith committed a crime?" Fuller asked.

Pip shook her head. "No, ma'am. I didn't know who owned the SUV until Agent Kincaid ran the plates."

"Why were you following the vehicle in the first place?" A slight mid-west twang laced the words.

"The day I found my friend Cindy's body, a black SUV nearly ran me off the road near her cottage. I saw a dust trail along her drive. I believe the SUV left the scene shortly before I arrived."

"You think whoever was in the SUV was involved in your friend's death?"

Pip shrugged and knew her expression betrayed her irritation.

"So you're just randomly following black SUVs around Georgia?" Agent Fuller didn't bother to hide her disdain.

"No. I'm trying to piece together who Cindy might have seen in her last days. I spoke to one of her exes and he mentioned seeing her with a man who drove a black SUV. I thought she might have gotten back together with Pete Dexter and decided to see if he happened to drive a black SUV."

"Because the ME found two different types of male DNA at her cottage? Contact DNA in the lounge. Semen in the bedroom." Fuller was looking at notes in a file in front of her.

A band of anger squeezed Pip's chest. That Cindy's life should be reduced to this... "Yes."

"Did she sleep with a lot of different guys?"

Pip was not going there. It didn't matter if Cindy slept with the entire state of Georgia. It only mattered if one of her lovers had force-fed her coke.

Fuller drew in a long breath when it was obvious Pip wasn't going to answer. "You have any idea why someone might have shot at you today?"

Pip had been considering it non-stop. "They might have been shooting at Agent Kincaid or the guard."

"We're checking the guard, but anyone trying to assassinate an FBI agent has to know their actions would bring down the wrath of the entire Bureau. We have dedicated a team of agents to this case, though Agent Kincaid probably wasn't the target."

A cold rush of air whipped over Pip's skin as the A/C kicked in. It didn't cause the goosebumps on her skin. Agent Fuller's words did. "Then someone doesn't like the questions I've been asking about Cindy's death."

"Who?" Fuller didn't hide her skepticism. "Two different Medical Examiners deemed your friend's death to be caused by asphyxiation due to drowning, with drugs as a contributing factor. The dealer who sold her the drugs is also dead. Who else would care?"

Pip recoiled.

"Do you know how he died?" asked Fuller.

"The drug dealer?" A chill of foreboding ran down Pip's spine. "He was shot in the head."

"We're running ballistics. You own a gun, Ms. West?"

Pip's mouth dropped open. "You think I shot him?"

"Did you?" Fuller's eyes didn't leave her face.

Pip felt persecuted. She shook her head. "No."

"Do you own a gun?"

Pip shook her head again then frowned. "I think I've just inherited two. Cindy's dad owned a gun. It's in the safe at the Atlanta house. And Cindy owned one too but I don't know where that is. Presumably at the cottage."

"What kind?"

"Black ones."

Fuller looked disgusted with her lack of firearms knowledge or maybe she thought Pip was being facetious. "You don't know the caliber?"

"I don't like guns." Pip could have mentioned Kincaid taking one off her last night but wasn't sure if that might get him into more trouble. Or her.

"Where were you between 10 PM last night and four this morning?"

"What?"

"I'm wondering if you have an alibi for the murder of the drug dealer who sold your friend the coke that killed her. You made it quite apparent your interest in the man."

Pip gaped. Apparently, she must have "assassin" tattooed on her forehead as this was the second time this week she was being accused of causing someone's death. She should probably call Adrian Lightfoot right about now.

So much for trying to keep Kincaid out of this. "I was in the hotel lobby until about eight, then went to my room until about ten thirty. I ordered room service. After that I went to Cindy's house in the city. Agent Kincaid turned up around eleven thirty and I was back at my hotel close to midnight." Just before she turned into a pumpkin. "Then Kincaid arrived again around 5 AM at my hotel room this morning to tell me about Sally-Anne Wilton. Talk to hotel security. They must have tapes or records."

"Why did Kincaid tell you about Sally-Anne? Were you friends with her, too?" The way Fuller said the word "friends" made it sound like a curse.

Had Kincaid thought she'd murdered Sally-Anne and the drug dealer too? She didn't want to believe it. "Kincaid came to the hotel yesterday afternoon, to the lobby," she clarified, "to tell me the results of Cindy's autopsy. Sally-Anne turned up just as he was leaving and Kincaid gave her his card. She stayed for an hour. After she left Cindy's lawyer turned up. The hotel must have security footage showing who enters and leaves the hotel."

The look in Fuller's eyes suggested she'd already checked. The agent was trying to trip her up.

"Is there anyone who might want to see you hurt?" Fuller asked.

Of course, there was. Pip felt sick. "If you're talking about Frank Booker, he's dead."

"What about his partner in the police force? A brother who loved him and thinks you framed him and got his family killed?"

Pip gritted her teeth. "I didn't frame him. I exposed him for the corrupt sonofabitch he was."

"A lot of cops who worked with him didn't believe the stories."

"They were wrong. I had enough evidence that even Frank knew he was going down."

"Whatever the cost?"

Pip leaned forward and narrowed her eyes. "If you're asking me if I wish things had happened differently then of course I do."

"Perhaps the wife had family who think you're responsible for her death and the death of her three children."

Pip shut her eyes. A fist closed around her trachea and she couldn't breathe. She'd warned Lisa to get out of the family home but the woman had been too terrified of Frank. She'd believed the only way she'd be safe was if Frank was locked up. But his colleagues had been slow to react to Pip's article, even though she'd warned them before it went to print.

Pip wasn't sure whether her editor had released the information about Lisa being her informant or not. She didn't know if it would make a difference to how she was perceived in Tallahassee. One thing had been clear—she could never again work there effectively as an investigative reporter. She wasn't sure she'd work anywhere as an investigative journalist again.

"It's possible someone targeted me for reasons related to my job," she conceded.

Which meant the guard had been hurt because of her. Nausea ground in her stomach.

"What did you see during the attack?" Fuller redirected her questions.

Pip huffed out a short gulp of air that sounded almost like a laugh. "I saw the gear shift and the foot well. Agent Kincaid was shielding me with his body."

"How well do you know Hunt?"

"Hunt?"

"Hunt Kincaid."

"Not well enough to know his given name, apparently." Pip's mouth went dry at that. She was getting way too attached to the agent.

Fuller's expression didn't change but Pip noticed her eyes got narrower. "He threw his body over yours at great danger to himself during a shooting, but you don't even know his first name?"

"Are you saying you'd need to be on first name terms

before you protected someone, Agent Fuller?" Pip crossed her arms, feeling pissed. "I assume he was doing what any federal agent would do in that situation."

The knowledge made her retreat further inside herself. She'd been doing a little falling for the man and he'd been doing his job. She was such an emotional mess she couldn't even tell the two apart.

Another thought struck her. Maybe Fuller was his girl friend. Sure, he'd said he wasn't married but what agent worth his salt would reveal his personal relationships to a potential suspect. Maybe Fuller was looking at Pip like she had crawled out from under a rock because she believed Pip was trying to poach her man.

Was Kincaid in trouble for being with her when he was supposed to be FBI-ing?

"We are not personally involved," she repeated, clearly. "Our relationship is strictly professional and related to the investigation into my friend's death."

Fuller pursed her lips but eventually nodded. She closed the folder. "I suggest you lay low until we've identified your attacker—"

"I have a funeral to arrange."

Fuller raised a finely plucked brow. "It might be a double one if you don't keep your head down until we figure out who shot at you and why."

Pip blinked at the callous phrasing. "You really think someone might be trying to kill me?"

Fuller stood. "I think you've made a lot of enemies and should watch your back."

Pip gave a bitter laugh. "That's your advice for someone who might be in danger? No offers of protection?" Pip stood, too. The interview was clearly over.

Fuller tilted her head to the side. "We could arrange protective custody until we have narrowed down a suspect if you wish."

Pip shook her head. Protective custody was too much like foster care.

The edges of Fuller's lips turned up in a small smile. "That's what I thought."

Fuller opened the door and Pip headed out, breathing a sigh of relief. Next time she was questioned she was getting a lawyer. Fuller led her down a corridor, right out to the front entrance. Pip wanted to ask after Kincaid but had the feeling Fuller wouldn't tell her anything anyway.

Her instincts proved correct when Fuller turned. "Do Agent Kincaid a favor and don't contact him again. If you have something to add to the investigation into the shooting or any questions regarding your friend's death, contact me." She handed Pip her business card. "Your vehicle is in evidence. Ask security to call you a cab." With that Agent Fuller walked away.

Pip raised her chin and stood as tall as her five-foot-one frame would allow. She'd been rejected before. Many, many times. Her opinions had been disregarded. And as a member of the press she'd been asked to leave before, too.

It didn't mean she was worthless or wrong.

The Resnicks had taught her that and she would not break faith with them even though they were all gone. She stepped outside into the hot sunshine and raised her face to the sky.

Someone had shot at her today and nearly killed her. Worse, other people had been caught in the crossfire.

The FBI didn't give a crap about Pip. Fuller had made that

more than clear. Pip dropped the female agent's business card in the nearest trashcan.

Being an investigative reporter had its dangers, but shining light on dark places was how you made the world a safer place. But she didn't want to put anyone else in danger. She pulled out her cell and called for a ride. She told herself not to think about Kincaid, or the fact he'd saved her life today. Instead she'd forget about the agent and go see how the guard was doing. And if she nursed a little ache at the unfairness of it all, that was her business. And she intended to keep it that way.

CHAPTER NINETEEN

"K INCAID!" FULLER YELLED at him as she strode across the bullpen. She glanced at Will who was still grilling him as he filled in his 302. The reports were a staple of FBI life. An FD 302 had to be filed for pretty much everything that happened except going to the bathroom.

Paperwork. Hunt detested it.

He ignored Fuller, wanting to get the shooting incident report finished. He held up his finger to ask her to wait. He could feel her seething annoyance as she and Will whispered to one another, about as subtle as warthogs on Peachtree Street.

He finished typing, pressed save, turning to face them both. "You want to question me?"

Mandy planted her hands on her hips and glared. "That your report on the shooting this morning?" She nodded at the 302 on the screen.

He switched files. "No, this is my statement on the shooting, ma'am." He gave her a tight smile to annoy her.

She read it over his shoulder while he sat there and watched her. "Doesn't mention here the fact you're involved with Pip West."

"Involved?"

"In a personal relationship."

"We don't have a personal relationship." But he'd like to. He acknowledged that to himself in some surprise. The woman had gotten under his skin despite being a reporter and despite his boss's warning.

"That's not what she said."

Hunt held Fuller's gaze for three long seconds before he knew for certain she was lying. "Bullshit."

She pulled her lips to one side and looked annoyed. "I guess you'll find out when the boss reads my report, won't you?"

He laughed and climbed to his feet.

"Maybe the reporter is trying to cause you trouble?" Will suggested, propping his hip against Hunt's desk.

"Fuller is lying," he told his friend. "The fact you can't tell makes me pity you."

Will looked at Mandy and swore. "That undercover stint gave you a whole new set of skills."

Fuller looked miffed they'd figured her out. "How'd you know?" she asked Hunt.

He gave her a pitying smile. "You tried to sell it too hard. Plus, Pip West has no reason to lie."

Hunt trusted the woman. The realization hit him hard in the solar plexus.

Was the fact he wanted to get *involved* with her, blinding him to everything else, everything that really mattered? Could she be part of the bioterrorism case? Regardless, she was still a reporter. But Hunt had learned this lesson and never shared classified data, and would certainly never discuss a case as sensitive as a renegade seller of a biological weapon.

But he liked Pip West.

Fuller tapped him on the back of the head. "Don't get

involved with her. She's bad news."

Hunt scowled at her for reading his mind.

"Mandy's right," Will said quietly. "She might be attractive but she's trouble."

Mandy's features became even more pinched.

They didn't get it. It wasn't Pip's good looks that attracted him. It was her tenacity, her search for the truth even though it wasn't her job and it wasn't convenient. She wasn't waiting for someone to come along and solve her problems. She was capable of doing that on her own, even without the authority of a badge.

He liked her independence. It was a turn on. He liked her spirit, her determination. He'd be lying if he pretended he didn't like the package it all came in.

"Hopefully you won't have to see her again."

"She's gone?" Hunt asked, disappointed they hadn't talked before she left—they had shared an experience today that he wouldn't forget in a hurry. Then he took in the mulish angle of Fuller's chin and knew exactly what had happened. "You just let her walk out of here? She could be in danger."

"We have a team searching for the driver of the truck who shot at you."

In the meantime, someone out there might take another shot at Pip. The idea worried him more than he wanted to admit.

"I offered her protective custody." Fuller looked at her fingernails in a relaxed manner that didn't fool him one bit.

"But you didn't insist."

"Judge would never sign off on it with what we've got so far."

"Something tells me you didn't try too hard to sell the

idea," Hunt said.

"I think she'll be fine as long as she keeps her nose out of things that don't involve her." With that she turned and walked away.

Hunt sat heavily in his chair, worried about Pip and unable to do a damned thing about it.

"She's right. That journalist is trouble," Will told him again.

He walked away before Hunt could tell him to shove it. Hunt picked up the phone and dialed Pip's cell but she didn't answer.

God, he was pissed.

So what if he was attracted? That wasn't the issue here. He had professional reasons to talk to Pip and they were treating him like some hormonal teenager who couldn't keep it zipped. He wasn't an idiot. Even though the idea of something physical with the woman was tempting, his job was more important. But she was part of that job.

Nothing meant more to him than the FBI and protecting people who were in danger. Why was Pip considered less worthy than anyone else?

"Saving the world" Pip had called it. She'd said he was like her friend and her friend was dead. He didn't want the same thing to happen to Pip.

Unbeknownst to his erstwhile colleagues he wanted to search Cindy's property for Dexter's keycard and see if the man's story was true. Unable to reach Pip, he called the FBI Laboratory and asked them to check Cindy's purse, which they'd grabbed with the electronics. Resnick's university keycard was in her wallet, but not Dexter's.

Maybe it was in the house in Atlanta or in the red SUV up

at the lake. He didn't necessarily want Pip to know *why* he was sniffing around Cindy's stuff. It was Dexter he was interested in, but he couldn't afford to let her know. She was already suspicious of the man. He didn't want her spooking him.

He called Libby Hernandez at SIOC. "Hernandez, did you find anything on the company Universal Biotech?"

"Well hello, Agent Kincaid. How's Atlanta?"

He could hear the analyst smiling as she typed in information.

"Hot."

"I hope you mean that in a totally non-biological weapon kind of way."

He grinned and scrubbed a hand through his still damp hair. At least someone was keeping their sense of humor. "I hope so, too."

"I didn't find out much beyond it being a corporation jointly owned by four individuals as we already discussed. We've been monitoring their phones and email since you visited them but nothing suspicious on the surface."

"Did you dig into their financials?"

"The firm's?" she asked. "They're still operating in the red but they've only been going two years. It's pretty early days for a firm like that to turn a profit."

"What about the individual owners?"

"That'll take more time."

"That's okay. It's probably nothing, but I'm curious."

"Curiosity is my middle name, Agent Kincaid."

He smiled.

"You want the results of the deeper background check on Pip West?"

He pressed his lips together and thought about it. After

everything that had happened between them he didn't want to intrude on Pip's privacy, but the information might be pertinent as to why someone had shot at her that afternoon.

"Email it to me."

"Do you think she's a suspect in the BLACKCLOUD investigation?" Hernandez asked carefully.

"You tell me?" His mouth went dry.

"Nothing came up to suggest any links to the dark web or suspicious activity or communications. According to the information I could access she routinely worked ninety-hour weeks and rarely took time off. She doesn't date. Her only intersection with our investigation is the dead friend."

Hunt squeezed his fingers into a fist. "She found her friend's body but has a solid alibi for TOD. Unless she was working with a third party..."

"But why stir things up? Why even turn up in Atlanta if she's involved with something as big as BLACKCLOUD?" Hernandez questioned.

It was good to hear his own arguments repeated back to him by an objective third party. Maybe he wasn't as blinded by lust as his colleagues all feared.

"Those were my thoughts, too. Thanks, Hernandez."

"Glad to help." The analyst rang off.

Hunt needed to keep moving forward. He'd contacted, albeit briefly and sometimes only via email, fifty percent of the people on his list of scientists. The only red flag so far was the use of Dexter's keycard at Blake, after the guy had graduated. Hopefully SIOC was seeing some other behind-the-scenes activities that would lead them straight to the bad guys.

He called Pip again. She still didn't answer.

Fuller would have warned her off. She'd probably roasted

Pip in the interview.

He picked up his leather jacket from the back of his chair and headed to his Bucar.

Will and Fuller might think they were protecting him, but in reality, they were slowing down his investigation and potentially jeopardizing a woman's life. Despite what they thought, he wasn't the one who needed to reassess his priorities.

ON THE RIDE to the hospital, Pip had reached out to her former editor in Tallahassee and told him about today's shooting. She wasn't giving interviews to anyone and the few calls she'd fielded had made her feel sick to her stomach about some aspects of her profession.

The police investigation in Florida was proceeding and the detective who was investigating the Booker case had taken her call, despite two weeks ago almost physically attacking her at the paper's office.

Apparently, Lisa Booker had left a letter with her attorney. One of those "in the event of my death" missives that only people in deep shit ever wrote. Lisa had confessed to being Pip's source and she'd professed her very deep fear of the man she was married to, the abuse she'd suffered, and her inability to leave him. She'd believed her only option had been to help send him to jail and she knew if he found out, he'd kill her.

The detective believed Frank Booker had figured it out. Booker might also have simply decided to kill his family when he realized he was going to jail. He would never have been able to relinquish the iron control he maintained over them.

Pip had tried to get Lisa to go to a shelter but she'd refused. On top of Cindy, it was another loss that still cut deep, especially when she remembered the faces of the Bookers' three young children.

Pip had arrived at the hospital to find the guard in surgery. He'd come through that first hurdle alive but still had a long way to go. His wife and mother were in the waiting room, consoling each other. They had no idea why anyone would open fire on him. He wasn't in trouble with gangs or involved with drugs.

Pip had left full of guilt, more convinced than ever she'd been the target. The fact Agent Kincaid had been in the car had probably saved her life—Kincaid, and her obsessive love of books.

Her cell rang as she walked into the lobby of her hotel. She stopped and checked the screen.

Kincaid.

He'd called her twice already but she decided it would be more sensible not to talk to him. The little flutter of sadness that settled around her shoulders reassured her it was the right move. She liked him too much. She didn't think she could cope with heartache on top of everything else she was experiencing right now.

Fool, Cindy whispered in her ear.

"Sensible." She was talking to herself in an anonymous hotel lobby and feeling a little lost.

"Hey." Kincaid stepped beside her and bumped her shoulder as they both stared up at the impressive roof of the atrium of the hotel. "Ghosting me?"

The smile that burst out on her lips was a very, very bad sign.

"How can I help you, Agent Kincaid?" She strove for cool.

His eyes twinkled and he looked about as handsome as any man ever had. "I think you should call me Hunt seeing as how we nearly perished together in a hail of bullets this afternoon."

"*Perished* makes it sound like some historical drama."

"Well, there was drama."

She looked at him sharply. "And I'm still mad at you for putting yourself in danger to protect me."

His eyes searched hers and didn't let her look away. Whatever he saw gave her away. "I'm sorry you were shot at, Pip. I'm more sorry Agent Fuller gave you hell. She's overprotective."

"Like an attack dog." She hardened her resolve. "You two dating?"

He laughed and the relief she felt staggered her. This wasn't good. This wasn't good at all.

"She's dating Will Griffin, who you met at the scene today. Fuller is not my type. I like women with less sharp edges."

The way he looked at her made her swallow hard.

Was that really how he saw her?

Not as harsh or abrasive, or jagged and suspicious? That was how she so often felt—like a razor's edge of broken glass. The events of the last few weeks had changed her. She hadn't imagined they'd changed her for the better, and she hated that she loved the idea of being softer.

Sharp edges were useful.

Sharp edges could protect you from danger.

She pulled her hair back off her overheated skin and his eyes followed the movement. The undercurrent of desire sparking between them was more obvious, as if it had been let out into the sunlight.

He cleared his throat. "I figured now might be a good moment to take a proper look around Cindy's house like we discussed earlier. See if I can help figure out who she was seeing."

"You'd do that for me, even though you think Cindy's death was accidental?"

He nodded.

She frowned. "I thought the Feds searched it already?"

He shook his head. He'd showered since the shooting. They both wore jeans and t-shirts now. He wore a leather jacket that concealed his shoulder holster.

"They just checked it for anthrax spores," he corrected quietly. "We didn't have a warrant to search the premises."

"You're looking for something." Her nose for a story started to twitch.

He held up his hands. "Not at all. It's after five o'clock and I wanted to help," he said. "You're the one who thinks there's more to her death than we've so far found."

Was she reading him all wrong? He looked like he was getting ready to leave. She didn't want to get involved with him but he was with the FBI. A good contact to have. If anyone could help solve the mystery it would be the premier law enforcement agency in the world.

Also, she wasn't ready to say goodbye. They'd been through a lot and she was still processing the shooting.

"We can go look around Cindy's house. I'll need to get a ride though. My car is in evidence."

Hunt laughed. "No kidding." Then he sobered. "I'm glad you didn't get hurt earlier but getting shot at can be devastating. Don't forget to seek help if you need it."

"A therapist?" she snorted.

"Don't be so dismissive." They started walking outside. "I've seen several therapists over the years."

"Yeah, so have I." Damp heat pressed against her skin as the sun glared down. She loathed therapists.

His ancient Buick sat half on the curb. The doorman tipped his cap in their direction and Hunt gave him a nod.

They got in and Hunt didn't need any direction across town to the old established Sherwood Forest neighborhood where Cindy had lived.

He parked in the driveway that curled up and around the side of the house. "It's a really nice place."

"It is." She shivered. "I can't believe that in theory it's mine."

"In theory?" He followed her around to the kitchen door.

"I keep expecting someone to tell me it's a mistake and hand over a very expensive hotel bill."

She unlocked the door, stepping inside to turn off the alarm code.

"Is that likely?"

She shook her head. "Doesn't mean I don't expect it."

He reached out and caught her hand and her heart stuttered. She pulled away. She didn't want his sympathy and didn't trust his pity.

"I know you've been here before but let me give you the full, official tour." She showed him around the kitchen, dining room and living rooms. He seemed particularly interested in the office and in the stack of things gathered in a basket on Cindy's dad's desk. He put on gloves to go through it.

"Should I be doing that?" She nodded to the gloves.

He shook his head. "Just a precaution. And a habit."

She made them both coffee in old familiar mugs and carried it back to him. He'd gone through all the drawers.

"Can I see her bedroom?" he asked.

Pip nodded and led the way, careful not to spill her hot drink. Up the stairs, along the corridor. She pointed out the various bedrooms. Dana and Bob's, Richie's.

Her throat tightened.

Richie had been a super nice kid. Pip had loved him dearly.

She forced the words out. "There are two guest rooms at the end of the hall. They actually deemed one my room and I still keep some stuff there." The familiar sense of grief swept over her again, more mellow than it had been. They'd all deserved to live long and happy lives. It sucked that they hadn't. "The other is a nice big spare room they kept for overnight guests. This is Cindy's room."

She pushed the door wide open and let him enter first.

The walls were a soft green and the bed was a double with a bright white eyelet duvet cover. Hunt walked over to the bureau, put his coffee down, and went through the things on top of it.

"You recognize all of these people?" He indicated the photos on the cork board.

She nodded.

His lips pressed into a firm line. He walked to the bedside table and opened the drawer.

"Cindy kept a diary. I took last year's from this drawer—I started to read it but I haven't got that far." Same with researching the phone bills she'd retrieved last night. She'd had a busy day. "I assume the current one is at the lake."

The leather of Hunt's jacket brushed the bare skin of her

arm and she jumped. She edged away. She didn't like the effect he had on her.

She hadn't dated in two years. A bad break up and then she'd been too busy. At least that's what she told herself. The older she got, the harder it was to meet single guys she was interested in. People had to prove themselves before she began to trust them and no one had time for that anymore. She wasn't outgoing and gregarious like Cindy had been. She was a wary loner.

But the heat in Hunt's eyes, and the corresponding jolt of desire it shot through her, suggested she wouldn't mind being alone with him.

She swallowed nervously and sipped her coffee. She kept forgetting this was business, not pleasure.

"Anyone else have a key to the house?" he asked.

Pip shrugged. "The cleaner. The lawyer. Apart from that I don't actually know. I guess I better find out. I'll talk to the neighbors. I need to talk to them about the funeral anyway."

The heat she'd felt earlier was washed away by the cold reality of this devastating loss.

God, it sucked.

Hunt went through Cindy's bedside table, but there was nothing more incriminating than a copy of *Vogue*. Then he stood and Pip was once again struck by how attractive he was.

She stubbed her toe on the corner of the drawers and that snapped her out of her thoughts. *Ouch*. They picked up their mugs and headed down the hall toward the kitchen.

"Should I call a cab or can you give me a ride back to the hotel?" she asked casually. She wasn't assuming anything. She was keeping this professional.

He frowned. "You don't have a car."

"Right." She raised one brow. "Not until the Feds release it and I'm not sure I want to drive around in a car with that many bullet holes in it anyhow."

He looked at her out of the side of his eye. "What about Cindy's car? The red one at the lake?"

She shrugged. "I guess theoretically I could drive it. Feels weird though." Like her friend was not coming back...

She blinked back tears.

He checked his wristwatch. "Call the lawyer and confirm you can drive it. Go grab the spare keys I see on the rack by the door and I'll give you a ride out to the lake to pick it up."

"Really?" she asked gratefully.

He nodded.

Pip hated the thought of going back there, but that was dumb. The lake was Cindy's happy place. In some ways it was a fitting place to die.

She called Adrian to confirm she could drive the SUV, and found Hunt in the kitchen rinsing their mugs and placing them on the draining board. It was a devastating combination, the man comfortable both washing dishes and throwing himself in front of bullets.

"Adrian said that was fine," she confirmed.

"Let's go." He dried his hands. "With luck we can get up there before dark."

Pip followed him, locking the house behind her. One of the neighbors sent her a sad, tentative wave and she raised her hand. Pip had met most of them over the years, at barbecues and Christmas parties, and funerals. She finally gave up on her wish that things could be different. They couldn't be. Cindy was gone. All the denial in the world wouldn't bring her back.

CHAPTER TWENTY

HUNT WANTED TO search for Pete Dexter's supposedly missing keycard. If he found the damn thing it would quiet the insistent niggle in the back of his mind and he'd have to assume Dexter was telling the truth. If Hunt didn't find it then it was a loose end that may or may not mean anything. All of the other entries into the lab seemed legit. It didn't mean that the legit scientists hadn't been doing nefarious deeds, but that was the next stage of the investigation.

It was also possible Cindy had handed the card back as Dexter claimed, and the secretary or some other admin person had lied about it. As much as he hated the idea, it was conceivable Lenore Daniels or one of her co-workers had sold it or provided it to a bioterrorist. Although, surely someone would have noticed a stranger hanging around the place?

Perhaps Cindy had given it back to her supervisor and Everson had used it as his own? Hunt would talk to the man again tomorrow—right now, Everson wasn't answering the phone.

As his boss had told him to avoid Pip, Hunt was conducting this search on his personal time, so had driven to his townhouse and switched out the Bucar for his truck before heading north. Nothing pissed off the Bureau more than misuse of official vehicles.

He glanced at Pip in the passenger seat. The fact he was attracted to her didn't factor into this. And if he kept telling himself that it just might make it true. Her hands were clenched into tight fists in her lap and she chewed her lip. She was so tense he was worried she'd shatter if she received another hit. He pushed aside the knowledge he was lying to her. His job was paramount and he didn't intend to compromise that.

But he cared about her, he realized with a sense of foreboding. Which was usually the moment he exited stage right, but they were stuck together in the short-term.

He didn't want to let her out of his sight.

"At least the SUV should be more reliable than your other car," he said, searching for something to break the tension that had built up between them.

Small talk. Awesome.

A dimple appeared in one cheek. "That Honda has been the most reliable car imaginable." Then she grimaced. "But it might have to retire, in light of recent events." She stared out the window at the unrelenting greenery. Endless woods running along the side of the road.

She turned back to him, her smile sad. "I helped Cindy pick out the SUV at Christmas. Her mom's old van finally packed it in and she traded it." She touched the window as if touching a memory. "She put me on the insurance so I could drive it when I was in town."

His ears sharpened. "So you spent the Christmas holidays together?"

"Every year since we met."

"Did Cindy go into work over the vacation?" God, that was about as subtle as a ballistic missile.

Pip didn't seem to notice. "Sure, she went in a couple of times to check on various experiments she had going. Recombinant vaccines. That's as much as I know."

That didn't help much.

"She'd call me when she was done and I'd go pick her up. We'd go out for drinks or home or to a movie."

He wondered if he could pin Pip down on the times without her getting too suspicious. Credit card details? Maybe they had someone who could isolate Cindy and Pip's cell phone data over that period. In fact, maybe they could monitor all the cell phones that had pinged off the tower nearest to Blake during those times when the stray keycard had been used to access the lab.

It was a good idea.

"How'd you end up in the FBI, anyway?" She glanced at the stainless steel ring he wore on the pinky finger of his right hand. "You were an engineer."

He glanced at her in surprise.

"I dated an engineer once." Her expression told him she'd been less than impressed.

He grinned. "I did an engineering degree before I applied to the FBI."

"Why join the FBI if you had a good job?"

"Why become a journalist?"

She sighed and looked out the window. Her hands rubbed up and down her thighs. It was wrong to imagine doing the same so he put his eyes back on the road, ignoring the shot of lust that rushed through him.

Not good.

"English was the only thing I was really good at in school. I loved telling stories, but I needed a way to pay the bills and enjoyed the college newspaper. Ended up taking journalism courses, discovered I enjoyed figuring out the puzzles, and exposing bad guys."

"Me, too."

She went silent and he knew it was his turn. "I was always going to be an FBI agent. It was my dream even as a little boy."

She watched him intently.

"My dad was killed during a bank robbery when I was a kid."

Her eyes reflected shock and pain, but she didn't say anything.

"That's when I met my first therapist." he admitted. "I stopped talking for a while. Shut down completely. My mom persuaded an FBI agent to come and talk to me and the guy promised he was going to catch these robbers and put them away."

"Did he?"

"Yes and no. Robbers were caught doing a job on a bank in Jersey. Cops surrounded the place. An HRT sniper took out both robbers without any hostages getting hurt. That's when I started talking again. After they were killed. That's when I decided to join the FBI."

She frowned. "Why do engineering first? If you knew as a kid you were going to be an agent, why not do criminology or become a cop?"

"It's complicated."

She gave a short laugh. "You wanna talk about the weather instead?"

"No." He grunted. He liked having a real conversation with her. Getting to know her without reading the damned background file even if he was the one doing most of the talking. "My mom met and married another guy, Tom. He had a daughter, Joanna. Jo.

"And she was killed in action," he continued gruffly. He'd already told her this. His stomach turned over. He understood grief. He understood Pip. Maybe that's why he liked her so much. "We weren't related by blood but we were close. All four of us were close even though Jo was six years older than me. Tom had been a good friend of Dad's. His wife walked out and left them."

Pip's jaw hardened.

"Jo joined the military at eighteen. When she died in combat, it broke them a little. My mother especially. She made me promise I wouldn't join the military, and would instead get a proper career." He shrugged. "I liked engineering and was able to work for a few years and pay off my student loans. Then I applied to Quantico. I only told Mom and Dad when I was about to graduate the academy. I planned it that way and didn't actually break any promises." His fingers flexed around the steering wheel. "I think she's finally forgiven me."

"How long ago?" Pip asked.

"Over five years now."

"Your parents sound great. The Resnicks were good people, too." She breathed in deeply and gave her head a little shake. "I'm sorry about your birth dad and your sister. It sucks to lose people you love."

Hunt nodded, wanting to ask her about her background. He hadn't read the file Libby Hernandez had sent him yet. He wanted Pip to tell him first.

They reached the road that led to the lake and she tensed.

"You don't have to come down to the cottage," he said. "I can walk in from the road and take a look around."

Pip shook her head. "I need to face it. I need to go back. I have a lot of happy memories here. I'd like to keep them from being tainted."

Hunt wasn't sure that would be possible, but he didn't say so.

They rode in silence and ten minutes later he turned onto the single track that led down to the lake. He could feel Pip bracing herself. He slowed just before the cottage came into view.

"You sure about this?" he asked.

Her dark eyes were huge, her bottom lip wobbled but still she nodded. He took her fingers in his. Her skin was freezing despite the warm air.

"It'll be okay. I'm here. I'll help you."

She nodded and held on tight to his hand for a few seconds before letting go.

He wasn't sure why he'd held her hand but it was something he wanted to do again. Not exactly how they taught FBI agents to behave during New Agents Training.

He pulled to a stop beside the outhouse and wood pile, and turned off the engine, exactly the same place he had on Monday morning.

They sat in the car without saying a word. Sunset was painting the lake with fingers of red and pink. There were no powerboats, no noise. Just someone fishing in the distance. It was an idyllic place.

But the beauty of the view was juxtaposed against the memory of a young woman's naked body pulled up out of the water just a few short days ago.

Silent tears streamed down Pip's cheeks. He was about to pull her against him to comfort her when she shoved open the door and got out of the car.

Slowly, he followed.

Pip walked down to the edge of the lake and stood with her arms wrapped tight around herself.

"Are you okay?"

She moved away. "No. I'm angry. I'm so damned angry. With Cindy. How could she have been so stupid?" She sobbed and he took another step toward her but she stepped away again. "I just need some time alone."

He nodded. "I'll go look around inside. Is that okay?"

She dug in her pocket and tossed him her keys. Then she walked to the end of the dock and sat, cradling her face in her hands. Her shoulders shook. He wanted to comfort her but sometimes people needed to be alone as they worked through the stages of their grief. Anger was a good sign, as long as she eventually got past it.

He headed inside the cottage and winced slightly at the grime of fingerprint powder on the door handles and light switches. He looked at the coffee table. Most of the coke residue had been cleaned off the surface. The cushions were in disarray—they would have been carefully vacuumed for any trace evidence.

Results from Cindy's electronics were due back in the morning, but her laptop power cord was still plugged into the wall.

He headed into the kitchen, donning latex gloves and leafing through piles of bills and letters on a small telephone table. No keycard. He headed into the office at the back of the house. Went quickly through the desk and drawers. Nothing.

He went up the stairs and checked the two bedrooms at the back of the house, one decorated in all dark plaid, the other painted a deep red. He was sure this was where Pip slept when she stayed here. She seemed to have an affinity for the color red.

He went to the main bedroom and quickly searched the bedside table. Condoms. Notepads. Pens. Books.

No diary. He needed to ask the national laboratory if she'd had it in her purse.

The bedding had been removed. He flicked through the books because some people would use a card as a bookmark. The corners of the pages were turned. His mother would have a fit.

He glanced at the vanity. Lots of makeup neatly lined up. And there were pictures tucked into the edge of the mirror. Cindy with her parents, her brother. Cindy and Pip horsing around. He didn't recognize everyone but there were group images with Sally-Anne, Pete Dexter, Angela Naysmith and the professor. There was a picture of a half-naked guy who had to be the dim but good-looking Dane. Mind, when you were a genius capable of Nobel Prize worthy leaps in vaccine development, Hunt figured he was just as dim and only half as handsome.

So was there another new guy?

Had she picked up guys at the local bar? Taken them home for one-nighters to relieve the stress of writing her thesis? Had one of them given her the coke? They'd found no evidence to suggest she'd tried to sell her vaccine on the black market. And why lodge a patent application if you planned to undermine yourself that way?

Hunt pulled out his phone and called the local detective, staring out the window down at the lone figure huddled at the end of the dock. Pip looked so small and alone. She was obviously used to working through her problems on her own. Hunt couldn't imagine having no one. His family had been through some rough times but they'd always been there for each other.

Detective Howell answered on the third ring.

"Agent Kincaid here. I was wondering if you'd come up with anything in the Cindy Resnick case?"

"I was wondering the same thing, Agent Kincaid."

That was a little reprimand for not calling sooner, but Hunt had been kind of busy. "Another girl who worked in the same department as Cindy Resnick died of a drug overdose late last night—coke and fentanyl mix. APD found the dealer they believe sold them the drugs. Brains blown out."

"Someone not happy with the product?"

"Apparently junkies like their high without the guaranteed added extra of a violent death."

"Can't say I blame them."

"APD is in charge of that case and said they'd be in touch with you."

The guy loosened up. Did he think Hunt had been sitting around with his feet up all day?

"So how can I help you, Agent Kincaid?"

"The lab found traces of spermicide on Cindy's body and some contact DNA. They also found traces of semen on the bed sheets from a different source. Did you hear of Cindy hooking up with anyone from the local bars?"

The detective made a long humming sound. "Not that anybody recalls. I checked the bars and spoke to some of her neighbors. They say she was always friendly but I didn't get the impression they had intimate relations with her. I can ask again. People don't always admit sexual relationships with individuals who die under suspicious circumstances."

"Let me know if anything comes up, will you?"

"Sure. Can I ask why?"

Hunt cleared his throat. "Just a loose end I'd like tied up. Her friend is insisting Cindy wouldn't have taken the drugs voluntarily."

"She thinks she was murdered?"

"Yeah, murder or manslaughter."

"We'll keep asking around." The detective would know how a loose end could niggle away at a man until it all but drove him crazy. He thanked the detective and rang off.

Pip climbed to her feet and Hunt watched her walk slowly back toward the cottage. Her eyes were red and swollen.

Not pretty, but there was no denying he was attracted to her. A gnawing hunger was starting to eat at him and it had Pip's name all over it.

The light was fading fast. He headed back downstairs, went out onto the deck and opened his arms wide. She came to him and leaned against his chest and held on tight, but she didn't cry. Something told him that despite the fact he'd seen her cry several times over her friend on that first day, Pip West rarely lost control of her emotions. He hugged her tight, enjoying the soft feel of her against him, her scent invading his senses—strawberries and sunshine mixed with a subtle hint of desirable woman.

"How's it look in there?" Her voice was rusty and deep.

Sexy as hell.

He cleared his throat. "There's fingerprint dust all over the walls. There are firms you can hire to clean it up…"

She shook her head. "I'll do it myself next time I come up."

Self-sufficient. Independent.

"You okay to drive back?" he asked.

She nodded and pulled out of his arms. "I'm sorry for falling apart. I guess I needed that. I'll be fine driving though. Just give me a minute." She looked up at him and her eyes were almost black in the twilight. His gaze dropped to her lips and the urge to kiss her hit him all over again.

Don't be a fool.

He wasn't being strictly honest. He couldn't be. He wasn't naive or stupid enough to jeopardize the case, but he could still show a little kindness to a woman he was starting to care about and not screw with her feelings when she was vulnerable.

"Give me the SUV keys and I'll make sure it starts."

She dug in her pocket, but said wryly, "I'm not an idiot. I can start a car." When he held out his hand, palm up, she handed over the keys with a resigned sigh. "Fine."

He got into the vehicle and turned the ignition. He did a quick sweep of the glovebox and the middle console and the pocket in the door. No key card.

The fact he couldn't find the thing meant maybe Pete Dexter was lying. Maybe the guy had sneaked into the lab to do something illegal—like make weaponized anthrax or vaccines. Or steal Cindy's work.

He backed the SUV out of its spot and pulled up beside his truck, where Pip stood waiting, composing herself.

He jumped out and helped her into the high seat, trying to keep his eyes off the molded jeans and skintight t-shirt.

Then his stomach growled loudly and Pip laughed. "Hungry?"

She had no idea.

Her eyes danced and those damned freckles made her look sweet and innocent and so goddamned cute.

He reached up and cupped the back of her head, pulling her toward him so he could kiss her. Electricity and heat flared between them.

He traced the seam of her lips with his tongue and she opened tentatively.

He wanted to take the kiss deeper but waited. Waited for her to hesitantly taste him and explore him. Let her lead.

They'd both almost died today and that basic need to prove that he was very much alive surged through him.

It was a natural reaction. He knew that.

She gripped his jacket and pulled him closer, mouth angling with a hunger that seemed to match his. She tasted rich and sinful, and sweet as sugar.

His hands slid up her sides and he was immediately hard as stone.

Dammit. What the hell was he thinking?

He gave a shuddering breath and pulled back. She blinked in surprise. Lips red and slick.

He shouldn't have kissed her.

She was upset. Emotional. His boss and his friends had all told him to steer clear. Even so, he wanted to kiss her again and never stop.

"Wow."

He laughed. "Yeah. Wow."

She swallowed. "You're a good kisser, Agent Kincaid."

He laughed again and moved a half step closer. "Pretty sure you should call me Hunt after that." He reached up and wiped a smudge of lipstick from the side of her mouth.

That mouth of hers gave him all sorts of ideas. X-rated ideas. Ideas that would get his ass kicked at work.

But, God, she was sexy. From virtually the day he'd met

her he'd wanted her. Which made him an asshole.

"You ruined my makeup. And there I was looking so good." She rolled her eyes.

Regardless of tears and smudged makeup, she was the prettiest girl he'd ever met.

She flipped down the sun visor to check the mirror and something small and plastic fell into her lap.

He reached out and picked it up using the edge of his t-shirt. Pete Dexter's goddamn plastic entry keycard for Blake University. "Mind if I take that?"

"What is it?" Pip looked confused then seemed to register it was an ID card. "Okay."

He couldn't explain, which made him feel doubly guilty for kissing her, especially as he'd used a ruse to search her friend's houses. An honest ruse, but a ruse all the same.

"I'll follow you back into the city." His stomach growled again. He wasn't sure when exactly he'd last eaten. "Wanna grab some dinner in Atlanta?"

Pip huffed out a mix between a groan and a laugh. "I probably shouldn't."

"It's only dinner, Pip."

Her gaze locked on his and her smile dropped. "We both know that's not true, Hunt Kincaid." Her voice suggested hot naked sex rather than food and Hunt fought the reaction his body had to the idea.

She'd called him on the bullshit he'd even been selling himself.

He nodded. "We should get going."

Dusk was falling. He didn't want to be on the road around here at night if he could avoid it. Too many chances for misadventure. He shut her door and stepped away.

Maybe she was right. Maybe they'd already crossed a line but they could still step back from taking it any further. He'd be lying if he said he didn't want to go there. He did. Although it was probably best for his career if he pretended she was just part of a case. Not someone whose scent aroused him beyond rational thought.

He got in his truck and slipped Pete Dexter's keycard into an evidence bag. Shit. He'd been sure he was onto something, but it looked like the guy had been telling the truth about giving Cindy the card after all.

Hunt turned his truck and followed Pip back along the track. Keeping his distance was probably a smart idea.

CHAPTER TWENTY-ONE

P IP'S LIPS BUZZED from the kiss she and the sexy FBI agent had shared. After the last few weeks it was a change to experience something other than grief or death. Her life had become a war zone. Forgetting the pain, even for a few moments, had been a welcome relief.

She signaled onto I-75 heading south to Atlanta, Hunt Kincaid following a safe distance behind. Cindy's SUV handled like a dream and reminded Pip of how excited her friend had been when she'd driven it off the lot four short months ago.

Warmth washed through her. There was comfort in being surrounded by memories of Cindy in happier times. Pip needed to hold onto that if she hoped to get through the next few weeks without losing her mind.

It wasn't the only thing she wanted to hold close.

That kiss had ignited a desire she hadn't felt in years, not since she'd fallen in love with Van whom she'd stupidly followed to Miami before he broke her heart. Hunt was turning into a temptation she didn't want to resist, something to keep her mind off the ugliness and emptiness of her reality. And she liked the fact she had gotten under the skin of his federal persona. She liked that a lot.

Five miles outside Atlanta Pip realized that not only did

she not want her time with Hunt to end, she was also starving. Her alternatives for dinner were a soulless hotel restaurant or lonely room service. The need for human company had her dialing his cellphone using the fancy Bluetooth setup in Cindy's SUV.

"I...hm...changed my mind. About dinner," she clarified. For now.

God, she was so out of practice with the whole "man" thing and was way out of her depth when it came to a guy like Hunt Kincaid. She didn't even remember the last time she'd gone on a date.

"Where do you want to eat?" she asked.

"Follow me."

He passed her in his big black truck that suited him way more than the tan Buick he drove for work. He took the next exit off I-75 and drove for ten minutes before pulling up behind a pale, square, brick building at the end of a row of shops that were now all closed.

She pulled up beside him, wondering if she was about to make a massive mistake. The butterflies in her stomach started to take off. She wanted more, and the thought terrified her.

He opened her car door and his gaze scanned her features. "Relax," he said. "It's just food."

She gave a little laugh that released most of the tension she'd been holding onto. He led her inside. The place had exposed brickwork and an enormous Stars and Stripes flag that almost covered one wall. It was cozy though, low lighting, lots of customers but not too rowdy. They could talk without yelling and had plenty of privacy.

Hunt asked for a corner booth and sat with his back to the wall.

They ordered immediately and the waitress brought them each a beer. He watched her lips as she took a sip and a sliver of something hot slid down her throat along with the brew. Her nipples tightened, clearly visible against the thin cotton of her t-shirt. Wonder Woman was getting excited. She pressed her thighs together to try and stop the effect he was having on her. It only made it worse.

A call came through to Hunt and he apologized even as he took it, talking quietly and using purposefully vague language to whoever was on the other end.

He mentioned finding Pete Dexter's university ID in Cindy's car but she couldn't read his reaction.

Why did Cindy have it? Had Pete accidentally left it behind? Had Cindy kept it as a keepsake? Had she still been hung up on the guy?

Pip liked the fact that Hunt's work was important to him. Being a journalist had been important to her, too, but the idea of going back to it, of cultivating new sources…

Her fingernail scraped the gold foil off the brown glass of her bottle. She'd taken pride in her job, weeding the bad guys out. But she didn't know if any of it had been worth it.

"Sorry." Hunt reached out and caught her hand, ran his thumb over the back of her knuckles. His touch sent shockwaves of sensation through her, and it beat the hell out of thinking about Frank Booker's murder spree.

The waitress arrived with their food and Pip moaned in appreciation. Burgers and fries. They smelled divine. She popped a fry into her mouth, flavor flooding her tongue as she moaned again.

"If you don't stop doing that I'm going to come over there and taste you rather than the food."

"Hah. No one is getting between me and this burger." She smiled because despite the heat in his eyes he was teasing her.

"You have a point. I haven't had much time for eating lately." He chewed and swallowed. "Even less for running, and I missed a training session with Will but he pissed me off, so…"

"Why did he piss you off?"

He pulled a face as he chewed and shook his head.

"Oh." Will had obviously said something about her. Probably echoing Agent Fuller's warning to stay away from her.

So why hadn't he?

The allure of forbidden fruit? Or something else?

"I used the treadmill at the hotel after you left this morning." She wiped her mouth and gave up trying to be delicate about eating the burger. "So at least I don't have to feel guilty about eating this."

"The fact you run makes you the ideal woman, you know." He was joking with her, not trying to sell her a line.

She laughed. Took a sip of beer. "Except I don't like guns."

"Definitely my favorite kind of date." He winked.

He had a dry sense of humor she liked. She hadn't noticed it before. Hadn't felt much like laughing. Cindy would have liked him, she realized. She didn't know why it mattered but it did.

"She went for a run the night she died. She went every day like clockwork. Five miles." Her mind drifted to her friend again and the humor died.

"So… I told you just about everything there is to know about me."

She rolled her eyes. "Sure."

He'd sensed her thoughts were turning morbid and wanted to distract her. And she was tired of being miserable. She was ready for some distraction, especially if it involved a honed body and an intelligent mind.

"Where'd you grow up?" asked Hunt.

"Don't pretend you haven't run a background check on me." She gave him a look.

"I have a background report on you. I haven't read it yet, but I know a few things," he admitted. She saw his eyes change. He looked like a man trying to figure out how to get to know a woman rather than an agent conducting an interrogation. "You grew up in foster care?"

"Mostly." Her fingers tightened on the bottle. "Near Tampa."

"You don't want to talk about it?"

She gave a heavy sigh. "It wasn't a happy time."

His eyes turned worried and he asked the hardest question, the one no one ever asked straight out. "Were you abused?"

She pressed her lips together. Shook her head. "No. I was lucky, but it's not the only issue with being a ward of the state."

He asked a thousand questions with his eyes, and saw way more than she wanted him to.

"Don't get me wrong. It wasn't all bad. The first foster family I had was fantastic. I was with them for four years, and I loved living with them."

A small line formed between his brows.

"My mother refused to give up her fight to get me back so I couldn't be adopted."

"Why were you removed from her care?"

She wiped her mouth on her napkin. Then played with the

label on her bottle some more. The last person she'd told this to was dead. It wasn't a story she shared very often, but it would all be in his file anyway. She'd rather she was the one to tell him than he read it in some antiseptic report.

"Mom was an alcoholic. My dad left when I was two or three. I don't really know. No idea what happened to him and I honestly don't care. Cops turned up one night after Mom and her latest boyfriend went on a bender and started smashing up the place. Found me in my bedroom hiding under the bed."

He didn't say anything, just watched her. Still eating. She did the same. It made the whole thing less heartbreaking to do this over food. Like they were talking about some other girl, a case, a story.

"Cops called social services and I ended up with a foster family in a town about thirty miles away." She smiled in reminiscence. "I loved it, actually. The first time I'd had clean clothes to go to school in. The first time I'd been fed on a regular basis." She waved a fry at him. "Probably accounts for my love of these.

"My mother didn't know where I lived." She brushed hair behind her ear. "I thought I'd landed in Heaven."

"What happened after four years?"

"Howard Briggs—the dad—got transferred to an office in San Francisco. They wanted me to come with them. Offered to adopt me, but Mom refused permission for me to move out of state." She shrugged like it hadn't killed her a thousand times over to be removed from the only safe home she'd known as a child. "The Briggs were fantastic and did everything they could to keep me with them, but... it didn't work out."

He took a sip of his beer and let the silence hang.

"By the time they moved away I was nearly thirteen which is not a good age for girls." She grimaced. "I acted like a brat. I was shuttled from one foster home to another. I got into trouble a few times, mainly wanting to fit in with the other kids. I tried weed and E, but I wasn't into it. Didn't like the kids who were. I didn't try sex, thank God."

It was a long time ago but it felt good to put all her hang ups out there. "I was nearly eight when I was removed from my mom's home but I remember seeing her having sex with different men. I think she was hooking to get money for booze and meth." She looked up to see if he was shocked, but his expression didn't tell her much. He'd probably seen or heard it all before. Her family was nothing special. She shrugged. "Cindy knew how badly drugs messed up my mom. She might have experimented once upon a time but she was vehemently against using and screwing up her brilliant brain."

"Even after she lost her entire family?"

Pip nodded. "Her work was too important to her."

They fell silent for a few seconds, before Pip continued. "I had some amazing teachers and counselors in high school and they helped. I qualified for scholarships and got into FSU. That's where I met Cindy and her family. They saved me."

He put his hand over hers and squeezed. "What happened to your mom?"

His hand felt good on hers. Warm and strong. His lips had felt even better on her mouth.

She looked away, hoping he couldn't read where her thoughts had drifted. She'd much rather think about kissing Hunt than talk about her mother. "She died when I was seventeen."

"Did you ever see her?"

Pip's gut clenched at the memory. She'd dealt with this. It wasn't her fault. It just felt like it sometimes.

"Yeah." Her voice was gravelly now. It did that when she got emotional. "A few days before she died." She ran her fingers through her hair. "She wanted me to move back in with her when I turned eighteen so we could try to reconnect." Her mother had begged her. Pip didn't like remembering that conversation. The shouting and emotional manipulation. Pip had been strong enough to say no, but a part of her had always wondered if things would have been different if she'd given her mother another chance. "I refused."

She took a final swallow of beer. "Cops found her dead in her apartment a few days later. Heart attack. The years of alcohol abuse hadn't helped. I blamed myself for a long time, until Cindy convinced me my mother had made her own choices. She'd had an illness she couldn't control. It wasn't up to me to save her."

Her mother had been dead to her for a long time, and yet, there was still a part of her who knew that if she could go back ten years she might now know how to deal with the situation better. Pip might have saved her.

She pushed her half-eaten plate of food away. She was full. Hunt had consumed every scrap of food in front of him and was eyeing hers as he finished his beer.

He opened his wallet and pulled out enough bills to cover both meals.

She dug into her pocket for her wallet.

"I've got this," he said.

She opened her mouth to argue.

"I've got this, Pip. Put your money away."

She let him because it wasn't worth fighting over. "I don't

like charity."

"You can pay next time."

It was a throwaway comment, a reflex on his part.

"Will there be a next time?" Hope and vulnerability were naked in her voice, though she tried to disguise them. But she needed to know what this was between them.

He looked at her and something changed in his eyes, heated and softened. "What do you think?"

He took her hand and tugged her gently out of her seat and toward the door. Once on the sidewalk he turned to face her and brushed her hair to one side. Then he lowered his lips to hers and kissed her again. A jolt of heat shot along her nerves. Tangy and sizzling. Alive. She held onto his forearms as he tilted her chin and deepened the kiss.

His tongue touched hers and she moaned and felt him smile against her lips. She tangled her tongue with his. He tasted like beer and salt and hot alpha male. Her fingers traced the hard planes of his chest, the warm cotton of his t-shirt. The scent of his leather jacket mixed with the musky scent of his skin made her knees go a little weak.

He pulled back, still cupping her face. Before she could think or speak he kissed her again and a tremor of longing ran through her. She curled her fingers into his t-shirt and pulled him tighter against her.

When they broke away they were both breathing hard.

"Come on." He took her hand and strode along the sidewalk, around the corner to their vehicles. He opened her door, boosting her into the seat, his hands lingering on her hips in a way that suggested he didn't want to let go.

"Come home with me," he said gruffly.

A wave of desire curled inside, tumbling her thoughts into

a mass of confusion. She wanted him, but she'd always been lousy at casual sex. But goddamn it, she'd almost died today and this was something she'd been thinking about since he'd come to her room that morning. And that was before he'd thrown himself over her to save her from flying bullets.

They were only alive thanks to a fickle dose of good luck.

Live a little.

Cindy's voice in her head dared her.

The dead woman was definitely haunting her now.

His eyes were dark with night shadows. "I want to show you something."

She snorted.

He grinned and took her hand, his fingers kneading the tension out of her joints. "That too, but if you're not interested or you change your mind at any point, I will make sure you get home safely. There is something else I'd like to show you. Something important."

She wasn't one to trust easily, but what did she have to lose? This would be a way to forget the sadness from the last few days. Unlike drugs or alcohol, sex with Hunt Kincaid wouldn't destroy her mind or body, though it might damage her heart.

But if she knew it was temporary going in, she could protect her heart. He'd be a distraction. Not an addiction.

She wanted this. She wanted him.

"Okay."

He kissed her fingertips and then got in his truck and left her to follow him through the city and into the outskirts, north of the city center.

He pulled up in the driveway of his neat little town house in Ansley Park. She parked by the curb.

She turned off the engine and the sounds of the night pulsed around her. Cars in the distance. People walking their dogs. Laughter. He got out and walked over to where she sat, watching him. Admiring him.

She squeezed the steering wheel, exasperated with herself.

It wasn't too late. She could still leave.

He opened the door and held out his hand, waiting for her to choose to get out of the SUV or drive away.

When she took his hand and turned toward him he lifted her and very gently placed her on the ground in front of him. His hands stayed were they were and she reached up to pull his mouth to hers, wanting that fire, wanting that burn of desire because she didn't want to change her mind. She wanted to forget all the bad things that had happened. She wanted *him*.

He hauled her against him, picked her up, and closed the door with a loud slam. He carried her all the way to his house, never breaking the kiss and she felt devoured by him, consumed by need.

He placed her down carefully on the front step and un-locked his door. He took her hand as they stepped inside and Pip shivered.

She was doing this.

The curtains were open and soft blue light showed a tidy living room. Dark masculine furniture. TV the size of Outer Mongolia on the near wall.

"What did you want to show me?" she asked with a smile.

He shook his head. "Not now. Later."

She kissed him again so he closed the door with his foot and her fingers dove around his waist, tugging his t-shirt from his jeans, finding smooth hot skin beneath the soft cotton.

His muscles clenched at her touch and she loved the way

he trembled as she moved her hands over hard abs, then ran her nails gently up the groove of his spine.

He groaned and worked her shirt free of her jeans. Clever fingers cupped the underside of her breast as his thumb brushed over rough lace, teasing the sensitive tips. She gasped as he rolled a taut nipple, a full body shiver making her hold on tight to his hips. He reached around her back and unclipped her bra in a move that spoke of a lot of practice.

She eyed him warily. "Smooth."

"Don't hold it against me." He nibbled her exposed throat as his attention returned to her now liberated breasts. "I try to be good at everything I do."

"Overachiever."

"I give everything my best effort." He laughed and she felt the slight scrape of stubble over the soft skin of her cheek.

Her heart gave a little skip. "I guess I'll find out, huh?"

He reared back. "You're sure?" He sounded uncertain all of a sudden.

She liked that. Liked that he'd been no more certain of her than she'd been of herself. This was sex and she'd learned a long time ago that sex and intimacy were not necessarily the same thing.

She pushed his jacket off his shoulders and he let it drop to the floor.

"Hang on." He locked the door, then slipped off his holster and put his gun in a drawer in a cabinet near the entrance. He came back, pressing her against the wall as he kissed her.

She lifted his t-shirt and he pulled it over his head and flung it away. She bit her lip and ran her hands over the satin-clad muscles. He had well-defined pecs and stomach that felt ridiculously sleek and hard.

"You obviously work out. A lot. Is that a general FBI thing?"

"I'm in training." His smile had a level of confidence that should have been irritating, but even a blind person could appreciate Hunt Kincaid's body. Especially a blind person. She closed her eyes and skimmed her palm from his collarbone all the way down to his jeans, slipping her fingers just inside the waistband where the skin was downy and delicate.

She wanted to ask what he was training for but it wasn't her business. She opened her eyes in time to watch his nostrils flare. "I'm a runner, not a gym rat. I've got a few curves." She wasn't apologizing.

"I like curves. Men like curves." His brows went high when she pulled a face. "Did you not see every guy in the restaurant eyeing your ass like they were imagining their hands on you?"

"Ew." She laughed. "No. I didn't see that, thank goodness. I think that's all in your head." Her heart was racing from desire and nerves. "Is that why you brought me home? Because you thought other men wanted me?"

He turned them so her back was pressed up against the wall.

"All I know is I wanted you from the moment I saw you being manhandled by Pete Dexter in his company lobby. Trust me, it was no more convenient then than it is now."

She punched him playfully in the arm. His eyes challenged her to deny the connection they both felt but ignored. She'd been too raw, too emotionally derelict, to even think about sex. He'd been too professional.

"Cindy would have told me to go for it with you. Especially after Agent Fuller warned me off."

He grinned. "Fuller told me the same thing."

"I guess we're both rule breakers then." Although she wasn't. She really wasn't. She leaned forward and placed an open-mouthed kiss above his heart. Then she trailed kisses over his chest, licking a flat brown nipple as his hands anchored her hips to his.

Their eyes met when she raised her head to meet his gaze. He lifted her t-shirt off and tossed it on the floor. She dragged off her bra and let it fall. His gaze dropped to her naked breasts and went from hot to combustible in a heartbeat.

He cupped one full breast, ran his thumb over the dusky nipple. "I like your curves."

She thought her knees might give out.

"You're beautiful." Moonlight carved out the solid jaw and wide shoulders. He was ridiculously gorgeous.

She gasped when he scooped her up in his arms and carried her along the hallway. He walked into his bedroom and placed her gently on the bed, coming down to lie next to her. He leaned over her and lowered his mouth to her breast, running his free hand over her waist and back up, homing in on her other nipple. She grabbed a handful of the dark sheets and closed her eyes at the sensation.

The suck and draw of his mouth and careful pinch of his fingers had pleasure shooting from her breasts to her core. She moaned. What he was doing to her felt better than anything she'd ever experienced before.

She ran her fingers through his hair, over his skull, over his shoulders as her head tipped back, overwhelmed with pleasure. Then his hands moved south and the sound of her zipper being lowered was followed by the slide of his hand into her panties.

He took her lips again as one finger dipped inside.

Oh, boy.

Her grip on his hair must have hurt but he didn't complain. She felt his laughter against her mouth before he returned to her breasts and started the torment all over again. Her body shook with sensation. Bulldozed with lust. His finger built an insistent rhythm inside her and her toes curled as the edge of his teeth scraped her skin. Her heart beat harder and harder against her ribs, pounding until she was sure he could feel the vibrations against his mouth. He still didn't stop. And she climbed higher and higher. Her heels dug into the mattress and she writhed, hips circling, thighs widening, wanting more, wanting all of him. The heat of his arousal pressed against her thigh, but he wouldn't let her touch him. Her hands roamed his back and his ass, but whenever she tried to touch his rigid cock he shifted away.

She growled in frustration. "I want you, Hunt Kincaid."

"Soon." He pressed the palm of his hand against her mound and zeroed in on that knot of flesh that swelled beneath his touch and she sucked in air, unable to exhale, then spasming around his fingers as she crashed over that ledge of pleasure, sobbing his name in the darkness.

CHAPTER TWENTY-TWO

H UNT DIDN'T THINK he'd ever seen a prettier sight than
Pip West climaxing in his bed. And they'd barely gotten
started. He moved to the bottom of the bed to tug off her
jeans.

"Up," he ordered and she obediently raised her hips. The
jeans came off and all that was left was a scrap of crimson silk
and lots of soft perfect skin with a tantalizing square of ink
above her left hipbone. "You have a tattoo."

NON DESISTAS
NON EXIERIS

"Never give up. Never surrender," she translated. Her
voice was deep with what he hoped was shocked pleasure.

"Figures." He gave her a grin, leaned forward and traced
his finger gently over the dark letters, which fit her personality
absolutely. He moved his attention to the thin strip of silk that
ran over the delicate skin of her hip. He remembered them
from the day he'd searched her belongings. The woman knew
her way around the lingerie department, that was for damned
sure. She lifted herself up on her elbows and he just stared.

She was so feminine and pretty, but so very strong and
determined. Her hair was mussed and her nipples matched her
lips, all pink and glistening from his mouth. She had the kind

of lush body his hands and mouth and eyes could feast on for hours and never tire.

And despite all the delectable naked beauty on display, it was her eyes that attracted him most. The sense of fierce pride shining there, not because of her appearance, but because of her courage. It conflicted with the uncertainty that also stirred in their depths. The aloneness.

That vulnerability made him want to drop his own emotional walls, but this was only sex. Satisfying the need to have her, the obsession that was starting to scratch at his brain and his body with equal insistence.

He knelt between her legs, spreading her thighs as he moved up the bed and then changed his mind about where to go next. She was like a feast to a hungry man and he wasn't sure where to start.

He leaned down and tasted her navel, enjoying the way she sighed and gasped whenever he touched her. He ran his tongue over the black lines of her tattoo and they tasted sweet.

When she fell back into the mattress he took advantage of the moment and moved lower, dipping between her legs and moving the panties to one side. He almost lost it when her scent surrounded him. He pushed her thighs further apart because he wanted to consume her.

Her moans grew desperate again—he'd never heard a sexier sound than Pip West's unconscious moans. He climbed back up her body, enjoying the shape and taste of every inch along the way.

"Why are you still wearing your pants?" she asked huskily as he settled between her thighs.

"Because I want to last more than five seconds."

The curve of her smile and laughter in her eyes were clear

in the moonlight. "Is that normally a problem for you?" she asked.

God, her voice got to him. All deep and throaty and seduced.

"Not usually," he told her with total sincerity. "I'm experiencing performance anxiety."

She laughed and he felt her shake beneath him.

Before tonight he hadn't dared think about having this woman in his arms. Now, it was all he could think about. He shouldn't be doing this yet he couldn't seem to stop. They'd both almost died today and he definitely felt the driving need to celebrate the fact he was alive and kicking. He felt like an animal. Feral and slightly out of control.

Having her in his arms was testing him. He couldn't get enough of her sweet body and wanted to make this as good for her as possible. She deserved better than the way he'd treated her this week—not that he'd had a choice.

His boss had called her dangerous and warned him not to get involved, but the man's issue was Hunt letting something slip about the BLACKCLOUD investigation, not with Pip herself.

It was insulting to both of them.

"You have a condom?" she asked, breathily.

"Stay there." He kissed her and went to grab a new box out of the bathroom cabinet. Pulling out a strip, he headed back. She'd moved—pity—and now lay propped against the pillows, still naked on his bed.

"You're gorgeous." Had he already told her that?

Her smile looked unconvinced.

"You are."

"Sure." She laughed at him.

He sat beside her and tossed the condoms on the bedside table. He was going to have to convince her, again, until she believed what he was saying.

He stretched out on the bed beside her. His hand hovered over her breast. "I especially like this bit." He moved his hand up as he said it and tipped her chin so he could capture her laughter and swallow it whole. She tasted sultry and spicy.

She took control of the kiss and he growled as he let her. For all her tenacity and guts, there was a sensitivity to Pip West that he didn't want to crush by doing something stupid.

And he was more than capable of doing something stupid when it came to women.

He didn't do relationships, but the idea of saying those words out loud made his brain rebel. But he couldn't not say anything. He wasn't built to lead people on.

"What are you waiting for, Hunt? A written invitation? Fuck me." She undid the snap of his jeans and carefully eased the zipper down, slipping her hands inside. He felt her moan of appreciation but as much as he loved the feel of her hands on him he took her hand and pressed it into the pillow beside her head. Then he took the other hand and placed it on the opposite side of her head.

She stared up at him mutinously.

Christ.

And then he kissed her mouth, and her neck where he found a sensitive spot beneath her ear. She giggled and he teased her unmercifully before making his way back to her breasts which were exquisitely sensitive to touch and had her writhing in his grip. He let go of one hand and splayed his across her stomach. She was so small. So much smaller than he was. He was a little worried about hurting her.

He swept his hands over her curves and over her hips, down her thighs. She wasn't skinny but she was toned and muscled and fit. He loved the light tan on her skin. The midnight silk of her hair. Those dark eyes that watched, transfixed, as his hands stroked her body.

He dipped his fingers into those frilly red panties again and found her wet. Her lips parted on a gasp and he couldn't wait any longer. He eased the lingerie down her legs, shucked his pants and grabbed a condom, settling between her thighs. They were nose to nose as he started to ease inside, gazes wide and intent on the other. Her ankles went over his hips and her nails dug into his back as he pushed inside for the first time.

They both froze, getting used to this new feeling, this primitive invasion. Slowly he felt the resistance of her muscles lessen and her breathing slow.

He leaned his forehead against hers. They were both sweaty and her hair clung to her cheek. "You okay?"

He could see her uncertainty and insecurity in the lines around her eyes and the downward pull of her mouth.

"It's been a while," she admitted.

He wondered how long, but didn't want to talk about former lovers. This was their time together. He rocked gently and she gasped.

"You feel amazing." He gritted his teeth against the need to rut.

Her nails dug a little harder. "You feel pretty amazing yourself."

He moved again, trying to keep the movement gentle and smooth, and oh, so good. He kissed her and she relaxed more and more. He took all his weight on one elbow and shifted her hips to get deeper and she tilted her pelvis and suddenly he was fully embedded and a fine sheen of perspiration broke out across his shoulders.

He slowly ground against her, wishing he could make this last forever, hoping it was making her feel even half as good as he felt. Her heels dug hard into his ass and her eyes closed and he could see her expression twist into a parody of pain as she lost herself in another orgasm. But the feel of her squeezing him blew a fuse inside and suddenly he wasn't thinking about anything anymore. He was driving toward release even as Pip continued to clench and come around him, making him feel better than he'd ever felt in his whole goddamn life. Blood pounding, heart-hammering, his climax finally hit him, slamming into his body with the impact of a meteorite. When he could breathe again he held her close, feeling her respond in kind as she wrapped herself around every part of his body and he wrapped his arms around her and squeezed tight.

Their hearts beat in unison and her hoarse breath brushed his ear.

Hunt didn't know exactly what had just happened, but he'd never experienced sex that passionate before.

This was a disaster.

He raised himself up on his elbows to stare down at her, but she wouldn't meet his gaze. She turned her face to the side. She was pulling away. He could feel it in the tension of her muscles as she unwrapped her legs from his hips and tried to shift. She was doing to him what he usually did to others, not because he was a rat bastard, but because he didn't want to risk falling for anyone. He couldn't be around to protect them 24-7 and knew the world was a dangerous place. Maybe when he was in the Hostage Rescue Team he'd settle down. Perhaps then he could let go of some of the fear of losing the people he loved.

Not that he loved Pip.

He squashed the little voice that whispered, "*yet.*"

He trapped her face between his hands and kissed her again, slowly, languorously.

It took a few seconds before she started to respond and relax into him again and he started revisiting all the places he'd visited before, acquainting and reacquainting himself with her body. He got rid of the condom, not leaving the bed because he knew the minute he left her she'd start thinking about all the reasons she shouldn't be here with him—the fact that their careers were incompatible, that there was no hope of a lasting relationship, that she might get hurt.

All true, but tonight he wanted more. It was selfish and greedy but he hadn't even begun to slake his hunger for her.

She touched him, running her hands over his sensitized skin, fingertips tracing the lines of his muscles, fingers curling around him, finding him hard again. She stroked him until he was aching with need and unable to bear another moment of not being inside her.

He grabbed a new condom and rolled it on, positioning himself against her entrance. She ran her hands down his back and urged him on but he paused, framing her face with his hands even as her hips tilted and took just the tip of him inside. It was torture and paradise combined, but he had something to say first. While he might not want something long term it didn't mean that this wasn't important to him. He opened his mouth to speak but she placed her finger over his lips.

"I don't want words, Kincaid. I don't want promises or confessions that might mean nothing tomorrow. Just fuck me as hard and as long as you can and make me forget everything except this, except you. Just you. Nothing else matters tonight."

THE RING OF a cell phone woke Pip slowly from a deep sleep. Her cheek was pressed against smooth, male skin. She frowned, then realized she was draped across Hunt's naked body and she rose and fell with his breathing. His arms were wrapped around her, holding her tight as he slept.

She didn't recognize the ring tone, and she knew most FBI agents carried two, a personal one and a work one. Knowing the call might be important given the nature of his work she pushed upright, breaking his hold.

"Hunt," she murmured. She enjoyed the shape of his name in her mouth. "Your cell phone is going off."

He groaned in denial then sat up in bed, rubbing his eyes with the heels of his hands. "What time is it?"

He was rumpled and deliciously naked. He'd taken her at her word and fucked her hard, but also slow and painstakingly tenderly.

She was left with an ache deep inside.

"Four AM," she told him softly.

She hadn't meant to fall asleep but he'd held onto her after that last time and his warmth and the sound of his heart beating against her ear had lulled her into oblivion.

He got out of bed and she watched, sitting up and gathering the sheets to her chest. The scar on his leg marred the perfection, but she'd always thought perfection was boring and didn't trust it. He was beautiful, and definitely not boring.

She'd never had sex like that before. It wasn't just physical. She'd never felt worshipped like a goddess on a pedestal—he had told her he was an overachiever.

But she wasn't a goddess. She was just a normal single woman, struggling to find her way in the world.

They'd had one perfect night and she didn't think it could ever get better than that. She wasn't sure she'd want to try. She certainly wasn't going to read more into it than it being great sex. Great sex was exactly what she'd needed to get her mind off her other problems, like the fact her best friend was dead, and someone had tried to kill her yesterday.

Hunt padded out the door in search of his cell, the rear view just as mouth-watering as the front. She made quick use of the facilities, conscious of the scent of him surrounding her. The shower beckoned but she needed to leave.

Self-conscious about her nakedness, she found a towel to wrap around herself. She opened the door and saw he'd already pulled on slacks and socks and was shoving an arm into the sleeve of a clean, white shirt.

"I have to go in," he said, doing up buttons and fastening a black, leather belt around his waist.

Disappointment arrowed through her.

Stupid.

But she nodded and scanned the room and saw her panties on the floor. She scooped them up. "I'll head back to the hotel."

Hunt frowned. "You don't have to leave. Stay the night."

The fact he offered made something inside her glow like oxygen kissing an ember. But she couldn't allow herself to get attached.

She knew Hunt's type. Handsome and ambitious. Not

looking for anything beyond the short-term. He wouldn't be around for long and she didn't want the heartbreak of falling in love with this man. Not right now.

She pulled away. "No. I'll head back. I've got a lot to do."

"Don't." An edge sharpened the word.

Her head snapped up at his tone. "Don't what?"

He walked toward her, forcing her backward until she hit the window, the glass frigid against her bare flesh.

"Run away." He gently tapped her forehead. "In here." Then he pressed his hand against her heart. "And here."

Her throat swelled in a familiar overload of emotion. "I'm not running away," she lied. "I'm just not making this into a big thing."

He tipped his head, his expression incredulous. "Seriously? Last night wasn't a big thing?"

"It was just sex."

He grunted.

Holding onto the towel, she slipped under his arm. "We just met. Under terrible circumstances," she added when he made another sound of frustration.

He tugged his shoulder holster over his arms. Everything about him was mesmerizing and she didn't want to fall victim to his appeal. Even if they fell in love—which was ridiculously fairytale—his job was dangerous. The idea that he might die and leave her alone, just like everyone else in her life had left her alone, wasn't something she could contemplate.

She couldn't do it.

She forced herself to find her clothes and get dressed, rather than just watch him with moonstruck eyes. She pulled on her jeans and t-shirt, giving up the search for her bra and other sock. She was lacing her running shoes when he came through into the living room looking like a just-got-laid, well-groomed, well-rested, G-man.

He smiled and her ovaries went bang.

She dragged a hand through her wild hair and decided the world really wasn't fair. He trapped her before she knew what was happening and kissed her again, hard, insistent, as if they had time for another round. Holding her against the wall until she melted. There was no other word for it, her bones dissolved as his mouth explored hers.

Oh, God. He wrung that response from her effortlessly, lust igniting like fireworks in her blood. Just as quickly he pulled back, his hand still lodged possessively in her hair, gently holding her nape. "I'll follow you back to the hotel."

She shook her head, put her hands against the cool, clean cotton of his shirt and pushed him away. "You'll be late."

"Someone tried to kill you yesterday, Pip. I want to make sure you get back safe and sound."

Was that why he'd brought her here? To protect her? She stared into those blue eyes of his, gold rings shadowed and muted.

"I don't need you looking out for me, Kincaid."

He released her and shrugged into his suit jacket. "I don't have time to discuss this."

There was an urgency in his voice, a firmness that told her he meant what he said and wasn't backing down.

"Fine."

She didn't have the energy to argue, not after the night they'd shared, especially knowing it was probably going to be the only time they'd be together like that.

They left the house and he armed his alarm and locked the door. The morning was quiet as Pip climbed into Cindy's SUV and started the engine. He followed her all the way to the hotel and flashed his headlights as she turned into the valet parking area. She sat and stared at the Buick as he headed past for the office, driving faster now that he'd fulfilled his responsibility in making sure she got home safely after a night in his bed.

She sighed, her body lax and sated.

"Stick with the program, West," she told herself firmly.

Give Cindy the best funeral she knew how and figure out who her friend had had sex with. Pip was convinced that the last person Cindy had seen was the person responsible for giving her the drugs. Pip would figure it out eventually. She just had to keep asking the right questions.

CHAPTER TWENTY-THREE

H UNT JOGGED UP the stairs to the SAC's office. Pip was right. He was late. But he'd needed to see her safely back to the hotel. He wasn't sure what he'd got into. Since he'd broken his leg last year, sex generally left him with a vague sense of dissatisfaction, not that he'd ever admit it. Sex had lost some of its appeal.

Not with Pip last night.

He'd been in plenty of short-term relationships, but this didn't feel like those. Maybe because, however obliquely, she was related to his job and he knew more about who she was under pressure than any other lover he'd ever had.

They'd been in complete sync for hours, each knowing what the other wanted, each pleasuring the other above their own wants and needs. Or maybe it was a temporary sexual blip, a reaction to their near-death experience yesterday. But there was no chance of a relationship for them. Not only was she career kryptonite, she constantly got herself into trouble.

A cold sweat broke out at just the thought of trying to keep her safe. He'd smother her and she'd hate him for it.

The office was dark, with pockets of activity in some of the gray cubicles that formed the bullpen. On the top floor Bourne's secretary sat behind her desk and told him to go right in.

McKenzie was on the screen. They all looked at him as he shut the door and threw himself into the empty seat.

"They sent us a video message," McKenzie said. "Show him."

Bourne turned a laptop toward him. There was a video file and Hunt pressed play.

A figure wearing a hoodie with the hood pulled low over his face sat in the shadows. It was impossible to make out features.

The figure began speaking. "The FBI are looking for the creators of the next great plague." The voice was electronically disguised and sounded sinister and evil.

Hunt's lips firmed. It was an old trick and he wasn't falling for cheap propaganda tools.

"You won't find us. We are smoke. We are shadow." The words reverberated menacingly. "We are everywhere and nowhere. Stop looking and we will be merciful. We will stop the plague before it begins."

The figure leaned forward although the shadows were too dark to make out features. The wall behind was dark gray painted breeze blocks. "If you don't stop your investigation we will release the plague in New York City and Miami, San Francisco and Houston. In every major city in the U.S. It will kill like the great plagues of Egypt. Death will be swift. Death will be excruciating. Death will be mercy. It will destroy millions of lives and taint the air for a thousand years."

Revulsion pulsed around Hunt's body.

"To prove we are telling the truth we have organized a demonstration." The hooded figure lifted his wrist as if to check his watch, but there was nothing there. "It just took off." The figure seemed to smile, layer upon layer of dark shadow.

"Cease your investigations. This is your one and only warning. Or we will release more, and soon. Millions will die."

The video went blank and Hunt sat there with his heart pounding.

"Any reports of sickness?" asked Hunt.

McKenzie shook his head. "We got this an hour ago. I've sent copies for image and linguistic analysis and have cyber experts trying to trace where it came from and where it was filmed. We have agents rushing to every airport with every rapid field test machine that we can use for anthrax. Nothing yet."

"So you're thinking airliner rather than missile?" asked Hunt.

McKenzie nodded. "No reports of any missiles fired. Military has been put on red alert."

"Thank Christ," Bourne added.

Hunt swore. "They're trying to blackmail us."

McKenzie nodded. "A foreign intelligence source sent us some fingerprint information last night they say is from the packaging used to mail the bioweapon to the arms dealer in France. Fingerprint came back to a freight handler at Atlanta airport. I want a team on him but it's likely he just handled the package as part of his job."

"It's a massive transportation hub." SAC Bourne nodded.

"But it's a lead that once again narrows down our focus to your neck of the woods. I just spoke to Dr. Place at the CDC. They're trying to mass produce the vaccine but, as he said yesterday, the procedure takes time. They are going to conduct tests today to see whether or not it's effective against the weaponized strain of anthrax the bastards tried to sell to terrorists."

Hunt thought about Cindy Resnick's work. The professor had seemed confident it would work on any strain. Had Jez Place looked through Cindy Resnick's thesis yet? Was her breakthrough legit, or hyperbole?

"These bad guys heard about our investigation. Does that mean it's someone we talked to?" Hunt asked.

McKenzie shook his head. "Hard to know. A week ago, the FBI ruined their little arms deal. They might have made the video then. They have to know we're investigating. Or maybe we are getting close and they're stalling for time."

"Why stall?" asked Hunt. "To produce more of their deadly anthrax? Why not just get out of the country and take their secrets with them? Set up somewhere else?"

"If they run, they risk revealing their identities," said Frazer who suddenly came on screen, looking out of breath. "Not just to us but also to the buyers of biological weapons. These are not nice people to have chasing you."

"And the last thing we want is the Russians or Iranians getting hold of this stuff or its creators," Hunt murmured.

"They have their own hot strains, but I bet they'd be interested in a vaccine that the sellers claim works against even the most aggressive form of the bacteria," mulled McKenzie out loud. "A vaccine that might neutralize all their biological weapons."

Hunt kept thinking about Cindy Resnick. Had her discovery really been as revolutionary as Professor Everson stated? Was it related to BLACKCLOUD, or a parallel discovery based on the same progressive technology?

"So you think these UNSUBs are staying in the U.S. because they're too cowardly to go elsewhere?" asked Bourne.

It was fucked up.

"They never expected the FBI to be onto them this fast. They expected to be rolling in cryptocurrency just about now, cracking open the bubbly. The fact we stopped that sale is a miracle," Frazer said. "Maybe they simply don't have the money to run."

The mention of champagne also reminded Hunt of Cindy.

"It strikes me whoever is doing this genuinely thinks they can get away with it," McKenzie put in.

"They think they're smarter than we are." And that pissed Hunt off. "Anything from the communications angle?"

"We've managed to exclude hundreds of people from the investigation, but whoever is doing this has been very careful to cover their tracks. But they just made a big mistake. They've given us a lot of fresh clues to follow by making this video," McKenzie said.

"Or they want to slow us down. Are they bluffing about this demonstration?" Hunt asked.

No one answered. It wasn't like the FBI would stop investigating a crime of this nature. They'd already been pretty subtle, to everyone except the people who knew they were after them.

McKenzie answered a call on his end then looked up at the screen. "A co-pilot just collapsed en route from Atlanta to Phoenix. We're having them divert the plane to a military base in Utah where we can isolate them and check for anthrax infection. I need to go deal with this."

"Do we stand down with this investigation?" Bourne asked.

"No, sir. You put every available agent on this. We just hit warp speed and I'm thinking Atlanta is ground zero. Kincaid is the case agent on this."

As hungry as he was for the honor, it would interfere with his plans for HRT. "I'm flattered sir," and it was a hell of a good opportunity, and possibly a career changing case, "but I've got a really good feel for some of these people. I think I'm of more use on the ground." And that was true, he realized. He'd be more useful poking scientists he'd established a relationship with just a little harder rather than coordinating an investigation that would be a full-time job for years to come.

McKenzie paused to consider him carefully. "I spoke to the Director before talking to you. This is the number one priority in the Bureau as of today and we're going to want most of the agents in the Atlanta FO working on this, but not one word of this can leak to anyone, especially not the press."

Hunt ignored the look his SAC threw at him. He had no intention of telling Pip about the bioweapon. It wasn't relevant to their relationship. And the fact he was calling it a relationship scared the ever-loving shit out of him.

"We'll figure out a cover story to tell the other airline passengers. The airbase in Utah is remote enough they might believe there's no tower coverage when locals tell them their cell phones won't work. If this thing is as fast-acting as these assholes claim we'll know if this is related to BLACKCLOUD by the end of the day. Hopefully the CDC can bulk generate the vaccine in time to circumvent a mass outbreak." Everyone's expression turned grim. "Let's reconvene in two hours."

McKenzie and Frazer cut the connection.

Bourne ran his finger around the inside of his collar. "We'll set up in the incident room. I want the blinds drawn and a total media blackout. Why don't you want the job, Kincaid?"

Hunt met the man's stare head-on. "The reason I stated." He cleared his throat. "Also because I plan to apply for HRT. I don't want to disrupt or slow this investigation if it's still ongoing."

Bourne nodded thoughtfully. "I don't want to be dealing with this until the day I retire. I want these people found and this case closed."

The sooner the better.

"I'm gonna put ASAC Levi in charge of this so let's call him in and get him up to speed," ordered Bourne.

Hunt nodded and went to the door and asked the secretary to call the man. Levi was a short, bullish guy with salt and pepper gray hair. He was also brilliant and had cut his teeth on undercover mafia cases in the New York Field Office.

A million thoughts whirled through Hunt's mind. He couldn't shake the idea that something had rattled the would-be anthrax producer into sending this video. Had Hunt spoken to him? Scared him? Was he stalling or did he mean what he said about the FBI backing off?

The bad guy had to know the FBI would never back off in the face of such a threat to public safety. A bit like Pip and her investigation into her friend's death.

Shit.

He hoped she was okay. He hoped what had happened between them last night hadn't freaked her out. He hoped she was taking precautions with her safety. He'd check on her later, but people's lives were at risk and he couldn't abandon his duty to protect them just because the woman he was starting to care about was relationship shy. The irony was staggering. He was usually the one running from any form of commitment but last night had been unlike anything he'd ever experienced. It wasn't just the mind-blowing sex. Getting her to commit to anything except a one-time thing might prove difficult. She was slippery and evasive. Still, he was good at what he did, and he was determined. Pip West had exploded into his life and he wanted to get to know her better even though the chance of a future together was remote.

He also wanted more mind-blowing sex, he admitted to himself. He might be an FBI agent but he was also a man, and the man wanted Pip in every possible way. But she probably needed a little time and space instead of more pressure from some over keen love interest.

Don't be that *guy, Kincaid.*

And he had a job to do. A very important job. Thirty minutes later ASAC Levi burst into the room and Hunt started filling the man in. The dawning look of horror on Levi's face reflected everyone's feelings.

This UNSUB was smart and desperate and didn't care who he sacrificed, as long as he didn't get caught. Catching him before anyone died was going to require a miracle.

AT NINE AM, Pip knocked on Cindy's advisor's door at Blake. She'd been emailing and calling the guy over the last couple of days but he hadn't replied.

After leaving Hunt's townhouse, she'd gone back to her hotel room and showered and tried to forget about how good it had felt to be in his arms.

What was wrong with her? Having sex with a guy she'd met over her friend's dead body. *Who did that?*

The rude noise in her head sounded like Cindy blowing a

raspberry.

What were you doing, Cindy? Who were you involved with? Why did you have to go and die?

She knocked on the door again and was about to turn and leave when she saw another professor walking down the hall towards her.

"Professor Everson has taken a few days off. You should have the email address of your TA—"

"I'm not a student," Pip interrupted quickly. "I'm a friend of Cindy Resnick's." Pip had actually met this woman after Cindy's family's funeral but didn't remember her name.

The professor's gaze cleared. She was carrying a polystyrene container under one arm. "Ah, I remember you now. Sorry, I'm really bad at recognizing people out of context. I am so very sorry about Cindy, and Sally-Anne." She balanced the container on one hip and unlocked a door with the name "Prof. K. Spalding. Departmental Head" on the door and went inside.

Pip hung around the open doorway.

Spalding put the white box on top of the papers and sat behind her desk. "I've been dealing with a lot of administration nightmares caused by Cindy and Sally-Anne's death and trying to make sure no one else does anything stupid."

Pip flinched.

Spalding eyed her critically. "It's a terrible thing. We're all in shock."

No kidding. Pip pushed on. "I was hoping to ask the professor to be one of her pallbearers and possibly do a reading at the service, but he hasn't answered my emails or phone messages."

"I can email him but I can't give you his number."

"I have his number," Pip admitted. She'd taken Cindy's address book from the house. "He's not answering the phone."

"I'm sorry," Spalding's eyes softened. "When is the funeral?"

"Sunday. Two o'clock at St. David's." Pip crossed her arms over her chest. "It's short notice but it's the church Cindy's parents attended and that's the only time available for the next week and, well…" She'd arranged almost everything else. The death certificate had been signed. The casket chosen. Adrian Lightfoot had taken care of most of the paperwork. The family burial plot was big enough to include Cindy so Pip hadn't had to worry about that either. She knew what flowers Cindy liked—roses, not lilies—and she'd chosen an outfit for her to be buried in—black pants and a long-sleeved designer blue blouse that had been Cindy's favorite. The music was Samuel Barber's "Adagio for Strings" that Cindy had chosen for her parents' service, and "Yesterday" by *The Beatles* because Cindy adored them.

Adrian had organized a caterer for a wake to be held after the service at the Resnicks' house. Pip wanted Cindy reunited with her family as quickly as possible and then she could figure out her next move and fully mourn her friend. Pip put her hand on her chest, hoping to shift the weight of grief, but it was wedged in like cardiac damage following a heart attack.

The funeral arrangements somehow seemed too easy. Death should be more difficult than this—especially when it ripped your insides out through your mouth.

Getting the word out and tracking down Cindy's advisor had been the only hiccup, barring someone shooting at her yesterday. The more she thought about that, the more she accepted that it probably had something to do with her job as a journalist rather than her questions about who Cindy might have been sleeping with. She had no doubt Agent Fuller would let her know when the FBI caught the shooter. The agent was too cocky not to come crowing like a rooster.

"I can promise to pass on the information, but Professor Everson is no more likely to pick up his phone at the cabin for me than for you. Trevor likes to disappear sometimes." Spalding smiled, not unsympathetically.

"That's fine." Pip didn't admit it but she knew where Everson's cabin was. She'd been in the car when Cindy had had to drop off a chapter of her thesis over Christmas. Pip would take a run up there and see if she could talk to the guy.

Pip cleared her throat. "I've asked some of her other friends if they'd be pallbearers. And the school secretary said she'd post a notice so everyone knows about the service." Sally-Anne's funeral had been planned for Wednesday next week.

Spalding frowned. "Maybe some of the people who used to work here might also want to pay their respects. I'll send out an email to the people I know to spread the word. I am sorry you're having to deal with this. Such a tragedy..."

Spalding's phone rang and she glanced at it and sighed. "The FBI." A small smile creased her cheeks. "I spoke to a very handsome agent on Monday morning. The highlight of a difficult week."

Pip frowned. "Monday *morning*?"

Spalding nodded, distractedly. "WMD coordinator for the Bureau. He was here when I heard about Cindy actually. I imagine he wants to finish his tour of the rest of the facility and speak to the other researchers."

Hunt. It had to be Hunt. Pip's heart gave a little leap of

excitement. WMD coordinator. *That's* why he'd been called on to investigate Cindy's death.

Spalding was looking at her and the box she'd been carrying, clearly eager to get on with her day. Pip backed away. "Thanks for your help. Anyone else who you think might want to know about the funeral I'd appreciate you passing on that information."

"I'm sorry about Cindy. I liked her. She was going to do great things in the world and now all that potential is cut short. Maybe we can get her Ph.D. awarded posthumously." Spalding pressed her lips together and shook her head. "It's a damned shame."

Pip said goodbye.

At the entrance to the building she paused. It was overcast and raining and she was exhausted. Probably because she'd spent the night having fabulous sex with that very hot FBI agent everyone liked to admire.

Hunt Kincaid.

She mulled the name over. It was a good name. Strong. Unpretentious. To the point. It suited him. She wondered how the FBI agent in question was feeling today. And what he wanted with Karen Spalding.

She shivered. Last night it seemed like they had an emotional connection but often in the light of day men seemed able to extinguish that connection with either carelessness or ignorance. This time it seemed she was the one doing it. Him telling her not to run away from whatever was between them had just about melted her resistance. And that wasn't good.

Was he regretting what happened now he had a little distance? She wouldn't blame him.

She probably shouldn't see him again. They weren't dating. They'd just hooked up after a completely shitty day. Agent Fuller had made it clear she should avoid him for his sake as much as hers.

To hell with Agent Fuller.

She dialed his cell, disappointed when it bounced to voicemail. He was probably still talking to Professor Spalding. She didn't leave a voice message.

She drew in a tight breath and decided to walk back to her hotel rather than get a cab. The exercise would do her good and then she could drive up and drop by the professor's cabin.

"Ms. West. Pippa!"

She looked over her shoulder in surprise and there was Adrian Lightfoot hurrying toward her. He was wearing an expensive-looking dark suit that made his blond hair shine. He really was a very attractive man.

"I have to go talk to some people here about a pending patent on Cindy's work. Do you want to join me?"

Pip's eyes were gritty from exhaustion and she had to suppress a yawn. "Not unless I have to."

He herded her in the circle of his arm and urged her toward a nearby coffee shop. "You and Cindy are very alike. She wasn't a morning person either."

"You knew her for a long time," she realized.

He nodded and gave her shoulders a quick squeeze before letting go. "Our families were friends. I was often dragged along as a teenager to barbecues at the Resnicks. I remember her as a little girl. Ridiculously smart even at a young age. But I was only interested in escaping the parentals and going to hang out with my buddies."

She smiled and touched his arm. "I was hoping you'd do a reading at the funeral."

He looked stricken all of a sudden and shook his head. "It doesn't feel right. I'm sure there are people who knew her better than I did." His voice caught and he looked away, almost embarrassed.

Pip ordered her coffee, a little disconcerted she'd overstepped some invisible boundary between attorney and client.

"I understand." But she really didn't. "Do you really think I need to come to this meeting with you?"

Adrian shrugged. "You don't have to, but…I'm fighting for Cindy's best interests, which are now also your best interests, so I thought you might want to be involved."

When he put it like that, how could she refuse?

CHAPTER TWENTY-FOUR

I T WAS ALMOST noon. Hunt sat in the SACs office waiting for McKenzie and Frazer to come on screen. He'd investigated Raz Perez, an employee of Hartsfield-Jackson Atlanta International Airport. The guy had worked as a mail handler for nearly seven years and was married to a nurse and they had two young children. No priors, no degree in microbiology, no known affiliations with any terrorist groups, no weird internet activity except for a propensity for streaming really bad sitcoms.

ASAC Levi sat in one corner of Bourne's office, taking everything in with a bleak expression. He already had people checking out the co-pilot's movements last night, his house, car, and gathering as much background information on the other passengers as possible.

Most of the agents in the FO had been pulled off their other cases in the short-term to work BLACKCLOUD. Luckily the white-collar crime sting had been wrapped up at the beginning of the week and most of the evidence had already been collected and submitted to the DA's office. Fuller had been ordered to stay on the shooting incident because that was an attack on a federal agent, but she was on her own now and pissed to be missing out on such a big case.

Ironically, considering the guy had questioned his professionalism, Will was also pissed Hunt hadn't confided more details about BLACKCLOUD.

McKenzie had mentioned sending more agents down to Atlanta, maybe even coming himself and basing the task force out of their office. McKenzie was more and more convinced the bad guys were in this part of the world.

Hunt wasn't sure how he felt about that. Worried because the UNSUBs could release deadly microbes in Atlanta or the surrounds, and pumped because he had the opportunity to make a difference and take these assholes down.

The video screens went live and McKenzie wasted no time. "We're not picking up any positive readings for anthrax in our rapid field tests anywhere on that commercial aircraft, but the co-pilot just died. Military doctor believes he died of anthrax."

Hunt swore.

"Anyone else sick?" Frazer asked.

"No," McKenzie said. "We've isolated the passengers in an old Quonset hut. They don't know about the co-pilot yet."

"Are we going to tell them about the anthrax threat?"

McKenzie pulled a face. "No. As far as they know there was a medical issue with one of the pilots and they had to make an emergency landing. We were able to get the man off the plane with the help of the other pilot and an air steward. Because we didn't find any contamination on the aircraft itself, the plan is to ask for saliva swabs as a precaution before getting the passengers back onboard and on their way."

"Hopefully they'll feel sorry enough about the co-pilot that they won't cause too much grief," said Bourne.

"Do we have any clear suspects?" asked ASAC Levi.

"What happened to that lead with the keycard being used at Blake to access the labs two years after the student left?"

asked Bourne.

Hunt pulled a face. "I found Pete Dexter's keycard in the sun visor of Cindy Resnick's SUV. It checks out with his story."

The SAC shot him a dark look.

"Pip West said Cindy Resnick worked in the lab over the Christmas vacation though I haven't firmed any times."

The dark look turned into a glare. "She gave you permission to search for the keycard?"

"I didn't tell her what I was looking for." Hunt hesitated. "Pip West refuses to believe her friend was foolish enough to take drugs. She thinks Cindy was date raped and the drugs were somehow forced on her friend. Pip was hoping I might find evidence to confirm that if I looked around." He ignored the guilt he felt for lying to Pip about what he was searching for. He kept his expression neutral, aware he'd spent hours last night getting to know Pip in intimate detail strictly against his boss's wishes. He was finding it hard to regret anything, except the fact their time together had been cut short. His work was important to him. He didn't resent it often.

"That's interesting." Frowning, McKenzie quickly rummaged through a pile of papers on his desk. "We just received Ms. Resnick's lab results. There're some peculiarities…"

"I'd like to hear it," Frazer said impatiently. He checked his watch. "CDC better come through with some results soon or I'm getting on a flight down there today."

They were waiting on the anthrax strain DNA results. Everyone was getting impatient.

"All right, all right," McKenzie muttered, pulling out another file. "Okay. A few things. One, there was a minute trace of Rohypnol in a water bottle at the scene and a small amount of cocaine in the champagne bottle."

Hunt blinked. *What...?* Had Pip been correct in her suspicions?

McKenzie carried on reading. "Neither male DNA profiles found at the scene were in CODIS nor were the fingerprints found in AFIS."

"Why would there be a sedative in her water bottle or cocaine in the alcohol?" asked Hunt.

"It's possible she used it to sleep? She was under a lot of stress, right?" the SAC suggested.

No one looked convinced.

"Here's the other thing that really bothered me. The files on her laptop are corrupted. Technicians are trying to restore the data," McKenzie told them.

"Maybe she had a system crash and didn't have a backup. Maybe losing a bunch of work made her decide to end it all," said Bourne.

"She sent the file to her printer back home, and I suspect she has cloud storage somehow," Hunt said thoughtfully, but he didn't know if anyone had checked it out.

"Doesn't really explain the Rohypnol," Frazer commented.

"So you think the reporter is on to something?" Bourne asked. "Maybe she's involved in something she's not telling us about? Someone tried to shoot her yesterday. Maybe she sold her friend's research—maybe they were in on it together?"

Hunt bristled. "Except her alibi for the death of her best friend is solid. And she's the one who's been pushing the fact her friend's death wasn't accidental, despite what we've been telling her."

The SAC shot him a look that made Hunt stop talking but he was pissed. Bottom line was, Pip couldn't win. Had Cindy's death been a murder staged to look like an overdose?

What about Sally-Anne? The drug dealer? Were they collateral damage? A diversion?

Hell of a fucking diversion, and no proof.

There was a knock on the door and Jez Place burst into the room wiping the sweat off his brow and looking generally harassed. His clothes were the same ones he'd worn yesterday and his hair stood on end.

He shut the door on the secretary who stood behind him. "Is this room shielded from electronic communications?"

That didn't sound good.

Bourne nodded.

The professor threw himself into a chair and opened the file in front of him. "We figured out the strain." He dabbed his forehead with a tissue.

"And?" McKenzie asked impatiently.

The scientist let out a gusty sigh. "It's one of ours."

Shit.

Everyone started talking at once.

"What do you mean, 'one of ours'?" McKenzie said loudly.

Frazer gritted out, "If you tell me we have a government weapons program I'm going to—"

Jez cut him off. "No, nothing like that, but prior to 1969? Definitely."

"I thought those strains were destroyed?" Hunt said carefully.

"Stockpiles were." Dr. Place nodded. "Most of the work done at USAMRIID was in reaction to the work of hostile nations around the world. But when we pulled the plug we didn't hamstring ourselves in the process. I mean we stopped developing new strains or better strains but we did keep some reference stocks we'd found in Nazi Germany and Japan after WWII."

The man looked around. "The parent strain of the bio-weapon uncovered in BLACKCLOUD is called SAHCAM45. It was isolated from a camel in the Sahara in 1945 at the tail end of the war. It was unlike any native varieties found in the region and the allies believed the Nazis had been testing it and wanted to observe it in the wild."

"We didn't know how fast it killed, but we didn't find just one dead camel, we found over a hundred. And not only the camels, but their owners and the Nazi guards. All found dead. Suggesting it acted so quickly everyone who came into contact with it died."

"Luckily we'd caught a prominent Nazi bioweapon scientist nearby and he was recognized. Soldiers from the US Army 12th Air Force wore protective suits when they went in. They took samples. The scientist tried to poison his guards and was shot dead before the Allies could debrief him."

"Samples went to USAMRIID and bodies were burnt and the ashes buried. At USAMRIID the strain was further enhanced as a bioweapon."

"Dear God," ASAC Levi said quietly.

"It's not a history to be proud of, but after WWII everyone was racing to find a balance of power between the east and west. Nuclear annihilation would have destroyed the planet."

"Whereas germ warfare only destroys living creatures," Frazer said dryly.

"I'm not agreeing with what happened but I think we need to remember they were different times back then," Jez said sharply. "Pandora's box was open and we couldn't simply ignore what was happening elsewhere. We still can't unless we want to risk getting wiped out by terrorists or rogue nations."

With sarin gas being used on civilians in Syria and nerve agents used for targeted assassinations around the world, Hunt wasn't sure where he stood on this stuff anymore. Except locking up forever anyone who used WMDs and hitting countries hard if they started releasing this shit.

"The specific enhanced strain that this anthrax came from was SAHCAM45-65 and was worked on by a government scientist trying to develop a vaccine to protect against it. He spent his entire life looking for something but never found it. His name was Vernon Grossman and he moved from Fort Detrick to the CDC and worked there from 1967 to 1981. He retired when he was sixty-eight years old and died in 2013. To my knowledge he never found a vaccine." Place looked deadly serious as he spoke.

"I'll get my people investigating everything there is to know about Vernon Grossman." McKenzie passed a note to an agent in the room.

"The thing is," Dr. Place continued, looking excited, "Grossman's widow, Elsa, is still alive. She's ninety-two and lives out in Decatur."

Hunt was out of his chair and heading for the door.

"I'm coming with you, Agent Kincaid," Jez said. "It's possible he stored samples at home and if that's so, I'll be able to assess the scene."

"Take Will Griffin with you," Bourne instructed.

"Yes, sir." Hunt nodded. "Send us the address."

He was secretly relieved they were moving away from Pip as a suspect although she might not forgive him for ignoring and discounting her theories about her friend's death. He realized he actually wanted to see where this thing with Pip went. He didn't want his bosses interfering with that just because none of them liked journalists. The Bureau demanded enough from him already.

He checked his cell. A missed call from Pip, but he didn't have time to call her back. He didn't intend to bend the rules, but he wasn't ready to give her up.

The net was closing and it seemed more and more likely that this awful bioweapon had some connection to Atlanta.

They headed downstairs.

"Let's take my vehicle. I keep protective equipment in the trunk," Jez told him, huffing after them.

Hunt nodded. "I'll grab my gear and a shotgun and Agent Griffin. Meet you out front." Hunt split off from the man from the CDC. He needed ammunition from his desk.

Mandy Fuller tried to stop him along the way.

"The guard looks like he's gonna pull through," she told him, hurrying to keep up.

"I know." Hunt had called the hospital earlier. "That's good news."

"I traced the truck, but the owner reported it stolen—"

"Mandy, I can't stop." He held up his hands in apology but she knew the investigation was critically important. "I'll come find you as soon as I have time."

Fuller looked pissed but he smiled determinedly at her. He felt like they'd made a giant leap forward. He just hoped the widow could help them solve this puzzle and that Pip would forgive him for not listening to her if Cindy's death somehow related. He also hoped he wouldn't end up arresting an old lady as a terrorist.

CHAPTER TWENTY-FIVE

T HEY PARKED ACROSS the street from the single-story home with its steep driveway overhung by tall sugar maples. The widow lived northeast of Decatur's downtown in an older style home that backed onto woods and a large cemetery. At the rear of the garden just visible through the overgrown shrubs was a garage-sized building with a metal chimney sticking out the roof. The sight of it made the hair on Hunt's nape stand on end.

"Think that's a summer house or a home laboratory?" Will asked Jez.

The scientist pulled a face.

"You don't take things home, right?" asked Hunt.

The man grinned. "Never, but would you like to come over for supper sometime?"

"Not in this lifetime." Hunt shook his head. Humor helped defuse the tension.

Hunt and Will both pulled on raid jackets, so they'd be easily identifiable as FBI agents while walking around the neighborhood with long guns.

They didn't want to scare anyone.

Jez handed them each a breathing apparatus and mask. They took the masks but didn't put them on yet. There was no obvious identifiable hazard.

It was quiet out. Kids would be in school. Most people at work.

"We're weighing wide scale panic versus personal risk. I think the mask is a sensible precaution. I'm definitely gonna wear mine if I go in there." Jez pointed at the shed.

Great.

"Give us five minutes and then join us," Hunt told the scientist.

To start with, Hunt and Will knocked on the front door, but after two minutes of no response they went around the side of the bungalow and stepped up to a screen door at the back of the property. Hunt pressed the doorbell again.

A strange hum filled the air, like someone had flicked on a lighter under a wasps' nest.

"You hear that?" he asked Will.

The other agent frowned, shook his head.

Hunt pressed the doorbell again and listened carefully. There was that weird hum again. A shiver ran over his flesh. "I've got a bad feeling about this."

The other agent nodded. "We can wait for backup."

Hunt felt stupid. "For one old lady?"

"For a group of bio-terrorists who may or may not be in the area."

Hunt grimaced. He carefully tried the knob but it was locked. He went to the window and pressed his nose to the glass. His heart did a swift kick against his ribs. "I figured out the noise."

Will came up beside him. "Flies?"

"Yep."

They both stared at a dark shadow on the floor. Something disturbed the dense mass and they rose in a thick cloud only to settle again after a few moments.

Jez came tentatively around the corner, wearing the protective headgear, carrying the little black box that was a rapid field tester for anthrax. He frowned when he saw them. He peered inside the house and swore colorfully. "Can't tell what she died of from here. If it's anthrax she's a perfect bioweapon bomb for anyone who goes inside and deals with the body. Even those flies need to be contained and killed before we go inside."

Something buzzed past Hunt's cheek and he batted it away. "Fuck."

The microbiologist checked his detector. "Not measuring anything and that is *good* news." He got on the phone, calling in evidence and decontamination teams from HMRU and CDC.

"Why do I get the feeling someone's cleaning house?" Hunt said tightly to Will.

"You don't think the widow could be in on it?"

Hunt shook his head. He doubted a ninety-two-year-old woman would want to kill hundreds of thousands of people with her husband's anthrax. But maybe she thought he was being ignored, or wanted him immortalized. Didn't make sense to him but he wasn't going to discount anything right now. He took another step away from the bungalow, convinced he could smell the decomposition even out here. There was nothing anyone could do for the widow—assuming it was Grossman's widow—but they needed to check the outbuilding.

Hunt called McKenzie and updated him while he waited for Jez to finish his preparations.

"We're gonna need a full biohazard team. Dr. Place just called it in to HMRU and CDC."

"Natural causes or murder?"

"Impossible to tell. Jez said she's a potential source of the disease so we didn't enter the main building." His stomach turned but he ignored it. HRT was looking better every day. "We're just about to enter a converted garage we're thinking might be the old man's laboratory."

"Keep me informed." McKenzie hung up.

Jez caught up with them as they approached the fancy shed in the back garden. They all put the breathing apparatus over their eyes, mouths and noses. Jez handed them gloves.

"But don't touch anything," the scientist ordered.

Hunt and Will nodded. They weren't stupid. Jez led the way, turning the door handle and finding it unlocked. He held up his hand and waited a few seconds, watching the display on his equipment.

Then he waved them forward, presumably free of anthrax.

Hunt and Will followed him inside a room that looked like a rudimental lab with a pot belly stove at one end of the room, probably for heat.

A big freezer sat against one wall. Jez touched it and checked the flex. "Someone turned it off."

He carefully opened the door and Hunt braced himself for loose powder or old vials, but there was nothing inside except the lingering scent of bleach.

Jez checked the display of his sensor and shook his head. "It's been cleared out."

"Now I know why they gave you a Ph.D.," Hunt joked.

"No one gave me shit," Jez said between gritted teeth. "And right now, I'm wishing I'd stopped at AP Bio."

They spread around the room, Jez heading to the fume hood tucked against the west wall, Will to the desk. Hunt drifted to a nearby wall covered in framed photographs and certificates. He used his cell to take copies, sending them to Hernandez at SIOC.

Hunt worked his way across the wall and finally got to a group shot probably taken in the seventies judging by the clothing. One tall guy at the edge of the group caught his eye, clenched fist planted firmly on a skinny waist. Hunt took a photograph, then called the other two men to him.

Jez peered closer. "Isn't that...?"

"Professor Trevor Everson." And suddenly Hunt really had to wonder about Cindy Resnick's death and all the things that didn't add up. Had the professor killed Cindy and Sally-Anne? Framed the drug dealer to divert the investigation? Killed the widow? All the clues were pointing firmly in his direction.

Whatever the truth was Hunt hoped to hell Pip was safe in her hotel room because things were starting to get ugly. She could kick his ass later, he just wanted her out of the cross-hairs.

PIP DROVE SLOWLY along a paved road south of Cartersville that skirted the Etowah River, about twenty minutes from Cindy's cottage. The professor's cabin was one of four or five tucked away from the road, near a farm and some stables, hidden by large leafy plots and hemmed in on the north side by the river. The properties were more rural and undeveloped than many of the surrounding subdivisions that had sprung up like clones over the last twenty years.

She thought she recognized the mailbox at the end of the

driveway and pulled up beside it. She hopped out of the cab and checked the name on a magazine sticking out.

Nature. And it was addressed to Trevor Everson. She was in the right place.

She shivered a little in the afternoon breeze and pulled her leather jacket on over her t-shirt. The sky was overcast and the temperature had cooled off overnight and they'd had intermittent rain, which suited her mood perfectly.

Hunt hadn't returned her call and it was ridiculous that she'd experienced a small sting of hurt. The man was working. Doing important things for his country. Hopefully putting the right bad guys in jail. And they'd made no promises. He'd accused her of running away, but it didn't mean he wanted a future together.

What did it matter? Hunt Kincaid wasn't her one true love and she'd do better by avoiding him altogether.

So why did the thought of never seeing him again hurt so damn much?

She debated for a moment whether to drive down to the cabin or just walk. But she could see the building just a hundred yards away through the trees and it felt lazy to take the car, and a little presumptuous. She pulled the professor's mail out of the mailbox, deciding to save him a trip, hoping the kindness would diminish any annoyance he might feel at her turning up uninvited.

She started off down the driveway, the crunch of gravel loud beneath her sneakers.

The meeting she'd had with the university IP department and Adrian Lightfoot had been eye opening. It looked like Cindy had been about to revolutionize vaccine research although Pip still didn't know exactly how. It would be a few years until the patent yielded any real money. If there was enough, Pip was thinking about starting a research fellowship in Cindy's name. It was something the professor might consider adding his name to as well, as a way of immortalizing their achievement.

A pair of blue jays bounded through the trees overhead and made her smile. Pip spotted two vehicles outside the small house. A silver hybrid and a dirty, gray truck.

She went to the back door, clutching the mail, and knocked.

She thought she heard voices inside. So she knocked again, louder this time. The voices stopped abruptly and she heard footsteps, then silence, though she couldn't see anyone. No one liked to be tracked down, especially when they were trying to escape. But the funeral was only a few days away. Surely, he wouldn't want to miss it?

She pressed her lips together, fighting a growing headache. "Professor? Professor Everson. It's Pip West, Cindy's friend. I wanted to tell you I've arranged the funeral for this coming Sunday." She raised her voice to be heard through the thick, wooden door. "I was hoping you could be a—"

Gravel crunched behind her and she swung around. Something heavy connected with her temple, and pain exploded through her skull. The world went black and she crashed to the ground.

CHAPTER TWENTY-SIX

T HEY WERE FLYING along the highway, ten minutes out from Everson's cabin when Hunt's cell rang. Libby Hernandez. Two more teams had been mobilized from the FBI's Atlanta FO, including the SWAT team but Hunt, Will and Jez were twenty-five minutes ahead of them. Jez Place had the accelerator pressed firmly to the floor.

"Three guesses as to the last post-doctoral research associate to work for Vernon Grossman?" Hernandez said without preamble.

"I'm way past guessing games, Libby," Hunt told her. The itch between his shoulder blades was becoming a full blown allergic reaction.

"Everson."

"Everson was a post doc of Grossman's," Hunt said to the others.

"They didn't publish any papers together so I had no idea," Jez exclaimed. "But it makes sense given their overlapping subject of expertise."

"Can you trace his cell and see where he is?" Hunt asked the analyst. "I spoke to his head of department and convinced her to give me the address of his cabin, but I don't know if he's there."

Other teams were mobilizing to raid his residence in Atlanta.

"Give me five minutes," Hernandez told him.

"We need to pick him up for questioning ASAP. And we need a CDC team at Blake, picking his lab apart."

"And probably another team up here," Jez added. "Just in case."

Dammit. The potential crime scenes were endless and they had to go slow until each scene had been cleared.

Just as they turned onto the road about a mile from Everson's cabin Hernandez called him back.

"Can't get a trace on his cell phone. Seems to be in a bit of a dead zone. You might lose comms there."

Hunt made a sound of frustration. This could be a giant waste of time but they wouldn't know until they knocked on the door. "Thanks anyway."

He disconnected and glanced up only to feel as if a bucket of ice water had been poured over his head.

"Up ahead." He pointed to the red SUV pulled up beside the mailboxes. "That's Pip West's vehicle."

"Any idea what she's doing here?" Will asked.

Hunt curled his fingers into fists. "Searching for answers about her friend's death."

Will shifted in the seat behind him. "Looks like she found them, unless she's involved—"

"She's not involved," Hunt snapped.

"You sure?"

"One hundred percent positive." And wouldn't he look like a bloody fool if he was wrong. But he wasn't.

Yes, she was a journalist. Yes, she was trouble. But she'd dedicated her life to figuring out the truth, not selling bioweapons, or blackmailing the government with the threat of unleashing deadly substances.

"Pull up here," Hunt told Jez. They were a hundred yards away from Pip's vehicle, closer to the neighbor on the east's driveway should Everson drive past unexpectedly.

He was anxious to get Pip out of there ASAP but not stupid enough to run into a situation blind. He had years of experience and training for raids, but not one of them had involved someone he cared about being smack bang in the middle.

They were already wearing ballistics vests and had spare ammo in their pockets. They paused only long enough to get Will's sniper rifle out the back of the truck and stuff their breathing apparatus into a duffle bag that Jez carried.

"You should stay here," Hunt told the scientist. "We don't know how dangerous this is."

Jez gave him a look. "Bullets are scary, but so are pathogens, Kincaid. Let's move it."

Hunt grinned but he wasn't feeling any humor. Pip was somewhere nearby and she might be in danger. If Everson spotted them and was involved he might try to take her hostage. They locked Jez's vehicle and headed into the woods, following as Will picked his way carefully toward the cabin. Hunt was aware how much noise he made, but Jez was like a bulldozer tromping through the forest.

Will held up his hand and raised the scope to his eye.

"I don't see any movement through the windows. A silver Prius in the driveway."

"Everson owns a Prius." Hunt confirmed. "You see Pip?"

Will shook his head.

Hunt tried to put his anxiety behind his training. It wasn't easy.

The overcast nature of the day helped them fade into the shadows, but they were still exposed and visible.

"Let's make our way through the woods using the trees for cover. I'm going to go first while you cover me," Will said. "When I get to that stump over there I should have a good visual of the back of the building and you can join me. I'll cover you from there."

Hunt nodded. He knew they should wait until backup arrived, but Pip was around here somewhere. Maybe she was having a perfectly normal conversation with Everson, or maybe he was feeding her chemicals so he could rape and murder her and stage her death as another overdose victim.

Had he really believed he could get away with this?

Hunt eased behind a big beech tree and took up position. He wished they had radios as their cells were useless. He waited until Will got into position then crept toward the cabin, cringing as Jez followed on his heels, as stealthy as a blind rhino.

Hunt moved cautiously until they reached a thick belt of trees. Out of sight he crouched and ran to where Will had set up.

"See anything?"

Will winced. "There's a figure lying on the ground just outside the backdoor. Looks like a woman."

Hunt felt himself go cold inside. "Let me look."

Will handed over the rifle and Hunt scanned the ground. He couldn't see the woman's face, but he recognized the shape and clothes and the glossy dark hair.

"It's Pip." He felt sick. She wasn't moving. He handed the rifle back. "I'm going in. Cover me."

Will gave him a hard stare then nodded. "Keep around the

back of the driveway. I don't see any windows on that side of the house."

Hunt was grateful the man didn't try to stop him. He ran, keeping low as he worked his way to the back of the building. Once at the driveway he hugged the shadows as he moved quickly over the ground. He ducked behind the car and then worked his way to where Pip lay unmoving.

He touched her neck, searching for a pulse and felt a slow rhythmic rush of blood that almost floored him. But he couldn't afford to drop his guard and he kept his weapon raised, eyes on the house.

The backdoor was slightly ajar.

He placed his hand on her back, trying to forget how her skin felt against his lips. Pip's chest rose and fell steadily. She was breathing and had a pulse. He ran his hand over her hair, coming across a wet, sticky patch with a bump to match.

Shit. Someone had hit her hard enough to knock her out.

Anger filled him but he pushed it aside. He needed a cool head to do his job. He didn't dare move her unless she was in imminent danger. He might cause irreparable harm if he did. He waved Will over. "She's breathing but unconscious. Go up to the road and call for an ambulance. I'm going to take a quick look around, see what I can see."

He didn't give Will time to argue. He eased around the eastern side of the cabin and slipped quietly up the stairs that led toward the deck. He crouched as soon as he had a visual. The entire front of the building was windows and he held still and peered inside, trying to make sense of the deepening shadows. It took time for his eyes to adjust to the semi-darkness. Nothing moved. Every second away from Pip felt like hours but he had to secure the scene and make sure it was safe for the paramedics to approach.

A movement caught his eye. Something sleek and feline. A white cat. The animal was lapping at something on the floor.

Ah, shit.

Hunt finally made out the shape in the chair. It was a person, and from the lack of movement they were also unconscious or dead.

He eased back down the steps and went back around the rear of the property.

Jez appeared out of the shadows, holding the anthrax detector aloft, taking measurements.

Hunt waited for Will to return, one hand on Pip's back trying to comfort her, the other holding his gun drawn, ready for trouble. A couple of minutes later, Will returned, blowing hard, lungs panting. Hunt handed him a set of breathing apparatus, and Will slung his rifle across his back, SIG Sauer in hand.

Hunt nodded silently and they both pulled on the masks. It had a clear plastic face plate with good vision. Backup wasn't far away. They didn't have time to hang around if Pip was going to get the help she needed. Hunt pushed her out of his head even as worry ate at him.

He used hand signals to tell the scientist to stay put. He and Will inched past Pip up the front stairs. Hunt kept his eyes off her lax form.

He and Will headed inside. Closing the door behind them as they entered. If there were anthrax spores here he didn't want them escaping.

His breathing sounded loud in his ears, his heart rate faster than he wanted. Worry for Pip was dragging at his concentration and he couldn't afford the distraction. Neither could his partner.

He waited a moment, settled his spinning brain and nodded at the other man when he was ready. They moved in rapid formation, clearing each room, looking for danger and UNSUBs. In the living room, Professor Everson was sitting in the chair, gun in his right hand. The cat looked up, blood on her whiskers and Hunt's stomach turned. The creature was lapping at the professor's blood. He snapped back to the moment, checking behind the kitchen island, the bathroom, up the stairs, moving quickly, efficiently.

Sweat ran down his back, his breath fogging up the inside plastic of the mask.

"It's clear," Will stated.

Lowering his weapon, Hunt jogged back down the stairs and checked Everson's pulse. Dead. Half his brain was missing so it was just as well.

A camera sat on the small table beside the recliner. A laptop computer was open on the kitchen island. Hunt went over and tapped a button, expecting a password request but instead opening to a Word file.

"Suicide note." Hunt scanned it quickly. "Says here he's the one who tried to sell the anthrax. Scene's secure. Let's get out of here and let Jez test the place while we get Pip the help she needs."

Will nodded and they headed out the way they'd come in, whipping off the heavy plastic and gulping in gallons of fresh air. Jez waved the wand of the machine over them both but nodded indicating they appeared anthrax free.

Hunt went to Pip's side and touched her cheek. Blood matted her hair. "Pip."

She groaned and it was pretty much the best sound he'd

ever heard, with or without clothes on.

"You're okay, Pip. Hang in there. We're gonna get you some help." Will had jogged back up to the road and Hunt knew he'd have the ambulance crew there ASAP.

Her eyes fluttered open. *Thank God.*

"What happened?" she asked.

He smiled. "I'm hoping you can tell me."

She tried to move and he pressed his hand to her shoulder. "Stay still. Paramedics are on the way."

She stilled but a frown formed between those dark eyes of hers. "I don't remember anything. I don't even know where I am."

"But you know who I am?" he asked cautiously.

She tried to laugh and winced. "I even remember you naked."

Hunt grinned, grateful Jez had gone inside to check for contamination. He wasn't ashamed of Pip. But this thing between them was new and it wasn't anyone else's business.

Seeing her hurt had made him appreciate he cared about her way more than he'd realized.

The sound of sirens and flash of lights as the cavalry arrived stopped him worrying about it. She was alive. The professor was the likely source of this anthrax and...and what? As soon as the call for selection went out he was off to Virginia.

But selection didn't last forever and when it was over maybe Pip would be interested in seeing him again.

And if he didn't make it into HRT...

He shook his head. He wasn't prepared to think that way. He had no intention of failing selection. Sure, they could still not pick him for the teams, but not because he failed.

Pip's hand snuck into his and squeezed. "Stay with me."

His heart gave a twist. "I need to do some things here first. I'll come to the hospital as soon as I can. Okay?"

Her mouth tightened and she blinked and withdrew her hand from his. "Okay."

He was pushed aside by a medic carrying a neck brace.

Hunt stood on the sidelines and watched them carefully move Pip onto a backboard and stretcher, and carefully load her onto the rig. She wouldn't meet his gaze and even though he wanted to be with her he couldn't. He had a job to do and part of that included figuring out what she was doing here and who the hell had hurt her. There was no weapon on the ground, nothing that looked like it could have been used to knock her unconscious.

If he had to guess he'd say the professor used his pistol to knock Pip unconscious before blowing his brains out, but the FBI didn't guess at evidence. They collected it. And because of his relationship with Pip he needed to take a backseat in this part of the case so he didn't jeopardize anything in court. He couldn't go with Pip either, until she'd been interviewed. Even talking to her just now could violate some procedure somewhere but he hadn't been about to stand by and watch her suffer.

She meant something to him.

Dammit.

So did his job.

The paramedics were about to close the doors.

"Wait!" He ran over and jumped inside and pressed a quick kiss to her brow. "As soon as I'm done here I'll be there, okay?"

Her eyes were clouded with pain as she smiled. "You better."

"Give me your car keys. I'll drive the SUV back for you."

He patted her jeans pocket and found her keys.

He jumped out of the rig and the ambulance sped away.

He was reminded of Monday morning when a rig had taken Cindy Resnick's body away from a lake not far from here. Had she been involved in this scheme? Or had the prof acted alone?

He'd figure it out so Pip didn't have to.

CHAPTER TWENTY-SEVEN

M ANDY FULLER GOT out of her silver sedan and approached the large detached house in the quiet, leafy Atlanta neighborhood. She swore when she checked her work cell, there was something wrong with the thing and it seemed to leech power. She needed to get a new one, but dammit, she didn't have time. And she'd stupidly left her personal cell at home.

She'd grabbed lunch on the way over, irritated that the team she'd had working with her yesterday had all been diverted onto this mysterious BLACKCLOUD investigation. Will had promised to fill her in on what he could that night.

Then she'd heard from a contact at the DMV that a truck matching the description of the one from the shooting yesterday had been found burned-out last night at an illegal dumping ground. It was registered to a soldier named Cory Slater who was currently deployed. The sister reported it stolen from her driveway when she'd gotten home from work last night.

It may or may not be the one she was looking for but it was worth asking a few questions. She made a note to contact the soldier. See if this was an insurance job or a personal grudge.

Mandy would be lying if she said she wasn't pissed to be

missing out on the excitement back at the office. The fact Hunt had been involved in tracking down a bioweapons terrorist and had still allowed himself to get distracted by the journalist pissed her off. You could bet your last cent she or the other female agents would have been kicked off the case if they'd gotten sidetracked by some good-looking dude.

This week, Mandy had already helped take down a major corruption ring and was now leading an inquiry into the shooting attempt of a federal agent. And would anyone remember that work in the months to come? Hell, no. It would all be swamped by the news of a potential biological weapon.

The wind rustled the leaves overhead and she blew out a matching sigh.

Women had to work twice as hard and fight three-times as dirty to achieve anything, and that went extra for law enforcement and military.

She hadn't wanted to date Will for that reason. She was ambitious. He was good at everything she was good at, and better at others. She didn't want to end up in his shadow.

She thought of his sexy grin. Damn if she wasn't smitten anyway. And the idea he thought she didn't know about his impending application to HRT?

She snorted out loud.

She could admit to herself she liked keeping him on his toes, but she wasn't sure how they'd handle a long distance relationship. They were about to find out.

She loved him.

Mandy checked out the property as she strode up the driveway. It was a really nice house. Sienna brown brickwork and red, painted shutters. Mandy would have to marry up or win the lottery to afford a place like this.

No one worked for the federal government for the big bucks.

There was a nice Merc pulled up next to the attached garage at the back of the house.

Mandy was convinced that yesterday's shooter had been targeting Pip West. She'd reviewed the woman's background and there were a few potential red flags. Pip came from a broken, abusive home and had grown up in foster care. Discounting her recent inheritance, she wasn't wealthy, but she didn't carry any significant debt either. And she did have an iron-clad alibi for her friend's death.

The journalist had a reputation for doing investigative work that had pissed off some very important people in Florida. Mandy had called Ms. West's editor but the guy had played hardball with information.

Maybe Hunt could get more out of her.

Her lip curled. Kincaid was a good agent, a hard worker, but in her experience, men were easy to manipulate. And if someone was involved with something dicey why wouldn't they cozy on up to the nearest handsome federal agent?

So what if she was cynical? Naivety got you killed.

She knocked on the front door and stood back, to the side, hands in front of her and close to her service weapon.

A woman with long, red hair, loose around her shoulders answered. She had a slight frame and was in workout gear, sweating slightly, as if she'd been running.

"Can I help you?" she asked politely, her eyes shooting to the creds Mandy held up in front of her.

"Beatrice Grantham?"

Two small lines marked the skin between her elegantly plucked brows. "That's me."

"You reported your brother's truck stolen yesterday."

"Wow." The woman's eyes went wide. "They sent the FBI?"

Mandy huffed out a quiet laugh. "I have a few questions and was wondering if I could come in for a moment?"

The woman wiped her brow on the sleeve of her gray tee. "It's not really a good time—"

"This will only take a minute."

The woman's shoulders bobbed as she sighed. "Fine. But I was in the middle of a workout. Come on in."

Mandy followed her inside, eyes huge as she took in the beautiful home. A TV blared in the background.

"Would you mind coming through to my home gym? I left the TV on back there."

"Your brother is in the Army."

Pursed lips showed her worry and disapproval. "Iraq. I was hoping to get his truck back quickly so he never has to know about this."

"Fond of it?"

The woman rolled her eyes. "You'd think they were dating."

They walked through an airy hallway and a white kitchen with wooden countertops. Mandy was having a major case of house envy.

Through the back of the house until they came to a gym area complete with weight machines, treadmill and workout mats. The TV was so loud Mandy had to resist the urge to protect her ears. She took a step farther into the room as Beatrice Grantham headed for the TV.

A fiery pain burst through her and she looked down to see blood blooming on the front of her shirt. Oh, God. She'd been shot! She tried to take a breath but the pain was crippling. She dropped to her knees and before her numb fingers could grapple with the snap, someone stepped up behind her and grabbed her Glock out of its holster.

"Watch out!" Mandy cried out in warning to the other woman.

Beatrice Grantham reduced the volume on the TV, turned and said calmly, "That's better."

She looked to whoever stood behind Mandy and nodded. Mandy closed her eyes. She'd made the classic mistake in underestimating a female based on her looks. She wished she'd told Will how much she loved him today. She wasn't going to get another chance.

CHAPTER TWENTY-EIGHT

PIP LAY IN the hospital bed and stared at the white tiles on the ceiling. She'd had an MRI and eight stitches. Apparently, she was very lucky. They'd given her something for the pain and now there was a dull thudding at the back of her skull.

Heaven help her when her luck ran out.

The electronic beep of machines and murmur of voices in the corridor formed a white noise that threatened to lull her to sleep. She frowned, desperately trying to remember what had happened. She'd been at Blake and spoken to Adrian Lightfoot and then she'd been driving, but after that she… Heck, she didn't remember much except waking up on the ground and Hunt holding his weapon like he expected to use it.

Her door opened and her heart leapt in stupid anticipation. It wasn't Hunt. One of his friends, the FBI agent she'd met yesterday at the shooting, came into the room. She couldn't remember his name. He had dark skin, a handsome face, intelligent eyes.

"Ms. West? Remember me? Will Griffin with the FBI. I'm a friend of Agent Kincaid's."

It felt weird hearing Hunt called by his official title again after spending last night naked in his bed. It was a good reminder of who and what he was.

"I was hoping this was a good time to ask you a few questions about what happened earlier today? We need to get a statement."

She tried to sit up but broke out in a cold sweat as a rush of vertigo swept over her. A wave of nausea followed but she managed not to throw up.

Yup, she was lucky all right.

"Steady." Will Griffin stepped forward and raised her bed a few inches. "Can I get you anything?"

"Where's Agent Kincaid?" Her voice came out crackly.

Will Griffin handed her a water glass. She drank greedily through a straw, the moisture relieving her parched mouth and throat.

"Agent Kincaid has been reassigned from your case."

"My case? What case?"

"Figuring out who hit you over the head." He smiled, dark eyes crinkling at the corners. "It's complicated."

She frowned and the action pulled the skin of her scalp. *Ouch.* "Does this have anything to do with my friend Cindy's death?"

He pulled up a chair and leaned toward her. "What do you remember from this morning?"

Was Hunt in trouble for sleeping with her? Why would he be? Was she on some sort of FBI *persona non grata* blacklist? She hated the idea of hurting his career. He'd told her how much his job meant to him.

"I went to the university first thing." Her thoughts cleared a little, though the fog didn't lift. "I was looking for Cindy's advisor and the head of department told me he was at his cabin." Her eyes went to Will Griffin's. "I didn't mention it, but I knew where that was because I'd driven there with Cindy over Christmas to drop something off."

"Why did you want to talk to the professor?"

Will Griffin had a lovely voice. Deep and soothing but she wished it was another agent asking her questions. She wanted to know what was going on.

"Cindy's funeral is this coming Sunday and I wanted to ask the professor to be a pallbearer." She touched her forehead and took another sip of water. "I have a vague recollection of driving to his cabin but then it just goes blank." The doctor had told her it was traumatic amnesia and said the memory may or may not return.

"Do you remember collecting the mail out of his mailbox?"

"No." Pip shook her head. "I just remember waking up when Hunt found me." Tears filled her eyes. Where was he? He'd told her not to run away from what was going on between them so why wasn't he here? She forced back the tears. He'd said he'd be here when they'd both been interviewed.

"You're lucky we turned up when we did."

"Why was the FBI there?" she asked. "Why did they want to talk to the professor?"

"I can't say."

Pip rolled her eyes and let out a big sigh. "You realize how irritating that is, right?"

He laughed. "Sometimes I have to be irritating to do my job properly."

"Me, too." She said it dryly.

He smiled but his eyes looked the way Hunt's had when they'd first met. Tainted by suspicion.

Pip didn't honestly feel like a reporter anymore. She'd lost the drive she'd once had, that the public had a right to know everything and make up its own mind. Maybe it was just the throbbing skull but something had shifted inside her over the last two weeks. Something fundamental. Guilt from the Booker case. Cindy's death. Realization that sometimes the public's best interest wasn't served by transparency. Should the public know the name of every spy? That was a crazy idea.

None of that mattered right now. "I wish I could tell you more about what happened or who hit me, but I don't remember." A sudden thought broke through the fog. "Is the professor okay?"

Will Griffin pursed his lips and shook his head. "I'm afraid the professor was found dead at his cabin."

"What?" Her mouth dropped in horror. "How is that possible?" Another terrible thought entered her mind. "Oh, my God. You don't think I did it, do you?" Was that why Hunt wasn't here? He thought she was a killer? Again?

"Honestly?" Will's dark brown eyes held hers and she didn't look away. "I don't know exactly what happened."

"You think I killed the professor and hit myself with a rock." She couldn't hide the bitterness in her voice.

"Did you?"

She pulled a face and tentatively touched the tender area of her scalp. "I'd have faked it less realistically." She didn't care what the Fed believed. She tried to work out what might have happened. "So someone hit me and killed him. Or killed the professor and then I turned up before they'd left so they hit me over the head." She frowned, trying to remember details but the harder she tried the more difficult it was to recall anything.

"Don't stress about this right now."

"Am I in danger?" Because this wasn't the first time someone had tried to kill her lately and it was getting a bit old.

He hesitated. "I don't believe so."

She nodded slowly, trying but failing to make sense of it all. "Does this have something to do with Cindy's death?"

"Let's just say you made us dig deeper into Ms. Resnick's circumstances and see the possibility that maybe there was more to it than originally met the eye."

"I don't understand." He was speaking in riddles. Not telling her anything. "Are you saying you think Cindy was murdered now? What about Sally-Anne and the drug dealer?"

Will climbed to his feet, obviously not about to confide. His lack of cooperation drove her crazy but she knew he had to be professional about his job. A bit like another federal agent she knew.

"Hunt's not coming, is he?" she asked quietly.

Will hesitated. "If you care about him at all it would be better if you didn't contact him again," he said softly before leaving.

The sharp sense of hurt was quickly squashed. It was nothing more than she'd expected.

Ironic that the FBI were now doing what she'd asked them to from the start. And because of that Hunt would have to stay away.

A wave of tears swept over her unexpectedly and she stared at the ceiling as they dripped down the sides of her face. She knew better than to let people get too close. God knew she'd been let down too many times to count.

She couldn't afford this sort of weakness.

She clenched her fists into the blanket. Thank goodness she'd figured it out now, before she'd lost her heart to him. She swallowed and ignored the swell of fresh tears.

Yeah, thank goodness.

———————

HUNT PACED OUTSIDE the professor's cabin. He wanted to go to Pip but he knew he couldn't. Not yet. The cabin and grounds were crawling with Feds and men in spacesuits as if an alien invasion had begun.

Jez Place had run the field testing equipment over the entire place and come up clean, but there were vials full of bone white powder in the refrigerator marked SAHCAM45-65. CDC had searched the professor's laboratory at Blake and come out with both spores and something that looked like the vaccine.

Again—nothing unexpected under the circumstances but only extensive tests would reveal whether or not they were the same as that being sold with the bioweapon.

According to the lab notes CDC had found, Cindy had been testing her new super vaccine against the SAHCAM45-65 strain that Everson had presumably gotten from Grossman.

According to those notes the vaccine had worked, which was the only good news in this shit-fest of disasters.

CDC had run some preliminary tests on cell cultures infected with the weaponized *Bacillus anthracis*. The vaccine they'd replicated from the BLACKCOUD source looked promising. They needed to compare the composition of it directly to that of Cindy's vaccine to confirm they were one and the same.

Current theory was Professor Everson had tried to sell the anthrax and vaccine to make some fast money and also to increase the value of his patent. If an enemy nation had access to this type of bioweapon and its antidote, then you could be damned sure the U.S. would want to mass produce the vaccine, too.

Hence, a big profit for the holders of the patent.

Another agent from the Atlanta Field Office—Kevin Christian—came out of the cabin carrying a plastic evidence bag. Inside was the camera Hunt had noticed on the table near the professor's body.

Kevin turned the display to Hunt and pressed play. There on the screen was the video that had been sent to the FBI late last night.

It was damning evidence.

"You find the voice modifier anywhere?" Hunt asked.

"Not yet. Suicide note on his laptop said he was sorry. It was extensive. Said he'd done terrible things, and everything got out of control. He'd killed Cindy to stop her submitting her thesis after he'd discovered the bioweapons arms deal was intercepted by the FBI. Tried to make it look like an overdose," Kevin told him.

"Prof figured it was only a matter of time before the CDC matched the anthrax source to SAHCAM45-65 and he knew Cindy wouldn't keep quiet about the fact that he had it in his lab, or that her vaccine had been successful at combatting the disease."

So Pip had been right the whole time he'd been blowing her off.

"Said he'd panicked and when the FBI started investigating Cindy's death he'd tried to make it look like part of a string of drug deaths. He'd slept with Sally-Anne in the past and knew where she bought her drugs. He said he'd put it in her drink so she'd OD then called the dealer to meet him in a place they'd met before. Guy never saw it coming."

Hunt remembered the scene at Sally-Anne's apartment. He'd done more than just feed her drugs. "That's quite the note."

"Full confession." Kevin nodded. "After that he talks about the fact he'd sent the video and infected the co-pilot—he didn't say how or where—and finally he'd realized it would never end. Said he couldn't carry on anymore. He knew the FBI would catch up with him eventually. Decided to take the easy way out."

Hunt had never figured putting a bullet in your own skull would be easy but he'd never been that desperate.

He handed the camera back to Kevin who put it in a sealed evidence canister in the trunk of an evidence technician's car.

"You believe it?" Hunt asked.

The guy shrugged. "It rings true. There's motive. Increasing desperation as every act snowballed..."

Hunt had spoken to the professor twice this week. So much for his instincts. "I need to talk to Pip."

Kevin shook his head. "She has to be questioned first and last I heard she was sleeping after an MRI."

The guy pre-empted Hunt's next question.

"MRI came back normal. She's got a sore head but no brain bleed or permanent damage that they can ascertain. There's blood on the base of Everson's weapon we can try to match to West. The Glock is registered to Cindy Resnick by the way."

Shit. All the times Hunt had blown Pip off with her theories about Cindy's death and it looked like she'd been right all along.

"Hey, if she's serious about you she'll understand you need

to do your job." Kevin eyed him with subtle amusement.

"The same way we're always so understanding of the press doing their jobs," Hunt said wryly.

"Hah," the agent laughed. "But you have to let the process work, else this situation will always hang over your head. She's in the hospital. Give us time to clear her. How much trouble can she get into in the hospital?"

"Knowing Pip? Plenty." But Kevin was right. He had to play this by the book if he didn't want it to mess up his career. The HRT at the FBI was all he'd *ever* wanted. Hunt let some of the tension ease out of him. Pip had to know how the process worked. Once the FBI had gathered all the evidence from the scene and questioned everyone involved independently he could go to her.

Not until.

If she cared about him at all she'd forgive him. If she didn't...better to find out now before either of them got more involved. It had been a rough few days. They were crazy for getting involved at all.

Kevin disappeared back inside and Hunt decided to head back to the city. He walked up to Cindy Resnick's old SUV and climbed in. Pip's purse was in the front seat.

Hunt started driving and after a minute or so found himself in range of a cell tower. His phone started pinging with messages so he pulled over to check them.

He called Hernandez back first, hooked up Bluetooth and carried on driving.

"Although Everson said he was at a conference when the Resnick woman died," the analyst told him, "he could have driven there and back to Nashville without anyone noticing."

"Any witnesses to say he was there?"

"We're questioning people but no one we talked to so far was with him that evening."

Hunt expelled a deep breath. Was it over? It seemed like it was over. The professor had tried to cover up his attempted illegal sale of a biological weapon by murdering the one person who'd be able to definitively link him to the strain. The connection to Cindy's work would have come out as soon as her thesis was submitted and her papers published.

He'd never have been caught if the FBI hadn't intercepted the weapons sale.

"Who kills three people to cover up committing a crime?"

"Four if he did the widow. And what sort of person tries to sell a biological agent that could kill thousands of innocents to an enemy of the United States?" Hernandez swore colorfully, then sighed. "We'll compare the ballistics of the bullets from the professor's gun to those that killed the dealer."

He voiced what was bothering him. "Everything seems neatly packaged, except for a few loose ends…"

He didn't know but the adrenaline surge had come and gone and right now he was exhausted. Time to head back to Atlanta and write up his report. He needed to hold onto his patience until he was cleared to visit Pip. He had a feeling he owed her a very large apology.

CHAPTER TWENTY-NINE

HUNT JOGGED UP the stairs to Bourne's office, grateful not to get waylaid by other agents wanting to know what had happened at the professor's house. What he really wanted was to go see Pip in the hospital, but instead his SAC wanted to see him. And, right now, he couldn't reach out to her no matter how much he wanted to. Not yet. Not until they'd figured out exactly what had gone down there and how her friend might be involved in their investigation.

He knocked on the door.

"Come in." Bourne looked up from a report he was reading. "Care to explain what the hell is going on."

Hunt told him exactly what had gone down at the professor's house. The fact Hunt could talk about it without throwing up proved he was a professional, because the thought of how close Pip had come to death was gut churning. "All appearances suggest the professor could be the bioweapons supplier. It looks like he hit West on the head and then shot himself."

"So this journalist turns up at the moment the professor decides to end it all," Bourne said, frowning. "And he gets pissed because she interrupts him and bumps her on the head? Why not shoot her, too?"

"I don't know," Hunt said.

"Maybe she's involved. Maybe she's the one selling anthrax."

Hunt widened his stance and crossed his arms. "She was seriously injured."

"She could have faked it. Killed the professor, knocked herself on the head with a rock."

The SAC hadn't seen the amount of blood she'd lost, Hunt reminded himself, holding on to his anger. "There was nothing near the body with blood on it. I don't see how she could have knocked herself out and got rid of the weapon."

Bourne stood and paced. "She could have hit herself just hard enough to split the skin and tossed the rock."

"Evidence techs think she was hit with the butt of the Glock the professor used to kill himself," said Hunt patiently.

"Did they find her blood inside the professor's cabin?"

Hunt shook his head. "They haven't had time to analyze the blood stains yet, sir."

"So it is possible?" Bourne pushed.

"And what? She offs the professor, hits herself on the head hard enough to bleed, copiously by the way, and then just went and laid down on the ground outside in the hopes we'd turn up? She had no way of knowing anyone would find her anytime soon." He hadn't told Pip where he was going or what he was doing today. Last time he'd seen her, before finding her injured, had been when he'd followed her back to the hotel that morning.

Bourne stared at him hard. "You know we have to look at all possibilities, no matter how improbable, right Kincaid?"

Hunt grudgingly nodded. Of course, they did. "West has been hounding me from day one to look more closely into her friend's death and even ordered a second autopsy. She was staking out her friend's ex-boyfriends trying to figure out where Cindy got the cocaine when all the time we were insisting it was accidental drowning complicated by an overdose and trying to get her to let it go." Hunt forced himself to keep his voice calm.

Bourne sat back down in his chair. "I agree, the fact that she's the one who demanded the second autopsy works in her favor, but that doesn't mean she couldn't have a different motive we haven't explored. And I think the fact that you can't see that means your objectivity where West is concerned is compromised."

Hunt gritted his teeth over what he wanted to say.

"She and the professor could have been working together and she might have worried they were close to getting caught. Maybe he's the one who shot at you yesterday? Maybe she tried to wheedle her way into the investigation by coming on to you."

Shit. Even though Hunt didn't believe Pip had deliberately tried to get close to him—and it was virtually impossible to get physically closer than they'd been last night—bad guys often insinuated themselves into investigations.

SAC Bourne's face set into stern lines. "What about this?"

His boss turned his computer monitor towards Hunt. The online headline screamed "*FBI and CDC probe suspicious deaths of bioweapon experts.*"

"Even if West isn't involved in the BLACKCLOUD investigation this headline probably persuaded the professor that it was all over. His threatening video hadn't worked and it was only a matter of time until he was exposed."

"I don't believe Pip leaked any information to the press."

Bourne scratched his head and Hunt knew he was totally

doubting Hunt's objectivity.

"Where'd the professor film the video he sent last night?" Hunt pushed.

"We don't know." Bourne admitted.

"How'd he infect the co-pilot?" asked Hunt.

"Still under investigation." Bourne leaned back in his chair and Hunt spotted the exhaustion marking the man's features. "We might never know now. The prime architect of this scheme appears to be dead. We don't know if he had stockpiles of anthrax or successfully sold off any other batches. Maybe he's sent packages in the mail. Maybe he's got some unknown accomplice who will release it from the top of a tall building in some major metropolitan area. But we won't know until it's too late now because he shot himself after someone leaked the story to the press and the heat was too much to bear. But hey," the SAC smiled without it touching his eyes, "at least the press has a great headline."

Shit. "Am I off the case?" Hunt asked, keeping his spine ramrod straight.

"Should you be?"

Hunt swallowed tightly. "I am involved with Pip West. I should probably remove myself from the BLACKCLOUD investigation." The loud explosion was his career imploding— all for a woman who might never want to see him again.

"Did you lie to me or just deliberately disobey orders, Agent Kincaid?"

"I never lied to you, sir. I do not believe Pip is guilty of anything except trying to discover the truth about her friend." Talking back to his SAC was probably going to get him in more trouble but damned if he wasn't going to defend himself after working his balls off.

Bourne crossed his arms and looked down at his large desk. "You're probably right, but we are playing this by the book. You're back on the white-collar squad. I will probably need to talk to the Office of Professional Responsibility about this."

Hunt's gut squeezed but fuck it, he hadn't done anything wrong and he didn't believe Pip had either. He refused to plead his case.

The worst thing about this whole scenario was all the hard work they'd put in and they were still unsure as to the extent of this bioweapon threat and clueless as to whether or not the danger was over. But Hunt was off the investigation so he couldn't even help figure it out. Not his business. Not anymore. It was over.

PIP WOKE TO darkness, but there was enough ambient light from the muted TV to see Hunt sprawled asleep in the uncomfortable looking chair beside her bed. Her heart clenched at the sight of his ruffled hair and scruff covered jaw.

She raised her bed with the automatic controls. She still had a headache but at least the fierce pain had dulled to a throb.

The slight buzz of the bed mechanism had Hunt slowly opening his eyes. "How are you feeling?"

He stretched out that magnificent body and her heart started beating harder and faster, which would have been fine if she was the only one who noticed.

Hunt glanced at the monitor and then at her heated cheeks and grinned. "I'm hoping that means you're a little better." His brows slid together in concern. "And not that you're about to go into cardiac arrest."

She closed her eyes and drew in a breath until she felt it all the way down in her solar plexus trying to center herself and her whirling emotions. She shouldn't be this happy to see him. "I didn't think you'd be allowed to visit."

"Allowed?" He scooted toward her and picked up her hand in both of his. "I told you I'd come as soon as I was able."

"Yeah, but I spoke to your buddy Will earlier and he said—"

"Will can be a dick."

She let out a huff. "I guess I should be grateful it wasn't Agent Fuller."

He leaned over her, still cradling her hand like he was scared he was gonna hurt her if he touched her anywhere else. "Don't think I didn't notice you didn't answer my question about how you're feeling. Trained federal agent, remember?"

She laughed properly this time and then winced. "I'm fine. I wanna go home."

Except she didn't have a home and that realization hit her hard. She was sick of staying in the hotel but didn't want to stay at Cindy's. The reminders of all she'd lost were too huge, too tangible.

"Let me talk to the nurse. If she approves we'll go back to mine and you can sleep."

She arched a brow although inside her heart melted just a little. "I don't remember much sleeping last time I was in your bed."

"Which is why I'm so goddamn tired today." He stroked her hand to the tips of her fingers. "But today you have a slight concussion so it'll be sleep and nothing else, young lady." He went to stand up but she gripped his forearm.

"Thank you. For rescuing me."

His eyes crinkled and she held on tight to her galloping pulse. "I'm grateful you were okay. When I saw you lying there…" His Adam's apple bobbed up and down his throat as he swallowed. "Fuck, Pip. At first I thought you were dead." He held her gaze, his pupils wide. "That sucked. So no need to thank me, just no more trying to give me a heart attack, okay? I get enough excitement in my job."

Something changed in his eyes then, but she couldn't read it.

She nodded, afraid that if she opened her mouth she'd spew tears and heartfelt pledges of love.

No one fell in love after a few days. It was crazy. Except, there was that whole love at first sight cliché. And clichés became clichés for a reason…

She shifted uncomfortably. There was too much going on in her life to even think about anything as dumb as falling in love with a guy she'd just met. A federal agent. A man who was probably already regretting the trouble she was causing him.

He came back into the room. "Nurse said they'd planned to keep you in for observation but if I promised to watch over you tonight you could sign out. I'm game if you are."

His grin was sinful and Pip's heart gave another little tumble. She could easily fall in love with him but the chances of him loving her back? Right up there with the Bucs winning the Super Bowl.

She knew these thoughts were crazy. She was twenty-eight years old, not eighteen. Eventually this would end the way every other relationship she'd ever had did. In heartbreak.

At least I'm not too terrified to date.

Cindy's voice reverberated in her mind. Pip was terrified. She didn't know how to handle letting anyone get close. But right now, she wanted to be with him and he seemed to want to be with her so she wasn't going to over think it or fight it. She was just going to try and be less terrified of life.

"Get me out of here. Please."

———————————

HUNT CARRIED PIP through his front door even though she insisted she could walk.

"This is my one chance to be chivalrous. Don't ruin it," he told her.

She was wearing cotton scrubs, her clothes having been taken into evidence. After Will had left she'd realized they'd be looking for blood splatter from Professor Everson, which they wouldn't find. She'd insisted someone come and test her hands for gunshot residue, too. She had nothing to hide.

She grabbed onto Hunt's leather jacket, enjoying the feel of those hard muscles and strong arms that lifted her with ease. Maybe there were some advantages to being petite. He shut the door with his foot and carried her straight through to the bed that was still unmade from last night.

It was weird to be back here, in his space.

He eased her down, propped pillows behind her and stood, looking uncertain and rubbing the back of his neck. "Are you hungry?"

She grimaced and shook her head. Her stomach growling but her spinning head was telling her not to risk eating yet. The idea of throwing up in front of anyone was embarrassing. She wasn't used to being taken care of when she got sick. She usually just curled up under a duvet for a few days and wallowed in self-pity.

"I'll get you some water and let you sleep." He went to back away and she almost let him.

"Wait." She swallowed nervously before asking, "Would you mind holding me?"

He stopped moving and nodded a little awkwardly, slipping off his jacket and his weapon holster, kicking off his boots before climbing in beside her and pulling her against him.

Her cheek settled against his chest and it felt like coming home—which made no sense because home for her had always been a solitary place that didn't involve listening to someone else's heartbeat. She put her hand on his chest. He stroked his carefully over her hair.

She could get used to this. A scary thought.

"What did you want to show me, yesterday?" she asked.

She expected a joke about sex, but he slipped out of bed and came back with a framed photograph before returning to his position as her favorite pillow. She touched the cool surface of the glass. A formal image of a man in a suit. Handsome. With the same distinctive blue eyes as Hunt. "Your father?"

She felt him nod.

"I was seven when he died. You said I wanted to save the world, but you were wrong. I just wanted to save him."

"Did you want to avenge him, too?" She wasn't judging him.

"Maybe," his voice was soft in the darkness. "But, like I told you, the FBI caught and killed his murderer years ago, during another bank robbery. Once I put on a badge I realized I didn't need to avenge him, but I could help make sure other kids didn't go through what I went through."

She gently stroked his hand. "Except there's always someone somewhere, willing to hurt others."

He nodded and was silent. He put the photograph on the bedside table behind the lamp.

"I'm sorry about your father. If it helps I expect he'd be very proud of what you've become."

He grunted and she let it drop. "I think I need to rearrange Cindy's funeral. Postpone it."

His breath brushed the top of her head. "How much do you have left to do?"

"I'd hoped to ask the professor to do a reading and be a pallbearer. That's why I was at his cabin."

His arms tightened around her.

"Did you find who killed him? Your friend Will said the FBI were going to look deeper into Cindy's death. Do they think I was right?"

He groaned. "I'm not supposed to talk about this."

She tensed. She understood. She really did. But this was Cindy's life. Cindy's death. She needed to know.

"I can tell you some of it though."

Her fingers curled into his shirt.

"The lab found some inconsistencies with Cindy's scene."

"What kind of inconsistencies?"

"Minute traces of Rohypnol in her water bottle."

Pip's mind raced so fast it started to throb again with pain. The last time she'd heard from Cindy her friend had been on her run and said she wasn't feeling well. Pip's mouth went dry at the implications. "Anyone who knew Cindy knew she ran every day and always took her water bottle."

"It's worse than that." Hunt's voice was low and deep. "Traces of coke were also found in the champagne."

Pip felt her heart beat harder. "Someone forced the drugs into her system." She'd been right. "Someone killed her."

"Probably dosed her up with drugs and took her down to the lake for a swim, hoping she'd drown."

Horror for her friend swept over her in a fresh wave of anguish. "Was she raped?"

"We don't know. We'll test DNA, but we might never know."

"Was it the same person who killed the professor? What about Sally-Anne? Was her death a coincidence?" Did they know who it was? Was it the same person who'd shot at her and Hunt yesterday? Was she in danger?

She felt Hunt swallow.

"Right now, it looks like Professor Everson killed himself. Most of us think, but don't know for sure, that he's the one who hit you on the head."

"What?" Pip struggled to sit up, but Hunt held tight.

"Evidence points to the professor being involved in Cindy's death."

"What? How? Why?" Pip gave up resisting and collapsed to his chest.

He stroked her arm. "I can't tell you."

God, Pip hated this. Her brain tried to catch up but it was all so awful. Cindy had a good relationship with the man. Not buddies, but a mutual respect. The idea he'd possibly murdered her friend, his student, and others, and had attacked her... *Why?*

"Is he the one who shot at us?" she asked.

"Pip," Hunt's voice was strained. "I really can't discuss this."

Frustration rushed through her, but he'd already told her

more than she'd expected. She didn't want to get him into trouble, but even so... "I promise I won't say anything. I know everyone thinks I'm going to write some exposé but I don't even have a job. I don't even know if I want to be a journalist—"

"It's a criminal investigation." There was an edge to his tone now. "We have reasons for not putting it all out there in the public realm. Moral reasons. Legal reasons. Procedural reasons."

She tried to pull away but he kept his arms firmly around her. "Are you suggesting I'd do something immoral or illegal just to get a story?"

"No." He ran a frustrated hand through his hair. "Shit. I don't know what I mean right now. I need sleep. You need sleep." He sounded exhausted and she felt bad for badgering him when he'd obviously had a rough day. They both had.

She tried to fight her fatigue for a few minutes but she was so tired and the drugs she'd been given in the hospital were still dragging through her system and making her drowsy.

"Hunt," she said, drowsily.

"Yeah?"

"Thank you. For everything."

CHAPTER THIRTY

HUNT WOKE WITH Pip sleeping on his chest. He'd been hit by a lot of things over the last twenty-four hours, the most striking this new relationship with Pip West that was both exciting and scary as fuck. He tried not to think about being taken off the BLACKCLOUD inquiry or his boss reporting him to OPR. He checked the clock. He'd been asleep for three hours which was pretty much the norm this week.

Pip frowned in her sleep and he wondered if she was in pain. He needed to wake her soon. The doctor said the chances were slim she'd slip into a coma, but it was possible. Remembering how it had felt for those few brief moments when he'd thought she might be dead...

This was why he didn't get close, dammit.

He wasn't impetuous or stupid. He always looked before he leaped, but God help him, this woman brought out every protective instinct he possessed and that scared the hell out of him. He couldn't protect her any more than he'd protected his dad or his stepsister. Or Cindy Resnick for that matter.

Pip's sharp brain and constant drive for answers didn't bode well for his career, and he'd already told her more than he should because he wanted her to have some closure about her friend.

Mistake.

He didn't want his relationship with her to cost him the FBI career he'd worked so hard for, but he did want to see where this thing with Pip led. And he did want to make sure she was okay after today's attack. She didn't have anyone else.

He shook his head at his own bullshit. Even if there had been someone else to take care of her, he wanted to be the one doing it. He wanted her in his bed, in his home. Things were moving too fast to get an emotional handle on how he was feeling. It was all new territory for him.

Removing himself from the BLACKCLOUD investigation sucked but had been necessary. Hunt had done everything by the book and had not jeopardized the search for the bioweapons dealer, but SAC Bourne had still looked like he'd wanted to wrap his hands around Hunt's throat. Pip being involved in the bioweapon production made little sense, but could she have given the newspaper that story?

No. No way.

But if he thought it, even for an instant, then everyone else at the Bureau would, too. If he stayed with the FBI, and with Pip, he'd spend his entire career defending her.

Professor Everson's cabin was still being processed but it seemed like a slam-dunk that the professor had hit Pip and then killed himself. His suicide note suggested the trail of bodies had become too great so perhaps he hadn't had the heart to finish Pip off, or he'd assumed she was already dead.

Hunt couldn't shake the sense of uneasiness.

They'd been fed too many clues in this enquiry, every one of which had subsequently proved to be false.

Pip's hair tickled his nose but he ignored it. He liked holding her in his arms.

It was after midnight. He should sleep some more. Just as

he was dropping off he heard his work cell vibrating. Gently he disengaged from Pip and slid out from the warmth of her embrace.

He waited until he was in the kitchen before he answered the call. It was Hernandez. She obviously hadn't heard that he was officially off the case.

HER CELL PHONE was ringing. Pip reached out and groped around on the bedside table until she found it, bringing it to her ear, groggy and confused.

"Hello," she said.

There was silence on the other end and it took a moment to remember she was in Hunt's house. In his bed. And this was his phone.

Crap. She thrust the covers off of her and slowly sat up. Her head was sore, but not blindingly painful.

"Why are you answering Hunt's phone?" It was Hunt's friend Will and he sounded pissed. "Don't bother saying anything. I mean it's obvious, isn't it? Despite everything I said earlier. Haven't you caused him enough trouble? He's just lost his place on the case and lost yet another collar. And now he's facing an internal investigation thanks to the story you leaked to the newspaper."

Pip sat stunned. "What do you mean?"

"Forget it. Where is he? I need to talk to him."

She looked up and there was Hunt standing in the doorway holding a different cell to his ear.

"I'll call you back," he said to whoever he was talking to. He held out his hand and she passed the cell over to him.

What had Will meant?

"What's up, asshole?"

Pip watched the expression on Hunt's face turn from annoyance to concern.

"No. Why?"

All she could hear was Hunt's half of the conversation.

"You guys have a fight?" There was a pause while Will presumably answered. "What was the last thing she was doing?"

The lines in Hunt's forehead creased deeper into worry. Something was wrong, but Pip was trapped in the thoughts that circled her brain like vultures waiting to pick apart a carcass. What had Will been referring to?

"You spoken to Bourne?" said Hunt.

"You call all her girlfriends?"

"Call Bourne. Tell him what you told me. I'll be in the office in twenty minutes." Hunt hung up.

She spoke first. "I didn't mean to answer your phone. Sorry." For a woman who never used to apologize she was getting better at it.

There was a flicker in his eyes she couldn't interpret. Did he not believe her?

"I was asleep." She looked down at her toes. "I wasn't sure where I was when it rang."

"It's okay," he said tersely. "Sorry about Will. He's worried."

"He said you were off the case?" Quietness settled around them, full of unanswered questions. Then Hunt moved, changing into a fresh t-shirt so fast she didn't have time to appreciate those sexy muscles.

"I removed myself from the case," he said, not looking at

her. "After we found you unconscious at Professor Everson's house it immediately became a conflict of interest."

Guilt churned inside her. "I never meant to cause trouble for you."

Something flickered in his eyes again, but he didn't say anything. Didn't he trust her? She gritted her teeth and then forced herself to speak. "Will said you faced an internal investigation because of a story I leaked?" She said it lightly as if someone wasn't making her bleed.

Hunt shook his head as he pulled his weapon's harness over the maroon tee. "I don't believe you leaked the story."

She formed her hands into fists and rested them together on her thighs. That was good. "What story?"

He pulled on a clean pair of socks, then a pair of heavy black boots.

"What story, Hunt?"

"Something about the FBI investigating the deaths of these scientists."

"Why would I do that?" She frowned.

"To try and gain more interest in investigating Cindy's death." He dragged his hand through his hair and made it stand up. "I don't think you leaked anything, but that's the motive someone could assign."

"I would never betray you like that..." She swallowed, trying to get moisture into her dry throat. She would never do that. A personal relationship would always trump a story, and she would never betray a source. If he didn't see that how could they ever hope to have a real relationship?

He knelt beside her and swept her hair behind her ear. "Like I said, I don't think you leaked anything. My boss hates reporters."

"So do you."

"Not anymore." He smiled and put his hands over hers. "I have to head in. Go back to sleep. I'll call you in a couple of hours to check you're okay. Things are a mess right now, but I do trust you."

His cell phones rang, one after the other, but he ignored them both as they silently stared at one another. She wanted to believe in him. She wanted to believe in them.

His landline rang shrilly. His voice filled the air, and she jolted even as she realized it was his answering machine. She could hear him clearly from another room.

"Agent Kincaid. I tried your work and cell numbers but you didn't answer so I'm trying the other number you wrote on your business card."

Hunt climbed to his feet and strode out of the room. Pip followed him into the kitchen.

"This is Karen Spalding from Blake." The woman sounded stressed. "I really must object to FBI agents and the CDC coming onto the campus and removing anthrax and other biological samples in armed raids. It crosses a line. I don't care if there's a threat. The CDC can't simply walk in here and take whatever they want and make us look like villains."

Hunt stood next to the machine and bowed his head. Pip had already heard enough. Spalding left her number and rang off.

Biological samples. Threat.

Pip put a hand on the counter to steady herself.

Biological threat.

Anthrax.

Her mouth went bone dry. All evidence had pointed to

this from the start. Hunt's job. The way scenes had been processed—she'd been too traumatized to figure it out.

"So, you created a cover story about new procedures when dealing with dead scientists because you were concerned, what, Cindy was developing a biological weapon?" She laughed as she said it but Hunt's expression told her she was right.

"Oh, my God." Pip swallowed. It seemed fantastical and unreal.

You don't know everything.

"No way would Cindy hurt anyone," she told him firmly. "I assume you now believe it was the professor? He killed Cindy to hide the fact he was, what, making anthrax?" The notion horrified her. "Why didn't you warn me? I would have backed off—"

He sank his hands into his hair. "It's classified—"

"I could have died!" she yelled so hard a pain shot through her head. She closed her eyes and turned away from him, resting both hands on the counter.

"You can't tell anyone about this. If the general population find out there could be a mass panic..."

She shut out whatever he was saying. Despite what he'd said just minutes ago, he didn't trust her. Even if he did, his colleagues didn't. Hence him being in trouble at work and Will giving her shit on the phone.

"I need to go," Hunt said. "Fuller is missing. Can we talk about this in the morning?"

Emotions welled up in her throat again and she blinked back tears. She nodded and held still when he kissed her on the temple. Then he was gone, and she forced herself to push aside the fatigue and lethargy and move. No way could she stay here alone in his space.

She wasn't strong enough to protect her heart the way she needed to and it would hurt too much when it all went horribly wrong. And it *always* went horribly wrong. So much for "Never Give Up. Never Surrender" being tattooed to her skin.

The front door banged shut and she strode to the bedroom and picked up her purse. She was barefoot and dressed in scrubs but didn't care. She couldn't stay here.

She picked up the keys to Cindy's SUV and let herself out. Hunt was gone. She climbed into the vehicle, gingerly putting her bare foot on the pedal as she started the engine, grateful for the blast of warm air from the heater.

She called him. She wasn't going to be a coward about this. She wasn't going to lie to him. But he didn't pick up and a gutless part of her gave a sigh of relief.

"Hunt. I'm heading back to the hotel. I'm not comfortable staying at your house alone and I think we should back off for a little while. I…" God, this was so hard. Just a few minutes ago she'd been snuggling in his bed. "I appreciate all your kindness but this *thing* between us isn't going to work. You deserve someone better than me. Someone braver. Goodbye." She hung up and immediately felt as if she was going to be sick, and it wasn't from the head injury. It was the self-imposed madness of walking—no, running—away from a man who might just be the love of her life.

But they could never be compatible. She wasn't sure she could cope with him having a job that meant he couldn't confide in her about what he did. And even if she could accept it, he'd spend his entire career defending and apologizing for her. She couldn't bear the idea of putting him through that ordeal. Of undermining the only job he'd ever wanted. Better she break it off now before they both had their hearts crushed.

CHAPTER THIRTY-ONE

C INDY'S HOUSE KEY was on the fob and she remembered she'd left a few clothes in the bedroom at the Resnick's house.

It wasn't that far away and beat the heck out of entering the hotel barefoot and looking like an extra for *The Walking Dead*.

Ten minutes later she was letting herself into Cindy's house, moving quietly around the place out of habit. Why hadn't the alarm been set? She'd have to have a long talk to the cleaner about security.

She padded silently up the carpeted staircase. Walked past Cindy's closed bedroom door to her old room and turned on the light. Everything was dear and familiar. It crystalized something else. Tomorrow she was moving out of the hotel and into this house until she figured everything out. She opened a drawer and pulled out an old FSU tee and a pair of ragged jeans. She also found a gray hoodie, socks and a pair of old running shoes in the closet. Her phone rang and she checked the number. It was Hunt. He must have gotten her message.

She drew in a deep breath, but before she could answer the call she heard the creak of a floorboard and whirled around. In the doorway stood Adrian Lightfoot. His eyes were red-rimmed and his suit was creased as if he'd slept in it.

"Adrian," she exclaimed.

"What are you doing here?" they said in unison.

"I needed some clothing," Pip said, feeling awkward.

His eyes were a little wild and she started to feel uncomfortable. "Why are you here, Adrian?"

Her phone went silent. Hunt had given up on her.

Adrian opened his mouth and closed it again, then ran his hand through his blond hair, making it stand on end.

"I came over earlier. Fell asleep. I'm so sorry. I heard a noise and thought a burglar had gotten in."

Pip stared at him. And suddenly some of the things Cindy and Dane had said clicked into place. "You were in love with her. With Cindy."

He sniffed loudly and blinked as he looked away. "I was. I thought she loved me back. We'd been seeing each other for a few months and she texted me to tell me she'd finished and planned to submit the next day. I decided to go to the cottage, surprise her with some flowers."

Another thing became clear. "It was your DNA on the bedsheets."

Why hadn't Cindy mentioned she was seeing him?

His lips twisted. "Probably. I'm not a hundred percent sure now."

"What do you mean?"

"Cindy was stringing me along. Seeing other men."

Pip frowned. "She wouldn't do that."

He tilted his head. "She started seeing me when she was still dating that clown Dane."

Pip shook her head. "She wouldn't have been sleeping with you both at the same time. Why didn't she tell me about you two?"

"I asked her not to. She's a client for God's sake, not to mention way too young for me."

"She was twenty-eight, old enough to make up her own mind about who she dated. You're not exactly ancient or hard on the eyes. And she could have gotten a new lawyer."

He looked stricken. "I wanted to take it slow. I told her to get someone else but she wanted me to handle the patent issues that were coming to a head."

Pip ignored the slight sting of hurt that Cindy had kept this from her.

Memories of their fight became clearer now. Sharper. More painful. Pip had accused Cindy of sleeping around when she was already in a relationship with this man. Cindy must have resented Pip's pious lecturing, especially if she'd promised Adrian she'd keep their relationship private.

His lip curled. "Stop pretending she was such an angel."

"She was—"

"Liar!" His voice cracked.

A tremor of fear raced through her. Had Hunt been wrong about who killed Cindy?

"That's what I thought too, until I saw her." He choked on a sob. "The night she died…"

A wave of ice crashed over Pip. Her fingers hovered over the redial button to Hunt's cell.

"She was fucking that asshole in the living room of the cottage."

"Wait. What?"

"Pete Dexter. That slimy bastard."

Pip's legs went from underneath her and she sat on the bed. "You saw her having sex with Pete Dexter the night she died?"

"She was naked. He had his clothes on." His voice was bitter. Pip could smell whiskey on his breath. "Trust me. She was having the time of her life—"

"No." Her stomach turned. Hunt thought the professor had killed Cindy. "Are you sure it was Pete? Not her advisor?"

"She was fucking her professor, too?" Adrian looked up at the ceiling. He was clutching a book. *Gone With the Wind*, she realized. It was in bad shape now, as if he'd been sleeping with it. Obviously, he'd been the one to give it to Cindy. It made sense now. He'd been in love with her. Had he also taken Cindy's journal so the authorities wouldn't question him?

"Why didn't you tell the cops about Pete?" Pip asked, incredulous.

"Because the autopsy said she died from drowning and drugs! I didn't want to destroy my career by admitting the affair. I didn't want the world to know I'd been a damned fool."

"But you're wrong about what happened." She wasn't sure she should tell him something Hunt had told her in confidence, but this man's pain cut through her and she needed him to understand Cindy hadn't betrayed him. "Someone roofied her water bottle when she went for a run. Then they force fed her champagne laced with cocaine."

Adrian frowned and swayed a little. "But I saw her…"

"You saw her being raped!" Fury erupted inside Pip.

Adrian's eyes widened. "What?"

"Someone drugged her and if what you're saying is correct"—because if he was lying she just realized she was alone in the house with a deranged lunatic who only had one reason to lie—"the same person raped her then fed her more cocaine."

Pete Dexter. Hatred filled her. She was going to kill the sonofabitch herself. "It's possible he either purposely led her to the lake, or just left her alone and in her altered state she decided to go for a swim."

Anguish followed by rage twisted Adrian's features. "I'm going to kill him."

She grabbed his arm but he shook her off and she fell to the floor. By the time she got over the immobilizing shock of the confrontation, Adrian was gone. She dragged herself upright, breathing heavily. Headed downstairs cautiously, following the lights that had been turned on throughout the house. She reached Cindy's dad's study and saw the safe was wide open. She checked inside. The gun was gone.

———————

PIP HAD CALLED Hunt's cell repeatedly and left messages that she urgently needed to talk to him about Cindy's death, but he wasn't returning her call. She'd called 911, but they hadn't taken her seriously, especially when she didn't know where Adrian or Pete were currently located. No way was she sitting and waiting all night for some busy detective to come and take a statement.

She drove to the apartment where Pete had lived when he was dating Cindy. It was in an exclusive neighborhood on the northeast side of the city. As far as she could tell from the databases she could access on her cell phone, he still lived here. She stared up at the window to the apartment but it was in darkness.

From what she remembered, Pete had been an early riser and went to bed early. It was now two in the morning and had already been a long day. She tapped her fingers on the steering wheel.

She couldn't see Adrian's car anywhere. If she called Pete to warn him about Adrian then she'd tip him off that they knew he'd raped Cindy and had probably been responsible for her friend's murder. And maybe he was involved in this anthrax thing the FBI was investigating.

Hatred welled up inside. No way would she let him wriggle out of receiving his full punishment. But she wanted it public. She wanted it legal. She wanted it *just*.

She decided to call his old landline and hoped the number hadn't switched to someone else. She masked caller information so he wouldn't see who was on the line. She just wanted to know where he was.

It rang four times before the answering machine kicked in. She called again.

Same lack of response. She sat in the car alone in the dark and suddenly realized what a fool she'd been. What a coward.

Hunt was investigating biological threats and murder. The fact he'd told her anything at all was a miracle of trust. That alone could cost him his job if his boss found out.

And she'd gotten scared because life had thrown some hard lessons at her. But shielding her heart by pushing people away didn't protect her, it just kept everyone on the other side. It kept her alone in the dark in the middle of the night trying to solve her friend's death when if she hadn't panicked and run she might be part of a team.

Loneliness crowded around her.

She dialed Hunt's number again and he didn't pick up. Had he already listened to her first message? The one she'd sent when in her fear she made herself unlovable so it would be easy to push her away?

She was such a mess.

She called again and left another message. She tried Pete's landline one more time but he didn't answer either. What if he was, at this very moment, trying to escape?

Her head had started to hurt again and a shiver ran over her shoulders and down her spine. She started the engine and blasted the air to wake herself up.

She'd take a drive past Pete's shiny company building and then onto the FBI Field Office and report what she'd learned.

She doubted she'd get another chance with Hunt but she couldn't let that get in the way of stopping Adrian from doing anything rash and bringing Pete Dexter to justice.

HUNT TOSSED DOWN the phone.

"Anything?" asked Will.

Hunt shook his head. This was not looking good.

Will leaned over his desk, mouth tense. Eyes worried.

Hunt had been furious with his buddy for trying to drive a wedge between him and Pip before they'd even had a chance at a relationship, but Fuller's disappearance was too serious to hold a grudge. Hunt had gone through Mandy's desk. She was gonna kill him when she saw the mess he'd made. But there was nothing to indicate where she'd been going that afternoon.

There was a BOLO out on her car. Local cops had been informed she was missing. Still nothing.

"She wouldn't disappear like this," said Will.

"You two didn't have a fight?"

Will shook his head. "Even if she was pissed with me she

wouldn't avoid me. More the other way around."

Hunt's phone rang. Pip. He gritted his teeth. He'd listened to her brush off earlier and he was still pissed and fucking *hurt* and had tried to call her back but she hadn't picked up. Kindness? She thought he was being fucking 'kind'? He didn't have time to deal with her insecurities right now. He'd put his ass on the line for her and she bailed at the first sign of trouble?

He let the call go to voicemail. He needed to take a step back right now. And maybe she was right. Maybe this thing wasn't going to work out between them and space would be a smart idea.

Sure. Whatever.

"What was the last phone call Fuller received?"

Will scrubbed his hand over his head. "I asked the switchboard but they don't know."

Hunt had an idea. He called SIOC. Libby Hernandez was still working. This anthrax threat meant everyone was pulling overtime. "We've lost an agent."

"Lost?" the analyst asked.

"Mandy Fuller. She's disappeared. Her boyfriend"—Will pulled a face at the description—"another agent at the Atlanta FO, hasn't heard from her since this morning. She isn't home, Bucar's not there either and we can't locate it. Her phone is turned off or dead. She wouldn't go dark like this. She was working the shooting from yesterday."

"You mean when someone tried to Swiss cheese your ass and you were saved by a bunch of romance novels?"

He sighed. "There were some thrillers in there, too." But this was going to become his FBI legend. He'd get romance novels every time he transferred offices. He'd get romance novels when he retired.

The craziest thing was he wanted to share the joke with Pip, but she'd run away because she was even more relationship-shy than he was.

None of it mattered. He was worried. About Mandy. About his career. About this thing with Pip. He knew she was scared. He was fucking scared. Like he didn't have everything that had ever mattered to him on the line. But Mandy was *missing*.

His phone beeped with a text.

"Last thing Mandy Fuller accessed on her work cell was an address." Hernandez reeled it off and he wrote it down and handed it to Will. "A truck matching the description of the one that was involved in yesterday's shooting was reported stolen from this address."

"Thank you. Can you tell me anything about who lives there?" Hunt pulled on his ballistics vest before grabbing his coat and heading out the door. Will followed close behind. They rushed out to the parking lot and took Will's Bucar which was a freaking Dodge Charger.

"Property and truck is listed as belonging to an active duty soldier named Cory Slater who is currently on deployment. House is jointly owned by his sister, Beatrice Grantham."

"Repeat that." Hunt didn't think he'd heard correctly.

"House owned by Cory Slater who is currently listed as being in Afghanistan and his sister Beatrice Grantham..."

"A Bea Grantham works for Universal Biotech Inc.," Hunt said quickly.

Will glanced at him as they pulled away.

"I don't like this. I don't like it at all. Call McKenzie and tell him. I'll talk to my SAC. Thank you," he added to

Hernandez.

"What? What is it?" Will's fists were wrapped around the steering wheel like he was going to rip it out.

"Let me fill in Bourne at the same time." Hunt dialed quickly and got his boss still in his office despite it being the middle of the night.

"Something weird came up. The last thing Fuller looked up on her cell is an address for a stolen truck that matched the description of the one used in the shooting yesterday. But the house belongs to a woman I met at Universal Biotech this week. Pete Dexter's personal assistant. At least, a woman with the same name," he corrected. No guarantee it was the same person.

Shit. This couldn't be a coincidence. The name wasn't a common one.

Bourne was quiet for so long Hunt thought he might have lost him. Finally, a drawn-out curse.

"I don't want anyone taking any chances with this. I want SWAT on the house. You and Griffin are not to go charging in there."

Will glared at him and Hunt's mood plummeted. "Did you figure out where the professor filmed that video yet? Or how he infected the pilot?"

"Not yet. It's early days, Kincaid, and you're off the case, remember."

Hunt knew that but those details ate at him.

"Stand down from going it alone to that house or I'll have both your badges. Send me the address and I'll have the SWAT there in twenty minutes."

Hunt blew out a big breath. "Yes, sir." He hung up on his boss and eyed Griffin. "You heard him."

"I am SWAT," Will growled.

"Not this time."

"I can't sit on the sidelines—"

"You don't have a choice if you want to keep your job." Hunt texted the address to his boss.

Will carried on driving and then pulled up on the side of the road with a screech of brakes. "I don't know what I'm going to do if something's happened to her."

Despair ate at Hunt. He knew it all too well. "Fuller's fine. She's probably downing margaritas at some fancy bar, unaware we're all freaking out."

But something wasn't right, not that he was going to worry his buddy with his sense of foreboding. Every time they thought they'd figured this case out it morphed into something else. Something more complicated.

Hunt felt his phone buzz in his pocket. It was Pip again with that unlistened-to voice message. He almost didn't bother with it because he needed to find Fuller and Pip's lack of faith hurt, but he wasn't a coward.

"Hunt, It's Pip. I went to Cindy's house to grab some clothes and ran into Adrian Lightfoot."

At this hour?

"I know I shouldn't have done it and I am so sorry I broke a confidence and I know you might not forgive me and think you were right all along, but... He was having an affair with Cindy. Listen, I know I'm rambling, but Adrian said he saw Pete Dexter having sex with Cindy that night and he thought she was cheating on him. And I told him, I know I shouldn't have. *God, I'm so stupid.* But I told him about the Rohypnol and then Adrian ran out of the house with Cindy's dad's gun and I know he's going to try to find Pete and kill him, which I'm okay with to a point. But what I really want is for Pete to pay for what he's done to Cindy, and God knows who else."

Hunt swore.

She was probably referring to Sally-Anne and the drug dealer. But what if Dexter's lies extended further beyond that? What if Dexter and his partners at Universal Biotech, along with Bea Grantham, were covering up a much greater crime and had framed the professor, the same way they'd framed the drug dealer earlier in the week?

Pip was still talking. "I figured I'd swing by Dexter's apartment and try to stop Adrian from confronting him, but the lights are out and I don't see any sign of anyone. I'm just sitting in the car now." He heard her swallow. "I realized you were the first person I wanted to call and it wasn't just because you're an FBI agent. I'm a screw-up when it comes to getting involved. I don't expect you to forgive me, but I am sorry for letting you down."

She hung up and he stared at the phone in shock. *Letting him down*? That was it? Shit.

"What is it?" Will asked urgently.

Hunt ignored his friend and dialed Pip's number but the call went straight to voicemail. His heart was beating so hard he could barely hear the beep to leave a message. "Do not approach Dexter. Go back to the hotel. The FBI is on the way. Pip..." Fuck, what could he say? He was suddenly convinced Dexter was responsible for trying to develop and sell bioweapons for financial gain and had killed at least five people to cover it up. He hoped to hell Fuller wasn't number six.

"Just, please, stay safe. I..." He tripped over things he wanted to say. Not confessions of love, surely, he'd only known her for a week. Not even. How could he *love* her? But there was something bubbling in his blood and it wasn't the fear for a friend. "I need you to be safe. Call me back."

He called Bourne again and told him what Pip had said as Will gritted his teeth, mute with worry. Hunt explained, "I'm thinking Dexter murdered Cindy because she was somehow in his way."

Dexter had been one of Professor Everson's students, too. Maybe they'd secretly tested their vaccines on that weaponized strain during their research studies. Maybe Dexter had taken a sample of the anthrax with him when he'd opened his company. And maybe Cindy was the only researcher capable of creating a vaccine against this even more deadly strain of the killer bacteria and after she'd served her purpose, they'd killed her?

Was that why Pete had dated Cindy, but screwed around with another woman? Maybe that other woman was the cute redhead?

"I'll get an arrest and search warrants for his house and company. SWAT are en route to the PA's house as we speak," Bourne told him.

"Yes, sir." Hunt hung up.

"What's the next move, Hunt? Where the hell is Mandy?" Will asked.

If he was right about Dexter then the guy had to know the plan was unraveling. Sure, the professor's apparent suicide would hold the investigation for a short time, but it wouldn't be long before the holes in the story became caverns.

"Pip said there was no one at Dexter's apartment. I think we should go check out the company headquarters. These assholes are going to make a run for it but they'll be taking their goodies with them." And even though it wasn't looking good for Mandy, he refused to lose hope. "And if Fuller isn't at Bea Grantham's house when the SWAT team arrives, she'll be at Biotech. Let's go find her."

CHAPTER THIRTY-TWO

T HE PAIN WAS overwhelming, but Mandy knew she couldn't give herself away by making a noise. She didn't know how she knew that, but the people she could hear shouting at one another clearly thought she was dead and were trying to figure out how to get rid of her body.

Fear made her shake. The tarp she was wrapped in made it hard to breathe. She'd been shot twice through the chest and it felt like someone continued to stab her with a red-hot poker. She felt nauseated, weak, and so very cold.

Yeah, she could definitely attest that slowly bleeding out via two bullet holes was not fun. She held back a sob of pain.

Had anyone missed her yet?

What about Will? But even if he had missed her, he was in the throes of a massive new case. He was busy. He'd never find her in time.

She could feel herself fading out of consciousness, and tried to concentrate on staying awake.

"Why the hell did you shoot her?" a voice asked. "You just had to say the truck was stolen and that was it. Now they'll be coming after us."

"I panicked." It was a male voice. "Doesn't matter now. We can't un-kill her."

"We have to get out of here before they figure out we are

the ones who tried to sell the bioweapon."

"Why?" The reply was sharp. A woman. There were four people all arguing over her dead body like she was nothing more than an inconvenience.

"The only blood at the house was on the gym mats which we hauled here with her. I got rid of her car in the quarry along with her cell and gun."

The FBI hated when agents lost their creds and guns.

"Tell the Feds she never came to your door. Tell 'em you weren't home or didn't hear the doorbell. No one knows she saw you."

"You really think we can get away with it?"

A male voice laughed and Mandy wanted to eviscerate him. "We've gotten away with everything else. In the meantime, we play it cool while we get the factory in Chile up to speed. By the time they figure it out we'll be long gone and probably have several government contracts to provide vaccines to the troops."

This mess was connected to the anthrax case, Mandy realized. How ironic she thought she'd got the shitty deal when in reality she'd honed straight in on the UNSUBs. They'd probably shot at Pip West because she was asking too many questions, then were blindsided by Hunt firing back at them.

"Oh, hell. Who the fuck is that?"

An alarm went off.

"That lawyer guy Cindy was seeing." One of the women shouted. "Simon, go get rid of him. I'll call the fire department and tell them it's a false alarm."

"I'll fire up the incinerator."

That last voice sent fear vibrating through her bones. Mandy closed her eyes and fought back a sob. No way in hell were they burning her alive. Someone dragged the tarp across the floor and she had to bite down so as not to scream in surprise and pain. God help her. She needed to figure out a way to escape.

CHAPTER THIRTY-THREE

P IP PARKED IN the same place she had when she'd surveilled Universal Biotech Inc. on Wednesday before she'd been shot at. It seemed like a million years ago now.

The SUV was higher off the ground than her noble little sedan, giving her a clear view when the cavalry turned up. She didn't intend to do anything stupid. If she saw Pete leave, she'd follow him at a safe distance and call the cops.

She scanned the scene. The guard house at the entrance was dark and presumably empty. Lights dotted various windows in the building. The main foyer was lit up like the midday sun.

A car parked in the lot looked a lot like the fancy Audi the bastard Pete Dexter drove. There was a big black SUV pulled up near the side loading bay. Her palms grew damp and she wiped them on her jeans. Angela Naysmith's? Was it the vehicle that had almost shoved her off the road on Monday morning before she found Cindy?

A squeal of brakes drew her gaze to the main road that separated her from the building. Someone was accelerating fast and swung into the access road without slowing down.

Oh, crap. Adrian.

The vehicle burst through the barrier and the tires screeched as he headed straight for the building. The car smashed into the glass door at the front, but clipped the edge of the concrete entrance with the crash and grind of steel. The car came to a shuddering halt.

"Oh, hell." She started the SUV and put it in gear, dialing Hunt with her left thumb.

"Hunt, I'm at Universal Biotech. I just saw Adrian Lightfoot plow straight into the front of the building there and I have to go see if he's okay. Send an ambulance. There are other vehicles here, too. I have the feeling something bad is happening..." As she said it she realized what that meant. These people were very dangerous. They hadn't just killed Cindy, they'd also been doing something despicable with pathogens, even if she didn't know exactly what that was.

She took her foot off the accelerator and hesitated. Then she saw the glow of flames under Adrian's car and remembered how Cindy's parents and brother had died. He might be trapped. Maybe even seriously hurt. She couldn't see anyone coming to his aid.

She realized she was still connected to Hunt's voicemail. "By the way. What I said earlier." She cleared her throat. "I was scared. Being alone at your place isn't the issue. I'm alone nearly all of the time. It was the fact I was falling for you that made me run, but maybe that isn't enough for a real relationship." She waited a beat. "Adrian's car is on fire and I'm going to help him get out. Sorry for being such a coward." She hung up and let out a big breath.

She drove through the shattered remains of the gate and pulled up around the side of the building far enough from Adrian's wrecked car that her SUV wouldn't catch fire, too. Flames flickered in the broken glass. She pushed down her fear and ran to the damaged car, terrified it was going to explode.

She glanced inside. Damn. He wasn't there.

The alarm started screaming. She spotted movement inside. Adrian, heading toward the elevators. He had a gun in his hand.

She made her way gingerly across the broken glass which crunched beneath her trainers.

"Adrian!" she yelled over the squealing alarm. The man looked back at her. "Don't do this!"

He simply shook his head and stepped into the elevator.

She backed away. She'd get back in her car and wait for the cops. The FBI were hopefully also on their way, and Pete Dexter would pay for whatever he'd done.

The fact Cindy had kept Adrian a secret suggested to Pip she'd cared a great deal for him and respected his wishes to keep their affair private. Cindy had loved the guy.

Emotion clogged Pip's throat. That her friend had been raped and murdered made her want to skewer Dexter, too, but prison would be better. Let the arrogant bastard rot. He could match wits with criminals and psychopaths. Show him he wasn't smarter than everyone else.

She gingerly stepped over shattered glass and mangled pieces of steel, keeping as far away from the wrecked car as possible because she was worried it was going to explode. Relief flooded her as the fresh breeze rushed over her and she drew in a deep breath and turned towards where she'd left the SUV.

Something connected with her skull and she went down with a silent scream of agony and curled up in a wretched ball. Someone rifled through her pockets, took her phone. Where was the fire department? Where was Hunt?

Her stomach tightened but she made herself limp and

unresponsive. She'd made a big mistake and it looked like she was about to join Cindy much sooner than she'd planned. And her biggest regret was not justice or revenge, it was walking out on Hunt Kincaid.

HUNT GOT PIP'S voice message just as they came in sight of the Universal Biotech building.

"Fuck. Pip's here. She says Adrian Lightfoot crashed his car into the building and she's gone to see if he's okay."

When he heard her telling him she'd run because she was falling for him he got that tight sensation in his chest.

His feelings for Pip couldn't be minimized or ignored just because they didn't fit in with his life plan. He understood her. He wanted her. He was terrified he was in love with her. And she was trying to prove something to him about the sort of person she was by running into a burning fucking building. He was so angry he could barely speak.

He called it in. Asked for immediate backup. Held on as Will careened around a corner and up through the broken barricades. The vehicle that had crashed into the doorway had flames licking under the hood. If the fuel tank blew it might set the whole building ablaze.

"Where's the extinguisher?" Hunt asked.

"Under your fucking seat." Will was barely keeping his shit together.

Hunt was worried, too. Mandy was missing and Pip was here somewhere. He looked around but didn't see her. Why the hell couldn't she have stayed safe in bed?

Because life didn't work that way, and even if someone

stayed home there was no guarantees they'd be safe.

He knew this. He *knew* it. But he'd fought that reality his whole life.

Pip's red SUV was parked around the side of the building. Lights were on upstairs and Hunt spotted a bay door open on the right.

The small extinguisher barely made a dent in the flames and he and Will were forced back by the intensity of the heat. He tossed the empty extinguisher aside.

"Leave it. Let's go find out where the hell our women are."

Will looked at him, startled, as Hunt pointed to the loading ramp. Will jumped in his Bucar and they pulled it in front of a white van that was parked there.

He and Will pulled their raid jackets over their vests. Will grabbed the shotgun from its rack above his head. They moved together, rolling under the bay door. It was dark inside the loading area, and cold. They headed toward the door and eased inside the main building. The door had been wedged open. Someone was hoping to make a quick getaway.

Hunt checked up and down the corridor. Empty.

"We'll cover more ground if we split up. You take the offices on the second floor and I'll take the labs in the basement." Hunt had been here before and knew his way around better than Will.

Will nodded. "I'll use the stairs and clear the floor. I'll call you if I find Mandy or Pip."

Hunt's throat tightened. His buddy hadn't reached the terrible realization yet that if Fuller were alive, she'd be leading this charge.

He took the stairs, grateful for the incessant noise of the fire alarms covering his progress, although it also masked everyone else's movements.

Where was Pip? Where was the lawyer? And where were all the bad guys?

The itch between his shoulder blades told him this was the endgame. But no way would these assholes get away with what they'd tried to do. No way would he lose Pip. Not today. Not when he'd just found her.

CHAPTER THIRTY-FOUR

P IP FOUND HERSELF on a cold, unforgiving floor, disorientated and confused. She must have passed out at some point. She squinted against the bright light. Pain streaked through her skull as an alarm sounded in the background. What the hell was going on?

A large blue tarp crinkled behind her. Then she noticed a long streak of blood glistening on the floor and a rush of horror crawled over her.

She moved her head, immediately rolled over and retched. Sweat broke out over her forehead as she wiped her mouth with the back of her hand.

Two head injuries in one day was two too many. She forced herself into a sitting position and swayed, her vision going in and out of focus. The jerk who'd brought her in here—had to be Pete Dexter, she realized—was climbing into a spacesuit and attaching it to an air hose.

Why?

Her brain had kicked into panic mode but her limbs were too shaky to follow orders. Her blurry gaze followed another blood trail—a thin line of drops across the floor, ending at a cupboard.

Weird. Her head rolled against the sealed floor.

And then she figured it out. Someone who was bleeding

had managed to crawl into that cupboard and hide.

Pip managed to get her feet beneath her and climb upright, holding onto a nearby bench.

Dexter eyed her but carried on working. He wore an insulated glove to protect one hand as he removed long, metal tubes from a liquid nitrogen store, which she recognized from visits to the laboratory with Cindy. He emptied the tubes onto the bench, then threw them into a Styrofoam box. Wisps of smoke were coming out of the top.

No, not smoke.

Dry ice.

He was loading up samples for transport.

"Why did you kill Cindy?" she asked, having to speak up over the stupid alarm that rang outside the glass walls of the lab. Everything pounded her brain and intensified the pain.

Was the building on fire?

It was a terrifying idea, but at least the emergency services should arrive soon, which was probably why Pete was grabbing samples as fast as his fingers could move.

Help was on the way. A surge of energy flowed through her. She could do this. She just had to survive until then.

"I didn't kill Cindy." He grinned. "She went for a swim and drowned."

Hatred moved inside her. He'd drugged her friend, raped her, and watched her die. And now he was laughing about it.

"You were jealous," Pip choked out. "Your ego couldn't cope with the fact she was so much smarter than you."

His expression twisted under his Plexiglas mask. "Didn't do her any good in the end, did it?"

"You're disgusting, you know that?"

He smiled. "Boo hoo. Poor little orphan Pippa. Such a

shame. Nobody wants her."

Not true. She didn't say it but she knew. Cindy had wanted her. And she was pretty sure Hunt wanted her, too. At least, he had before she'd pushed him away.

Keep Pete talking, she reminded herself. Feds were on their way. Hunt would get her message and Dickster would be brought to justice. "You're the one nobody wants. You cheated on Cindy because even her love wasn't enough for a narcissist like you."

He sneered. "I started dating Cindy simply to keep an eye on what was happening in Everson's lab. We chose the weakest link. Seduce her. Pretend to love her. It was easy until she found Bea's underwear in my pocket."

Pip straightened. She loathed this monster. Her headache and pain all but faded into insignificance compared to the anger that surged through her at what he'd done to her friend. "You stole her research."

"She built her ideas on the work of others. I just refined it further."

Pip paced and he had to twist to look at her. "No. She's the one who refined it. She did something amazing, didn't she? And you didn't want her to get the credit. You're a jealous little worm."

An ugly sound came out of his mouth. "I didn't want her to get the cash." He picked up a gun she hadn't noticed on the bench and pointed it at her. "Sit back on the tarp and keep the dead FBI agent company."

Pip's entire being froze. Could it be Hunt? No. He'd been called into work. She clenched her fists. *It couldn't be him.* Fuller…

"You killed an FBI agent?" She could barely get the words

out. "They'll be swarming this place."

"And I won't be here." Pete pulled another set of samples from the liquid nitrogen store. "But you will be."

"What about Sally-Anne and the professor?" she asked. "Did you stage their deaths, too?"

His lips curled behind the mask. "Wasn't difficult. Sally-Anne enjoyed it. She had a good time right until the end." Pip wanted to puke. "The professor was starting to figure it out. When you got the Feds involved, he had to die."

Was he really trying to blame this on her?

"Angela Naysmith almost ran me off the road on Monday morning heading to Cindy's cottage. Are she and Simon Corker involved in this plot?"

Pete left a metal rod on the bench and she inched closer.

He shrugged. "I forgot to leave my Blake keycard in Cindy's truck the way we'd planned so Angela took it up for me. We all needed this thing to work."

That was the keycard Hunt had seemed very interested in when they'd come across it. A lot of things were starting to make more sense now. He'd been searching for a bioterrorist. "Your company not doing so well, Pete?"

He glared at her. "Those bastard Feds ruined everything."

"I think it's their job," she said wryly. "What happened? You tried to sell anthrax on the black market, didn't you? And Cindy's vaccine, too."

He and his cronies were monsters. They didn't care who they put in danger.

He pointed the gun straight at her head. "We decided to stir up the demand for our product by increasing the threat levels. But once the FBI intercepted the sale of our weaponized anthrax we had to go to plan B and try to deflect any attention away from us."

Plan B being kill anyone who might suspect them and get the hell out of Dodge. This was why Hunt had been so secretive. This case was way more important than any issues of trust between the two of them.

"As soon as the Feds got their hands on the samples we'd tried to sell, Cindy and the professor both had to die."

And now it was *their* fault?

His grip changed on the weapon. "Go and sit back on the floor like I told you. I don't have much time."

Pip would rather die fighting than sit still while someone used her for target practice. She snatched up the nearest metal rod and hit him with it. The handle was so cold it burned her skin but she didn't care. She hit him again. The gun went off and she felt the heat of a bullet brush her cheek.

Crap. She jerked and fell to the floor, catching herself with her forearms.

Pete dropped an open vial a yard from where she lay.

White powder floated into the air, then dissipated.

He started laughing, then grabbed the polystyrene box to his chest with one arm, gun pointed unwaveringly in her direction. "That vial is full of a virulent form of anthrax that Professor Everson and myself pulled out of his old supervisor's Cold War freezer. The old man's widow asked Trevor for help cleaning his home office. Naturally Trevor wanted to use free student labor and made me help. Bet he wished he'd done it all on his own now." The words were snide.

Pip stared in horror at the bone white powder scattered across the floor.

She swallowed tightly. "Give me the vaccine."

Pete backed towards the exit. "We shipped it all to our

new location the day after Cindy died. Don't worry. It won't take long, but it will hurt. We tested it on a few volunteers before we decided to sell it to the highest bidder. We filmed their violent deaths and we filmed the girl who lived. That's why the buyers were so ready to part with so much money." He shook his head as she moved toward him. "Uh, uh. If you follow me you'll spread the spores throughout Atlanta and who knows how many people will die."

Pip froze in indecision and within seconds he was gone.

Shit. Shit. Shit.

She tried the door he'd backed through but he'd locked it from the outside. Dammit.

She snatched up a face mask and positioned it over her mouth and nose. Too little too late probably. She grabbed a couple of paper towels and laid them over the broken vial to try and contain the spores. Then she rushed to the cupboard and threw open the doors.

Agent Fuller was inside, curled up in a tiny ball. Blood covered her clothes and smeared the veneer of the cabinet. The agent tried to open her eyes but they immediately started to droop again. She was obviously weak from loss of blood and who knew what internal damage.

Pip dragged her out of the cupboard. "Wake up, Agent Fuller. I need you to wake up." She tapped the woman's cheek and was rewarded with a groggy glare. And maybe she should have left her in the cupboard, because as things stood they were both going to die. She hooked Fuller's arm over her shoulder and started shuffling them to the door of the lab.

It was amazing how the yawning maw of imminent death made all the regrets and mistakes focus with unprecedented clarity. Pip would give anything to go back in time and not run from Hunt's place, not tell him she didn't want to even try to see where this thing between them might lead.

But his job was dangerous and he dealt with this sort of situation on a daily basis. She didn't think she could cope with the idea of losing him if she did let herself fall in love.

"We need to find a way into another lab and then we need to contact your colleagues so we can get out of here." The longer they stayed the more likely they were to be exposed, but there was no point worrying Fuller. The woman was barely clinging to life.

CHAPTER THIRTY-FIVE

H UNT CHECKED EVERY room. The floor was a sprawling mass of labs and he didn't want to miss Pip if she was hiding somewhere or had gotten lost.

His work cell vibrated and he put it to his ear, though he could barely hear above the noise.

Will yelled, "I'm outside. I've got a man and a woman under arrest—Simon Corker and Angela Naysmith. The second floor is on fire."

"You find Fuller or Pip?" Hunt asked.

"No. I hoped you had. Nor Pete Dexter, Bea Grantham or the lawyer. I'm gonna secure these two and head down to the basement with you. The fire department is on their way but they might not enter the facility when they don't know what the fuck flammables or biological agents are inside."

"And turn that goddamned alarm off before you come down here. I can't hear a thing."

Hunt stuffed his cell in his pocket and continued clearing each room as quickly as possible. Then, up ahead, a figure in scrubs appeared with a Styrofoam box in one hand and a gun in the other. Hunt froze and hugged the shadows.

Dexter.

That's when he noticed the gray painted breeze-block walls. Just like in the video. These guys had killed Cindy, Sally-

Anne, Grossman's widow, and probably the drug dealer, and the professor, too. Who knew when they'd infected the co-pilot. And they'd filmed the video right here. Hunt debated shouting to the man striding away from him down the corridor that he was under arrest. Instead he sprinted, knowing the guy wouldn't hear him over the alarm.

He got to within a few feet and jabbed his SIG into Dexter's spine. "Hands up," he yelled. "You're under arrest."

Hunt took the gun out of Dexter's hand and stuffed it into a pocket. "Put the box carefully on the floor, asshole. It's all over."

Dexter put the box down and tried to run. Hunt was on him in seconds and smashed him into the floor. He yanked Dexter's arms behind his back and slipped the metal cuffs over the bastard's wrists.

The alarm finally stopped ringing and the silence seemed to reverberate around them.

Dexter started laughing. "You got me. Bravo. Intrepid FBI agent finally nailed the man who's been leading him around by his dick all week. Pity you didn't do it before I killed the witless female FBI agent or Cindy's stupid little friend."

Hunt's heart stopped. *God, no.* He dragged Dexter to his feet and jammed his arm up against Dexter's throat. "Where are they?"

"Like that, is it?" Dexter laughed mockingly. "They're in the containment lab. Pippa isn't dead yet, but she will be. Just like you will be." He kicked at the box on the floor, clearly meaning to break the contents, but Hunt anticipated the move. He blocked the kick with his leg and shoved Dexter farther down the corridor away from whatever deadly microbes were in the box.

Hunt threw Dexter back to the floor, not caring when he landed on his face with no way of breaking his fall. Hunt used his boot to scoot the box into the nearest lab and closed the door on it.

"What did you give them?" Crouching, Hunt jammed his gun against Dexter's temple.

Dexter smiled but Hunt saw the fear light his eyes. "Anthrax. But you can't do anything to stop it. We already shipped the vaccine out of the country."

"What if I pour a vial down your throat, asshole? Will you find the vaccine then?"

Dexter sneered. "I already took the vaccine, so go ahead." He started smirking and then Hunt stuck his gun in the man's mouth, desperate to end the evil little shit. The thought of losing Pip brought back every reason he'd had for keeping lovers at arm's length over the years. Loving people was easy, but losing them? That fucking sucked.

Footsteps ran toward them. Hunt eased the gun back against the man's cheek.

"He's threatening to kill me!" Dexter yelled.

Hunt climbed to his feet as Will approached. "Asshole says he exposed Fuller and Pip to the anthrax and doesn't have any vaccine here."

Will swore. "What the hell did you do to Agent Fuller?"

Dexter sneered again and his face grated on Hunt's nerves so much his trigger finger itched.

"She's been dead for hours. Waltzed in like a lamb to slaughter. Bled like a pig—uff."

Will kicked the man in the stomach, but Hunt held him back from beating Dexter more. "He's a lying sack of shit. Don't lose hope. Get him out of here." Even though he'd love to hurt the guy, they needed to know where Dexter had shipped the vaccine and any other nasties. Hunt pulled out his cell and called Jez Place from CDC. "Jez? I'm gonna need some of that vaccine you've been making. Enough for three adults. And we need it immediately down at Universal Biotech. Meet Will at the side bay door. Bring an ambulance and medical doctors. ASAP."

Dexter looked smug. "If this is Cindy's stuff from the lab it won't work. I substituted it with serum."

"It isn't Cindy's stuff," Hunt said calmly. In reality he was anything but calm about what he was about to do, but he was gonna do it anyway. "Get him the fuck out of here," he told Will. "I'll be at the side bay door in fifteen minutes. Meet me there with Jez. Don't let anything stop him getting through. No Bureau bullshit. No crime scene blockade."

Will nodded. "Bring her back to me alive, Hunt." Will hauled Dexter to his feet and shoved him along the corridor, moving stiffly, clearly terrified for Fuller but doing his job.

Hunt ran back to the side corridor where Dexter had come out of. He remembered it from his tour. The containment labs. He ran along the corridor and spotted the crash door but he couldn't get inside. He moved to the window and spotted Pip with Fuller draped over her shoulders trying to get out the main door. There was no time for that. He banged hard on the window, making her startle and turn toward him. Her brown eyes filled with happiness before they turned distressed. She dragged Fuller with her, but his fellow agent was in bad shape. She was covered in blood and barely conscious.

He pointed at the exit for the crash door but Pip shook her head and mouthed back "anthrax."

"I have the vaccine," he yelled. He gave her the hand signals to get her to move it. He was lying but he didn't care. He needed to get her out of there and to Jez as fast as possible. Smoke was starting to fill the corridor. He didn't want them all burning to death on top of everything else the women had suffered.

He watched Pip pull in a deep breath and push the big red button. The door opened, the fire doors sealed either side of them and the shower came on as both she and Fuller fell into his waiting arms.

CHAPTER THIRTY-SIX

P IP COULDN'T BELIEVE she was in Hunt's embrace. Steaming hot water poured over their heads, soaking them. The smell of bleach came from spray down near their ankles. She coughed as fumes filled her lungs.

Hunt took Fuller's weight and held her upright. The water turned bright red as blood washed out of her clothes.

"They thought she was dead," Pip told him, starting to shiver despite the heat of the water.

"Fuller's too stubborn to die." Worry dimmed his smile even as she was captivated by the intensity of his blue eyes, which ran quickly over her. He touched her cheek.

"Where's the vaccine?" she asked.

Hunt winced.

Oh, God.

"I didn't lie," he forestalled her. "I have a CDC doctor arriving at the side door with it as we speak. How long ago were you exposed?"

Pip's teeth started to chatter, which made her head hurt worse, and at first, she thought it was being soaked through while dressed, but then she realized she wasn't feeling well. She didn't know if it was the head injuries, the anthrax or something else. "About five, ten minutes ago."

"The shower is on a short timer that cannot be overridden,

but it will make sure no anthrax leaves with us."

Pip tried not to worry while helping to take Fuller's weight. "She lost a lot of blood."

Hunt nodded. He raised Fuller's shirt and revealed two seeping bullet holes.

"I think the fact she isn't dead already means it didn't hit anything vital." Pip was searching for something positive to get out of this situation. There was still a very good chance this woman might die. It reminded her of how much good law enforcement agents risked when they headed to work every single day.

Hunt checked Fuller's pulse. "Weak, but there."

"It's a miracle." Her lungs felt tight. "Did you find Adrian?" She caught a faint whiff of smoke and wanted to cling to Hunt and never let go.

"Not yet."

She forced herself to say calmly, "The building is on fire I take it?"

Hunt nodded.

"You came looking for us anyway." She smiled. "I don't know whether to be horrified or impressed."

"Please be impressed." His gaze held hers, more focused this time.

"I'm sorry for leaving your house." She glanced around wildly. "Really sorry."

He nodded again.

"I'm so sorry I betrayed your confidence with Adrian. He was acting a little unhinged and I was trying to calm him down and convince him Cindy hadn't cheated on him."

Hunt nodded. "We'll talk about it later."

That sounded ominous but considering he'd risked exposure to freaking *anthrax* to save her and Fuller she couldn't complain. The water slowed, then stopped. A quiet snick as the doors released.

"Okay, let's get the hell out of here."

Hunt carried Agent Fuller, but made Pip hold onto his belt as the smoke started to get thicker. "I don't want to lose you."

She told herself not to read anything into those words. What future could they hope for after this mess?

She stumbled along behind him, following blindly through a maze of gray corridors thick with smoke. Finally, they got to a door with an exit sign and he went through it backwards.

It opened into a cavernous loading bay and precious fresh air. Flashing lights appeared. Uniformed cops and firefighters milled around, staring as the three of them stumbled through the doorway.

Someone wrapped a blanket around her and rolled up her sleeve, driving a needle home. She was so numb it didn't even hurt. She was hustled onto a stretcher and loaded inside an ambulance. She watched a group of people hovering around the female agent. Fuller was getting a vaccination shot, as was Hunt. Someone was setting up an IV. Activity seemed to intensify and all of a sudden someone was starting compressions.

It took her right back to finding Cindy's body on Monday morning and trying to revive her dead friend.

"Please live." Pip closed her eyes and prayed. She opened them and they were whisking Fuller into the back of a different ambulance, someone riding astride trying to get Fuller's heart beating again. The bravery of these people, the constant danger they faced every day they went to work hit her with renewed force. The prospect of facing that worry for Hunt every single day...

Her throat burned from holding back emotion.

She turned her head and spotted Dexter in the back of a squad car, smirking. Out of nowhere, Adrian Lightfoot walked up to the window of the police car and fired three shots into the man who'd killed her best friend. She jolted in time with each bullet. He raised his hand and Pip was terrified he was going to blow his own brains out but instead he dropped the gun onto the roof of the squad car and put his hands on his head. He fell to his knees and was swarmed by armed officers. A woman screamed.

A redhead Pip remembered as Pete's PA tried to run towards Dexter. The woman he'd been seeing behind Cindy's back their entire relationship, she recalled. She was in handcuffs. Judging from her grief she'd actually cared about the asshole.

Pip stared out at the low hung moon shining bright in the sky, same moon she and Cindy had lain on the deck and watched so many times at the cottage. "See you soon, Cindy."

A star shot across the sky just as she started to fall asleep.

"Oh, no you don't, Pip." Hunt's voice cut through the dense fog that was trying to take over her brain. Her throat hurt.

He went to kiss her, but she turned away. "Don't. I might infect you."

He leaned over her and suddenly she realized the ambulance was moving and they were traveling fast, sirens blaring.

"What the hell were you thinking going there without backup?" he asked, angry now.

She frowned. It had seemed to make sense at the time, but looking back? Maybe not the most sensible thing she'd ever done. She caught his gaze. "I guess I wanted to prove I wasn't the bad guy. I wanted to prove I had guts."

His lips disappeared as he visibly held back emotion. "If you weren't so sick I'd tell you how full of shit that is. You didn't need to prove yourself. Not to me. Not to the FBI. You hadn't done anything wrong."

She squeezed his fingers. "I'm sorry." Apparently, the words were easier to say with practice. "How is Agent Fuller?"

Hunt's expression became even more grim. "She's alive. That's all I know right now."

"She's strong." Pip tried to comfort him. "She'll come through this."

Her eyes started to close, no matter how hard she tried to keep them open. What she did know was Hunt held her hand all the way to the hospital.

HUNT WAS READY to punch the agent they'd put on Pip's room. She had a fever and had been placed in complete isolation. He'd changed, made his report, and rushed back to the hospital, only to find the room barred and a guy the size of the Empire State Building guarding the door.

Hunt was pretty sure he could take him.

But then he'd lose his job for sure. And he wanted to keep his job and keep Pip. He wanted it all.

The fire department had been unable to gain control of the fire at Universal Biotech. Although Simon Corker denied it, the arson investigator figured someone had poured gasoline somewhere on the second floor and purposefully lit up the building. Given the nature of everything inside they'd decided to let it burn, killing the hazardous microbes in the raging inferno that developed.

Simon Corker, Bea Grantham, Angela Naysmith and Adrian Lightfoot were all in custody. Pete Dexter was DOA.

Not that Hunt gave a shit. He hoped the sonofabitch roasted in hell.

"How is she, Doc?" Hunt caught a specialist coming out of Pip's room. He could see inside but she was covered by a plastic tent so he couldn't see her features.

"She's sleeping, Agent Kincaid. She has a fever and a concussion so we are monitoring her carefully. She's received more vaccine, which should defeat any pathogens in her system before they start producing toxins, but it's going to take a few days to know for certain. How are you feeling?"

Hunt looked sideways at the WWF bouncer. "Thwarted."

The doctor grinned and patted his arm. "Look, it's going to take time and there is really nothing you can do here. If you write her a note I'll make sure she gets it."

Hunt nodded. Good idea. Maybe he could get on paper some of what he was feeling.

Mollified, he went in search of Will Griffin.

Fuller was still in surgery. He put his arm over his buddy's hunched frame as the agent sat in the waiting room, skin waxy with worry.

"I don't know what I'm going to do if she dies, Hunt."

"She's not going to die."

But the clock ticked loudly as they continued to wait for the surgeon to get out of the operating room. Bourne came in a few minutes later and gave them a look. Although, really, what else could they have done? Hunt and Pip had helped save their fellow agent, but the longer the surgery dragged on, the more worried they all became.

Finally, the surgeon entered the room, but they knew it was bad news even before the man opened his mouth. Mandy Fuller had died on the operating table. The bullets had fragmented and severed two veins, one fragment lodging in her lung and another nicking her kidney. Despite everything they'd tried to do for her, she'd lost too much blood. She was gone.

Hunt stood, dazed. Mandy was gritty and determined, as capable and as strong as any of them. A coldness washed over him at this devastating loss. Will squatted on the floor. Hunt tried to comfort him but no one could get past the grief. Other agents swarmed into the waiting room as news filtered out.

Shell-shock reflected on every face. The idea they'd lost one of their own…

Hunt slumped into a chair and tried not to lose it. Mandy had been an incredible agent. Smart. Tenacious. The idea this was his fault…but it wasn't. It was the job. She'd be pissed if he tried to take responsibility for her decisions.

He started to shake with that old familiar fear. That knowledge of how impotent he was when it came to keeping people he cared about safe.

People died. He had to figure out a way to understand that it wasn't his fault. Death was a basic fact of life. He remembered what he'd put Pip through on Monday when he'd questioned her just yards from where her best friend lay lifeless. His stomach turned.

He might love his job, but sometimes it sucked.

He held his face in his hands and didn't know he was crying until he felt a hand on his back.

He looked up. Bourne sat next to him. "Not your fault,

Kincaid. It was a miracle Fuller lasted as long as she did. Corker has made a deal to avoid the death penalty. He told us she turned up at Bea Grantham's house unexpectedly and Dexter panicked and shot her. They'd been quietly moving their operation to Chile. Corker told us where all their samples were shipped to. We have agents en route to intercept and make sure they don't fall into enemy hands. We found videos online of human subjects they tested the vaccine on. These people are all going down."

Hunt stared at him blankly.

"We caught the bad guys, son. We're going to track down every move they've made since they climbed out of diapers. Agent Fuller's death will not go unavenged."

Hunt forced himself to nod. His gaze found Will's but his friend seemed like an empty husk. He wasn't even in the room.

Hunt recognized the reaction and couldn't blame the man, but Hunt wasn't going to run this time. Not mentally or physically. Not from Pip. She deserved better. Maybe he did, too. He pushed to his feet and went back to watch over Pip from the corridor outside her room. He wasn't leaving her. He wasn't going anywhere.

CHAPTER THIRTY-SEVEN

P IP SAT UP in bed, writing on the pad of legal paper Hunt had sent her a few days ago when she'd finally felt well enough to keep her eyes open for more than five minutes.

Her headache had taken a couple of days to disappear and since then she'd been bored stiff inside her little plastic tent that had allowed her to see only blurry outlines of people. Hunt had started sending her things. She apparently wasn't allowed electronics. A legal pad. A pen. Books—including a copy of Margaret Mitchell's *Gone With the Wind*, which she'd never read, and a new copy of Rachel Grant's *Firestorm* that had a bullet-hole right in the middle of the "O." The book had literally saved her and Hunt's life.

He sent her poetry, messages, and quotes from the books. The first had been: *"You're the strongest person I know. Fierce. Determined. But if you do shatter, I will hold you until you're back together."*

Then, "Please don't die" with a love heart and the initial H written in shaky handwriting beside it.

She'd held that note against her chest for two whole days. Later, when the doctors were optimistic she was going to survive she allowed herself to hope and think about the future. About Hunt. About her friend, and what had happened. It was Cindy's work on vaccines that had saved her life, and Pip knew her friend would be happy at the thought.

Hunt kept on writing to her. Cindy would have been happy with that, too.

"I just know that when I'm with you, I get a charge of energy, pleasure. A zing that's missing without you. And when I'm inside you, I feel a connection. More than sex. Deeper. More intense. More than I expected. More than I want."

The second part of the quote arrived just before Hunt went home that same night. She heard his voice as he spoke to the nurses and saw the pale outline of his body near the observation window. The message he sent made her hot and weepy.

"You're addictive in a way that scares me. You're like a drug I'll never get enough of. I want that zing. That intensity. The thrill of being with you. In you. And that scares the hell out of me given the risks you take."

She could barely breathe after she read it because she felt exactly the same way.

"I'm afraid of how I feel about you. Afraid to care. Afraid to love."

He added, "I love you" to the note and her heart pinged against her ribs when she realized those words weren't from the book.

Yesterday, he'd written:

"I've waited for you longer than I've waited for any woman."

She eventually found those words in Margaret Mitchell's epic Civil War-era novel. Pip wrote back that he'd waited *five* days.

He'd replied with a sad face and she giggled.

She was curious about what he'd come up with next and

stared at her watch, willing it to get to six o'clock when he usually turned up. He didn't sleep here but he was here more than any sane person should be.

And she loved him for it.

She just hadn't figured out how to tell him or what to do about it.

This time he'd have a surprise when he arrived. She'd been declared anthrax free and noncontagious. She'd had all those uncomfortable tubes removed and her tent had been taken away.

Now she sat in bed in a pair of pajamas Hunt had picked up for her from the hotel. His notes sat on the bedside cabinet, beside the books. His presence had made the last few days bearable, especially when one of the nurses had told her about Agent Fuller. Pip had sobbed when she'd heard. They'd tried so hard to save her and the woman had fought so valiantly for life. It didn't seem real. Or fair.

She still wasn't sure she could deal with the fact that as a federal agent, dangerous situations were the norm for Hunt. How could she watch him walk out the door every single day, not knowing whether or not he'd return?

And she worried the adorable little things Hunt had been doing were borne of guilt and a reaction to Fuller's death. Maybe when he recovered from the shock of what had happened to his colleague, he'd realize the emotions he felt were fleeting and not real. She wasn't sure she could cope with that either. Being alone, guarding her heart, was so much easier.

Hunt had postponed Cindy's funeral.

There was a lot to sort out but Adrian had been doing what he could for her from jail. She had no idea what would

COLD BLOODED

happen to him, but would be willing to testify on his behalf. The guy had clearly suffered a breakdown. He hadn't been sane or rational when he'd shot Pete Dexter.

The world was strangely ignorant about the facts of the events of that day. The public didn't know about the super-deadly anthrax or Cindy's amazing vaccine that had saved Pip's life. Pip had no intention of revealing any details that might upset the delicate balance in the fight against biological weapons. She was writing again, but it wasn't articles for a paper. It was fiction. She'd found herself penning a tale that involved a deadly virus and a beautiful researcher who just happened to fall in love with an FBI agent investigating a suspicious death.

She wasn't sure what it would lead to but it was better than staring at the wall.

A figure appeared behind the glass of the window and Pip's breath caught while her heart gave a little squeeze. She'd brushed her hair and even slicked on a little lip gloss. She smiled and Hunt grinned at her, looking so handsome, tie askew, hair sticking up on end. He turned to speak to someone and suddenly the door was opening and there he was walking towards her.

Her heart started pounding again. Not in panic. Not in fear. In anticipation. He took her hand in his and rubbed her fingers, before leaning over and brushing his lips against hers.

The connection was shocking and made her gasp. He smiled against her mouth and held her for a moment.

"Pip," he said finally, softly.

He pulled back and she ran her hand over his jaw, the stubble just starting to break through the skin.

"I missed you," she said.

413

He kissed her again, hungrily. Her notepad dropped onto the floor with a slap. She wrapped her arms around his neck and held on tight.

A few seconds later, a loud cough interrupted them and they pulled apart.

"Maybe you two should continue this conversation at home?" the nurse said with a grin, handing Pip back the notepad.

"I can leave?" asked Pip excitedly. She couldn't believe she was actually escaping.

The nurse nodded and Hunt jumped up to pull the curtain around the bed. He'd brought in some clothes for her when he'd fetched her PJs. She dragged everything out of the cabinet. Leggings. T-shirt. Socks. Sneakers. She looked up suspiciously. "You forgot my underwear."

He bobbed a brow and gave her an exaggerated wink. "I sure did."

She laughed. "You were not thinking about sex when you packed my clothes."

"No, but I might have been if I'd gone through your lingerie. Anyway," he said, suddenly serious, "you don't need them. Doctors said at least three full days of bed rest. That was a condition of early release."

"Fine." She was just happy to be let out. He stepped outside the curtain when the nurse stepped inside. Pip quickly pulled on her clothes—*sans* bra and panties—and gathered the books, all the notes, and other things Hunt had sent over the last few days and placed them carefully into a plastic bag. Funny how those notes and that notepad had become more precious to her than diamonds or prestige. She said thank you to the nurse and the other staff who'd cared for her so wonderfully.

When she was finished Hunt held out his bent arm to her and cocked his brow. They hit the exit and kept walking. She was desperate to put this chapter of her life behind her.

"You're keeping the notes I sent?" He eyed the bag she refused to relinquish.

Pip brought it protectively to her chest and channeled her inner goddess. "They are mine."

"As long as you don't tell anyone I can quote Yeats."

"I have spread my dreams under your feet," she murmured with a sigh.

He stopped and pulled her against him. "Tread softly because you tread on my dreams." He lowered his mouth to kiss her, but when he pulled back he had a worried expression on his face. "You want a coffee? We need to talk."

There was a small café and he steered her that way.

A wave of fear and uncertainty washed over her. He had something important to tell her. She could tell by the grip of his fingers and the worried lines around his mouth.

He drew her to a small empty table with two chairs.

"What is it?" she asked. She'd gotten to the point where she didn't want any lingering pain. If this was all some big lie just to get her through her stay in the hospital she'd rather he told her now.

"I know I told you I love you, but—"

The pain in her chest felt like a knife being twisted.

"But you never actually told me how you feel about me."

She blinked rapidly. How could he not know?

"And I, well, I took a few liberties when you were admitted. And, if you don't feel the way about me that I feel about you you're going to think this is some weird stalker shit and probably want a third party to protect you from me."

Her mouth opened. "I never told you how I feel?"

Those rings of gold in the blue of his eyes shone and then dimmed. "I'm not pressuring you. You were kind of busy, being infected and worried about dying…"

She stared at him openmouthed, unable to talk. He'd done all this for her, brought her books, kept her company, sent her love notes without knowing she was crazy about him. She tried to think what she'd written on those pieces of paper back to him. Not words of love. Funny things. Thankful things, but never once had she written, "I love you."

How could she have been so insensitive?

Because she still hadn't truly believed he loved her. She still thought of herself as someone fundamentally unworthy.

She was quiet too long.

"I also love my job. I know being a journalist will mean I can't always discuss certain things, but I think we can make it work. I'm applying to the Hostage Rescue Team and if I get in I'll be based more or less in one place."

"Virginia," she said.

He held her hand, even now. He held her hand and didn't give up on her even though she hadn't told him how she really felt.

He started to say more but she placed her finger over his lips and he stopped talking.

"The idea of you doing something so dangerous scares me. A lot. I've guarded my heart for years because the idea of opening up and then losing someone is painful."

He gathered her hands in his and kissed her fingers. "I know exactly. But I've finally found something I've never had before and the idea of pushing you away just so I don't get hurt if anything happens to you..." He swallowed. "I don't think I can live without you. I don't want to try."

Her vision blurred. She hadn't imagined FBI Agent Hunt Kincaid would be such a romantic when she'd first met him, but he'd given her everything a woman could ever ask for. "I think I first fell in love with you when you threw yourself between me and flying bullets. And then again when you risked dying of anthrax to save me from a burning building."

His face lost its worried expression.

"But the defining moment was when you sent me love notes. Any man who has the balls to quote Romance novels to woo a woman is amongst the bravest of the brave. I love you. I thought I'd said it in the ambulance or at some point on the phone." She looked deep into his pretty eyes. "I'm working on my insecurities. I'm working on being more open and less scared of being hurt, but it won't happen overnight."

With a relieved grin, he hooked her hair behind her ear. "We've got time."

"I hope so." She caught his hand again, unable to stop touching him. "I don't think I'm going to go back to journalism. At least not yet."

"Don't give it up for me."

"Why not for you?" she asked. "Who else would I make a sacrifice for?"

He drew in a deep breath, clearly unsure what to say.

She smiled at his uncertain expression. "But I'm not giving it up for you. I don't think I can ever go back to being the person I was before Lisa Booker and her children were murdered. Even if Cindy hadn't died..."

He pulled her against him so their heads rested on one another's shoulders.

"But she did." Pip drew in another deep breath and told him the secret desire that had begun to bloom in that boring hospital bed. "I'm going to try to write a novel."

His eyes lit up. "Romance?"

He sounded intrigued by the idea.

She laughed. "Maybe. Or a thriller. I haven't decided yet."

"I think that's a great idea and I will support you every step of the way. Come on." He pulled her to her feet, took her hand and led her to his truck in the basement garage.

When he headed north she corrected him. "The hotel is back that way." She pointed over his shoulder.

"Yeah, that's one of the crazy things I told you about. I went to the hotel and grabbed all your stuff and brought it back to my place." He grimaced. "I know you might want to go stay at Cindy's but I wanted you close—"

She ran her hand over his forearm. "We'll figure it out."

"And I lied to the hospital staff and told them we were engaged so they'd let me hang out after visiting hours were done."

A deep sense of longing shook her.

"And I told my mother about you and she and my stepdad are coming to visit in a couple of weeks to meet you."

She blinked in surprise. She hadn't really thought about the fact he had a family.

She bit her lip.

"Freaked out yet?" he asked, sparing her a quick glance.

"A little." *A lot, actually.* Would they like her? What if they didn't?

"My mother is a force of nature, but don't worry, she's going to love you. I'm the one who's gonna get hassled about treating you right. So, if it's all a bit overwhelming to start with just give it time." He sounded nervous. This big, strong FBI agent sounded unsure of himself and she loved him all the more for showing her that vulnerability.

"I intend to. I intend to give it as much time as we both need to get used to the idea of *you* and *me* being an *us*."

He reached over and cupped her cheek. "I love you, Pip West."

"I know." She took his hand and kissed his fingers. "I love you, too, Special Agent Hunt Kincaid. Take us home."

A COLD DARK PLACE

Cold Justice Series Book 1

Justice isn't always black or white.

Former CIA assassin Alex Parker works for The Gateway Project, a clandestine government organization hell-bent on taking out serial killers and pedophiles before they enter the justice system. Alex doesn't enjoy killing, but he's damn good at it. He's good at dodging the law, too—until a beautiful rookie agent has him wondering what it might be like to get caught.

FBI Special Agent Mallory Rooney has spent years hunting the lowlife who abducted her identical twin sister eighteen years ago. Now, during an on-going serial killer investigation, Mallory begins to suspect there's a vigilante operating outside the law. She has no choice but to take him down, because murder isn't justice. Is it?

Sometimes it's cold and dark.

When Mallory starts asking questions, The Gateway Project management starts to sweat, and orders Alex to watch her. As soon as they meet, the two begin to fall in love. But the lies and betrayals that define Alex's life threaten to destroy them both—especially when the man who stole her sister all those years ago makes Mallory his next target, and Alex must reveal his true identity to save the woman he loves.

COLD PURSUIT

Cold Justice Series Book 2

Single mom Vivi Vincent is thrust into her worst nightmare when she's trapped inside a mall during a terror attack along with her eight-year-old son. With the help of Jed Brennan, an FBI special agent on enforced leave, Vivi and her son survive the assault. But the danger is far from over.

Vivi's son may have witnessed critical details of the terrorists' future plans and is targeted for death, but he's mute, and he's traumatized. Still someone launches a strike against the FBI's safe house, and Jed fears the bad guys have an inside man. No longer knowing who to trust, he hides mother and son in a log cabin deep in the heart of the Wisconsin Northwoods. There Jed and Vivi try to figure out how to unlock the information inside her son's head. What they don't bargain for is the red-hot attraction that flares between them, or the extent of the sinister plot that threatens to rip apart not only any chance of happiness they might have together, but also the very fabric of American society.

COLD LIGHT OF DAY

Cold Justice Series Book 3

Physicist Scarlett Stone is the daughter of the man considered to be the most notorious Russian agent in FBI history. With her father dying in prison she's determined to prove he's innocent, but time is running out. Using a false identity, she gains access to the Russian ambassador's Christmas party, searching for evidence of a set-up.

Former Navy SEAL, now FBI Special Agent, Matt Lazlo, is instantly attracted to Scarlett but life is too complicated to pursue a politician's daughter. When he discovers she lied to him about her identity, he hunts her down with the ruthless efficiency he usually reserves for serial killers.

Not only does Scarlett's scheme fail, it puts her in the sights of powerful people who reward unwanted curiosity with brutality. The FBI—and Matt—aren't thrilled with her, either. But as agents involved in her father's investigation start dying, and the attempts to stop Scarlett intensify, Matt and his colleagues begin to wonder. Could they have a traitor in their midst?

As Scarlett and Matt dig for the truth they begin to fall passionately for one another. But the real spy isn't about to let anyone uncover their secrets, and resolves to remain firmly in the shadows—and for that to happen, Matt and Scarlett have to die.

COLD FEAR

Cold Justice Series Book 4

When old evidence turns up on a fresh corpse, ASAC Lincoln Frazer is determined it won't delay the execution of a convicted serial killer. But when more young women are brutally slain, it becomes clear—this new killer is intimately familiar with the old murders.

Former Army Captain Dr. Isadora Campbell helped her mother conceal a terrible crime. After her mother's death, Izzy resigned her commission and returned to the Outer Banks to raise her rebellious teenage sister. But it doesn't take long for Izzy to suspect that someone knows exactly what she did, all those years ago.

With pressure mounting to reopen the old case, Frazer will use any means possible to catch the killer. Thrust together during the investigation, he and Izzy find themselves reluctantly attracted to one another, and begin an affair. Meanwhile the killer is much closer than they think. Izzy's confession of her secret drives Frazer away as he struggles with her deception. By the time he realizes he's fallen in love with the stubborn woman, the killer has her. Now the race is on to save Izzy, and any chance of a future they might have together.

COLD IN THE SHADOWS

Cold Justice Series Book 5

CIA Officer Patrick Killion is on a secret mission to hunt down the ruthless female assassin hired to kill the Vice President of the United States. The trail leads him to the Colombian rainforest and an earnest biologist, Audrey Lockhart, whose work on poison dart frogs gives her access to one of the deadliest substances on earth—the same substance used to murder the VP.

When Audrey is attacked by the local drug cartel, Killion steps in and hustles her out of harm's way, determined to find out what she knows. His interrogation skills falter somewhere between saving her life and nursing her back to health as he realizes she's innocent, and he ends up falling for her. Audrey has a hard time overlooking the fact that Killion kidnapped her, but if she wants to get her life back and track down the bad guys, she has to trust him. Then someone changes the rules of their cat and mouse game and now they're the ones being hunted—by a cold-blooded killer who is much closer than they think.

COLD HEARTED

Cold Justice Series Book 6

Hunting For A Killer...

Detective Erin Donovan expects life to quiet down after the arrest and conviction of a serial rapist who terrified her university town last summer. Then two young women are brutally slain and the murders bear all the hallmarks of the campus rapist. Did Erin arrest an innocent man? Now her job is at stake and tensions are high and just when it looks like things can't get worse, her department gets the help it needs to solve the double homicide—in the form of a man Erin has never been able to forget.

Who Doesn't Play By The Rules.

FBI Agent Darsh Singh has no interest in reliving the past. Three years ago, his feelings for Erin Donovan had him breaking all his rules about getting involved. Now his only interest in the former NYPD detective is figuring out if she screwed up a rape investigation and helped send an innocent man to prison. But being forced to work together rekindles their old attraction, and as Darsh and Erin fall for each other, the campus predator fixates on Erin. The race is on to identify the ruthless killer before he makes Erin his final victim.

COLD SECRETS

Cold Justice Series Book 7

When an international ring of sex traffickers kidnaps an eight-year-old girl in Boston, FBI Agent Lucas Randall heads undercover. But his rescue operation goes disastrously wrong and Lucas barely escapes with his life. Now the ruthless traffickers are hunting him down, along with everyone else who threatens their operation.

Computer expert Ashley Chen joined the FBI to fight against evil in the world—evil she experienced firsthand. She has mad skills, and deadly secrets, and once she starts working with Lucas, she also has big trouble, because after years of pushing people away, she's falling for the guy. The feeling is more than mutual, but as Ashley intensifies her online pursuit of the trafficking ring, her traumatic past collides with her present and suddenly Lucas can't tell which side she's on. And as the case escalates into a high-stakes game of cat and mouse, it turns out Ashley isn't the only one with something to hide.

If neither can trust the other with their secrets, how can they trust each other with their hearts?

COLD MALICE

Cold Justice Series Book 8

ASAC Steve (Mac) McKenzie is out to prove himself by leading a task force investigating a series of murders in the heart of Washington, DC. His undercover work in an antigovernment compound twenty years earlier is related—as is the sweet, innocent girl he befriended back then. Now that girl is a beautiful woman, and she has something to hide.

Tess Fallon spent a lifetime trying to outrun her family's brand of bigotry, but someone is threatening her anonymity by using the anniversary of her father's death to carry out evil crimes and she's terrified her younger brother is involved. She sets out to find the truth and comes face-to-face with a man she once idolized, a man she thought long dead. As the crimes escalate it becomes obvious the killer has an agenda, and Tess and Mac are running out of time to stop him.

Will the perpetrator use a decades-old dream of revolution to attack the federal government? And will the fact that Tess and Mac have fallen hard for each other give a cold-hearted killer the power to destroy them both?

A COLD DARK PROMISE

Cold Justice Series Book 9

In the midst of wedding preparations, a shadowy figure from Alex Parker's past reappears and threatens the joy he's found with Mallory Rooney.

Four years ago, Jane Sanders's rich and powerful ex-husband kidnapped their young daughter and Jane hasn't seen her since. Now she finally has a lead on her location and she knows just the man to help her get her daughter back. Trouble is, he's an assassin. And he terrifies her.

Despite his upcoming nuptials, Alex agrees to help, but it doesn't take long for the routine operation to turn complicated—and deadly. Can the former CIA operative make it home in time to marry the woman he loves, or will his dark past destroy all hope for their future?

COLD JUSTICE SERIES OVERVIEW

COLD JUSTICE SERIES
A Cold Dark Place (Book #1)
Cold Pursuit (Book #2)
Cold Light of Day (Book #3)
Cold Fear (Book #4)
Cold in The Shadows (Book #5)
Cold Hearted (Book #6)
Cold Secrets (Book #7)
Cold Malice (Book #8)
A Cold Dark Promise (Book #9~A Wedding Novella)
Cold Blooded (Book #10)

COLD JUSTICE – THE NEGOTIATORS
Cold & Deadly (Book #1)
Colder Than Sin (Book #2)
Cold Wicked Lies (Book #3)
Cold Cruel Kiss (Book #4)
Cold as Ice (Book #5)

COMING SOON...
Cold Silence

The *Cold Justice Series* books are also available as **audiobooks** narrated by Eric Dove, and in various box set compilations.

Check out all Toni's books on her website
(www.toniandersonauthor.com/books-2)

ACKNOWLEDGMENTS

In May 2017, I was lucky enough to visit Atlanta, Georgia for the second time. I took advantage of the opportunity and called up another romance writer who happens to work at the Centers for Disease Control and Prevention (CDC) and arranged a tour of the museum there. Although I didn't use the location as much as I'd anticipated, I did get a great feel for the area and the essential work they do. Thanks, Jennifer McQuiston!

Many thanks again go to Angela Bell of the FBI for answering my strange questions—I think she's used to me by now. I appreciate all her hard work and dedication.

Kathy Altman deserves a medal for being my critique partner. This book reads somewhat coherently because she is patient and brilliant and a miracle worker. I love her. I also love Rachel Grant for the fabulous beta-read where she picked up all sorts of weird-Toni-ness that had crept in. And those lovely quotes at the end of the book? They really are from her book FIRESTORM which releases July 10. It rocks. Buy it!

Thanks to my editors, Alicia Dean, and Joan Turner at JRT Editing, for the fresh eyes. My cover artist, Syd Gill, who nailed this fabulous cover in one shot. And Paul Salvette (BB eBooks) who formats my books with such care and professionalism. Thanks to my publicity person Tara Gonzalez at Inkslingers PR for helping me get the word out.

And I want to thank my husband for not rolling his eyes

too hard when I told him this really was the worst book I'd ever written and that I was done as a writer. Love you!

Being a writer is a crazy roller coaster of woe and elation and I love it despite all the pain, blood, sweat, and tears. So, my heartfelt thanks go to my readers for buying the books!

DEAR READER

Thank you for reading *COLD BLOODED*. I hope you enjoyed Hunt and Pip's story. Please note, this is *not* the last book in the *Cold Justice Series* although I am planning a little side trip for our next adventure.

1. If you have time, please help other readers find this book by writing a review. Thank you!
2. Sign up for my Newsletter (www.toniandersonauthor.com/newsletter) on my website to hear about new releases, special offers, and receive a FREE EBOOK!
3. Check out my website for exclusive short stories and extra content.
4. Interested in a writer's life? Come chat with me on Facebook (facebook.com/toniandersonauthor), follow me on Twitter (@toniannanderson), or check out some of my visual inspiration on Pinterest (pinterest.com/toniannanderson).

ABOUT THE AUTHOR

Toni Anderson writes gritty, sexy, FBI Romantic Thrillers, and is a *New York Times* and a *USA Today* bestselling author. Her books have won the Daphne du Maurier Award for Excellence in Mystery and Suspense, Readers' Choice, Aspen Gold, Book Buyers' Best, Golden Quill, National Excellence in Story Telling (NEST) Contest, and National Excellence in Romance Fiction awards. She's been a finalist in both the Vivian Contest and the RITA Award from the Romance Writers of America. More than two million copies of her books have been downloaded.

Best known for her "COLD" books perhaps it's not surprising to discover Toni lives in one of the most extreme climates on earth—Manitoba, Canada. Formerly a Marine Biologist, Toni still misses the ocean, but is lucky enough to travel for research purposes. In January 2016, she visited FBI Headquarters in Washington DC, including a tour of the Strategic Information and Operations Center. She hopes not to get arrested for her Google searches.

Sign up for Toni Anderson's newsletter:
www.toniandersonauthor.com/newsletter-signup

Like Toni Anderson on Facebook:
facebook.com/toniannanderson

See Toni Anderson's current book list:
www.toniandersonauthor.com/books-2

Follow Toni Anderson on Instagram:
instagram.com/toni_anderson_author

Made in the USA
Columbia, SC
15 February 2022